THE
SECRET
SPEECH

Also by Tom Rob Smith

Child 44

Praise for *The Secret Speech*:

'As a study of betrayal at every level *The Secret Speech* is masterly. It brilliantly portrays a society stripped of every element of love, trust and respect; compassion is a weakness to be exploited and denunciation is accepted with resignation . . . Read this and shiver' *Sunday Telegraph*

'In Smith's hands [the] scenes attain a pulse of exhilaration worthy of Dickens by way of Conrad . . . a broadening of moral scope and thematic richness' Dennis Lehane, *New York Times*

'An epic journey across the blasted Siberian landscape to the dreaded Gulag 57. As with *Child 44*, Smith's historiography is exact and his early career as a scriptwriter shows in his feel for the necessary rhythms of plot. The feints, bluggs and reveals keep it all rattling along' *The Herald*

'Smith's plotting is elaborate, and his pacing is relentless. His characters are wonderfully drawn, and the near-nonstop action is utterly gripping' *Booklist*

'A superb thriller, full of pitch-perfect atmosphere' *Kirkus Reviews* (starred review)

'Tom Rob Smith has created another insanely exciting story, while making you feel you're learning a bit of history along the way' *Independent on Sunday*

Praise for *Child 44*:

'*Child 44* telegraphs the talent and class of its writer from its opening pages, transporting you back to the darkest days of post-war Soviet Russia with assured efficiency and ruthlessly drawing you into its richly atmospheric and engrossing tale'
Raymond Khoury, bestselling author of *The Last Templar* and *Sanctuary*

'Achingly suspenseful, full of feeling and of the twists and turns that one expects from Le Carré at his best, it's a tale that grabs you by the throat and simply never lets you go' Robert Towne

'This is a truly remarkable debut novel. *Child 44* is a rare blend of great insight, excellent writing, and a refreshingly original story. Favourable comparisons to *Gorky Park* are inevitable, but *Child 44* is in a class of its own' Nelson DeMille

'This stellar debut from British author Smith offers appealing characters, a strong plot and authentic period detail . . . The evocation of the deadly cloud-cuckoo-land of Russia during Stalin's final days will remind many of *Gorky Park* and *Darkness at Noon*, but the novel remains Smith's alone, completely original and absolutely satisfying' *Publishers Weekly*

'Astounding . . . The phrase "master storyteller" is horribly overused. In the case of young, first-time novelist Tom Rob Smith, it simply cannot do him justice. *Child 44* is not only a thriller of the highest quality – addictive, pacey, frighteningly unpredictable – but also a magnificently written novel with far more to offer than carefully managed tension and twists' Fiona Atherton, *Scotsman*

'A memorable debut . . . The atmosphere of paranoia and paralysing fear is brilliantly portrayed and unremittingly grim' *Sunday Telegraph*

'Smith's plain, elegant prose powerfully evokes the bleakness of the era, and sympathetic characterisation gives the story flesh without slowing the plot. Impressive stuff' *thelondonpaper*

'The action tears along at a relentless pace . . . This is a perfectly plotted, utterly terrifying adventure – unadulterated crack cocaine for thriller addicts' *Daily Mail*

'Tom Rob Smith's debut novel is stunning . . . Smith captures the bleak Russia of 1953. The fear and mistrust engendered by the regime is palpable . . . The characterisations are pinpoint accurate, leaving the reader as paranoid as the protagonists . . . This is heart-stopping stuff . . . It's little wonder that Ridley Scott snapped up the film rights. There's nothing as gripping, chilling or as intense out there' *Gay Times*

'This is a compelling detective story that I read in the proverbial single sitting . . . I can think of few novels that have touched so eloquently on the complex moral climate of life in the Soviet Union while delivering all the pleasures of a brilliant airport read' *Guardian*

'This gripping thriller has everything you could wish for in a holiday read – and more. A real page-turner, its murder mystery plot acts as a device to explore the terrible workings of Stalinism . . . Bleak but compelling, this is just the thing to make a long-haul flight fly by' The 50 Best Summer Reads, *Independent*

'A tale of redemption but deliciously laced with a gritty, grimy under-current of repression and harsh Soviet reality. It is an accomplished, smoothly-told tale' *Daily Express*

'The novel's atmosphere of paranoia and delusion owes something to Orwell and Kafka but the action is as violent and fast as James Ellroy or Dan Brown . . . the phrase "action packed" hardly does it justice – you could not want for more danger and drama' *Evening Standard*

'Martin Cruz Smith watch your back, here comes Tom Rob Smith . . . Tom has created a *Gorky Park* for the 21st century . . . Tense, atmospheric, inventive and surprisingly timely, *Child 44* is one of those books that reminds you just how entertaining reading can be' *Daily Mirror*

THE
SECRET
SPEECH

TOM ROB SMITH

POCKET
BOOKS

LONDON • SYDNEY • NEW YORK • TORONTO

First published in Great Britain by Simon & Schuster UK Ltd, 2009
This edition first published by Pocket Books, 2010
A CBS COMPANY

Copyright © Tom Rob Smith, 2009, 2010

3 5 7 9 10 8 6 4 2

Simon & Schuster UK Ltd
1st Floor
222 Gray's Inn Road
London
WC1X 8HB

www.simonandschuster.co.uk

Simon & Schuster Australia
Sydney

A CIP catalogue record for this book
is available from the British Library

ISBN 978-1-84739-160-5
Export edition: ISBN 978-1-84739-844-4

Typeset by M Rules
Printed by CPI Cox & Wyman, Reading, Berkshire RG1 8EX

To my sister and brother,
Sarah and Michael.

SOVIET UNION
MOSCOW

During the Great Patriotic War he'd demolished the bridge at Kalach in defence of Stalingrad, rigged factories with dynamite, reducing them to rubble, and set indefensible refineries ablaze, slicing the skyline with columns of burning oil. Anything that might be requisitioned by the invading Wehrmacht he'd rushed to destroy. While his fellow countrymen wept as hometowns crumbled around them, he'd surveyed the devastation with grim satisfaction. The enemy would conquer a wasteland, burnt earth and a smoke-filled sky. Often improvising with whatever materials were at hand — tank shells, glass bottles, siphoned petrol from abandoned, upturned military trucks — he'd gained a reputation for being a man the State could rely on. He never lost his nerve, never made a mistake even when operating in extreme conditions: freezing winter nights, waist deep in fast-flowing rivers, under enemy fire. For a man of his experience and temperament, today's job should be routine. There was no urgency, no bullets whistling overhead. Yet his hands, renowned as the steadiest in the trade, were trembling. Sweat rolled into his eyes, forcing him to dab them with the corner of his shirt. He felt sick, a novice again as this was the first time that fifty-year-old war hero Jekabs Drozdov had ever blown up a church.

There was one more charge to be set, directly before him, positioned in the sanctuary where the altar had once stood. The bishop's throne, icons, menalia – everything had been removed. Even the gold leaf had been scraped from the walls. The church stood empty except for the dynamite dug into the foundations and strapped to the columns. Pillaged and picked clean, it remained a vast and awesome space. The central dome, mounted with a crown of stained-glass windows, was so tall and filled with so much daylight that it seemed part of the sky. Head arched back, mouth open, Jekabs admired the peak some fifty metres above him. Rays of sunlight entered through the high windows illuminating frescos that were soon to be blasted apart, broken down into their constituent parts: a million specks of paint. The light spread across the smooth stone floor not far from where he sat as if trying to reach out to him, an outstretched golden palm.

He muttered:

— *There is no God.*

He said it again, louder this time, the words echoing inside the dome:

— *There is no God!*

It was a summer's day; of course there was light. It wasn't a sign of anything. It wasn't divine. The light meant nothing. He was thinking too much, that was the problem. He didn't even believe in God. He tried to recall the State's many anti-religious phrases.

Religion belonged in an age where every man was for himself
And God was for everyman.

This building wasn't sacred or blessed. He should see it as nothing more than stone, glass and timber; dimensions, one hundred metres long and sixty metres wide. Producing nothing, serving no quantifiable function, the church was an archaic structure, erected for archaic reasons by a society that no longer existed.

Jekabs sat back, running his hand along the cool stone floor smoothed by the feet of many hundreds and thousands of worshippers attending services for many hundreds of years. Overwhelmed by the magnitude of what he was about to do, he began to choke as surely as if there was something stuck in his throat. The sensation passed. He was tired and overworked – that was all. Normally on a demolition project of this scale he'd be assisted by a team. In this instance he'd decided his men could play a peripheral role. There was no need to divide the responsibility, no need to involve his colleagues. Not all of them were as clear-thinking as he was. Not all of them had purged themselves of religious sentiments. He didn't want men with conflicted motivation working alongside him.

For five days, starting at sunrise, finishing at sunset, he'd laid every charge – explosives strategically positioned to ensure the structure collapsed inwards, the domes falling neatly on top of themselves. There was order and precision to his craft and he was proud of his skill. This building presented a unique challenge. It wasn't a moral question but an intellectual test. With a bell tower and five golden cupolas, the largest of which was supported on a tabernacle eighty metres high, today's controlled, successful demolition would be a fitting conclusion to his career. After this, he'd been promised an early retirement. There'd even been talk about him receiving the Order of Lenin, payment for a job no one else wanted to do.

He shook his head. He shouldn't be here. He shouldn't be doing this. He should've feigned sickness. He should've forced someone

3

else to lay the final charge. This was no job for a hero. But the dangers of avoiding work were far greater, far more real than some superstitious notion that this work might be cursed. He had his family to protect – a wife, a daughter – and he loved them very much.

*

Lazar stood among the crowd, held back from the perimeter of the Church of Sancta Sophia at a precautionary distance of a hundred metres, his solemnity contrasting with the excitement and chatter around him. He decided they were the kind of crowd that might have attended a public execution, not out of principle, but just for the spectacle, just for something to do. There was a festive atmosphere, conversations bubbling with anticipation. Children bounced on their fathers' shoulders, impatient for something to happen. A church was not enough for them: the church needed to collapse for them to be entertained.

At the front of the barricade, on a specially constructed podium to provide elevation, a film crew were busy setting up tripods and cameras – discussing which angles would best capture the demolition. Particular attention was paid to ensure they caught all five cupolas and there was earnest speculation whether the timber domes would smash in the air as they crashed into each other, or not until they hit the ground. It would depend, they reasoned, on the skill of the experts laying the dynamite inside.

Lazar wondered if there could be sadness too among the crowd. He looked left and right, searching for like-minded souls – the married couple in the distance, silent, their faces drained of colour; the elderly woman at the back, her hand in her pocket. She had some item hidden in there, a crucifix perhaps. Lazar wanted to divide this crowd, to separate the mourners from the revellers. He wanted to stand beside those who appreciated what was about to be lost: a three-hundred-year-old church. Named and designed after the Cathedral of Sancta Sophia in Gorky, it had survived civil wars, world wars. The recent bomb damage was a reason to preserve, not to destroy. Lazar had contemptuously read the article in *Pravda* claiming *structural instability*. Such a claim was nothing more than a pretext, a spoonful of false logic to make the deed palatable. The State had ordered its destruction, and what was worse, far worse, the order had been made in agreement with the Orthodox Church. Both parties to the crime claimed it was a pragmatic decision, not ideological. They'd listed a series of contributing factors. Damage by Luftwaffe raids. The interior required elaborate renovations that couldn't be paid for. Furthermore, the land, in the heart of the city, was needed for a crucial construction project. Everyone in power was in agreement. This church, hardly one of Moscow's finest, should be torn down.

Cowardice lay behind the shameful arrangement. The ecclesiastical authorities, having rallied every church congregation behind Stalin during the war, were now an instrument of the State, a ministry of the Kremlin. The demolition was a demonstration of that subjugation. They were blowing it up for no reason other than to prove their humility: an act of self-mutilation to testify that religion was harmless, docile, tamed. It didn't need to be persecuted any more. Lazar understood the politics of sacrifice: wasn't it better to lose one church than to lose them all? As a young man he'd witnessed seminaries turned into workers' barracks, churches turned into anti-religious exhibition halls. Icons had been used as firewood; priests imprisoned, tortured and executed. Continued persecution or thoughtless subservience: that had been the choice.

*

Jekabs listened to the sound of the crowd gathered outside, the bustle as they waited for the show to begin. He was late. He should've finished by now. Yet for the past five minutes he hadn't moved, staring down at the final charge and doing nothing. Behind him, he heard the creak of the door. He glanced over his shoulder. It was his colleague and friend, standing at the doorway, on the threshold, as if fearful of entering. He called out, his voice echoing:

— *Jekabs! What's wrong?*

Jekabs replied:

— *I'm almost done.*

His friend hesitated before remarking, softening his voice:

— *We will drink tonight, the two of us, to celebrate your retirement. In the morning you'll have a terrible headache but by the evening you will feel much better.*

Jekabs smiled at his friend's attempt at consolation. The guilt would be nothing worse than a hangover. It would pass.

— *Give me five minutes.*

With that, his friend left him alone.

Kneeling in a parody of prayer, sweat streaming, his fingers slippery, he wiped his face, but it made no difference, his shirt was soaked and could absorb no more. *Finish the job!* And he'd never have to work again. Tomorrow he'd take his little daughter for a walk by the river. The day after he'd buy her something, watch her smile. By the end of next week he would've forgotten about this church, about the five golden domes and the sensation of the cold stone floor.

Finish the job!

He snatched hold of the blast cap, crouched down to the dynamite.

*

Stained glass shot out, every window shattering simultaneously, the air filling with coloured fragments. The back wall transformed from a solid mass to a rushing dust cloud. Ragged chunks of stone arced up then crashed to the ground, chewing up the grass, skidding towards the crowd. The flimsy barrier offered no protection, swatted aside with a shrill clang. To Lazar's right and left people dropped as their legs were knocked out from under them. Children on their fathers' shoulders clutched their faces, sliced by whistling stone and glass shards. As though it was a single entity, a great shoal, the crowd pulled away in unison, crouching, hiding behind each other, fearful that more debris would rip through them. No one had been expecting anything to happen yet; many hadn't even been looking in the right direction. The film cameras weren't set up. There were workers within the blast perimeter, a perimeter hopelessly underestimated or an explosion misjudged.

Lazar stood, his ears ringing, staring at the plumes of dust, waiting for it to settle. As the cloud thinned it revealed a hole in the wall twice the height of a man and equally wide. It was as if a giant had accidentally put the tip of his boot through the church and then retracted his foot apologetically, sparing the rest of the building. Lazar looked up at the golden domes. Everyone around him followed suit, a single question on everyone's mind: would the towers fall?

Out of the corner of his eye Lazar could see the film crew scrambling to get the cameras rolling, wiping the dust off the lenses, abandoning the tripods, desperate to capture the footage. If they missed the collapse, no matter what the excuse, their lives would be on the line. Despite the danger, no one ran away, they remained fixed to the spot, searching for even the slightest movement, a tilt or jolt – a tremble. It seemed as if even the injured were silent in anticipation.

The five domes did not fall, aloof from the petty chaos of the world below. While the church remained standing, scores in the crowd were bleeding, wounded, weeping. As surely as if the sky had clouded over, Lazar sensed the mood change. Doubts surfaced. Had some unearthly power intervened and stopped this crime? Spectators began to leave, a few slowly, then others joined them, more and more, hurrying away. No one wanted to watch any more. Lazar struggled to suppress a laugh. The crowd had broken apart while the church had survived! He turned to the married couple, hoping to share this moment with them.

The man standing directly behind Lazar was so close they were almost touching. Lazar hadn't heard him approach. He was smiling but his eyes were cold. He didn't wear a uniform or show his identity card. However, there was no question that he was State Security, a secret-police officer, an agent of the MGB – a deduction possible not from what was present in his appearance but what was absent. To the right and left there were injured people. Yet this man had no interest in them. He'd been planted in the crowd to monitor people's reactions. And Lazar had failed: he'd been sad when he should've been happy and happy when he should've been sad.

The man spoke through a thin smile, his dead eyes never moving from Lazar.

— *A small setback, an accident, easily fixed. You should stay: perhaps it will still happen today, the demolition. You want to stay, don't you? You want to see the church fall? It will be quite spectacular.*

— *Yes.*

A careful answer and also the truth, he did want to stay, but no, he didn't want the church to fall and he certainly wouldn't say so. The man continued:

— *This site is going to become one of the largest indoor swimming pools in the world. So our children can be healthy. It is a good thing, our children being healthy. What is your name?*

The most ordinary of questions and yet the most terrifying.

— *My name is Lazar*

— *What is your occupation?*

No longer masquerading as casual conversation, it was now an open interrogation. Subjugation or persecution, being pragmatic or principled — Lazar had to choose. And he did have a choice, unlike many of his brethren who were instantly recognizable. He didn't have to admit that he was a priest. Vladimir Lvov, former chief procurator of the Holy Synod, had argued priests need not set themselves apart by their dress and that they might — *throw off their cassocks, cut their hair and be changed into ordinary mortals.* Lazar agreed. With his trim beard and unremarkable appearance, he could lie to this agent. He could disown his vocation and hope that the lie would protect him. He worked in a shoe factory or he crafted tables — anything but the truth. The agent was waiting.

In their first weeks together, Anisya hadn't given the matter much thought. Maxim was only twenty-four years old, a graduate of Moscow's Theological Academy Seminary, closed since 1918 and recently reopened as part of the rehabilitation of religious institutions. She was older than him by six years, married, unattainable, a tantalizing prospect for a young man whom she supposed to have limited, if any, sexual experience. Introspective and shy, Maxim never socialized outside of the Church and had few friends or family, at least none that lived in the city. It was unsurprising that he'd developed something of an infatuation. She'd tolerated his lingering stares, perhaps even been flattered by them. But in no way had she encouraged him. He'd misunderstood her silence, inferring permission to continue courting her. It was for that reason that he now felt confident enough to take hold of her hand and say:

— *Leave him. Live with me.*

She'd been convinced he'd never find the courage to act upon what could only ever be a childish daydream – the two of them running off together. She'd been wrong.

Remarkably he'd chosen her husband's church to cross the line from private fantasy into open proposition: the frescos of disciples, demons, prophets and angels judged their illicit moves from the shadowy alcoves. Maxim was risking everything he'd trained for, facing certain disgrace and exile from the religious community with no hope of redemption. His earnest, heartfelt plea was so misjudged and absurd that she couldn't help but react in the worst possible way. She uttered a short, surprised laugh.

Before he had time to reply the heavy oak door slammed shut. Startled, Anisya turned to see her husband – Lazar – hurrying towards them with such urgency that she could only presume he'd misconstrued the scene as evidence of her infidelity. She pulled away from Maxim, a sudden movement that only compounded the impression of guilt. But as he drew closer she realized that Lazar, her husband of ten years, was preoccupied with something else. Breathless, he took hold of her hands, hands which only seconds ago had been held by Maxim.

— *I was picked out of the crowd. An agent questioned me.*

He spoke rapidly, the words tumbling out, their importance brushing aside Maxim's proposal. She asked:

— *Were you followed?*

He nodded.

— *I hid in Natasha Niurina's apartment.*

— *What happened?*

— *He remained outside. I was forced to leave through the back.*

— *Will they arrest Natasha and question her?*

Lazar raised his hands to his face.

— *I panicked. I didn't know where else to go. I shouldn't have gone to her.*

Anisya took him by the shoulders.

— *If the only way they can find us is by arresting Natasha, we have a little time.*

Lazar shook his head.

— *I told him my name.*

She understood. He wouldn't lie. He wouldn't compromise his

11

principles, not for her, not for anyone. Principles were more important than their lives. He shouldn't have attended the demolition: she'd warned him it was an unnecessary risk. The crowd was inevitably going to be monitored and he'd be a conspicuous observer. He'd ignored her, as was his way, always appearing to contemplate her advice but never heeding it. Hadn't she pleaded with him not to alienate the ecclesiastical authorities? Were they in such a position of strength that they could afford to make enemies of both the State and the Church? But he had no interest in the politics of alliance: he only wanted to speak his mind even if it left him isolated, openly criticizing the new relationship between bishops and politicians. Stubborn, headstrong, he demanded that she support his stance while giving her no say in it. She admired him, a man of integrity. But he did not admire her. She was younger than him and was only twenty years old when they'd married. He was thirty-five. At times she wondered whether he'd married her because being a White Priest, a married priest, taking a monastic vow, was itself a reformist statement. The concept appealed to him, fitting with his liberal, philosophical scheme. She'd always been braced for the moment when the State might cut across their lives. However, now that the moment had come, she felt cheated. She was paying for his opinions, opinions that she'd never been allowed to influence or contribute to.

Lazar put a hand on Maxim's shoulder.

— *It would be better if you returned to the theological seminary and denounced us. Since we're going to be arrested the denunciation would only serve to distance you from us. Maxim, you're a young man. No one will think worse of you for leaving.*

Coming from Lazar, the offer to run was a loaded proposition. Lazar considered such pragmatic behaviour beneath him, suitable for others, weaker men and women. His moral superiority was stifling. Far from offering Maxim a way out, it trapped him. Anisya interjected, trying to keep her voice friendly.

— *Maxim, you must go.*

He reacted sharply.

— *I want to stay.*

Slighted by her earlier laugh, he was stubborn and indignant. Speaking in a double meaning invisible to her husband, she said:

— *Please, Maxim, forget everything that has happened, you will achieve nothing by staying.*

Maxim shook his head.

— *I've made my decision.*

Anisya noticed Lazar smile. There was no doubt her husband was fond of Maxim. He'd taken him under his wing, blind to his protégé's infatuation with her, alert only to the deficiencies in his knowledge of scripture and philosophy. He was pleased with Maxim's decision to stay, believing that it had something to do with him. Anisya moved closer to Lazar.

— *We cannot allow him to risk his life.*

— *We cannot force him to leave.*

— *Lazar, this is not his fight.*

It was not her fight either.

— *He has made it his. I respect that. You must too.*

— *It is senseless!*

In modelling Maxim on himself, the martyr, her husband had chosen to humiliate her and condemn him. Lazar exclaimed:

— *Enough! We don't have time! You wish him to be safe. I do too. But if Maxim wants to stay, he stays.*

*

Lazar hurried towards the stone altar, hastily stripping it bare. Every person connected to his church was in danger. He could do little for his wife or Maxim: they were too closely connected to him. But his congregation, the people who'd confided in him, shared their fears – it was essential their names remain a secret.

With the altar bare, Lazar gripped the side.

— *Push!*

None the wiser but obedient, Maxim pushed the altar, straining at the weight. The rough stone base scratched across the stone floor, slowly sliding aside and revealing a hole, a hiding place created some twenty years ago during the most intensive attacks on the church. The stone slabs had been removed, exposing earth that had been carefully dug and lined with timber supports to stop it subsiding, creating a space one metre deep, two metres wide. It contained a steel trunk. Lazar reached down and Maxim followed suit, taking the opposite end of the trunk and lifting it out, placing it on the floor, ready to be opened.

Anisya lifted the lid. Maxim crouched beside her, unable to keep the amazement out of his voice.

— *Music?*

The trunk was filled with handwritten musical scores. Lazar explained:

— *The composer attended services here, a young man – not much older than you, a student at the Moscow Conservatory. He came to us one night, terrified that he was about to be arrested. Fearing that his work would be destroyed, he entrusted us with his compositions. Much of his work had been condemned as anti-Soviet.*

— *Why?*

— *I don't know. He didn't know either. He had nowhere to turn, no family or friends he could trust. So, he came to us. We agreed to take possession of his life's work. Shortly afterwards, he disappeared.*

Maxim glanced over the notes.

— The music . . . is it good?

— We haven't heard it performed. We dare not show it to anyone, or have it played for us. Questions might be asked.

— You have no idea what it sounds like?

— I can't read music. Neither can my wife. But, Maxim, you're missing the point. My promise of help wasn't dependent on the merits of his work.

— You're risking your lives? If it's worthless . . .

Lazar corrected him.

— We're not protecting these papers; we're protecting their right to survive.

Anisya found her husband's assuredness infuriating. The young composer in question had come to her, not him. She'd then petitioned Lazar and convinced him to take the music. In the retelling of the story he'd smoothed over his doubts, anxieties — reducing her to nothing more than his passive supporter. She wondered if he was even aware of the adjustments he'd made to the history, automatically elevating his own importance, re-centring the story around him.

Lazar picked up the entire collection of unbound sheet music, maybe two hundred pages in total. Included among the music were documents relating to the business of the church and several original icons that had been hidden, replaced with reproductions. He hastily divided the contents into three piles, checking as best he could that complete musical compositions were kept together. The plan was to smuggle out a more or less equal share. Divided in three, there was a reasonable chance some of the music would survive. The difficulty was finding three separate hiding places, three people who'd be prepared to sacrifice their lives for notes on a page even though they'd never met the composer or heard his music. Lazar knew many in his parish would help. Many were also

15

likely to be under suspicion of some kind. For this task they
needed the help of a perfect Soviet, someone whose apartment
would never be searched. Such a person, if they existed, would
never help them. Anisya threw out suggestions.

— *Martemian Syrtsov.*

— *Too talkative.*

— *Artiom Nakhaev.*

— *He'd agree, take the papers and then panic, lose his nerve and
burn them.*

— *Niura Dmitrieva.*

— *She'd say yes but she'd hate us for asking. She wouldn't sleep.
She wouldn't eat.*

In the end, two names – that's all they could agree upon. Lazar
decided to keep one portion of the music hidden in the church,
along with the larger icons, returning them to the trunk and
pushing the altar back into position. Since Lazar was the most
likely to be followed, Anisya and Maxim were to carry their share
of the music to the two addresses. They would leave separately.
Anisya was ready.

— *I'll go first.*

Maxim shook his head.

— *No. I will.*

She guessed his reason for offering: if Maxim got away then the
chances were that she would too.

They unlocked the main door, lifting up the thick timber beam.
Anisya sensed Maxim hesitate, no doubt afraid, the danger of his
predicament finally sinking in. Lazar shook his hand. Over her
husband's shoulder, Maxim looked at her. Once Lazar was done,
Maxim stepped towards her. She gave him a hug and watched him
set off into the night.

Lazar closed the door, locking it behind him, reiterating the plan:

— *We wait ten minutes.*

Alone with her husband, she waited near the front of the church. He joined her. To her surprise, rather than praying, he took hold of her hand.

*

Ten minutes had passed, they moved to the door. Lazar lifted the beam. The papers were in a bag, slung over her shoulder. Anisya stepped outside. They'd already said goodbye. She turned, watching in silence as Lazar shut the door behind her. She heard the beam lowered back in place. Walking towards the street, she checked for faces at the windows, movement in the shadows. Suddenly a hand gripped her wrist. Startled, she spun around.

— *Maxim?*

What was he doing here? Where was the music he was carrying? From behind the back of the church a voice called out, harsh and impatient:

— *Leo?*

Anisya saw a man dressed in a dark uniform – an MGB agent. There were more men behind him, clustering like cockroaches. Her questions melted away, concentrating on the name called out: *Leo.* With the tug of a single word the knot of lies unravelled. That was why he had no friends or family in the city, that was why he was so quiet in lessons with Lazar, he knew nothing of scripture or philosophy. That was why he'd wanted to leave the church first, not for her protection but to alert the surveillance, to prepare for their arrest. He was a Chekist, a secret-police officer. He'd tricked her and her husband. He'd infiltrated their lives to gather as much information as possible, not just on them but on the people who sympathized with them, dealing a blow against the remaining pockets of resistance within the Church. Had attempting to

17

seduce her been an objective handed down by his superiors? Had they identified her as weak, gullible, and instructed this handsome officer to form a persona – *Maxim* – to manipulate her?

He spoke quietly, intimately, as though nothing had changed between them:

— *Anisya, I give you one more chance. Come with me. I've made arrangements. They're not interested in you. They're after Lazar.*

The sound of his voice, tender and concerned, was appalling. The offer he'd made earlier, to leave with him, hadn't been a naive fantasy. It hadn't been romantic. It had been the calculation of an agent. He continued:

— *Take the advice you gave me, denounce Lazar. I can lie for you. I can protect you. It's him they want. You will achieve nothing by remaining loyal.*

*

Leo was running out of time. Anisya had to understand that he was her only chance of survival, no matter what she thought of him. She would gain nothing by clinging to her principles. His superior officer Nikolai Borisov walked towards them. Forty years old, he had the body of an ageing weight-lifter, still strong but slackening with an excess of drink.

— *Is she cooperating?*

Leo stretched out his hand, his eyes pleading with her to hand him the bag.

— *Please?*

In reply she cried out as loud as she could:

— *Lazar!*

Nikolai stepped forward, slapping her with the back of his hand. He called out to his men:

— *Go!*

Axes were brought against the church door.

Leo saw hatred in Anisya's face. Nikolai pulled the bag from her.

— *He tried to save you, ungrateful bitch.*

She leaned forward, whispering into Leo's ear:

— *You genuinely believed that I might end up loving you. Didn't you?*

Officers grabbed her arms. Pulled back, she smiled at him, a vicious smile:

— *No one will ever love you. No one!*

Leo turned his back on her, desperate for her to be taken away. Nikolai put a consoling hand on his shoulder.

— *It would've been complicated explaining how she wasn't a traitor anyway. It's much better this way. Better for you. There are other women, Leo. There are always others.*

Leo had completed his first arrest.

Anisya was wrong. He was already loved — by the State. He didn't want the love of a traitor: that was no love at all. Deception, betrayal — these were an officer's tools. He had a legitimate right to them. His country depended upon betrayal. A soldier before he became an MGB agent, he'd experienced savage necessity in the defeat of Fascism. Even the most terrible of things could be excused by the greater good that they served.

He entered the church. Instead of attempting escape, Lazar was kneeling near the altar, praying, awaiting his fate. Seeing Leo, his proud defiance melted away. In that moment of understanding he seemed to age several years.

— *Maxim?*

For the first time since they'd known each other he looked to his protégé for answers.

— *My name is Leo Stepanovich Demidov.*

For several seconds Lazar remained silent. Finally he said:

— *You were recommended to me by the Patriarch . . .*

— *Patriarch Krasikov is a good citizen.*

Lazar shook his head, refusing to believe it. The Patriarch was an informer. His protégé was a spy sent to him by the highest religious figure. He'd been sacrificed to the State just as the Church of Sancta Sophia had been sacrificed. He was a fool, warning others to take care, preaching caution, when standing beside him, taking notes, was an MGB officer.

Nikolai stepped forward.

— *Where are the remaining papers?*

Leo gestured at the altar.

— *Underneath.*

Three agents pushed it aside, revealing the trunk. Nikolai asked:

— *Did he give you any other names?*

Leo answered:

— *Martemian Syrtsov. Artiom Nakhaev. Niura Dmitrieva. Moisei Semashko.*

He caught sight of Lazar's face: shock turned to disgust. Leo stepped up to him:

— *Keep your eyes on the floor!*

Lazar didn't turn away. Leo pushed his face down.

— *Eyes on the floor!*

Lazar lifted his head again. This time Leo punched him. Slowly, with his lip split open, Lazar lifted his head, dripping blood, looking up at him, disgust mingled with defiance. Leo replied, as if Lazar's eyes had asked him a question:

— *I am a good man.*

Holding his mentor by the hair, Leo didn't stop, punch after punch, continuing mechanically like a clockwork soldier, repeating the same action over and over until his knuckles hurt, until his arms ached and the side of Lazar's face turned soft. When he finally stopped and released him, Lazar slumped to the floor, blood pooling around his mouth, shaped like a speech bubble.

Nikolai hung an arm around Leo's shoulder, watching as Lazar was carried out, leaving a trail of blood from the altar to the door. Nikolai lit a cigarette.

— *The State needs people like us.*

Numb, Leo wiped the blood on his trousers, remarking:

— *Before we go I'd like a moment to check the church.*

Nikolai accepted the proposal at face value.

— *A perfectionist, that's good. But hurry up. Tonight we get drunk. You haven't had a drink in two months! You've been living like a monk!*

Nikolai laughed at his own joke, patting Leo on the back before heading out. Alone, Leo walked to the displaced stone altar, staring into the hole. Caught between the side of the trunk and the earth wall there was a single sheet of paper. He reached down, picked it up. It was a page of music. His eyes ran across the notes. Deciding that it would be better not to know what had been lost, he raised the sheet above the flame of a nearby candle, watching the paper turn black.

SEVEN
YEARS
LATER

MOSCOW

The manager of a small academic printing press, Suren Moskvin had become renowned for producing textbooks of the poorest quality, using ink that smeared and the thinnest paper, all held together with a glued spine that began to shed pages within hours of opening. It wasn't that he was lazy or incompetent. Far from it, he'd start work early in the morning and finish late at night. The reason the books were so shabby was due to the raw materials allotted by the State. While the content of academic publications was carefully monitored, they were not a resource priority. Locked into a quota system, Suren was forced to produce a large number of books from the lowest grade of paper in the shortest time. The equation never changed and he was at its mercy, acutely embarrassed that his reputation had sunk so low. There were jokes – with ink-stained fingers, students and teachers quipped that Moskvin's books always stayed with you. Ridiculed, he'd been finding it difficult getting out of bed. He wasn't eating properly. He was drinking throughout the day, bottles stashed in drawers, behind bookshelves. Aged fifty-five, he'd discovered something new about himself: he didn't have the stomach for public humiliation.

Inspecting the Linotype machines, brooding over his failures, he noticed a young man standing at the door. Suren addressed him defensively:

— *Yes? What is it? It's not normal to stand there unannounced.*

The man stepped forward, in typical student attire, a long coat and a cheap black scarf. He was holding a book, outstretched. Suren snatched it from his hands, bracing himself for more complaints. He glanced at the cover: Lenin's *The State and Revolution*. They'd printed a new volume only last week, distributed a day or so ago, and this man, it would seem, was the first to spot something amiss. A mistake in a seminal work was a grave matter: during Stalin's rule such a mistake would be enough to warrant arrest. The student leaned forward and opened the book, flicking to the front. Printed on the title page was a black-and-white photo. The student commented:

— *The text at the bottom says it's a photo of Lenin but . . . as you can see . . .*

The photo was of a man who looked nothing like Lenin, a man standing against a wall, a stark white wall. His hair was wild. His eyes were wild.

Suren slammed the book shut and turned to the student:

— *You think I could have printed one thousand copies of this book with the wrong photo? Who are you? What is your name? Why are you doing this? My problems are due to the limits of my materials, not carelessness!*

Pushed back, the book jabbed at his chest, the scarf around the student's neck came loose, revealing the edge of a tattoo. The sight made Suren pause. A tattoo was incongruous with the typical appearance of a student. No one, except the *vory*, the professional criminals, would mark their skin in such a way.

With the impetus taken out of Suren's indignation, the man

exploited his hesitation and hurried out. Half-heartedly, Suren followed, still holding the book, watching the mysterious figure disappear into the night. Uneasy, he shut the door, locking it. Something bothered him: that photograph. He took out his spectacles, opened the book and scrutinized the face a little more closely: those terrified eyes. Like a ghost ship slowly emerging from dense fog, the identity appeared to him. His face was familiar. His hair and eyes were wild because he'd been arrested and dragged from his bed. Suren recognized the photograph because he had taken it.

Suren hadn't always run a printing press. Previously, he'd been employed by the MGB. Twenty years of loyal service, his career with the secret police had spanned longer than many of his superiors. Fulfilling a variety of banal tasks – cleaning cells, photographing prisoners – his low rank had been an asset and he'd been savvy enough not to push for more responsibility, never getting noticed, evading the cyclical purges of the upper echelons. Difficult things had been demanded of him. He'd done his duty unswervingly. Back then he'd been a man to be feared. No one made jokes about him. They wouldn't have dared. Ill-health had forced him to retire. Though well remunerated and comfortable, he'd found idleness impossible. Lying in bed with no purpose to his day, his mind had wandered, drifting over the past, remembering faces like the one now stuck into this book. The solution was to remain busy, appointments and meetings. He needed an occupation. He didn't want to reminisce.

Closing the book, he slipped the volume into his pocket. Why was this happening today? It couldn't be mere coincidence. Despite his failure to produce a book or journal of any quality, he'd unexpectedly been asked to publish an important State document. He hadn't been told it's nature, but the prestige of the assignment meant high-quality resources – good paper and ink. Finally he'd been given the opportunity to produce something he could be proud of. They were to deliver the document this evening. And someone with a grudge was trying to undermine him just as his fortunes were about to change.

He left the factory floor, hurrying to his office, carefully smoothing his wispy grey hair to the side. He was wearing his best suit – he only had two, one for everyday use and one for special occasions. This was a special occasion. He hadn't needed help getting out of bed today. He'd been awake before his wife. He'd shaved, humming. He'd eaten a full breakfast, his first for weeks. Arriving at the factory early, he'd taken the bottle of vodka from his drawer and poured it down the sink before spending the day cleaning, mopping, dusting – wiping away the flecks of grease from the Linotype machines. His sons, both university students, had paid him a visit, impressed by the transformation. Suren reminded them that it was a matter of principle to keep the workplace spotless. The workplace was where a person took their identity and sense of self. They'd kissed him goodbye, wishing him luck with the enigmatic new commission. At last, after the many years of secrecy and the recent years of failure, they had reason to be proud of him.

He checked his watch. It was seven in the evening. They'd be here any minute. He should forget about the stranger and photograph, it wasn't important. He couldn't let him distract him. Suddenly he wished he hadn't poured the vodka away. A drink would've calmed him. Then again, they might have smelt it on his breath. Better not to have any, better to be nervous – it showed he took the job seriously. Suren reached for the bottle of Kvass, a non-alcoholic rye-bread brew: it would have to do.

In his haste, his coordination shaky from alcohol withdrawal, he upended a tray of letter moulds. The tray fell from the desk, the letters scattering across the stone floor.

Clink Clink

His body went rigid. No longer in his office, Suren was standing in a narrow brick corridor, a row of steel doors on one side. He remembered this place: Oriol Prison, where he'd been a guard at the outbreak of the Great Patriotic War. Forced to retreat from the rapidly approaching German army, he and his fellow guards had been ordered to liquidate the inmate population, leaving behind no sympathetic recruits for the Nazi invaders. With the buildings strafed by Stukas and shelled by Panzers, they'd faced the logistical conundrum of eliminating twenty cells crowded with hundreds of political criminals in minutes. They didn't have time for bullets or nooses. It had been his idea to use grenades, two dropped into each cell. He'd walked to the end of the corridor, pulled back the small steel grate and tossed them in – *clink, clink* – the sound of the grenade casing on a concrete floor. He'd slammed the grate shut so that they couldn't be tossed out, running back down the corridor to get away from the blast, imagining the men fumbling for the grenades, their filthy fingers slipping, trying to throw them out of the small, barred window.

Suren placed his hands tight over his ears as if this could stop the memory. But the noise continued, louder and louder, grenades on the concrete floor, cell after cell.

Clink Clink Clink Clink

He cried out:
— *Stop!*
Removing his hands from his ears, he realized someone was knocking on the door.

The victim's throat had been savaged by a series of deep, ragged cuts. There were no injuries above or below what remained of the man's neck, giving the contradictory impression of frenzy and control. Considering the ferocity of the attack, only a small amount of blood had spread right and left from the incisions, pooling into the shape of fledgling angel wings. The killer appeared to have knocked the victim to the floor, pinned him down, continuing to slash long after Suren Moskvin – aged fifty-five and the manager of a small academic printing press – had died.

His body had been found early this morning when his sons, Vsevolod and Akvsenti, had entered the premises, concerned that their father hadn't come home. Distraught, they'd contacted the militia, who'd found a ransacked office: drawers pulled out of the desk, papers on the floor, filing cabinets forced open. They'd concluded that it was a bungled robbery. Not until the after-noon, some seven hours after the initial discovery, had the militia finally contacted the Homicide Department headed by former MGB agent Leo Stepanovich Demidov.

Leo was accustomed to such delays. He'd created the Homicide Department three years ago using the leverage he'd gained from solving the murders of over forty-four children.

Since its conception the department's relationship with the regular militia was fraught. Cooperation was erratic. The very existence of his department was considered by many militia and KGB officers to imply an unacceptable degree of criticism of both their work and the State. In truth, they were correct. Leo's motive in forming the department was a reaction against his work as an agent. He'd arrested many civilians during his previous career, arrests he'd made based upon nothing more than typed lists of names passed down from his superiors. In contrast, the Homicide Department pursued an evidential truth, not a politicized one. Leo's duty was to present the facts of each case to his superiors. What they did with that truth was up to them. Leo's private hope was that one day he'd balance his arrest ledger, the guilty outweighing the innocent. Even at a conservative estimate, he had a long way to go.

The freedoms granted to the Homicide Department resulted in their work being subject to the highest level of secrecy. They reported directly to senior figures in the Ministry of the Interior, operating as a covert subsection of the Main Office for Criminal Investigations. The population at large still needed to believe in the evolution of society. Falling crime rates were a tenet of that belief. Contradictory facts were filtered from the national consciousness. No citizen could contact the Homicide Department because no citizen knew it existed. For this reason Leo couldn't broadcast requests for information or ask witnesses to come forward since such actions would be tantamount to propagandizing the existence of crime. The freedom that he'd been granted was of a very particular kind and Leo, who'd done everything in his power to put his former career in the secret police behind him, now found himself running a very different kind of secret police force.

31

Uneasy with the first-glance explanation behind Moskvin's death, Leo studied the crime scene, his eyes fastening on the chair. Positioned, unremarkably, in front of the desk, the seat was at a slight angle. He walked up to it, crouching down, running his finger over a thin fracture line on one of the wooden legs. Tentatively testing his weight, pushing down on the back, the leg immediately gave way. The chair was broken. If anyone had sat on it, it would have collapsed. Yet it was positioned at the desk as though suitable for use.

Returning his attention to the body, he took hold of the victim's hands. There were no cuts, no scratches — no sign of self-defence. Kneeling, Leo moved close to the victim's neck. There was hardly any skin left except on the back, the area touching the floor, protected from repeated slashes. Leo took out a knife, prising it under the victim's neck and lifting the blade up, exposing a small stretch of skin that hadn't been destroyed. It was bruised. Lowering the flap of skin, retracting the knife, he was about to stand up when he caught sight of a pocket on the dead man's suit. He reached in, taking out a slim book — Lenin's *The State and Revolution*. Even before opening the book, he could see that there was something unusual with the binding: a page had been glued in. Turning to the page in question he saw a photo of a dishevelled man. Though Leo had no idea who he was, he recognized the type of photograph — the stark white background, the suspect's disorientated expression. It was an arrest photo.

Puzzled by this elaborate anomaly, Leo stood up. Timur Nesterov entered the room, glancing at the book.

— *Something important?*

— *I'm not sure.*

Timur was Leo's closest colleague and friend. The friendship they'd developed was understated. They didn't drink together, banter or talk very much except about work – a partnership typified by long silences. To cynics there was reason to suppose resentment in their relationship. Almost ten years younger, Leo was now Timur's superior, despite the fact that he'd previously been his subordinate, always formally addressing him as General Nesterov. Objectively Leo had benefited more from their joint success. People had insinuated that he was a profiteer, individualistic and career-minded. But Timur showed no jealousy. The issue of rank was incidental. He was proud of his job. His family was provided for. In moving to Moscow he'd finally, after languishing on waiting lists, been appointed a modern apartment with running hot water and a twenty-four-hour electricity supply. No matter how their relationship might outwardly seem, they trusted each other with their lives.

Timur gestured towards the main factory floor where the towering Linotype machines stood, giant mechanical insects.

— *The sons have arrived.*

— *Bring them in.*

— *With their father's body in the room?*

— *Yes.*

The sons had been allowed to leave, sent home by the militia before Leo could question them. He would apologize that they had to see their father's body again but he had no intention of trusting second-hand information passed to him by the militia.

Summoned, Vsevolod and Akvsenti – both in their early twenties – appeared at the door, side by side. Leo introduced himself.

— *I'm Officer Leo Demidov. I understand this must be difficult.*

Neither of them looked at their father's body, keeping their eyes on Leo. The older son, Vsevolod, spoke.

— *We answered the militia's questions.*

— My questions won't take long. Is this room as you found it this morning?

— Yes, it's the same.

Vsevolod was doing all the talking. Akvsenti remained silent, his eyes occasionally flicking up. Leo continued:

— Was this chair at the table? It might have been knocked over, in the struggle perhaps?

— The struggle?

— Between your father and the killer?

There was silence. Leo continued:

— The chair's broken. If you sat on it, it would collapse. It's odd to have a broken chair in front of a desk, isn't it? You can't sit on it.

Both sons turned towards the chair. Vsevolod replied:

— You've brought us back to talk about a chair?

— The chair is important. I believe your father used it to hang himself.

The suggestion should have been ludicrous. They should have been outraged. Yet they remained silent. Sensing his speculation was on target, Leo pressed his theory:

— I believe your father hanged himself, maybe from one of the overhead beams in the factory. He stood on the chair and then kicked it from under his feet. You found his body this morning. You dragged him here, replaced the chair, not noticing that it had been damaged. One of you, or both of you, cut his throat in an attempt to conceal the scarring from the rope burns. The office was staged as if there was a break-in.

They were promising students. The suicide might end their careers and destroy their prospects. Suicide, attempted suicide, depression — even vocalizing the desire to end your life — all these things were interpreted as slanders against the State. Suicide, like murder, had no place in the evolution of a higher society.

The sons were evidently deciding whether or not it was possible to deny the allegation. Leo softened his tone.

— *An autopsy will reveal that his spine is broken. I have to investigate his suicide as rigorously as I would his murder. The reason for his suicide concerns me, not your understandable desire to cover it up.*

The younger son, Akvsenti, answered, speaking for the first time.

— *I cut his throat.*

The young man continued:

— *I was lowering his body. I realized what he'd done to our lives.*

— *Do you have any idea why he killed himself?*

— *He was drinking. He was depressed about work.*

They were telling the truth yet it was incomplete, either through ignorance or calculation. Leo pressed the matter.

— *A fifty-five-year-old man doesn't kill himself because his readers got ink on their fingers. Your father has survived far worse troubles than that.*

The older son became angry.

— *I've spent four years training to be a doctor. All for nothing — no hospital will hire me now.*

Leo guided them out of the office, onto the factory floor, away from the sight of their father's body.

— *You didn't become alarmed that your father hadn't come home until the morning. You expected him to be working late or you would've become concerned last night. If that is the case, why are there no pages of type ready to print? There are four Linotype typesetting machines. No pages have been set. There's nothing to indicate any work was being done here.*

They approached the enormous machines. At the front of each one there was a typewriter-like device, a panel of letters. Leo addressed the sons.

— Right now you're in need of friends. I can't dismiss your father's suicide. I can petition my superiors to stop his actions from impacting on your careers. Times are different now: the mistakes of your father need not reflect on you. But you must earn my help. Tell me what happened. What was your father working on?

The younger son shrugged.

— He was working on some kind of State document. We didn't read it. We destroyed all the pages he'd set. He hadn't finished. We thought maybe he was depressed because he was going to print another badly produced journal. We burnt the paper copy. We melted down the typeset pages. There's nothing left. That's the truth.

Refusing to give up, Leo pointed at the machine.

— Which machine was he working on?

— This one.

— Show me how it works.

— But we've destroyed everything.

— Please.

Akvsenti glanced at his brother, evidently seeking permission. His brother nodded.

— You operate the machine by typing. At the back the device collects the letter moulds. Each line is formed of individual moulds grouped together with space moulds in between. When the line is finished it's cast from a mixture of molten lead and tin. It forms a slug. Those slugs are placed on this tray, until you have an entire page of text. The steel page is then covered in ink and the paper is rolled over – the text is printed. But, like we said, we melted all the pages down. There's nothing left.

Leo walked around the machine. His eyes followed the mechanical process, from the collection of letter moulds to the assembly line. He asked:

— When I type, the letter moulds are collected in this assembly grid?

— Yes.

— There are no complete lines of text. You destroyed those. But in the assembly grid, there's a partial line, a line that hasn't been finished.

Leo was pointing at an incomplete row of letter moulds.

— Your father was halfway through a line.

The sons peered into the machine. Leo was right.

— I want to print these words.

The eldest son began tapping the space bar.

— If we add spaces to the end of the line, it will be of complete length and ready to cast as a slug.

Individual space moulds were added to the incomplete line until the assembly grid was full. A plunger depressed molten lead into the mould and a narrow rectangular slug dropped out – the last words Suren Moskvin set before taking his own life.

The single slug lay on its side, its letters tilted away from view. Leo asked:

— Is it hot?

— No.

Leo picked up the slug line, placed it on the tray. He covered the surface with ink and placed a single sheet of white paper over the top, pressing down.

Seated at his kitchen table, Leo stared at the sheet of paper. Three words were all that remained of the document that had resulted in Suren Moskvin taking his own life:

Under torture, Eikhe

Leo had read the words over and over again, unable to take his eyes off them. Out of context, their effect was none the less hypnotic. Breaking their spell, he pushed the sheet of paper aside and picked up his case, laying it flat on the table. Inside were two classified files. In order to obtain access to them he'd needed clearance. There'd been no difficulty regarding the first file, on Suren Moskvin. However, the second had prompted questions. The second file he'd requested was on Robert Eikhe.

Opening the first set of documents, he felt the weight of this man's past, the number of pages accumulated on him. Moskvin had been a state security officer – a Chekist – just like Leo, for far longer than Leo had served, keeping his job while thousands of officers were shot. Included in the file was a list: the denunciations Moskvin had made throughout his career:

Nestor Iurovsky. Neighbour. Executed
Rozalia Reisner. Friend. 10 years
Iakov Blok. Shopkeeper. 5 years
Karl Uritsky. Colleague. Guard. 10 years

Nineteen years of service, two pages of denunciations and nearly one hundred names – yet he'd only ever given up one family member.

Iona Radek. Cousin. Executed

Leo recognized a technique. The dates of the denunciations were haphazard, many falling in one month and then nothing for several months. The chaotic spacing was deliberate, hiding careful calculation. Denouncing his cousin had almost certainly been strategic. Moskvin needed to make sure it didn't look as if his loyalty to the State stopped at his family. To suffuse his list with credibility the cousin had been sacrificed: protection from the allegation that he only named people who didn't matter to him personally. A consummate survivor, this man was an improbable suicide.

Checking the dates and locations of where Moskvin had worked, Leo sat back in surprise. They'd been colleagues: both of them were employed at the Lubyanka seven years ago. Their paths had never crossed, at least not that he could remember. Leo had been an investigator, making arrests, following suspects. Moskvin had been a guard, transporting prisoners, supervising their detention. Leo had done his utmost to avoid the basement interrogation cells, as if believing the floorboards shielded him from the activities that carried on below, day after day. If Moskvin's suicide was an expression of guilt, what had triggered such extreme feelings after all this time? Leo shut the folder, turning his attention to the second file.

Robert Eikhe's file was thicker, heavier, the front cover stamped CLASSIFIED, the pages bound shut as if to keep something noxious trapped inside. Leo unwound the string. The name seemed familiar. Glancing at the pages he saw that Eikhe had been a party member since 1905 – before the Revolution – at a time when being a member of the Communist Party meant exile or execution. His record was impeccable: a former candidate for the Central Committee Politburo. Despite this, he'd been arrested on 29 April 1938. Plainly, this man was no traitor. Yet Eikhe had confessed: the protocol was in the file, page after page detailing his anti-Soviet activity. Leo had drafted too many pre-prepared confessions not to recognize this as the work of an agent, punctuated with stock phrases – signs of the in-house style, the template to which any person might be forced to sign their name. Flicking forward, Leo found a declaration of innocence written by Eikhe while imprisoned. In contrast to the confession, the prose was human, desperate, pitifully heaping praise on the party, proclaiming love for the State and pointing out with timid modesty the injustice of his arrest. Leo read, hardly able to breathe:

Not being able to suffer the tortures to which I was submitted by Ushakov and Nikolayev – especially by the former, who utilized the knowledge that my broken ribs have not properly mended and caused me great pain – I have been forced to accuse myself and others.

Leo knew what would follow next.

On 4 February 1940 Eikhe had been shot.

*

Raisa stood, watching her husband. Engrossed in classified files, he was oblivious to her presence. This vision of Leo – pale, tense, shoulders hunched over secret documents, the fate of other people in his hands – could have been sliced from their unhappy past. The temptation was to react as she'd done so many times before, to walk away, to avoid and ignore him. The rush of bad memories hit her like a kind of nausea. She fought against the sensation. Leo was not that man any more. She was no longer trapped in that marriage. Walking forward, she reached out, resting a hand on his shoulder, appointing him the man she'd learnt to love.

Leo flinched at her touch. He hadn't noticed his wife enter the room. Caught unawares, he felt exposed. He stood up abruptly, the chair clattering behind him. Eye to eye, he saw her nervousness. He'd never wanted her to feel that way again. He should have explained what he was doing. He'd fallen into old habits, silence and secrets. He put his arms around her. Resting her head on his shoulder he knew she was peering down at the files. He explained:

— *A man killed himself, a former MGB agent.*

— *Someone you knew?*

— *No. Not that I remember.*

— *You have to investigate?*

— *Suicide is treated as—*

   I mean . . . does it have to be you?

Raisa wanted him to pass it over, to have nothing to do with the MGB, even indirectly. He pulled back.

— *The case won't take long.*

She nodded, slowly, before changing the subject.

— *The girls are in bed. Are you going to read for them? Maybe you're busy?*

— *No, I'm not busy.*

He put the files back in his briefcase. Passing his wife he leaned in to kiss her, a kiss that she gently blocked with a finger, looking into his eyes. She said nothing, before removing her finger and kissing him — a kiss that felt as if he was making the most unbreakable and sacred of promises.

Entering his bedroom, he placed the files out of sight, an old habit. Changing his mind, he retrieved them, leaving them on the side table for Raisa should she want to read them. He hurried back down the hallway on his way to his daughters' bedroom, trying to smooth the tension from his face. Smiling broadly, he opened the door.

Leo and Raisa had adopted two young sisters. Zoya was now fourteen years old and Elena, seven. Leo moved towards Elena's bed, perching on the edge, picking up a book from the cabinet, a children's story by Yury Strugatsky. He opened the book and began to read aloud. Almost immediately, Zoya interrupted:

— *We've heard this before.*

She waited a moment before adding:

— *We hated it the first time.*

The story concerned a young boy who wanted to be a miner. The boy's father, also a miner, had died in an accident and the boy's mother was fearful of her son continuing in such a dangerous profession. Zoya was right. Leo had read this before. Zoya summarized contemptuously:

— *The son ends up digging more coal than anyone has ever dug before, becomes a national hero and dedicates his prize to the memory of his father.*

Leo shut the book.

— *You're right. It's not very good. But, Zoya, while it's OK for you to say whatever you please in this house, be more careful outside. Expressing critical opinions, even about trivial matters, like a children's story, is dangerous.*

— You going to arrest me?

Zoya had never accepted Leo as her guardian. She'd never forgiven him for the death of her parents. Leo didn't refer to himself as their father. And Zoya would call him Leo Demidov, addressing him formally, putting as much distance between them as possible. She took every opportunity to remind him that she was living with him out of practical considerations, using him as a means to an end – providing material comforts for her sister, freeing her from the orphanage. Even so, she took care that nothing impressed her, not the apartment, not their outings, day trips or meals. As stern as she was beautiful, there was no softness in her appearance. Perpetual unhappiness seemed vitally important to her. There was little Leo could do to encourage her to shrug it off. He hoped that at some point relations would slowly improve. He was still waiting. He would, if necessary, wait for ever.

No, Zoya, I don't do that any more. And I never will again.

Leo reached down, picking up one of the *Detskaya Literatura* journals, printed for children across the country. Before he could start, Zoya cut in:

— Why don't you make up a story? We'd like that, wouldn't we, Elena?

When Elena arrived in Moscow she was only four years old, young enough to adapt to the changes in her life. In contrast to her older sister, she made friends and worked hard at school. Susceptible to flattery, she sought her teachers' praise, trying to please everyone, including her new guardians.

Elena became anxious. She understood from the tone of her sister's voice that she was expected to agree. Embarrassed at having to take sides, she merely nodded. Leo, sensing danger, replied:

— There are plenty of stories we haven't read, I'm sure I can find one we like.

Zoya wouldn't relent.

— *They're all the same. Tell us something new. Make something up.*

— *I doubt I'd be very good.*

— *You're not even going to try? My father used to make up all kinds of stories. Set it on a remote farm, a farm in winter, with the ground covered in a layer of snow. The nearby river is frozen. It could start like this. Once upon a time there are two young girls, sisters . . .*

— *Zoya, please.*

— *The sisters live with their mother and their father and they're as happy as can be. Until one day a man, in a uniform, came to arrest them and—*

Leo interrupted:

— *Zoya? Please?*

Zoya glanced at her sister and stopped. Elena was crying. Leo stood up.

— *You're both tired. I'll find some better books tomorrow. I promise.*

Leo turned the light off and closed the door. In the hallway, he comforted himself that things would get better, eventually. All Zoya needed was a little more time.

*

Zoya lay in bed, listening to the sound of her sister sleeping – her slow, soft intakes of breath. When they'd lived on the farm with their parents, the four of them shared a small room with thick mud walls, warmed by a wood fire. Zoya would sleep beside Elena under their coarse, hand-stitched blankets. The sound of her little sister sleeping meant safety: it meant their parents were nearby. It didn't belong here, in this apartment, with Leo in the room next door.

Zoya never fell asleep easily. She'd lie in bed for hours, churning thoughts before exhaustion overcame her. She was the only person who cherished the truth: the only person who refused to forget. She eased herself out of bed. Aside from her little sister breathing, the apartment was silent. She crept to the door, her eyes already adjusted to the darkness. She navigated the hallway by keeping her hand on the wall. In the kitchen, street lighting leaked in through the window. Moving nimbly, like a thief, she opened a drawer and took hold of the handle, feeling the weight of the knife.

Pressing the blade flat against her leg, Zoya walked towards Leo's bedroom. Slowly she pushed open the door until there was enough space to sidestep inside. She moved silently over the wooden floor. The curtains were drawn, the room dark, but she knew the layout, where to tread in order to reach Leo, sleeping on the far side.

Standing directly over him, Zoya raised the knife. Although she couldn't see him, her imagination mapped the contours of his body. She wouldn't stab him in the stomach: the blankets might absorb the blade. She'd plunge it through his neck, sinking it as far as she could, before he had a chance to overpower her. Knife out-stretched, she pressed down with perfect control. Through the blade she felt his arm, his shoulder – she steered upwards, making small depressions until the knife tip touched directly onto his skin. In position, all she had to do was grip the handle with both hands and push down.

Zoya performed this ritual at irregular intervals, sometimes once a week, sometimes not for a month. The first time was three years ago, shortly after she and her sister moved into this apart-ment from the orphanage. On that occasion she had every intention of killing him. That same day he'd taken them to the zoo. Neither she nor Elena had been to a zoo, and confronted with exotic animals, creatures that she'd never seen before, she'd forgotten herself. For perhaps no more than five or ten minutes, she'd enjoyed the visit. She'd smiled. He hadn't seen her smile, she was sure of that, but it didn't matter. Watching him together with Raisa, a happy couple, imitating a family, pretending, lying, she understood that they were trying to steal the place of her parents. And she'd let them. On her way home, on the tramcar, her guilt had been so intense she'd thrown up. Leo and Raisa had blamed the sweet snacks and the motion of the tram. That night, feverish, she lay in bed, crying, scratching her legs until they bled. How could she have betrayed the memory of her parents so easily? Leo believed he could win her love with new clothes, rare foods, day trips and chocolate: it was pathetic. She vowed that her lapse would never happen again. There was one way to make sure: she took the knife and resolved to kill him. She stood, as she stood now, ready to murder.

The same memory that had driven her into the room, the memory of her parents, was the reason she hadn't killed him. They wouldn't want this man's blood on her hands. They would want her to look after her sister. Obedient, silently crying, she'd allowed Leo to live. Every now and then she'd come back, creeping in, armed with a knife, not because she'd changed her mind, not for revenge, not to murder, but as a memorial to her parents, as a way of saying she had not forgotten them.

The telephone rang. Startled, Zoya stepped back, the knife slipping from her hand, clattering to the floor. Dropping to her knees she fumbled in the pitch black frantically trying to find it. Leo and Raisa were stirring, the bed straining as they moved. They'd be reaching for the light. Working by touch alone Zoya desperately patted the floorboards. As the telephone rang for the second time she had no choice but to leave the knife behind, hurrying around

TOM ROB SMITH

the bed, running towards the door, slipping through the gap just
as the light came on.

*

Leo sat up, his thoughts sluggish with sleep, intermingled dreams
and reality – there had been movement, a figure, or perhaps there
hadn't. The phone was ringing. It only ever rang because of work.
He checked his watch: almost midnight. He glanced at Raisa. She
was awake, waiting for him to answer the phone. He mumbled an
apology and got up. The door was ajar. Didn't they always close it
before they went to sleep? Maybe not, it didn't matter, and he
headed into the hallway.

He picked up the receiver. The voice on the other end was
urgent, loud.

— *Leo? This is Nikolai.*

Nikolai: the name meant nothing to him. He didn't reply.
Correctly interpreting Leo's silence, the man continued:

— *Nikolai, your old boss! Your friend! Leo, don't you remember? I gave you your first assignment! The priest, remember, Leo?*

Leo remembered. He hadn't heard from Nikolai in a long time.
This man was of no relevance to his life now and he resented him
calling.

— *Nikolai, it's late.*

— *Late? What's happened to you? We didn't start work until
about now.*

— *Not any more.*

— *No, not any more.*

Nikolai's voice drifted off, before adding:

— *I need to meet you.*

His words were slurred. He was drunk.

— *Nikolai, why don't you sleep it off and we'll talk tomorrow?*

— It has to be tonight.

His voice cracked. He was on the verge of crying.

— What's going on?

— Meet me. Please.

Leo wanted to say no.

— Where?

— Your offices.

— I'll be there in thirty minutes.

Leo hung up. His annoyance was tempered by unease. Nikolai wouldn't have got back in contact unless he had cause. Returning to the bedroom, Raisa was sitting up. Leo shrugged an explanation.

— A former colleague. He wants to meet. Says it has to be tonight.

— A colleague from when?

— From . . .

Leo didn't need to finish the sentence.

— Out of nowhere, he calls?

— He was drunk. I'll speak to him.

— Leo . . . ?

She didn't finish. Leo nodded.

— I don't like it either.

He grabbed his clothes, hastily getting changed. Almost ready to leave, tying his shoelaces, he saw something under the bed, something catching the light. Curious, he moved forward, crouching down. Raisa asked:

— What?

It was a large kitchen knife. Near it was a notch in the floor.

— Leo?

He should show it to her.

— It's nothing.

As Raisa leaned over to look he stood up, hiding the knife behind his back and turning the light off.

In the hallway he laid the blade flat across his palm. He glanced at his daughters' bedroom. He stepped towards the door and gently pushed it open. The room was dark. Both girls were in bed, asleep. In the process of retreat, silently shutting the door, he smiled at the slow, shallow breathing of Elena sleeping. He paused, listening carefully. He couldn't hear any noise coming from Zoya's side of the room. She was holding her breath.

Driving too fast, Leo skidded into a turn, the tyres slipping across black ice. He eased off the gas pedal and brought the car back to the centre of the road. Agitated, his back damp with perspiration, he was relieved to arrive at the Homicide Department. He pulled up, resting his head against the steering wheel. In the unheated interior his breath formed a thin mist. It was one in the morning. The streets were deserted, layered with patchy snow. He began to shiver, having forgotten gloves or hat as he hurried out to get away from the question of why the bedroom door had been ajar, why his daughter had been pretending to sleep and why there'd been a knife under his bed.

Surely there were explanations, simple, mundane explanations. Maybe he'd left the door open. Maybe his wife had gone to the bathroom, forgetting to shut the door on her return. As for Zoya pretending to be asleep: he'd misheard. In fact, why did she need to be asleep? It made sense that she was awake, she'd been woken by the telephone and she'd been lying in bed, trying to get back to sleep, justifiably annoyed. As for the knife . . . He didn't know, he just couldn't think, but there had to be an innocent reason, even if he had no idea of what it might be.

He stepped out of the car, shut the door, moved towards his offices. Located in the Zamoskvareche district, south of the river, an area with a high concentration of factories, his Homicide Department had been designated space above a vast bakery. There was mockery in the location as well as the message that its work was to remain invisible. The offices had been marked as Button Factory 14, prompting Leo to wonder what went on in the other thirteen factories.

Entering the ramshackle reception, the floor criss-crossed with flour footsteps, Leo climbed the stairs, running over in his mind the events of the night. He'd successfully dismissed two out of three occurrences but the third – the knife – resisted attempts to explain it away. The matter would have to wait until the morning when he could talk to Raisa. Right now Nikolai's unexpected phone call was a greater concern. Leo needed to focus on why a man he hadn't spoken to in six years was calling, drunk, in the middle of the night, begging for a meeting. There was nothing between them, no bond or friendship, nothing except that year, 1949 – his first year as an MGB agent.

Nikolai was waiting for him at the top of the stairs, slouched in the doorway like a vagrant. Seeing Leo arrive he stood up. His winter coat was well tailored, perhaps even foreign-made, but tatty with neglect. His shirt had come unbuttoned, his stomach overflowing. He'd gained weight, lost hair. He was old and tired-looking, his face pinched with worry, scrunched up around the eyes. He stank of smoke and sweat and booze which, combined with the ever-present smell of baking and dough, formed a rancid combination. Leo offered his hand. Nikolai pushed it aside, embracing him, clinging on as if he'd been rescued from a mountainside. There was something pitiful about the hug – this from a man who'd built a reputation on being pitiless.

Leo's attention was suddenly snatched away as he remembered the notch in his floor. Why had he forgotten that detail? It was unimportant, that's why. Any number of things could have caused it. It might have been there for some time, it wasn't something he'd necessarily notice, a scratch caused by furniture being moved. Yet in his gut he knew the knife and the notch were connected.

Nikolai had begun talking, rambling, slurring his words. Leo was barely paying attention as he opened the department, leading his guest through to his office. Seated, Leo clenched his hands together, leaning his elbows on the table, watching Nikolai speak but hearing almost nothing, tuning in and out, catching occasional fragments — something about being sent photographs.

— Leo, they're photographs of the men and women I arrested.

Leo's mind had no space for the things Nikolai was saying. A single, terrible realization was growing inside him, shunting every other thought aside. The knife had been dropped, the tip cutting into the floor before ricocheting under the bed, dropped because whoever was holding it had panicked, alarmed by a sudden noise, an unexpected telephone call. The person fled the room, leaving the door open, in too much of a rush to close it behind her.

HER

Even now, with all the pieces in place, he struggled to articulate the only logical conclusion: the person holding the knife had been Zoya.

He stood up, walking to the window and throwing it open. Cold air rushed over his face. He wasn't sure how long he remained in this position, staring out at the night sky, but hearing a noise behind him he remembered that he was not alone. He turned around, about to apologize. He swallowed his words.

Nikolai, a man who'd taught him that cruelty was necessary and good, was crying:

— *Leo? You're not even listening.*

Tears still on his cheeks, Nikolai started to laugh, a noise that took Leo back to their obligatory post-arrest drinking celebrations. Tonight Nikolai's laughter was different. It was brittle. The swagger and confidence were gone.

— *You want to forget? Don't you, Leo? I don't blame you. I would pay anything to forget it all. What a wonderful dream that would be . . .*

— *I'm sorry, Nikolai; my mind is elsewhere, a family matter.*

— *You took my advice . . . A family, that's good. Families are important. A man is nothing without the love of his family.*

— *Can we talk tomorrow? When we're less tired?*

Nikolai nodded and stood up. At the door he paused, looking at the floor.

— *I am . . . ashamed.*

— *Think nothing of it. We all drink too much from time to time. We'll talk tomorrow.*

Nikolai stared at him. Leo thought he was going to laugh again but this time he turned around, heading towards the stairs.

Leo was thankful to be alone and able to concentrate. He couldn't pretend any longer. He was an ever-present reminder of Zoya's terrible loss. He'd never spoken about what happened that day, when her parents had been shot. He'd tried to brush the past aside. The knife was a cry for help. He had to act to save his family. He could fix this. Talking to Zoya: that was the solution. He had to talk to her right now.

Nikolai stepped outside, his boots sinking into the thin snow. Feeling the chill on his exposed stomach, he tucked his shirt into his trousers – his eyes barely able to focus, his body swaying as though he was on the deck of a boat. Why had he phoned his former protégé? What had he expected him to do? Perhaps he'd just come for companionship, not just any companionship such as a fellow drunk; he'd come for the company of a man who shared his shame, a man who couldn't pass judgement without also passing that same judgement on himself.

I am ashamed.

Those were words that Leo should have understood better than anyone. Mutual shame should have brought them together and made them brothers. Leo should've put his arms around him and said: *Me too.* Had he forgotten their history so easily? No, they merely had different techniques for dealing with it. Leo had embarked on a new and noble career, scrubbing his bloody hands in a basin of warm, soapy respectability. Nikolai's technique had been to drink until he blacked out, not for the thrill but as an attack on his memory.

Someone wouldn't allow him to forget, sending him

photographs of men and women taken against a white wall, cropped so that they were just a face. At first he hadn't recognized the subjects although he'd realized that they were arrest photographs, the kind required by any prison bureaucracy. They arrived in batches, once a week, then once a day, every day, an envelope left at his home. Going through them he'd begun to remember names, conversations – tattered memories, a crude collage with one citizen's arrest spliced with another's interrogation and another's execution. As the photographs accumulated, holding them heaped in his hands, he questioned whether he'd arrested so many. In truth, he knew, he'd arrested far more.

Nikolai wanted to confess, to ask for forgiveness. But no demands were sent, no requests for an apology, no instructions on how to repent. The first envelope had been marked with his name. His wife had brought it to him. He'd opened it casually in front of her. When she'd asked what it contained he'd lied, hiding the photos. From then on, he'd been forced to open them in secret. Even after twenty years of marriage, his wife didn't know about his work. She knew he'd been a State Security officer. But she knew little more. Perhaps she was being wilfully ignorant. He didn't care whether it was wilful or not, he cherished her ignorance – he depended upon it. When he looked into her eyes he saw unqualified love. If she knew, if she'd seen the faces of the people he'd arrested, if she'd seen their faces after two days of questioning, there would be fear in her eyes. The same was true for his daughters. They laughed and joked with him. They loved him and he loved them. He was a good father, attentive and patient, never raising his voice, never drinking at home – a home where he remained a good man.

Someone wanted to steal this from him. Within the last couple of days the envelopes were no longer marked with his name.

Anyone could have opened them: his wife, his daughters. Nikolai had become afraid to go out in case something should arrive in his absence. He'd made his family swear to bring to him any package or letter whether it was marked with a name or not. Yesterday he'd gone into his daughters' room to find an unmarked letter on their bedside table. He'd lost his temper, wild with anger, furiously asking if the girls had opened it. They'd cried, confused by the sudden transformation, assuring him they'd put it on the table for safekeeping. He'd seen fear in their eyes. It had broken his heart. It was the moment he'd decided to seek Leo's help. The State must catch these criminals that were senselessly persecuting him. He'd given many years of service to his country. He was a patriot. He'd earned the right to live in peace. Leo could help: he had an investigative team at his disposal. It would be in their mutual interest to hunt down these counter-revolutionaries. It would be just like old times. Except Leo hadn't wanted to know.

The early morning workers were already arriving at the bakery. They stopped, staring at Nikolai in the doorway. He snarled:

— *What?*

They said nothing, remaining huddled, some metres away, not passing him.

— *You judge me?*

Their faces were blank, men and women waiting to bake the city's bread. He had to get home, to the one place, the only place where he was loved and where his past meant nothing.

Living nearby, he staggered through the deserted streets, hoping that another package of photographs hadn't arrived in his absence. He stopped walking: his breathing was shallow and heavy, like an old, unhealthy dog. There was something else, another noise. He turned around, looking behind him. Footsteps — he was sure of it, the tap, tap of hard heels on stone pavements. He was being followed. He lurched towards the shadows, searching for outlines, straining his eyes. They were after him, his enemies, stalking him: hunting him as he had once hunted them.

He was running now, home, as fast as he could. He stumbled before regaining his balance, his coat flapping about his ankles. Changing tack, he spun around. He'd catch them at this game. He knew these tricks. They were his tricks. They were using his methods against him. Staring at the dark corners, the murky enclaves, the hiding places where he'd trained MGB recruits to move, he called out:

— *I know you're there.*

His voice echoed down the seemingly empty street. Empty to a layman, but he was an expert in such matters. His defiance was brief, melting away.

— *I have children, two daughters. They love me! They don't deserve this. You hurt me and you hurt them.*

His children had been born while he'd been an MGB officer. After arresting fathers, mothers, sons and daughters, every night he'd gone home and kissed his own family goodnight.

— *What about the others? There are millions of others, if you killed us all, there'd be no one left. We were all involved!*

People were appearing at the windows, drawn out by his shouting. He could point to any building, any house, and inside there'd be former officers and guards. The men and women in uniform were the obvious targets. There were also the train drivers who took the prisoners to the Gulags, the men and women who processed paperwork, stamped forms, the people who cooked and cleaned. The system required the consent of everyone, even if they consented by doing nothing. Nothing was enough. They'd depended upon a lack of resistance as much as they'd depended on volunteers. He would not be a scapegoat. This wasn't his burden alone. Everyone carried a collective guilt. He was prepared to feel remorse from time to time, to spend a minute each day thinking over the terrible things he'd done. The people hounding him weren't satisfied with that. They wanted more.

Fearful, Nikolai turned and ran, wildly this time, as fast as he could. Tangled up in his coat, he fell over, crashing down into the slushy snow, his clothes soaking up the filthy water. Slowly getting up, his knee throbbing, his trousers ripped, he ran again, water streaming from his coat. It wasn't long before he fell again. This time he began to cry, exhausted, awful sobs. Rolling onto his back, he pulled himself free from his coat, now impossibly heavy. He'd bought it many years ago from one of the restricted stores. He'd been proud of it. It was proof of his status. He didn't need it any more: he'd never go out again, he'd stay at home, lock the door and pull the curtains shut.

Reaching his apartment block, he entered the hallway panting and sweating, dirty water dripping from his clothes. Soaking wet, pressed against the wall, leaving an impression of his body, he checked the street, waiting to catch a glimpse of his pursuers. Unable to see anyone – they were too sly – he climbed the stairs, his feet slipping, then scrambled up on all fours. The closer he got to home, the more he relaxed. They couldn't reach him through these walls, his sanctuary. As if he'd swallowed a soothing tonic, he began to think rationally. He was drunk. He'd overreacted, that was all. Of course he'd made enemies over the years, people with grudges, bitter at his success. If all they could do was send him a couple of photographs he didn't need to worry. The majority – society – respected and valued him. He breathed deeply, reaching his landing and groping for his key.

Outside his front door was a package, roughly thirty centimetres long, twenty centimetres wide and ten centimetres deep, wrapped in brown paper, neatly bound with string. There was no name, no label, just an ink drawing on the paper, a crucifix. Nikolai dropped to his knees. His hands trembled as he pulled the string free. Inside was a box. The top of the box was marked:

NOT FOR PRESS

He lifted the lid. There were no photographs. Instead, there was a stack of neatly printed pages, a substantial document, over a hundred pages long. On the top rested an accompanying letter. He picked it up, scanning the words. It wasn't addressed to him: it was an official State letter declaring that this speech was to be distributed to every school, every factory, every workers' group and youth group up and down the country. Confused, he put the letter down, taking up the speech. He read the first page carefully. He began shaking his head. This couldn't be true. It was a lie, a malicious fabrication, intended to drive him insane. This could never have been published by the State: they would never distribute such a document. It was impossible.

INNOCENT

VICTIMS

TORTURE

These words couldn't exist in black and white, printed, State-sanctioned, distributed to every school and factory. When he caught the perpetrator of this hoax, this well-informed hoax, he'd have them executed.

Involuntarily Nikolai scrunched up the page he was reading and tossed it aside. He began to tear at the next page, and the next, ripping them into shreds, tossing the scraps aside. He stopped, bending forward, curling into a ball, his head resting on the unread pages, muttering to himself:

— *It can't be true.*

How could it be? But it was here, with a State-stamped letter, containing information only the State would know, with sources, quotes, references. The conspiracy of silence, which Nikolai had presumed would last for ever, was over. It was no trick.

The speech was real.

Nikolai stood up, leaving the papers scattered. He unlocked the door and entered his apartment, abandoning the papers to the communal hallway. It didn't matter if he locked the door behind him and pulled the curtains shut, his home was no longer a sanctuary. There were no sanctuaries any longer. Soon everyone would know, every schoolchild and every factory worker would read the speech. Not only would they know, they'd be allowed to talk openly, encouraged to discuss.

He pushed open the bedroom door, staring down at his wife, asleep, on her side, her hands under her head. She was beautiful. He adored her. They lived a perfect, privileged life. They had two wonderful, happy daughters. His wife had never known disgrace. She'd never known shame. She'd never known Nikolai in any other guise than that of a loving husband, a tender man who'd die for his family. He sat on the edge of the bed, running a finger along her pale arm. He couldn't live with her knowing the truth, changing her opinion of him, pulling away, asking questions or worse still remaining silent. Her silence would be unbearable. All her friends would ask questions. She'd be judged. How much did she know? Had she always known? Better that he should not live to see her shamed. Better that he should die now.

Except his death would change nothing. She would still find out. She would wake to find his body and she would cry and grieve. Then, she would read the speech. Although she'd attend his funeral she would wonder at the things he'd done. She would rethink the moments they'd spent together, when he'd touched her, when he'd made love to her. Had he murdered someone hours before? Had her home been bought with blood? Perhaps, eventually, she would even come to believe that he deserved to die and that taking his life had been the right thing to do, not just for him but also for their daughters.

He picked up the pillow. His wife was strong and she would struggle but even though he was out of shape he was confident of his ability to overpower her. He positioned himself carefully and she moved accordingly, sensing his body, no doubt pleased he was home. She rolled onto her back, smiling. He couldn't look at her face any more. He had to act now before he lost his nerve. He lowered the pillow, quickly, not wanting to catch sight of her opening her eyes. He pressed down as hard as he could. Quickly she grabbed at the pillow, at his wrists, scratching. It was no good, he wouldn't let go – she couldn't pull loose. Rather than trying to break his grip, she tried to wriggle out from underneath. He straddled her, locking his legs around her stomach, keeping her fixed in position and unable to move while he kept the pillow in place. She was pinned down, helpless, weakening. Her hands no longer scratched, they merely held his wrists until they went slack and fell by her side.

He remained in the same position, on top of her, holding the pillow for some minutes after she stopped moving. Finally, he eased back, letting go, leaving the pillow across her face. He didn't want to see her bloodshot eyes. He wanted to remember her expression as being full of love. He reached under the pillow to shut her eyelids. His fingertips roamed her face, getting closer and closer until he touched her pupil – the faintly sticky surface. He carefully closed her eyelids and lifted the pillow, looking down at her. She was at peace. He lay beside her, his arms around her waist.

Exhausted, Nikolai almost fell asleep. He shook himself awake. He was not finished yet. Standing up, neatening the sheets, he picked up the pillow and walked out into the living room, turning towards his daughters' bedroom.

Zoya and Elena were asleep: Leo could hear the rise and fall of their breathing. Adjusting to the darkness, he carefully shut the door behind him. He couldn't fail at being a father. Let the Homicide Department close, let him be stripped of his apartment and privileges, there had to be some way of saving his family, nothing mattered more. And he was sure that this family, despite its problems, offered the best chance for all of them. He refused to imagine a future where they wouldn't be together. It was true that both girls were far closer to Raisa than they were to him. Clearly the obstacle wasn't the adoption but his past. He'd been naive in thinking that his relationship with Elena and Zoya merely required time, which, like a trick of perspective moving far enough away from the incident, would make it appear smaller and less significant. Even now he used a euphemism — *the incident* — for the murder of her parents. Zoya's anger was as vivid as the day they had been shot. Instead of denial, he had to confront her hatred directly.

Zoya was sleeping on her side, facing the wall. Leo reached over and took hold of her shoulder, gently rolling her onto her back. The intention had been to ease her out of her sleep but instead she sat up straight, tensing, pulling away from his touch. Without realizing exactly what he was doing he placed his other hand on her shoulder, stopping her from moving away. He did it for the best of reasons, for both of their sakes. He needed her to listen. Attempting to maintain a measured, reassuring tone he whispered:

— *Zoya, we need to talk, the two of us. It can't wait. If I wait till morning I'll find some excuse and I'll delay till tomorrow. I've already delayed for three years.*

She said nothing, remaining motionless, her eyes fixed on him. Although he'd spent at least an hour in the kitchen trying to work out exactly what to say, those carefully planned words disappeared.

— *You were in my bedroom. I found the knife.*

He'd opened on the wrong topic. He was here to talk about his failings, not to criticize her. He tried to turn the conversation around.

— *First, let me make clear, I'm a different person now. I'm not the officer that came to your parents' farm. Also, remember, I tried to save your parents. I failed. I will live with that failure for the rest of my life. I can't bring them back. But I can give you and your sister opportunities. That's how I see this family. It's an opportunity. It's an opportunity for you and for Elena, but also for me*

Leo stopped, remaining silent, waiting to see if she'd ridicule the notion. She didn't move or speak. Her lips were clamped together: her body was rigid.

— *Can't you . . . try?*

Her voice trembled, her first words.

— *Let go.*

— *Zoya, don't get upset: just tell me what you're thinking. Be honest. Tell me what you want me to do. Tell me what kind of person you want me to be.*

— *Let go.*

— *No, Zoya, please, you have to understand how important this is.*

— *Let go.*

— *Zoya . . .*

Her voice became higher, strained – desperate.

— *Let go!*

Stunned, he pulled back. She was whining like a wounded animal. How had this gone so wrong? In disbelief he watched as she recoiled from his affection. This wasn't how it was supposed to be. He was trying to express his love for her. She was throwing it back in his face. Zoya was ruining this, not just for him. She was ruining it for everyone. Elena wanted to be part of a family. He knew she did. She held his hand: she smiled, laughed. She wanted to be happy. Raisa wanted to be happy. They all just wanted to be happy. Except for Zoya, stubbornly refusing to recognize that he'd changed, childishly clinging to her hatred as if it was her favourite doll.

Leo noticed the smell. Touching the sheets, he discovered they were damp. Even so, it took him a second or two to understand that Zoya had wet the bed. He stood up, stepped back, muttering:

— *That's OK. I'll clean it up. Don't worry. That's my fault. I'm to blame.*

Zoya shook her head, saying nothing, scrunching her hands against her temples, clawing at the sides of her face. Leo became short of breath, perplexed that his love could create such misery.

— *Zoya, I'll take the sheets.*

She shook her head, clutching the piss-stained sheets as if they were protecting her from him. By now Elena was awake and crying.

Leo turned to the door and then turned back again, unable to leave her in such a state. How could he fix the problem when he was the problem?

— *I just want to love you, Zoya*.

Elena was looking from Zoya to Leo. Her being awake resulted in a change in Zoya. She regained her composure, calmly telling Leo:

— *I'm going to wash my sheets. I'm going to do it myself. I don't need your help*.

Leo left the room, leaving the young girl he'd hoped to win over sitting in piss and tears.

*

Entering the kitchen, Leo paced the room, drunk on catastrophe. While he'd tidied away the files, the sheet of paper from Moskvin's printing press was as he'd left it:

Under torture, Eikhe

An appropriate companion: a reminder of his former career, a career that was going to shadow him for ever. Picturing Zoya's reaction in the bedroom, Leo was forced to contemplate something he'd only minutes ago dismissed as unthinkable. The family might have to be broken apart.

Had his desire to hold them together become a blind obsession? It was forcing Zoya to pick at the scab of a wound that would never heal, infecting her with hatred and bitterness. Of course, if she couldn't live with him then neither could Elena. The sisters were inseparable. He'd have no choice but to find them a new home, one with no connection to the State, perhaps outside Moscow in a smaller town where the apparatus of power was less visible. He and Raisa would need to search for suitable guardians, meeting prospective parents and wondering if they could do a better job, if they could bring the girls happiness, something Leo had so utterly failed to provide.

Raisa appeared at the door.

— *What's going on?*

She'd come from their bedroom. She didn't know about the bed-wetting, the conversation, referring instead to Nikolai, the phone call, the midnight meeting. Leo's voice was cracked with emotion.

— *Nikolai was drunk. I told him we'd talk when he was sober.*

— *That took all night?*

What was he waiting for? He should sit her down and explain.

— *Leo? What's wrong?*

He'd promised there would be no more secrets. Yet he couldn't admit that after three years of trying to be a father he had nothing but Zoya's hatred to show for it. He couldn't admit that he woken her in the middle of the night, pathetically petitioning to be her father. He was afraid. The division of their family might make Raisa wonder which side she wanted to be on. Would she remain with the girls or with him? For the years he'd been an MGB officer she'd despised him and everything he represented. In contrast, she loved Elena and Zoya without qualification. Her love for him was complicated. Her love for them was simple. In making her decision she might choose to remember the man he was, the man he used to be. Part of him was convinced that his relationship with Raisa depended upon him proving himself as a father. For the first time in three years he lied to her.

— *Nothing is wrong. It was a shock seeing Nikolai again. That's all.*

Raisa nodded. She looked down the hall.

— *Are the girls awake?*

— *They woke up when I came back. I'm sorry. I said sorry to them.*

Raisa picked up the sheet of paper taken from the printing press.

— *You'd better move this before the girls sit down.*

Leo took the sheet to their room. He perched on the bed, watching as Raisa left the kitchen to wake the girls. Nervous, nearly sick, he waited for her to discover the truth. His lie had bought him a temporary reprieve and no more than that. She would listen as Zoya explained what had happened.

He looked up, stunned to see Raisa casually emerge from the girls' bedroom, returning to the kitchen without saying a word. Seconds later Zoya emerged, carrying her sheets to the bathroom where she deposited them in the bath, running the hot water. She hadn't told Raisa. She didn't want Raisa to know. The only thing she hated more than Leo was the idea that he'd been able to embarrass her in this way.

Leo stood up, entering the kitchen and asking:

— *Zoya's washing the sheets?*

Raisa nodded. Leo continued:

— *She doesn't need to do that. I can arrange to have them cleaned.*

Raisa lowered her voice.

— *I think she had an accident. Just leave her, OK?*

— *OK.*

Elena entered first, her shirt buttoned up incorrectly, taking her seat. She was silent. Leo smiled at her. She studied his smile as if it was something unknown and threatening. She did not smile back. He could hear Zoya's footsteps. They stopped. She was standing out of sight, waiting in the hall.

Zoya stepped into view. She faced Leo directly, looking at him from across the room. She glanced at Raisa, who was busy stirring the oats, then at her sister, who was eating. She understood that he hadn't told them either. The knife was their secret. The bed-wetting was their secret. They were accomplices, complicit in this false family. Zoya wasn't ready to tear the family apart. Her love for Elena was stronger than her hatred of him.

Gingerly, like an alley cat, Zoya moved towards her seat. She didn't touch her breakfast. In turn, Leo ate nothing, churning the oats in the bowl, unable to look up. Raisa was unimpressed.

— *Neither of you are going to eat?*

Leo waited for Zoya to reply. She said nothing. Leo began to eat. As soon as he did, Zoya stood up, depositing her untouched bowl in the sink.

— *I feel sick.*

Raisa stood up, checking her temperature.

— *Are you well enough for school?*

— *Yes.*

The girls left the kitchen. Raisa moved close to Leo:

— *What is wrong with you today?*

Leo was sure, if he opened his mouth, he'd start to cry. He said nothing, his hands clenched under the table.

Shaking her head, Raisa moved off to help the girls. There was bustle around the front door: final preparations to leave, coats being put on. The door was opened. Raisa returned to the kitchen, carrying a parcel wrapped in brown paper, tied with string. She placed it on the table and walked out. The front door slammed shut.

Leo didn't move for several minutes. Then, slowly, he reached forward, pulling the parcel towards him. They lived inside a min-isterial compound. Letters were normally left at the gate: this had been left on his doorstep. The parcel was about thirty centimetres long, twenty centimetres wide and ten centimetres deep. There was no name, no address, just an ink drawing of a crucifix. Ripping the brown paper he saw a box, the top of which was stamped:

NOT FOR PRESS

The metro carriage wasn't crowded, yet Elena took hold of Raisa's hand, gripping it tightly, as if fearful they were about to be separated. Both girls were unusually quiet. Leo's behaviour this morning had unsettled them. Raisa couldn't understand what had come over him. Normally so careful around the girls, he'd seemed to accept that they were about to sit down for breakfast and witness him preoccupied by that word: *torture*. When she'd asked him to take the sheet of paper away, his cue to pull himself together, he'd obeyed only to return to the kitchen in exactly the same dishevelled state, staring at the girls and not saying a word. Bloodshot eyes, a haunted, ragged look: she hadn't seen that expression for years, not since his return from all-night assignments as a secret-police officer, exhausted and yet unable to go to bed. He'd slump in the corner, in the dark, brooding, silent, as though the events of the previous night were playing over and over in his mind. During that period he'd never spoken about his work yet she'd known what he was doing, arresting indiscriminately, and she'd secretly hated him for it.

Those times were past. He'd changed – she was sure of it. He'd risked his life to break from a profession of midnight arrests and forced confessions. The State security apparatus still existed, renamed the KGB, remaining a presence in everyone's life but Leo played no part in its operations, having declined the offer of a high-ranking position. Instead, taking a much greater risk, he'd opened his own investigative department. Every night he shared stories of his working day partly because he sought her advice, partly to show how different his department was to the KGB, but mostly to prove there were no more secrets between them. Yet her approval wasn't enough. Observing him around the girls, it struck Raisa that he behaved as if he was cursed, a character in a children's fairytale, and only the words – *I love you* – spoken by both girls, could break the dark magic of his past.

Despite his frustrations, he'd never shown any jealousy of Raisa's easy relationship with Elena and Zoya even when Zoya deliberately tormented him by being openly affectionate to her and cold to him. Over the past three years he'd withstood rejection and rudeness, never losing his temper, soaking up hostility as if he considered it nothing less than he deserved. In the face of this, he'd made the girls his only hope of redemption. Zoya knew it and reacted against it. The more he sought her affection, the more she hated him. Raisa couldn't point out the contradiction, or tell him to relax. Once fanatical about Communism, he was now fanatical about his family. His vision of Utopia had been made smaller, less abstract and though it now encompassed only four people, rather than the entire world, it remained just as elusive.

The train pulled into TsPkiO station, abbreviated from its full name, Tsentralnyl Park Kulturyi Otdykha Imeni Gorkovo. The first time the girls had heard it formally read out over the tannoy system they'd started to laugh. Caught unawares by this chance absurdity, Zoya had revealed a beautiful smile that she'd kept locked out of sight. In that moment Raisa caught a glimpse of the child that had been lost – playful and irreverent. Within seconds her smile was wiped away. Raisa felt an intense pain. She was no less emotionally involved. She and Leo had been unable to have children of their own: adoption was her only hope of motherhood. However, she was by far the better at concealing her thoughts, even if Leo had been trained by the secret police. She'd made a tactical decision, careful that the girls should not be constantly aware of how important they were to her. She treated them without fuss or ceremony, establishing functional foundations – school, clothes, food, going out, homework. Though they both went about it in different ways, she shared Leo's dream – the dream of creating a loving, happy family.

Raisa and the girls exited the station on the corner of Ostozhenka and Novokrymskiy on their way to their respective schools, following a path dug through the snow. Raisa had wanted to enrol the girls at the same school, where, ideally, she would also have taught so the three of them could be together. However, the decision had been made, either by the school authorities or at a higher level, that Zoya would attend Lycée 1535. Since it only accepted secondary-school students, Elena was forced into a separate primary school. Raisa had resisted since the majority of schools accepted both primary and secondary students and there was no need to split them up. Her request had been declined. Siblings were at school to create a relationship with the State not to shelter within family ties. According to that rationale, Raisa was lucky to get a job at Lycée 1535 and so she'd relinquished the demand in order to preserve the advantage. At least this way she was able to keep an eye on Zoya. Although Elena was younger and had been more obviously nervous about the prospect of a new school in a large city, Zoya concerned Raisa far more. She'd fallen further behind academically, her village school not being up to Moscow's standards. There was no question that she was intelligent. But it was unpolished, directionless, ill-disciplined and, unlike Elena, Zoya steadfastly refused to make any efforts to fit in, as if it was a matter of principle that she remain isolated.

Outside the primary school, a converted pre-Revolutionary aristocratic town house, Raisa took an unnecessary amount of time tending to Elena's uniform. Finally, holding her close, she whispered:

— *Everything's going to be OK, I promise.*

For the first few months Elena had cried when she'd been separated from Zoya. Though she'd gradually adjusted to spending eight hours apart, at the end of every school day, without exception, she'd stand by the gates eagerly awaiting their reunion. Her excitement at seeing her older sister return hadn't diminished, a reunion as full of joy as if a year had passed.

After Zoya had given her sister a hug, Elena hurried into school, pausing at the doors to wave goodbye. Once she was inside, Zoya and Raisa walked in silence towards the Lycée. Raisa resisted the urge to question Zoya. She didn't want to agitate her before class. Even the simplest of enquiries risked putting her on the defensive, setting off a chain of disruptive behaviour that rippled throughout the day. If she asked about schoolwork it was an implicit criticism of her academic achievements. If she asked about her classmates it was a reference to her refusal to make any friends. The only subject open to discussion was Zoya's athletic abilities. She was tall and strong. Needless to say she hated team sports, unable to take orders. Individual sports were a different matter — she was an excellent swimmer and runner, the fastest in the school for her age. But she refused to compete. If entered into a competition she would deliberately forfeit the race, although she had enough pride not to come last. She'd aim for fourth and since she occasionally mistimed it, or forgot herself in the heat of the moment, she might come in third or even second.

Built in 1929, Lycée 1535 was angular and stark in design, intending to embody an egalitarian approach to learning, a new kind of architecture for a new kind of student. Twenty metres from the gates Zoya stopped walking, remaining fixed to the spot and staring straight ahead. Raisa crouched down.

— *What is it?*

Zoya dropped her head, speaking under her breath.

— *I feel sad. I feel sad all the time.*

Raisa bit her lip, trying not to cry. She put a hand on Zoya's arm.

— *Tell me what I can do.*

— *Elena can't go back to that orphanage: she can't ever go back.*

— *No one is going anywhere.*

— *I want her to stay with you.*

— *She will. You both will. Of course you will. I love you very much.*

Raisa had never dared to say that aloud. Zoya looked at her carefully.

— *I could be happy . . . living with you.*

They'd never spoken like this. Raisa had to be careful: if she said the wrong thing, gave the wrong reply, Zoya would close down and she might not get another chance.

— *Tell me what you want me to do.*

Zoya considered.

— *Leave Leo.*

Her beautiful eyes seemed to swell, soaking up every detail of Raisa's reaction. Zoya's expression was filled with hope at the notion of never seeing Leo again. She was asking Raisa to divorce Leo. Where could she have learnt about divorce? It was rarely spoken about. The State's initially permissive attitude had hardened under Stalin, making divorce more difficult, expensive and stigmatized. In the past, Raisa had considered a life without Leo many times. Had Zoya detected the remnants of that embittered relationship and drawn hope from it? Would she have dared ask if she didn't think there was a chance Raisa would have said yes?

— *Zoya . . .*

Raisa was gripped by an intense desire to give this girl anything she wanted. At the same time, she was young – she needed guidance, she couldn't make outlandish demands and expect them to come true.

— *Leo's changed. Let's talk, you and me and him, together, tonight.*

— *I don't want to talk to him. I don't want to see him. I don't want to hear his voice. I want you to leave him.*

— *But, Zoya . . . I love him.*

The hope drained from Zoya's face. Her expression became cold. Without saying another word she broke into a run, leaving Raisa behind, hurrying through the main gates.

Raisa watched as Zoya disappeared into the school. She couldn't run after her: there was no way they could speak in front of the other students and anyway it was too late. Zoya would remain silent, refusing to answer. The moment had passed, the opportunity was gone, Raisa had given her reply – *I love him.* Words greeted with a grim stoicism, like a convict hearing a death sentence confirmed. Cursing herself for responding so definitively, Raisa entered the school grounds. Ignoring the students and teachers passing her, she considered Zoya's dream – a life without Leo.

Inside the school building she entered the staff room, unable to concentrate, dizzy and distracted. Raisa found a parcel waiting for her. There was a letter attached. She ripped it open, glancing at it. She was to read the enclosed document to all her students, every year group. The letter was from the Ministry of Education. Tearing off the brown paper wrapped around the parcel she glanced at the top of the box:

NOT FOR PRESS

She lifted the lid, taking out the thick stack of neatly typed pages. As a politics teacher she was regularly sent material and instructed to convey it to her students. Having read the covering letter, she tossed it into the bin only to see that the bin was filled with identical letters. Copies must have been sent to every teacher, every class must be having the speech read to them. Already running late, Raisa picked up the box, hurrying out.

Arriving at class, she saw the pupils talking, making the most of her delay. There were thirty students, aged between fifteen and sixteen. She'd taught many of them for the full three years she'd been at the school. She put the pages down on the table, explaining that today they'd be hearing a speech by their leader Khrushchev. After the applause died down, she read aloud.

— *Special report to the 20th Congress of the Communist Party of the Soviet Union. Closed session. 25th February 1956. By Nikita Sergeyevich Khrushchev, First Secretary, Communist Party of the Soviet Union.*

It was the first Congress since Stalin's death. Raisa reminded her class that the Communist Revolution was worldwide and that at these gatherings were emissaries from international workers' parties as well as Soviet leaders. Braced for an hour of platitudes and self-congratulatory declarations, her thoughts focused on the unlikely hope that Zoya would make it through the day without getting into a fight.

Very quickly her attention was brought back to the material she was reading. This was no ordinary speech. It opened with none of the normal descriptions of startling Soviet successes. Midway through the fourth paragraph, her hands tight around the paper, she stopped, unable to believe the sentences set out before her. The class was silent. In an uncertain voice she read:

— *The cult of the person of Stalin has been gradually growing, the cult which became the source of a whole series of exceedingly serious and grave perversions of Party principles, of Party democracy, of Revolutionary legality.*

Amazed, she flicked forward, wondering if there was more, reading silently:

The negative characteristics of Stalin, which, in Lenin's time, were only incipient, transformed themselves during the last years into a grave abuse of power . . .

She'd spent her entire career propagandizing the State, teaching these children that the State was always right, good and just. If Stalin had been guilty of fostering a cult, Raisa had been instrumental in that. She'd justified teaching such falsehoods since it was necessary that her students learn the language of adulation, the vocabulary of State worship without which they'd be vulnerable to suspicion. The relationship between a student and teacher depended upon trust. She believed she'd upheld that premise, not in the orthodox sense that she'd told the truth, but she'd told them the truths they needed to hear. These words made her a cheat. She looked up. The students were too confused to understand the implications immediately. But they would eventually. They would understand that she was not an enlightened role model but a slave to whoever happened to be in charge.

The door was flung open. Iulia Peshkova, a teacher, was standing in the doorway, her face bright red — her mouth open, startled, unable to speak. Raisa stood up:

— *What is it?*

— Come quickly.

Iulia was Zoya's teacher. Fear struck Raisa. She put down the pages, telling her class to remain in their seats, and followed Iulia down the corridor, down the stairs, unable to get a sensible answer.

— What happened?

— It's Zoya. It's the speech. I was reading and she . . . you must see for yourself.

They reached the classroom. Iulia stood back, allowing Raisa to go in first. She opened the door. Zoya was standing on the teacher's desk. The desk had been pushed up against the wall. All the other students were at the opposite end of the room, bunched up, as far away as possible, as if Zoya had some contagious disease. Around her feet were the pages of the speech and shards of glass. Zoya was standing proud, triumphant. Her hands were bloody. They clasped the remains of a poster taken down from the wall, an image of Stalin with the words printed underneath:

FATHER TO ALL CHILDREN

Zoya had climbed onto the table to take the picture off the wall: she'd smashed the frame, cutting her hand before ripping the poster in two, decapitating the image of Stalin. Her eyes were ablaze with victory. She raised the halves of the poster, streaked with her blood, as if brandishing the body of a vanquished foe:

— He's not my father.

In the communal corridor outside Nikolai's apartment were the remains of the speech. Seeing the ripped pages, glancing at the words, Leo drew his gun. Behind him, Timur did the same. Paper scrunching under foot, Leo reached out, taking hold of the door handle. The apartment was unlocked. He nudged open the door, the two of them stepping into the empty living area. There was no sign of a disturbance. The doors to the other rooms were closed except for one — the bathroom door.

The bath was full to the rim, the bloody water's surface broken only by the emergence of Nikolai's head and the island of his plump, hairy stomach. His eyes and mouth were open, as if amazed that an angel and not a demon had welcomed him to death. Leo crouched beside his former mentor, a man whose every lesson Leo had spent the past three years trying to unlearn. Timur called out:

— Leo . . .

Noting his deputy's tone, Leo stood up, following him to the adjacent bedroom.

The two girls appeared to be sleeping, the blankets pulled over their bodies up to their necks. Had it been night, the stillness of the room would've felt natural. But it was midday and sunlight was pushing through the gaps in the curtains. Both girls were facing the walls; their backs turned to each other. The eldest daughter's long glossy hair was spread over the pillow. Leo swept it back, touching her neck. The faintest trace of warmth remained, preserved by the thick eiderdown that she'd been lovingly tucked under. There was no sign of any injury on her body. The younger daughter, no more than four years old, was positioned identically. She was cold. Her small body had lost its warmth quicker than that of her sister's. Leo closed his eyes. He could've saved these girls.

Next door, Nikolai's wife, Ariadna, was arranged, as her daughters had been, in a semblance of sleep. Leo had known her a little. Seven years ago, after an arrest, Nikolai used to insist that Leo eat with him. No matter how late, Ariadna had always made dinner, offering hospitality and civility after Leo and Nikolai's mutual savagery. The dinners had been intended as a demonstration of the value of domestic space where the details of their bloody employment did not exist, where he could maintain the illusion of being nothing more than an ordinary loving husband. Sitting at her dressing table, Leo regarded the ivory and bone hairbrush, perfumes and powders – luxuries that Ariadna had accepted as payment for her unquestioning devotion. She hadn't realized that ignorance wasn't a choice: it was a condition of her existence. Nikolai wouldn't tolerate his family in any other form.

Never tell your wife anything.

As a young officer Leo had interpreted that warning, whispered to him after he'd made his first arrest, as referring to the need for caution and secrecy, a lesson in not trusting even those closest to him. But that was not what Nikolai had meant at all.

Unable to stay in the apartment any longer, Leo stood up, unsteady on his feet. Leaving the bodies behind, he hurried to the communal hallway, leaning against the wall, breathing deeply and staring down at the remains of Khrushchev's speech, delivered and positioned outside Nikolai's front door with lethal intent. Returning home last night, Nikolai had read a small fraction; most of it was still untouched in the box. Had Nikolai believed he could destroy these words? If that thought had crossed his mind, the accompanying letter would've ended it. The speech was to be copied and distributed. The inclusion of the official letter was a message to Nikolai that the secrets of his past were no longer his to control.

Leo glanced at Timur. Before joining the Homicide Department he'd been a militia officer, arresting drunks and thieves and rapists. The militia had not been excluded from making politicized arrests. However, Timur had been fortunate, no such demands had been placed on him, at least not that he'd ever admitted to Leo.

A man who rarely lost control of his emotions, Timur was visibly angry.

— *Nikolai was a coward*.

Leo nodded. It was true. He'd been too scared to face disapproval. Nikolai's life was his family. He couldn't live without them. He couldn't die without them either.

Leo picked up a page from the speech, regarding it as if it were a knife or a gun — the most effective of murder weapons. He'd read the speech this morning, after it had been delivered to him. Shocked at the outspoken attack, it had taken Leo very little time to realize that if he'd been sent the speech, Nikolai would have too. The intended target was clear: the people responsible for the crimes described.

The clump of footsteps filled the stairway. The KGB had arrived.

*

KGB officers entered the apartment regarding Leo with open contempt. No longer one of them, he'd turned his back on their ranks. He'd refused a job in order to run his Homicide Department, a department they'd been lobbying to shut down since its inception. Prizing loyalty above all else, in their eyes he was the worst of things – a traitor.

Taking charge was Frol Panin, Leo's superior officer from the Interior Ministry, the office of Criminal Investigations. Some fifty years old, Panin was handsome, well tailored, charming. Though Leo had never seen a Hollywood movie, he imagined Panin was the type of man they'd cast. Fluent in several languages, he was a former ambassador who'd survived Stalin's reign by remaining abroad. It was rumoured that he didn't drink, that he exercised daily and had his hair cut once a week. In contrast to many officials who prided themselves on their modest background and indifference to anything as bourgeois as appearances, Panin was brazenly immaculate. Softly spoken, polite, he was a new breed of official who no doubt approved of Khrushchev's speech. Behind his back he was frequently bad-mouthed. It was claimed that no man as effete as he was would have lasted under Stalin. His hands were too soft, his nails too clean. Leo was sure that Panin would accept it as a compliment.

Panin briskly studied the crime scene before addressing the KGB officers:

— *No one leaves the building. Head-count all the other apartments, check them against residential records and make sure every person is accounted for. No one goes to work; those who have already left, bring in for questioning. Interview everyone – find out what they saw or heard. If you suspect they're lying, or holding back, take them into a cell and ask them again. No violence, no threats, just make them understand that our patience has limits. If they do know something . . .*

Panin paused, adding:

— *We'll deal with that on an individual basis. Also, I want a cover story. Agree the details among yourselves but no mention of murder. Is that understood?*

Thinking better of giving them responsibility for a plausible lie, he continued:

— *These four citizens were not murdered. They were arrested, taken away. The children have been sent to an orphanage. Begin to sow talk of their subversive attitudes. Use the people you have at your disposal in nearby communities. It is imperative no one catches sight of the bodies when they're taken out. Clear the street if you have to.*

It was better that society believe an entire family had been arrested, never to be seen again, than know that a retired MGB officer had murdered his family.

Panin turned to Leo.

— *You met Nikolai last night?*

— *He phoned around midnight. I was surprised. I hadn't spoken to him in over five years. He was upset, drunk. He wanted to meet me. I agreed. I was tired. It was late. He was incoherent. I told him to go home and we'd talk when he was sober. That was the last I saw of him. When he got home, he found Khrushchev's speech on his doorstep. It was put there as part of a campaign against him, instigated I believe by the same people who put the speech on my doorstep this morning.*

— *Have you read the speech?*

— *Yes, it's the reason I came here. It seemed too much of a coincidence that it was delivered to me at the same time as Nikolai getting in touch.*

Panin turned, staring at Nikolai in the bloody bath water.

— *I was in the Kremlin Palace when Nikita Khrushchev*

delivered the speech. Several hours and no one moved, silence, disbelief. Only a very small number of people worked on it, select members of the Presidium. No warning was given. The Twentieth Congress began with ten days of unremarkable talks. Delegates were still applauding Stalin's name. On the last day, the foreign delegates were getting ready to go home. We were called in for a closed session. Khrushchev showed a certain relish for the task. He's passionate about admitting the mistakes of the past.

— To the entire country?

— He argued that these words couldn't go beyond the confines of the hall or it would damage our nation's reputation.

Leo failed to keep the anger out of his voice.

— Then why are there millions of copies in circulation?

— He lied. He wants people to read it. He wants people to know that he was the first person to say sorry. He's taken his place in history. He's the first man to criticize Stalin and not be executed. The notice that it is not to be printed in the press was a concession to those who opposed the speech. Of course, the stipulation is absurd in the context of the wider distribution plans.

— Khrushchev rose up under Stalin.

Panin smiled.

— We are all guilty, yes? And he feels it. He's confessing, selectively. In many ways, it's an old-fashioned denunciation. Stalin is bad: I'm good. I'm right: they're wrong.

— Nikolai, myself, we are the people he's telling everyone to hate. He is making monsters of us.

— Or showing the world the monsters we really are. I include myself in that, Leo. It is true for everyone who was involved, everyone who made the system tick. We're not talking about a list of five names. We're talking about millions of people, all of them either actively involved or complicit. Have you considered the

possibility the guilty might outnumber the innocent? That the inno-cent might be a minority?

Leo glanced at the KGB officers examining the two daughters.

— *The people who sent this speech to Nikolai must be caught.*

— *What leads do you have?*

Leo opened his notepad, taking out the folded sheet of paper retrieved from Moskvin's printing press.

Under torture, Eikhe

Panin examined it while Leo retrieved a page from Nikolai's copy of the speech. He pointed at a line:

> *Under torture, Eikhe was forced to sign a protocol*
> *of his confession prepared in advance by the*
> *investigative judges.*

Spotting the duplication of the three words, Panin asked:

— *Where did the first sheet come from?*

— *From a printing press run by a man called Suren Moskvin, retired from the MGB. I'm sure the speech was delivered to him. His sons claim that he had an official contract with the State to print ten thousand copies, but I can find no evidence of that con-tract. I don't believe it existed: it was a lie. He was told it was a State contract and then he was given the speech. He worked through the night, typesetting it. By the time he got to these words he'd decided to kill himself. They gave him the speech knowing the effect it would have, just as they gave it to Nikolai, just as they gave it to me. Yesterday, Nikolai said he was being sent photo-graphs of the people he'd arrested. Moskvin was also harassed with photographs of the people he'd come into contact with.*

Leo took out the modified volume of Lenin's text, holding up the arrest photo glued into the front instead of Lenin's.

— *I'm sure one person connects all three of us – Suren, Nikolai and me – someone recently released from imprisonment, a relative of a . . .*

Leo paused before adding the word:

— *A victim.*

Timur asked:

— *How many people did you arrest as an MGB officer?*

Leo considered. On occasions, he arrested entire families – six people in one night.

— *Over three years . . . Many hundreds.*

Timur couldn't hide his surprise. The number was high. Panin remarked:

— *And you think the perpetrator would send a photograph?*

— *They're not afraid of us, not any more. We're afraid of them.*

Panin clapped his hands, calling together the various officers.

— *Search this apartment. We're looking for a batch of photographs.*

Leo added:

— *Nikolai would've hidden them carefully. It was essential that his family never find them. He was an agent so he was good at hiding things and good at knowing where people might look.*

Systematically searching every room, the luxurious apartment Nikolai had spent years furnishing and decorating took two hours to dismantle. In order to search under the beds and rip up the floorboards, the bodies of his murdered children and wife were heaped in the centre of the living room, wrapped in bed linen. Around them, wardrobes were smashed, mattresses torn open. No photos were found.

Frustrated, Leo stared at Nikolai in the bath of bloody water.

Struck by a thought, he stepped up to the bath and without taking off his shirt sank his arm into the water. He felt Nikolai's hand. His fingers were locked around a thick envelope. He'd been clutching it when he'd died. The paper had softened and broke apart as soon as Leo touched it, the contents floating to the surface. Timur and Panin joined Leo, watching as one by one the faces of men and women rose up from the bloody bottom of the bath. Soon a film of photographs, hundreds of overlapping faces, bobbed up and down. Leo's eyes darted from old women to young men, the mothers and fathers, sons and daughters. He recognized none of them. Then one face caught his eye. He picked it out of the water. Timur asked:

— *You know this man?*

Yes, Leo knew him. His name was Lazar.

A crucifix had been drawn on the outside of the envelope, a careful ink drawing of the Orthodox cross. The drawing was small, roughly the size of his palm. Someone had taken time over it: the proportions were correct, the inkwork competent. Was it supposed to engender fear, as if he were a ghoul or a demon? More likely it was intended ironically, as a commentary on his faith. If so, it was misjudged — amateurish in its psychology.

Krasikov broke the seal, emptying the contents onto his desk. More photographs . . . He was tempted to toss them in the fire as he'd done the others but curiosity stopped him. He put on his glasses, straining his eyes, studying this new batch of faces. At a glance they meant nothing. He was about to put them aside when one of them caught his attention. He concentrated, trying to remember the name of this man with intense eyes.

Lazar.

These were the priests he'd denounced.

He counted them. Thirty faces, had he really betrayed so many? Not all of them had been arrested while he'd been Patriarch of Moscow and All Russia, the leading religious authority in the country. The denunciations had pre-dated that appointment, spread over many years. He was seventy-five years old. For a life-time, thirty denunciations were not so many. His calculated obedience to the State had saved the Church from immeasurable harm — an unholy alliance, perhaps, yet these thirty priests had been necessary sacrifices. It was remiss of him not to be able to remember each of their names. He should pray for them every night. Instead, he'd let them slip from his mind like rain running off glass. He found forgetfulness easier than asking for forgiveness.

Even with their photographs in his hands he felt no regret. This wasn't bravado. He suffered no nightmares, experienced no anguish. His soul was light. Yes, he'd read Khrushchev's speech, sent to him by the same people who had sent these photos. He'd read the criticisms of Stalin's murderous regime, a regime he'd supported by ordering his priests to praise Stalin in their sermons. Undoubtedly there'd been the cult of dictator and he'd been a loyal worshipper. What of it? If this speech pointed to a future of pointless intro-spection then so be it — but it wouldn't be his future. Was he responsible for the Church's persecution through the early decades of Communism? Of course not, he'd merely reacted to the circum-stances in which he found himself and his beloved Church. His hand had been forced. The decision to surrender some of his colleagues was unpleasant although not difficult. There were individuals who believed they could say and do as they pleased simply because it was the work of God. They were naive and he'd found them tire-some, eager to be martyrs. In that sense, he'd merely given them what they wanted, the opportunity to die for their faith.

Religion, like everything else, had to compromise. The Pomestny Sobor, the Council of Bishops, had shrewdly put him forward as Patriarch. They'd needed someone who could be polit-ical, flexible, shrewd, which was why his nomination had been State-approved and why the State had allowed elections in the first place, elections duly rigged in his favour. There had been those who had argued that his election was a violation of canon law; Church hierarchy was not supposed to be consecrated by secular authorities. To his mind, that was an obscure academic argument at a time when the number of churches had shrunk from twenty thousand to less than one thousand. Were they supposed to disappear altogether, proudly clinging to their principles, as a captain might cling to the mast of his sinking ship? His appointment had been intended to reverse that decline and stem their losses. He'd succeeded. New churches had been built. Priests were trained rather than shot. He'd done what had been required, no more. His actions had never been malicious. And the Church had survived.

Krasikov stood up, weary of these recollections. He picked up the photos and piled them on the fire, watching them curl, blacken and burn. He'd accepted reprisals were a possibility. There was no way to govern an organization as complex as the Church, manage its relationship with the State, and not create enemies. A cautious man, he'd taken steps to protect himself. Old, infirm, he was Patriarch only in name, no longer involved in the day-to-day running of the Church. He now spent much of his time working in a children's sanctuary he'd founded not far from the Church of the Conception of St Anna. There were those who considered his sanctuary a dying man's attempt at redemption. Let them think that. He didn't care. He enjoyed the work: there was no more mystery than that. The hard graft was done by the younger members of staff while he provided spiritual guidance to the one hundred or so children they had space for, converting them from a path of addiction to *chiffr*, a narcotic derived from tea leaves, to a life of piety. Having dedicated his life to God, a dedication which forbade him from having children of his own, this was compensation of a kind.

He shut the door to his office, locking it, descended the stairs to the main sanctuary hall where the children ate and were schooled. There were four dormitories: two for the girls, two for the boys. There was also a prayer room with a crucifix, icons and candles – a room where he taught matters of faith. No child could remain in the sanctuary unless they opened themselves to God. If they resisted, refused to believe, they were expelled. There was no shortage of street children to choose from. According to secret State estimates, to which he was privy, some eight hundred thousand homeless children were scattered across the country, mainly concentrated in the major cities – living in train stations, or sleeping in alleyways. Some had run away from orphanages, some from forced-labour colonies. Many had travelled in from the countryside, subsisting in the cities like packs of wild dogs – scavenging and stealing. Krasikov wasn't sentimental. He understood that these children were potentially dangerous and untrustworthy. He therefore employed the services of former Red Army soldiers to keep order. The complex was secure. No one could get in or out without his permission. Everyone was searched upon entry. There were guards inside, circling, and two always on the front door. Ostensibly these men were employed to keep the hundred children in check. However, these men provided a secondary service: they were Krasikov's bodyguards.

Krasikov surveyed the hall, searching the grateful faces for his newest intake, a young boy, perhaps only thirteen or fourteen years old. He hadn't given his age, refusing to say very much. The boy had a terrible stammer and a peculiarly adult face as if each year on earth had aged him by three. It was time for the boy's induction, to decide if he was sincere about his commitment to God.

Krasikov gestured for one of his guards to bring the child over. The boy shied away like a mistreated dog, wary of human contact. He'd been found not far from the sanctuary, in a doorway, huddled in rags, clutching an earthenware figure of a man sitting on the back of a pig, riding the pig as though it were a horse. It was a comic piece of household porcelain, suggesting a provincial background. Once brightly coloured, the paint had faded. Remarkably, it was unbroken except for the pig's chipped left ear. The boy, sinewy and strong, never let it out of his sight and never let it go. It had some sentimental value, perhaps, an object from his past.

Krasikov smiled at the guard, politely dismissing him. He opened the door to the prayer room, waiting for the boy to follow. The boy didn't move, clutching his painted man on a pig as tightly as if it was filled with gold.

— *You don't have to do anything you don't want. However, if you can't let God into your life, you can't stay here.*

The boy glanced at the other children. They'd stopped what they were doing: watching to see what decision would be made. No one had ever said no. The boy tentatively entered the prayer room. As he passed by Krasikov asked:

— *Remind me of your name.*

The boy stammered:

— *Ser . . . gei.*

Krasikov shut the door behind them. The room had been prepared. Candles were burning. The afternoon light was fading. He knelt before the crucifix, not giving Sergei any instructions, waiting for the boy to join him, a simple test to see if the child had any religious background. Those with experience would join him: those with none would remain by the door. Sergei didn't move, remaining by the door.

— *Many of the children were ignorant when they arrived. That is no crime. You will learn. I hope God will one day take the place of that toy figure you hold so dear.*

To Krasikov's surprise the boy replied by locking the door.

Before he could query the action, the boy strode forward, pulling a length of wire from the chipped pig's ear. At the same time, he raised the earthenware figure above his head, throwing it down with all his strength. Krasikov instinctively turned away, expecting it to hit him. But the porcelain figure missed, smashing at his feet, breaking into several large, uneven pieces. Shocked, he peered at the porcelain fragments. There was something else beside the remains of the pig – cylindrical and black. He bent down, picking it up. It was a flashlight.

Confused, he tried to get up, off his knees. Before he could, a noose slipped over his head, down around his neck – thin steel wire secured in a knot. The boy was holding the other end, coiled around his hand. He tugged: the wire tightened, Krasikov gasped as his breath was squeezed from him. His face turned red, the blood constricted. His fingers slipped over the wire, unable to get underneath. The boy tugged again, speaking in a cool, composed voice with no trace of his previous stammer.

— *Answer correctly and you'll live.*

*

At the entrance to the children's sanctuary, Leo and Timur were denied access, held back by two guards. Frustrated with the delay, Leo showed the men the photo of Lazar, explaining:

— *It's possible that everyone involved in this man's arrest is a target. Two men are already dead. If we're right, the Patriarch might be in danger.*

The guards were unimpressed.

— *We'll pass the message on.*

— *We need to speak to him.*

— *Militia or not, the Patriarch has given us instructions not to let anyone in.*

Commotion broke out upstairs: the sound of shouting. In an instant the guards' complacency turned to panic. They abandoned their post, climbing the stairs, followed by Leo and Timur, bursting into a large hall filled with children. The staff had huddled around a door, shaking it, unable to get in. The guards joined the fray, taking hold of the door handle, listening to the overlapping explanations:

— *He went in there to pray.*

— *With the new boy.*

— *Krasikov's not replying.*

— *Something smashed.*

Leo cut through the discussion.

— *Kick the door down.*

They turned to him, unsure.

— *Do it now.*

The heaviest and strongest of the guards rushed forward, shoulder smashing against the frame. He charged again, the door broke apart.

Clambering through the splintered opening, Leo and Timur entered the room. A young voice called out, authoritative, assured.

— *Stay where you are!*

The guards stopped moving, fierce men rendered helpless by the scene before them.

The Patriarch was on his knees, turned towards them, his face as red as blood, his mouth open — his tongue protruding, obscene, like a twisted slug. His neck was pinched: thin steel wire stretched to the hands of the young boy. The boy's hands were wrapped in rags: the wire coiled round and round. A master with a dog on a leash, the boy exercised absolute and lethal control: he need only apply more tension and the wire would either choke the Patriarch or slice into his skin.

The boy took a careful backwards step, almost at the window, keeping the wire tight and ceding no slack. Leo emerged from the pack of guards who'd become paralysed at their failure to protect. There were maybe ten metres between him and the Patriarch. He couldn't risk running forward. Even if he reached the Patriarch there was no way to get his fingers underneath the wire. Addressing Leo, sensing his calculations, the boy said:

— *Any closer, he dies.*

The boy threw open the small window, clambering up onto the ledge. They were on the first floor, too great a height to jump. Leo asked:

— *What do you want?*

— *This man's apology for betraying priests who trusted him, priests he was supposed to protect.*

The boy was speaking words as if reading from a script. Leo glanced at the Patriarch. Surely the threat of death would make him compliant. The boy's orders were to extract an apology. If those were his orders he'd obey them: that was the only leverage Leo had.

— *He'll say sorry. Loosen the wire. Let him speak. That's what you've come to hear.*

The Patriarch nodded, indicating that he wanted to comply. The boy considered and then slowly loosened the wire. Krasikov gasped, a strangled intake of breath.

Supreme resilience glistened in the old man's eyes and Leo realized that he'd made a mistake. Summoning his strength, spraying spit with each word:

— *Tell whoever sent you . . . I'd betray him again!*

Except for the Patriarch, all eyes turned to the boy. But he was already gone. He'd jumped from the window.

The wire whipped up, the full weight of the boy catching on the old man's neck, pulling the Patriarch with such force that he rose up from his knees like a puppet jerked by strings before falling onto his back, dragged across the floor and smashing the small window. His body caught in the window frame. Leo darted forward, grabbing the wire around the Patriarch's neck, trying to relieve the pressure. But the wire had cut through skin, severing muscle. There was nothing he could do.

Looking out of the window he saw the boy on the street below. Without saying a word Leo and Timur ran out of the room, abandoning the distraught guards, through the main sanctuary hall, the crowd of children, downstairs. The boy was skilled and nimble but he was young and he would not be able to outrun them.

Reaching the street, the boy was nowhere to be seen. There were no alleys, no turnings for some distance, he couldn't have cleared the length of the street in the short time it had taken them to get outside. Leo hurried to the window where the wire was hanging. He found the boy's footprints in the snow and followed them to a manhole. Snow had been brushed aside. Timur lifted the manhole cover. The drop was deep – a steel ladder leading to the sewage system. The boy was already near the bottom, rags tied around his hands. Seeing the light above him, he glanced up, revealing his face to the daylight. In response to seeing Leo he let go of the ladder, falling the last distance and disappearing into the dark.

Leo turned to Timur.

— *Get the flashlights from the car.*

Not waiting, Leo grabbed the ladder, climbing down. The rungs were icy cold and without gloves his skin stuck to the steel. Each time he let go of the rungs his skin began to rip. There were gloves in the car but he couldn't delay his pursuit. The sewage system was a labyrinth of tunnels: the boy could disappear down any of them, one unsighted turn and he'd be free. Gritting his teeth at the pain,

Leo's palms began to bleed as patches of skin tore off. His eyes watering, he looked down, judging the remaining distance. It was still too far to jump. He had to continue, forced to press his raw flesh against the iced steel. He cried out, letting go of the ladder.

Landing awkwardly on a narrow concrete ledge, his feet sliding under him, he almost toppled into a deep stream of filthy water. He steadied himself and examined his surroundings – a large brick tunnel, roughly the size of a metro tunnel. A pool of sunlight from the manhole above illuminated a small patch of ground around him but little more. In front of him it was dark except for a flicker of light, like a firefly, some fifty metres ahead. It was the boy: he had a flashlight, he'd prepared for this escape.

The flicker of light disappeared. Either the boy had turned his flashlight off or he'd gone down another tunnel. Unable to follow in the dark, unable to see the ledge, Leo looked up at the manhole, waiting for Timur – each second was vital.

— *Come on . . .*

Timur's face appeared at the top. Leo called out.

— *Drop it!*

If he failed to catch the flashlight it would hit the concrete and smash and he'd have to delay chasing after the boy until Timur climbed down. By that time the boy would be gone. Timur stepped back so that he wasn't blocking the light. His arm appeared outstretched holding a flashlight, positioning it in the centre of the hole. He let it fall.

Leo's eyes tracked it as it began to turn, glancing against the wall, knocking outwards again, the movement now entirely unpredictable. He took a step forward, reached up and caught the handle, his red-raw palms stinging as he gripped. Fighting against the instinct to let go, he flicked the switch. The bulb still worked. He shone the light in the direction the boy had disappeared, revealing a ledge that ran alongside the tunnel above the slow-flowing stream of filth. He set off, his speed limited by ice and slime, his clunky boots slipping on the precarious surface. Tempered by the cold, the smell was not unbearable and he limited himself to short, shallow breaths.

Where the boy had disappeared, the ledge stopped altogether. There was a secondary tunnel, much smaller – only a metre or so wide – the base appearing at shoulder height. This side tunnel fed into the stream below. There was excrement streaked across the wall. The boy must have climbed up. There was no other choice. Leo had to crawl into the tunnel.

He put the flashlight up first. Bracing himself, he gripped the oozy sides, his open wounds roaring in pain as exposed flesh mingled with dirt and shit. Dizzy with pain, he tried to pull himself up, aware that if he lost his grip he'd fall into the stream below. But there was nothing to grab onto further inside the tunnel – he reached out, his hand splashing down on the smooth, curved surface. The toe of his boot gripped the brickwork: he pushed up, into the tunnel, lying on his back, trying to wipe the filth off his hands. In the confined space the smell was overwhelming. Leo retched. Managing not to throw up, he took hold of the flashlight, shining the beam down the tunnel and crawling on his stomach, using his elbows to propel himself along.

A series of rusted bars blocked the way forward: the space between them was less than the width of his hand. The boy must have gone another way. About to turn back, Leo stopped. He was certain: there was no other way. Wiping off the grime, he examined the bars. Two of them were loose. He gripped them, tugging. They could be pulled free. The boy had scouted this route, that's why he had the flashlight, that's why he knew to wear the rags – he'd always intended to escape through the sewers. Even with the two bars removed Leo had trouble squeezing through the gap. Forced to take off his jacket to fit, he emerged into a cavernous chamber.

Lowering his feet, the floor seemed to move. He shone the light down. It was alive with rats, three or four deep, crawling over each other. His disgust was moderated by his curiosity – they were all travelling in one direction. He turned his light in the direction they were running from, scrambling away from a larger tunnel. Inside that tunnel Leo could see the boy, about a hundred metres between them. The boy wasn't running: he was standing by the wall, his hand flat against it. Cautious, sensing something was wrong, Leo moved forward.

The boy swung around and seeing his pursuer set off again He'd hung his flashlight around his neck by a piece of string, freeing both hands. Leo reached out, feeling the tunnel wall. The vibrations were so intense his fingers trembled.

The boy was sprinting, water splashing around his ankles. Leo tracked his movements with his flashlight. Nimble as a cat, the boy used the curved walls, jumping and propelling himself off the sides, leaping upwards. His target was the bottom rung of a ladder that emerged from a vertical tunnel overhead. The boy missed the lowest rung, landing with a splash on the floor. Leo ran forward. Behind him, he could hear Timur crying out in disgust, no doubt at the mass of rats. The boy was up on his feet, preparing himself for another jump at the ladder.

Suddenly the thin stream of stagnant water started to swell, surging, rising in volume. A tremendous rumbling filled the tunnel. Leo raised his torch upwards. The beam of light caught white foam: the breaking tip of a wall of water crashing towards them less than two hundred metres away.

With only seconds remaining, the boy made another run for

the ladder, jumping at the wall and reaching for the bottom rung. This time he caught it, hanging by both hands. He pulled himself up, clambering into the vertical tunnel, out of the water's reach. Leo turned around. The water was closing. Timur had just entered the main tunnel.

Arriving at the base of the ladder, Leo clamped the flashlight between his teeth and jumped, catching hold of the steel bar, his hands stinging as he pulled himself up. He could see the boy moving up above him. Ignoring the pain, he sped up, closing on the boy. He grabbed the boy's foot. Keeping a lock as the boy tried to kick free, Leo directed the beam of light down. At the bottom of the shaft, frantic, Timur dropped his flashlight, jumped. He caught the bottom rung with both hands just as the water crashed around him, white foamy water exploding up into the vertical tunnel.

The boy laughed.

— *If you want to save your friend you'll have to let me go!*

He was right. Leo had to let the boy go, scale down and help Timur.

— *He's going to die!*

Timur emerged from the water, gasping, lifting himself up, wrapping an arm around the next bar and pulling himself free of the foam. The bulk of his body was still submerged but his grip was good.

Relieved, Leo didn't move, keeping a grip on the boy's ankle as he kicked and thrashed. Timur pulled himself up to Leo's position, taking the flashlight from Leo's mouth and pointing it at the boy's face.

— *Kick again and I'll break your leg.*

The boy stopped: there was no doubting that Timur was serious. Leo added:

— We climb up together, slowly, to the next level. Understood?

The boy nodded. The three of them climbed up, slowly, awkwardly, a mass of limbs, moving like a deformed spider.

At the top of the ladder, Leo remained stationary, holding the boy's ankle while Timur scrambled up over both of them, reaching the passageway above.

— Let him go.

Leo let go and climbed up. Timur had the boy's arms pinned. Leo took hold of the flashlight, using his fingertips to avoid touching his bloody palms. He shone the light in the boy's face.

— Your only chance of staying alive is by talking to me. You've murdered a very important man. A lot of people are going to be calling for execution.

Timur shook his head.

— You're wasting your time. Look at his neck.

The boy's neck was marked with a tattoo, an Orthodox cross. Timur explained:

— He's a member of a gang. He'd rather die than talk.

The boy smiled.

— You're down here while up there . . . your wife . . . Raisa . . .

Leo's reaction was instant, stepping forward, grabbing the boy by his shirt, pulling him free from Timur and lifting him off his feet. It was all the opportunity the boy needed. Like an eel, he slipped out of his shirt, dropping to the floor and darting to the side. Left holding the shirt, Leo turned the flashlight, finding the boy crouched by the edge of the shaft. The boy stepped out, falling into the water below. Leo lunged but too late. Looking down he saw no sign of the boy — he'd fallen into the fast-flowing water, swept away.

Frantic, Leo assessed his surroundings: a closed concrete tunnel. Raisa was in danger. And there was no way out.

Raisa was seated opposite the school's *director*, Karl Enukidze – a kind man with a grey beard. Also with them was Iulia Peshkova, Zoya's teacher. Karl's fingers were knotted under his chin, scratching backwards and forwards, glancing at Raisa and then at Iulia. For the most part Iulia avoided eye contact altogether, chewing her lip and wishing that she was anywhere but here. Raisa understood their trepidation. If the smashing of Stalin's portrait were investigated, Zoya would be placed under the scrutiny of the KGB. But so would they. The question of guilt could be reconstituted: do they blame the child, or the adults who influenced the child? Was Karl a subversive, encouraging dissident behaviour in his students when they should be fervently patriotic? Or perhaps Iulia's lessons were deficient in Soviet character? Questions would arise as to what kind of guardian Raisa had been. Possible outcomes were being hastily calculated. Breaking the silence, Raisa said:

— *We're still behaving as though Stalin were alive. Times have changed. There's no appetite for the denunciation of a fourteen-year-old girl. You've read the speech: Khrushchev admits the arrests have gone too far. We don't need to take an internal school matter to the State. We can deal with it. Let's see this for what it really is: a troubled young girl, a girl in my care. Let me help her.*

Judging from their muted reaction, a lifetime of caution was not wiped away by a single speech, no matter who was speaking and what was being said. Adjusting the emphasis of her strategy, Raisa pointed out:

— *It would be best if this were never reported.*

Iulia looked up. Karl sat back. A new set of calculations began: Raisa had tried to silence the matter. Her proposal could be used against her. Iulia replied:

— *We're not the only people who know what happened. The students in my class saw everything. There are over thirty of them. By now they will have spoken to their friends, the number will grow. By tomorrow I would be surprised if the entire school wasn't talking about it. The news will travel outside the school. Parents will find out. They will want to know why we did nothing. What will we say? We didn't think it was important? That is not for us to decide. Trust in the State. People will find out, Raisa, and if we don't talk, someone else will.*

She was right: containment wasn't possible. On the defensive, Raisa countered:

— *What if Zoya left school with immediate effect? I'd speak to Leo; he could speak to his colleagues. We'd find another school for her. Needless to say I would also leave.*

There was no way Zoya could continue her education here. Students would avoid her. Many wouldn't sit next to her. Teachers would resist having her in their classes. She'd be an outcast as surely as if a cross were daubed on her back.

— *I propose that you, Karl Enukidze, make no statement about our leaving. We would simply disappear: no explanation given.*

The other students and teachers would presume the matter had been taken care off. The sudden absence would be translated as the culprits being punished. No one would want to talk about it because the consequences would be so severe. The topic would close, the subject would disappear — a ship sinking at sea while another ship passed by, all the passengers looking in the opposite direction.

Karl weighed up the proposal. Finally he asked:

— *You'd take care of all the arrangements?*

— *Yes.*

— *Including discussing the issue with the relevant authorities? The Ministry of Education, you have connections?*

— *Leo does, I'm sure.*

— *I don't need to speak to Zoya? I don't need to have any dealings with her at all?*

Raisa shook her head.

— *I'll take my daughter and walk out. You carry on as normal, as though I'd never existed. Tomorrow neither Zoya nor I will attend classes.*

Karl looked at Iulia, his eager eyes recommending the plan. It now depended on her. Raisa turned to her friend.

— *Iulia?*

They'd known each other for three years. They'd helped each other on many occasions. They were friends. Iulia nodded, saying:

— *That would be for the best.*

They would never speak to each other again.

*

Outside the office, in the corridor, Zoya was waiting, leaning against the wall — nonchalant, as though she'd merely failed to hand in homework. Her hand was bandaged: the cut had bled profusely. With the negotiations concluded, Raisa shut the office door, exhaustion sweeping over her. Much would now depend upon Leo. Walking to Zoya, she crouched down.

— *We're going home.*

— *Not my home.*

No gratitude, just disdain. Close to tears, Raisa couldn't manage any words.

Leaving the school building, Raisa stopped at the gates. Had they been betrayed so quickly? Two uniformed officers walked towards her.

— *Raisa Demidova?*

The eldest of the officers continued:

— *We've been sent by your husband to escort you home.*

They weren't here about Zoya. Relieved, she asked:

— *What's happened?*

— *Your husband wants to be sure you're safe. We can't go into the details except to say there has been a series of incidents. Our presence is a precaution.*

Raisa checked their identity cards. They were in order. She asked:

— *You work with my husband?*

— *We're part of his Homicide Department.*

Since the department was a secret, even that admission went some way to satisfying Raisa's suspicions. She handed back the cards, pointing out:

— *We need to pick up Elena.*

As they walked towards the car, Zoya tugged her hand. Raisa lowered her head. Zoya's voice was a whisper.

— *I don't trust them.*

*

Alone in his office, Karl stared out of the window.

Times have changed.

Maybe that was true, he wanted to believe it and put the entire affair out of his mind, as they'd agreed. He'd always liked Raisa. She was intelligent and beautiful and he wished her well. He picked up the telephone, wondering how best to phrase the denunciation of her daughter.

In the back of the car, Zoya glared at the militia officers, following their every movement as if imprisoned with two venomous snakes. Though the officer in the passenger seat had made a cursory attempt at being friendly, turning round and smiling at the girls, his smile had smashed up against a brick wall. Zoya hated these men, hated their uniforms and insignia, their leather belts and steel-capped black boots, making no distinction between the KGB and the militia.

Glancing out of the window, Raisa approximated where they were in the city. Evening had set. Street lights flickered on. Unaccustomed to being driven home, she slowly pieced together her location. This was not the way to their apartment. Leaning forward, trying to smooth out the urgency in her voice, she asked:

— *Where are we going?*

The officer in the front passenger seat turned around, his face expressionless, his back creaking against the leather upholstery.

— *We're taking you home.*

— *This isn't the way.*

Zoya sprang forward.

— *Let us out!*

The guard scrunched up his face.

Zoya didn't ask twice. With the car still in motion she unlocked the latch, throwing the door wide open into the middle of the road. Bright headlights flashed through the window as an oncoming truck swerved to avoid a collision.

Raisa grabbed hold of Zoya, clutching her waist, pulling her back inside just as the truck clipped the door, smashing it shut. The impact crumpled steel and shattered the window, showering the interior with glass. The officers were shouting. Elena was screaming. The car thumped into the kerb, running up onto the pavement, before skidding to a stop by the side of the road.

A stunned silence elapsed, the two officers turned round, pale and breathless.

— *What is wrong with her?*

The driver added, tapping his temples:

— *She's not right in the head.*

Raisa ignored them, examining Zoya. Unharmed, her eyes were blazing. There was a wildness about her: the primeval energies of a feral child brought up by wolves and captured by man, refusing to be tamed or civilized.

The driver got out, examining the damaged door, scratching and shaking his head.

— *We're taking you home. What's the problem?*

— *This isn't the way.*

The officer pulled out a slip of paper, handing it to Raisa through the gap where the window had been. It was Leo's writing. She stared blankly at the address before recognizing it. Her anger evaporated.

— *This is where Leo's parents live.*

— *I didn't know whose apartment it was. I just follow orders.*

Zoya wriggled free, climbing over her sister and out of the car. Raisa called after her:

— *Zoya, it's OK!*

Unappeased, Zoya didn't return. The driver moved towards her. Seeing him about to grab her, Raisa called out:

— *Don't touch her! Leave her! We'll walk the rest of the way.*

The driver shook his head.

— *We're supposed to stay with you until Leo turns up.*

— *Then follow behind.*

Still seated on the back seat, Elena was crying. Raisa put an arm around her.

— *Zoya's OK. She's not hurt.*

Elena seemed to absorb those words, checking on her older sister. Seeing that she was unhurt, her tears stopped. Raisa wiped away the remaining few.

— *We're going to walk. It's not far. Can you manage that?*

Elena nodded.

— *I don't like being driven home.*

Raisa smiled.

— *Nor do I.*

Raisa helped her out of the car. The driver threw up his hands, exasperated at the exodus of passengers.

Leo's parents lived in a low-rise modern block to the north of the city, home to numerous elderly parents of State officials, a retirement home for the privileged. In the winter, residents would play cards in each other's living rooms. In the summer, they'd play cards outside, on the grass strip. They'd shop together, cook together, a community with only one rule – they never spoke about their children's work.

Raisa entered the building, leading the girls to the elevator. The doors closed just as the militia officers caught up, forcing them to take the stairs. There was no chance Zoya would remain in a confined space with those two men. Reaching the seventh floor, Raisa led the girls down the corridor to the last apartment. Stepan – Leo's father – answered the door, surprised to see them. His surprise quickly transformed into concern.

— *What's wrong?*

Leo's mother, Anna, appeared from the living room, equally concerned. Addressing both of them, Raisa answered:

— *Leo wants us to stay here.*

Raisa gestured at the two officers approaching from the stairway, adding:

— *We have an escort.*

There was fear in Anna's voice.

— *Where is Leo? What's going on?*

— *I don't know.*

The officers arrived at the door. The more senior of the two, the driver, out of breath from climbing the stairs, asked:

— *Is there any other way into the apartment?*

Anna answered:

— *No.*

— *We'll remain here.*

But Anna wanted more information.

— *Can you explain?*

— *There have been reprisals. That's all I can say.*

Raisa shut the door. Anna wasn't satisfied.

— *But Leo is OK, isn't he?*

With gritted teeth, Zoya listened to Anna, watching the loose skin of her chin wobble as she spoke. She was fat with doing nothing all day long, fat with her son's provision of rich and rare foods. Her worries about Leo were excruciating, her voice strangled with concern for her murdering son:

Is Leo OK? Leo is OK, isn't he?

Are the people he arrested, the families he destroyed – are they OK? They doted on him as if he was a child. Worse than concern was their parental pride, excited by every story, hanging on every word he had to say. The displays of affection were sickening: kisses, embraces, jokes. Both Stepan and Anna were willing and eager participants in Leo's conspiracy to pretend that they were a normal family, planning day trips and visits to the shops, the restricted shops, rather than those with long queues of people and limited supplies. Everything was nice. Everything was comfortable. Everything was designed to conceal the murder of her father and mother. Zoya hated them for loving him.

Anna asked:

— *Reprisals?*

She repeated the word as if the concept were nonsensical and baffling, as if no one could possibly have any reason to dislike her son. Zoya couldn't help herself, stepping into the discussion and directing her words at Anna.

— *Reprisals for arresting so many innocent people! What did you think your son was doing all these years? Haven't you read the speech?*

In unison Stepan and Anna turned to her, shocked by the mention of the speech. They didn't know. They hadn't read it. Sensing her advantage, Zoya twisted her lips into a smile. Stepan asked:

— *What speech?*

— *The speech about how your son tortured innocent victims, about how he forced them to confess, about how he beat them, about how the innocent were sent to the Gulags while the guilty lived in apartments like this.*

Raisa crouched down in front of her, as if trying to block her words.

— *I need you to stop. I need you to stop right now.*

113

— Why? It's true. I didn't write those words. I was read them as part of my education. I'm only repeating what I was told. It's not for you to censor Khrushchev's words. He must have wanted us to talk about it otherwise he wouldn't have allowed us to read it. It's not a secret. Everyone knows. Everyone knows what Leo did.

— Zoya, listen to me . . .

But Zoya was in mid-flow, unstoppable:

— You think they shouldn't know the truth about their wonderful son? The wonderful son who found them this wonderful apartment, who helps them with the shopping – their wonderful murdering son.

Stepan's face went pale, his voice quivered with emotion.

— You don't know what you're saying.

— You don't believe me? Ask Raisa: the speech is real. Everything I've said is true. And everyone is going to know your son is a murderer.

Anna's voice was a whisper.

— What is this speech?

Raisa shook her head.

— We don't need to talk about it right now.

Zoya wasn't about to back down, enjoying her new-found power.

— It was written by Khrushchev and delivered at the Twentieth Congress. It says your son, and every officer like him, is a murderer. They acted illegally. They're not police officers! They're criminals! Ask Raisa, ask her if it's true. Ask her!

Stepan and Anna turned to Raisa.

— There is a speech. In it there are some critical things about Stalin.

— Not just about Stalin, it's about the people that followed his orders, including your son, your murdering son.

Stepan walked up to Zoya.

— *Stop saying that.*

— *Stop saying what? Murderer? Leo the Murderer? How many deaths do you think he's responsible for, aside from my parents?*

— *That's enough!*

— *You knew all along! You knew what he was doing for a living and you didn't care because you liked living in a nice apartment. You're as bad as he is! At least he was willing to get blood on his hands!*

Anna slapped Zoya, a stinging blow.

— *Young girl, you don't know what you're talking about. You speak like that because you've been spoiled. For three years you've been allowed to get away with anything. You can do whatever you want and have whatever you want. You've never been told off. We've watched it happen and said nothing. Leo and Raisa have wanted to give you everything. Look at you now, look at what you've become – ungrateful, hateful, when all anyone is trying to do is love you.*

Where she'd been smacked, Zoya felt her skin burn hot, a sensation which spread through her body, every part of her stinging from her fingertips to the back of her neck. She reached out and scratched Anna, digging her nails in as deep as they could go, tearing as much skin as she could.

— *Fuck your love!*

Anna retreated, crying out. But Zoya wasn't finished, lunging at her, fingers arched like claws. Raisa caught hold of her waist, spinning her away. Uncontrollable, Zoya's anger sought a new target, redirected towards Raisa. She bit her arm, sinking her teeth as far as they'd go.

The pain was so intense Raisa felt light-headed, her legs about to buckle and give way. Stepan grabbed hold of Zoya's jaw, prising it open as if dealing with a savage, rabid dog. Blood streamed from the deep teeth marks. Zoya was twisting and thrashing. Stepan threw her to the floor where she fell, teeth bared and bloody.

A knock on the door: the guards had heard the commotion. They wanted to come in. Raisa examined the bite – it was bleeding heavily. Zoya was still on the floor, eyes wild but no longer seeking a fight. Stepan hurried to the bathroom, bringing back a towel, pressing it against Raisa's arm. There was a second knock. Raisa turned to Anna, who was standing in almost exactly the same position as when she'd been attacked, dumbstruck, scratches down her face, four bleeding lines.

— *Anna, get rid of the officers, tell them they don't need to interfere.*

Anna didn't react. Raisa had to raise her voice.

— *Anna!*

Anna opened the door, turning her injured face away from view, ready to reassure the guards. Expecting to see two officers, she was startled to find four standing outside as if, like bacteria, they'd divided and multiplied. The two new officers were wearing different uniforms. They were KGB.

The KGB agents stepped into the apartment, taking in the scene before them, the girl on the floor with bloody teeth and bloody lips, the woman with a bleeding arm, the elderly woman with a scratched face.

— *Raisa Demidova?*

Despite the element of grim farce, Raisa tried to keep her voice steady and calm, the towel around her bite marks turning red.

— *Yes?*

— *Your daughter needs to come with us.*

Their attention fixed on Zoya.

Raisa's plan had failed. Iulia, or the director of the school, had betrayed her. Despite her injury, despite everything that had just happened, Raisa instinctively, protectively moved in front of Zoya.

— *Your daughter smashed a portrait of Stalin.*

— *That matter is being taken care of.*

— *She needs to come with us.*

— *She's being arrested?*

Seeing that the two KGB officers were determined to carry out their orders Raisa addressed the timid militia, the officers Leo had sent to protect them.

— *They're going to have to wait until my husband comes back, isn't that correct?*

The older of the two KGB agents shook his head.

— *Our orders are to bring your daughter in for questioning. Your husband has nothing to do with this.*

— *Those men have orders to make sure we stay here, together, until Leo gets back.*

The militia officer meekly stepped forward. Raisa's heart sank.

— *These are KGB officers . . .*

— *Leo won't be long. We stay here, together, until he gets back – he can sort this out. She's a fourteen-year-old girl. There's no rush to take her anywhere. We can wait.*

The KGB officer stepped closer, raising his voice.

— *She's going to have to come with us right now.*

Something about their impatience was wrong. The dynamic of these agents was wrong. The older agent was doing all the talking, the other man merely stood in silence, uneasy, his eyes darting from person to person as if he expected someone to attack him. They were both awkward in their uniforms. How was it possible they were here so quickly? It would take hours for the KGB to put together a plan and authorize an arrest. Even more peculiar, why were they at this address? How would they have known Raisa wouldn't be at home? Fuelled by these discrepancies, Raisa's eyes focused on the agent's neck. A mark rose above his shirt collar: the tip of a tattoo.

These men weren't KGB.

Raisa glanced at the militia officers, attempting to communicate the danger they were in. However, the militia officers were stupefied by the guise of these agents, scared at the very mention of the KGB. In her efforts to catch their attention, she caught the eye of the impostor. Whereas the militia were dumb to her signals, he was not. Before Raisa could raise her hand to warn the militia the tattooed man had drawn his weapon. Turning, he fired twice, a shot into the forehead of each officer. As they collapsed to the floor, the man turned the weapon on Raisa.

— *I'm taking your daughter.*

Raisa stepped closer to the barrel of the gun, in front of Zoya who was still crouched on the floor.

— *No.*

The gun was turned on Elena.

— *Give me Zoya. Or I will kill Elena.*

A shot rang out.

The bullet missed Elena, embedding into the apartment wall, a warning. Looking into his eyes, Raisa had no doubt this man would kill a seven-year-old as easily as he'd shot the two officers. She had to choose. She stepped out of the way, allowing them to take Zoya.

The man scooped Zoya in his arms.

— *Struggle and I'll knock you unconscious.*

He threw her over his shoulder, carrying her towards the door and calling out:

— *Stay in the apartment!*

The keys were taken: the apartment door was shut and locked.

Raisa ran to Elena, dropping to her side. She was on her knees, staring at the floor, her body shaking and her eyes vacant. She took hold of Elena's head, directing her eyes up, trying to get through to her:

— *Elena?*

But she didn't seem to hear, didn't respond.

— *Elena?*

Still no reply, no recognition or awareness, her body was slack. Transferring Elena to Anna's care, Raisa stood up, taking hold of the front door handle, unable to get out. She pulled back, moving to the bodies of the dead officers, taking one of their guns and tucking it into the back of her trousers. She hurried through the living room, opening the door to the small balcony. Stepan grabbed her.

— *What are you doing?*

— *Look after Elena.*

She stepped out onto the balcony, shutting the door behind her.

They were on the seventh floor, some twenty metres above street level. There were identical balconies each directly below the other. They could serve as a step to the next. She could climb down from balcony to balcony. If she fell, thin heaps of snow would do little to break the fall.

Kicking off her smooth-soled shoes, Raisa scaled the rail. She'd not taken into account the bite on her arm. It was still bleeding. The arm felt weak, her grip less secure. Unsure whether she could carry her weight, she lowered herself to the outer rim of the balcony. Gripping the freezing concrete ledge, she was hanging by her fingers, blood dripping onto her shoulder. Even at full stretch her toes didn't reach the sixth-floor balcony rail below. She hazarded a guess at the distance being no more than a couple of centimetres. There was no choice other than to let go.

A split-second fall, then her feet made contact with the rail. Trying to keep her balance, rocking from side to side, she heard Zoya's voice. Looking over her shoulder, she saw the men leaving the front entrance, one carrying Zoya. The other had his gun trained on her. Balancing on the narrow rail she was helpless.

The man fired. She heard glass smash. Raisa was falling towards the snow.

Unwashed, still stinking of the sewers, Leo was driving the car at top speed. Cumbersome and slow, incongruous with his urgency, it was the first vehicle they'd been able to requisition after he and Timur had emerged from a manhole almost a kilometre due south from where they'd originally descended into the sewers. His hands a bloody mess, Leo had refused Timur's offer to drive, putting on a pair of gloves, taking hold of the steering wheel with his fingertips, eyes watering each time he changed gear. He'd driven to his parents' apartment only to discover the area closed down by the militia. Elena, Raisa and his parents had been taken to the hospital. Elena was being treated for shock. Raisa was in a critical state. Zoya was missing.

Reaching Municipal Emergency Hospital 31, he skidded to a stop, leaving the car on the verge – door open, keys in the ignition – and running inside with Timur just behind. Everyone was staring, appalled by the sight and smell of him. Indifferent to the spectacle, demanding answers, Leo was eventually directed to the surgery where Raisa was fighting for her life.

Outside the operating theatre a surgeon explained that she'd fallen from a significant height and was suffering from internal bleeding.

— *Will she live?*

The surgeon couldn't be sure.

Entering the private ward where Elena was being treated, Leo saw his parents standing by her bed. Anna's face was bandaged. Stepan seemed unhurt. Elena was sleeping, her tiny body lost in the middle of a white hospital bed. She'd been given a mild sedative, having become hysterical when she'd realized Zoya was gone. Peeling off his bloody gloves, Leo took hold of Elena's hand, pressing it against his face, pitifully, wanting to tell her how sorry he was.

Timur put a hand on his shoulder.

— *Frol Panin is here.*

Leo followed Timur to the office commandeered by Panin and his armed retinue. The office door was locked. It was impossible to enter without first announcing your name. Inside there were two uniformed armed guards. Though Panin appeared unruffled, neat as always, the additional protection was testament to the fact that he was scared. He caught the observation in Leo's eyes.

— *Everyone is scared, Leo, at least everyone in power.*

— *You were not involved in Lazar's arrest.*

— *The issue stretches beyond your prime suspect. What if this behaviour triggers a pattern of reprisals? What if everyone wronged seeks revenge? Leo, nothing like this has ever happened before: the execution and persecution of members of our State Security services. We simply don't know what to expect next.*

Leo remained silent, noting Panin's interest was not the welfare of Raisa, Elena or Zoya, but the wider implications. He was a consummate politician, dealing with nations and armies, borders and regions, never the mere individual. Charming and witty, yet there was something cold about him, revealed in moments like these when any ordinary person would have offered some words of comfort.

There was a knock on the door. The guards moved for their guns. A voice called out:

— *I'm looking for Officer Leo Demidov. A letter was delivered to reception.*

Panin nodded at the guards, who cautiously opened the door, guns raised. One took the letter while the other searched the man who delivered it, finding nothing. The envelope was handed to Leo.

On the outside was a carefully drawn ink crucifix. Leo tore open the envelope, pulling out a single sheet of paper.

Church of Sancta Sophia
Midnight
Alone

Thirty minutes past midnight. Leo was waiting where the Church of Sancta Sophia had once stood. The domes and tabernacles were gone. In their place was a vast pit, ten metres deep, twenty metres wide and seventy long. One of the walls had collapsed, forming an uneven slope that led down to a muddy basin of brown snow, black ice and oozy water. The remaining walls were near collapse, slipping inwards, creating the impression of a mouth closing around a monstrous black tongue. No work had taken place since 1950: it was a construction site with no construction, sealed off and closed down. Along the steel perimeter fence were faded signs warning people to keep out. After the initial, botched attempt, when one demolition expert had died and several of the crowd had been injured, the church had been successfully destroyed and cleared away, loaded on trucks, the remains dumped outside the city, a rubble corpse now bound together with weeds. Preliminary work had begun for what was to be the nation's largest water-sports complex, including a fifty-metre pool and a series of *banya*, one for men, one for women and one marble chamber for State officials.

Excitement had been manufactured by a saturation media campaign. The design schematics had been reprinted in *Pravda*, footage had run in the cinemas showing real people superimposed against a matte drawing of the completed baths. While the propaganda geared up, work had shuddered to a halt. The ground beside the river was unstable and susceptible to slippage. The foundations had begun to move and tear, causing the authorities to regret not examining the ancient foundations of the church more carefully before scooping them up and tossing them aside. Some of the best minds in the country had been called in and, after careful consideration, declared it unsuitable for a complex that required deep networks of pipes and drains, dug further down than the church had ever extended. Those experts had been dismissed and more pliable experts brought in who, after a different kind of careful consideration, declared the problem fixable. They merely needed more time. That was the answer the State had wanted to hear, not wishing to admit to a mistake. These experts had been housed in luxury apartments where they drew diagrams, smoked cigars and jotted down calculations while the deep pit filled with rain during the autumn, snow during the winter and mosquitoes during the summer. The propaganda footage was pulled from the cinemas. Shrewd citizens understood that it would be best to forget about the project. Imprudent citizens wryly commented that a watery trench made a poor substitute for a three-hundred-year-old church. In the summer of 1951 Leo had arrested a man for making such a quip.

Leo checked his watch. He'd been waiting for over an hour. Shivering and exhausted, he was near mad with impatience. He had no idea if his wife had survived surgery and, cut off from communication, had no means of finding out. There was no question that the decision to leave Raisa's side and meet Lazar was the correct one. There was nothing he could do in the hospital. No matter how much Zoya hated him, no matter how she behaved, no matter if she wanted him dead, he'd taken responsibility for her, a responsibility he'd promised to uphold whether she loved him or not. In preparation for the meeting he'd gone home, showered, scrubbed off the smell of the sewer and changed out of his uniform. His hands had been dressed at the hospital. He'd refused painkillers, fearing that they might dull him. He was wearing civilian clothing, conscious that the trappings of authority might provoke a vengeful priest.

Hearing a noise, Leo turned, searching the gloom for his adversary. There was residual light from nearby buildings outside the fenced perimeter. Precious machinery – cranes, diggers – stood abandoned, left to rust because no one dared admit defeat and redeploy them where they could be put to use. Leo heard the noise again: the clang of metal against stone. It wasn't coming from inside the construction site: it was coming from the river.

Cautiously, he approached the stone ledge, tentatively leaning over and peering down towards the water. A hand reached up not far from where he was standing. A man nimbly pulled himself up, squatting on the ledge before jumping down to the construction site. To his side another man climbed up. They were crawling out of the mouth of a sewer tunnel, clambering up the wall, like a disturbed ant colony responding to a threat. Leo recognized the young boy who'd murdered the Patriarch clambering out, expertly using finger- and toe-holds in the brickwork. Watching him move with such agility, it was unsurprising that he'd survived his dive into the torrent.

The gang searched Leo for weapons. There were seven men and the boy, tattoos on their necks and hands. Several items of their clothes were well tailored while others were threadbare, mismatched as if wearing a haphazard selection from the wardrobes of a hundred different people. Their appearance left no question. They were part of a criminal fraternity, the *vory* – a brotherhood forged during their time in the Gulags. Despite Leo's profession, he rarely encountered *vory*. They considered themselves apart from the State.

The gang members spread out, examining the surroundings, making sure it was safe. Finally the boy whistled, giving the all-clear. Two hands appeared on the ledge. Lazar climbed up, towering above his *vory*, silhouetted by the lights on the other side of the river. Except that this wasn't Lazar. It was a woman – Anisya, Lazar's wife.

Anisya's hair was cropped short. Her features were sharp. All the softness in her face and body had been lost. Despite this, she seemed more intensely alive, more striking and vivid than ever before, as if some great energy emanated from her. She was wearing loose trousers, an open shirt and a short, thick coat – dressed much like her men. There was a gun on her belt, like a bandit. From her triumphant position she looked down at Leo, proud that her arrival had surprised him. Leo could manage only one word, her name:

— *Anisya?*

She smiled. Her voice was cracked and deep, no longer melodic, no longer the voice of a woman who used to sing in her husband's choir.

— *That name means nothing to me now. My men call me Fraera.*

She jumped down from the ledge not far from Leo. Standing up straight, she studied his face intently.

— *Maxim . . .*

She addressed him with the alias he'd taken.

— *Answer me this, and don't lie, how often did you think of me? Every day?*

— *Honestly, no.*

— *Did you think of me once a week?*

— *No.*

— *Once a month . . .*

— *I don't know . . .*

Fraera allowed him to taper off into embarrassed silence before remarking:

— *I can guarantee you that your victims think about you every day, every morning and every night. They remember your smell and the sound of your voice – they remember you as clearly as I see you now.*

Fraera raised her right hand.

— *This was the hand you touched when you made me your offer, that I leave my husband. Isn't that what you said? I should let him die in the Gulags while I slipped into bed with you?*

— *I was young.*

— *Yes, you were. Very young and yet you were still given power over me, over my husband. You were a boy with a crush, little more than a teenager. You thought you'd done a decent thing in trying to save me.*

This was a conversation she'd practised a thousand times, words shaped by seven years of hate.

— *I had a lucky escape. If fear had taken hold of me, if I had faltered, I would've ended up as your wife, the wife of an MGB officer, an accomplice to your crimes, someone to share your guilt with.*

— *You have every reason to hate me.*

— *I have more reason than you think.*

— *Raisa, Zoya, Elena: they have nothing to do with my mistakes.*

— *You mean that they are innocent? When has that mattered to officers like you? How many innocent people have you arrested?*

— *You intend to murder every person who wronged you?*

— *I didn't murder Suren. I didn't murder your mentor Nikolai.*

— *His daughters are dead.*

Fraera shook her head.

— *Maxim, I have no heart. I have no tears to shed. Nikolai was weak and vain. I should've guessed he would die in the most pathetic of fashions. However, as a message to the State, it was certainly more powerful than him merely hanging himself.*

Just as the Church of Sancta Sophia had been destroyed and replaced with a dark, deep pit, Leo wondered if the same was true of her. Her moral foundations had been ripped up and replaced with a dark abyss.

Fraera asked:

— *I take it you have made the connection between Suren, the man who ran the printing press, Nikolai, the Patriarch and yourself? You knew Nikolai: he was your boss. The Patriarch was the man who enabled you to infiltrate our Church.*

— *Suren worked for the MGB but I didn't know him personally.*

— *He was a guard when I was interrogated. I remember him standing on tiptoe, looking into the cell. I remember the top of his head, his curious eyes, watching as if he'd snuck into a movie theatre.*

Leo asked:

— *What is the point of this?*

— *When the police are criminals, the criminals must become the police. The innocent must live underground, in the shit of the city, while the villains live in warm apartments. The world is upside down: I'm merely turning it the right way up.*

Leo spoke out.

— *What about Zoya? You'd kill her, a young girl who doesn't even like me? A girl who only chose to live with me to save her sister from an orphanage?*

— *You are mistaken in your attempts at appealing to my*

129

humanity. Anisya is dead. She died when her child was taken from her by the State.

Leo didn't understand. Answering his evident confusion, Fraera added:

— *Maxim, I was pregnant when you arrested me.*

With the precision of a surgeon Fraera probed this newly inflicted cut, prising it open, watching him bleed.

— *You never even took the time to find out what had happened to Lazar. You never took the time to find out what had happened to me. Had you looked through the records you would've discovered that I gave birth eight months into my sentence. I was allowed to nurse my son for three months before he was taken from me. I was told to forget about him. I was told I would never see him again. When I was released, granted an early reprieve after Stalin's death, I searched for my child. He'd been placed in an orphanage but his name had been changed and all record of my motherhood erased. This is standard, I was told. It is one thing to lose a child: it is another to know that they're alive, somewhere, ignorant of your existence.*

— *Fraera, I can't defend the State. I followed orders. And I was wrong. The orders were wrong. The State was wrong. But I have changed.*

— *I know about the changes you've made. You're no longer KGB, you're militia. You deal only with real crimes, not political ones. You've adopted two beautiful young girls. This is your idea of redemption, yes? What does any of it mean to me? What of the debt you owe me? What of the debt you owe to the men and women you arrested? How is that to be paid? Are you planning to build a modest stone statue to commemorate the dead? Will you put up a brass plaque with our names written in tiny letters so they all fit in? Will that suffice?*

— *You want to take my life?*

— *I have thought about it many times.*

— *Then kill me and let Zoya live. Let my wife live.*

— *You would gladly die to save them. It would make you noble; it would scrub you clean of your crimes. You still believe that you can lead your life as a hero? Take off your clothes.*

Leo remained silent, unsure if he'd heard correctly. She repeated her instructions.

— *Maxim, take off your clothes.*

Leo took off his hat, his gloves, his coat, dropping them to the ground. He unbuttoned his shirt, shuddering in the cold, placing it on the heap in front of him. Fraera raised her hand.

— *That's enough.*

He stood, shivering, his arms by his side.

— *You find the night cold, Maxim? It is nothing compared to the winters in Kolyma, the frozen corner of this country where you sent my husband.*

To his surprise, Fraera also began to undress, taking off her coat, her shirt, revealing her naked torso. Tattoos covered her skin: one under her right breast, one on her stomach, tattoos on her arms, her hands, fingers. She stepped closer to Leo.

— *You want to know what has happened to me these past few years? You want to know how a woman, the wife of a priest, came to be in charge of a* vory *gang? The answers are written on my skin.*

She took hold of her breast, lifting it up, drawing Leo's attention to the tattoo. There was a lion.

— *It means I will avenge all who wronged me, from the lawyers to the judges, from the prison guards to the police officers.*

In the centre of her chest, rising up between her breasts, was a crucifix.

— *This has nothing to do with my husband, Maxim – it represents my authority, as the Thief-in-Law. Perhaps this one you'll understand.*

She touched the tattoo on her stomach. It showed a heavily pregnant woman – a cross-section revealing the inside of her extended belly. Instead of an unborn child, the pregnant stomach was filled with barbed wire, coiled round and round like one long, jagged umbilical cord.

— *Maxim, you have the blank skin of a child. To me, and to my men, it appears dishonest. Where are your crimes? Where are the things you have done? I see no trace of them. I see no marks on you. I see none of your guilt written on you.*

Fraera took another step closer, her body almost touching his.

— *I can touch you, Maxim. Yet if you lay a finger on me, you will be killed. My skin is the same as my authority. For you to touch me would be a violation, an insult.*

She pressed against him, whispering:

— *Seven years later, it is my turn to make you an offer. Lazar is still in Kolyma, working in a gold mine. They refuse to release him. He's a priest. Priests are hated again, now there are no wars the State needs them to promote. He's been told he'll have to serve his full sentence – twenty-five years. I want you to get him out. I want you to put right that wrong.*

— *I have no such power.*

— *You have connections.*

— *Fraera, you murdered the Patriarch. They blame you for the murder of two agents, Nikolai and Moskvin. They will never negotiate with you. They will never release Lazar.*

— *Then you must find another way to get him out.*

— *Fraera, please – if you had asked me a week ago, perhaps it would've been feasible. But after what you have done, it is impossible. Listen to my voice. I would do anything for Zoya, anything within my power. However, I cannot free Lazar.*

Fraera leaned forward, whispering:

— *Remember, I can touch you, but you must not touch me.*

With that warning she kissed him on the cheek. Tender at first before her teeth gripped his skin, closing tight, digging in, increasing in pressure – drawing blood. The pain was intense. Leo wanted to push her away but if he touched her he would be killed. He could do nothing except suffer the pain. Finally, she opened her mouth, stepping back and admiring the bite marks.

— *Maxim, you have your first tattoo.*

With his blood on her lips, she concluded:

— *Free my husband, or I will murder your daughter.*

THREE
WEEKS
LATER

WESTERN PACIFIC OCEAN
SOVIET TERRITORIAL WATERS
SEA OF OKHOTSK
STARY BOLSHEVIK PRISON SHIP

7 APRIL 1956

Standing on deck, Officer Genrikh Duvakin used the tips of his teeth to pull off his coarse mittens. His fingers were icy numb, slow to respond. He blew on them, rubbing his hands together, trying to restore circulation. Exposed to the biting wind, his face was deadened – his lips bloodless and blue. The outermost hairs in his nose had frozen and when he pinched his nostrils, brittle hairs broke like miniature icicles. He could tolerate such minor discomforts because his hat was a miracle of warmth, lined with reindeer fur and stitched with the care of someone who appreciated that the wearer's life might depend on the quality of their work. Three long flaps covered his ears and the back of his neck. The earflaps, tied tight under his chin, gave him the appearance of a child wrapped up against the cold, an effect compounded by his soft, boyish features. The pounding salt air had failed to crack his smooth complexion while his plump cheeks had proved resilient to poor diet and lack of sleep. Twenty-seven years old, he was often mistaken for younger, a physical immaturity that did not serve him well. Supposed to be intimidating and fierce, he was a daydreamer, an unlikely guard on board a prison ship as notorious as the *Stary Bolshevik*.

Roughly the size of an industrial barge, the *Stary Bolshevik* was a workhorse vessel. Once a sea-battered Dutch steamer, it had been bought in the nineteen-thirties, renamed and customized by the Soviet secret police. Originally intended for colonial exports – ivory, pungent spices and exotic fruits – it now ferried men destined for the deadliest labour camps in the Gulag enterprise. Towards the bow there was a central tower four storeys high that included living quarters for the guards and crew. At the top of the tower was the bridge where the captain and crew navigated, a close-knit group autonomous from the prison guards themselves, wilfully blind to the business of this ship, pretending that it was no responsibility of theirs.

Opening the door, the captain stepped out from the bridge, surveying the stretch of sea they were leaving behind. He gestured down to Genrikh on deck, giving him a nod and announcing:

— *All clear!*

They'd passed through the Pérouse Strait, the only point on the journey where they neared Japanese islands and risked international contact. Precautions were taken to ensure that the vessel appeared to be nothing more than a civilian cargo ship. The heavy machine gun on the centre deck was dismantled, uniforms hidden beneath long coats. Genrikh had never been entirely sure why they took such efforts to conceal their true nature from the glances of Japanese fishermen. In idle moments, he wondered if there were similar prison ships in Japan with similar men to him.

Genrikh reassembled the machine gun. He directed the barrel at the reinforced steel hatch. Below it, in the darkness, cramped on bunks like matches in a box, was a cargo of five hundred men – the first convict-laden voyage of the year from transit camp Buchta Nakhodka on the south of the Pacific coastline to Kolyma in the north. Though the ports were located on the same stretch of coastline the distance between them was vast. There was no way to reach Kolyma by land: it was accessible only by plane or ship. The northern port of Magadan served as the entry point for a network of labour camps that had spread like fungal spores up along the Kolyma highway into the mountains, forests and mines.

Five hundred was the smallest prisoner cargo Genrikh had ever supervised. At this point in the year under Stalin's rule the ship would have held four times as many in an attempt to ease the backlog at the transit camps built up over the winter as the *zek* trains, the prisoner-filled wagons, continued to deliver but the ships remained docked. The Sea of Okhotsk was only passable when the ice floes melted. By October it was frozen again. A mistimed voyage meant being encased in ice. Genrikh had heard of ships that had ventured too late in winter or left too early in the spring. Unable to turn back or reach their destination, the guards had made good their escape, trekking across the ice, dragging sleighs loaded with canned meats and bread while the abandoned prisoners were left in the hold to starve or freeze, whichever came first.

Today no prisoners would be allowed to starve, or freeze, nor would they be summarily executed, their bodies tossed overboard. Genrikh hadn't read Khrushchev's Secret Speech condemning Stalin and the excesses of the Gulags. He'd been too scared. There were rumours that it was designed to flush out counter-revolutionaries, a ploy so that people might let their defences slip and join in the criticism only to be arrested. Genrikh wasn't convinced by this theory: the changes seemed real. The long-established practice of brutality and indifference with no accountability had been replaced by confused compassion. At the transit camp prisoners' sentences were hastily reviewed. Thousands destined for Kolyma had been suddenly granted their freedom, returned to civilization as abruptly as they'd been taken from it. These free men — most of the women had been granted freedom in the amnesty of 1953 — had sat on the shore, staring out at the sea, each clutching a five-hundred-gram chunk of black rye bread, a freedom ration, intended to sustain them until they reached home. For most, home was thousands of miles away. With no possessions, no money, just their rags and their freedom bread, they'd stared out at the sea, unable to comprehend that they could walk away and not be shot. Genrikh had shooed them from the shoreline as if they were pesky birds, encouraging them to make the journey home but unable to tell them how.

Genrikh's superiors had spent the weeks panicking that they were going to be brought before a tribunal. In an attempt to show how much they'd changed, they had issued extensive reviews and overhauls of regulations, frantic signals to Moscow that they were synchronized with this new fashion for fairness. Genrikh had kept his head down, doing as ordered, never questioning and never offering an opinion. If he were told to be tough with prisoners he'd be tough. If he were told to be nice he'd be nice. As it happens with his baby face, he'd always been better at being nice than tough.

After years of shipping thousands of political prisoners convicted under Article 58, men and women who'd said the wrong thing, or been in the wrong place, or known the wrong people, the *Stary Bolshevik* had a new role — to carry a more select cargo, only the most violent and dangerous criminals, men for whom everyone could agree: there was no question of them ever being released.

*

In the pitch-black belly of the *Stary Bolshevik*, among the stinking bodies of five hundred murderers and rapists and thieves, Leo lay on his back, resting on the narrow, rickety top bunk, his shoulder pressed against the hull. On the other side was a vast expanse of sea, a mass of freezing water held back by a steel plate no thicker than his thumbnail.

The air was stale and putrid, boiled by the shuddering coal engine secured in the adjacent compartment. The convicts had no access to the engine, but its heat seeped through the timber partition wall, a crude addition to the ship's original design. At the beginning of the journey, when the hold was freezing cold, prisoners fought for the bunks nearest the engine. Within days, as temperatures soared, those same prisoners were fighting for bunks further away. Divided into a grid of narrow passageways, with high rows of wooden bunks on either side, the sub-deck cargo hold had been transformed into an insect hive, infested with prisoners. Leo had a top bunk, a space he'd fought for and defended, prized for its elevation from the sick and shit slopping on the floor. The weaker you were, the lower you were – as if they'd been shaken through a filtering process, separating into Darwinian layers. Lanterns that had for the past week emitted a dim, sooty glow – like stars seen through city smog – were now out of kerosene, creating darkness so complete that Leo couldn't see his hands even as they scratched his face.

Tonight was the seventh day at sea. Leo had counted the days as carefully as he could, making the most of infrequently permitted toilet visits to regain some sense of time. On deck, with a mounted machine gun directed at them, prisoners queued to use the hole intended for the anchor, a drop straight into the ocean. Trying to maintain balance on the choppy seas, whipped by icy winds, squatting and shuffling, the process became an awful pantomime. Some inmates, unable to queue, lost control of their bowels, soiling themselves, lying in their own excrement, waiting until it was crust before they started moving again. The psychological importance of cleanliness was self-evident. A person could lose their sanity after only seven days down here. Leo comforted himself that these conditions were temporary. His primary concern was maintaining his edge. Many prisoners had been weakened by months in transit, their muscles softened by inactivity and poor food, their minds softened by the prospect of ten years working in the mines. Leo exercised regularly, keeping his body taut and his mind focused on the task at hand.

After Leo's encounter with Fraera on the excavated grounds of the Church of Sancta Sophia he'd returned to hospital to discover that Raisa had survived surgery and that the doctors were confident of a full recovery. Waking up, her first question was about Zoya and Elena. Seeing how pale and weak she was, Leo promised that he was concentrated entirely on his kidnapped daughter. Listening to him explain Fraera's demands Raisa merely said:

— *Do whatever it takes.*

*

Fraera had gained control of a criminal gang. As far as Leo could tell she was no *torpedy*, no mere foot soldier — she was the *avtoritet*, the leader. Members of a criminal gang, the *vory*, were typically contemptuous of women. They wrote songs about their love for their mothers, they killed each other over insults to their mothers, but nurtured no belief in women being equals. Somehow the wife of a priest, a woman who'd spent her life in her husband's shadow, assisting his career, had managed to penetrate the *vorovskoi mir*. Even more astounding was that she had risen to the top. Fraera was integrated into their rituals: her body covered with tattoos, her birth name tossed aside and replaced with a *klikukha*, a *vory* nickname. Sheltered within the highly secretive *vorovskoi mir*, her operations were probably funded by pickpockets and black-market trade. If revenge had been her intention from the outset then she'd chosen her allies well. The *vory* gangs were the only organizations the State had no control over. There was no chance of infiltrating their ranks: it would take too much time – requiring an officer to spend years undercover, to murder and rape in order to prove himself. It wasn't that the State couldn't find a suitable candidate but rather that it had always considered the *vory* an irrelevance. The gangs were motivated by their own internal, closed system of loyalty and reward. None of them had ever shown any interest in politics, until now, until Fraera.

Had Fraera's demand – the release of her husband – come before her murders, it might have been achievable. The penal system was in upheaval following Khrushchev's speech. Regarding Lazar's twenty-five-year sentence, Leo could have applied for a special dispensation, a dismissal or an early parole. The complication would have been Khrushchev's renewed anti-religious campaign. However, after the murders there was no chance of negotiating for Lazar's release. No deal would be struck. Fraera was a terrorist, to be hunted down and killed irrespective of whether or not Zoya had been taken hostage. Fraera's gang had been classified as a counter-revolutionary cell. To make matters worse she'd made no attempt to curtail her blood lust. In the days directly after Zoya's kidnapping Fraera's men had murdered several officials – men and women who'd served under Stalin. Some had been tortured as they'd tortured others. Faced with a reflection of their own crimes, the upper echelons of power were terrified. They were demanding the execution of every member of Fraera's cell and every man and woman who aided them.

Fortunately Leo's boss, Frol Panin, was an ambitious man. Despite the KGB and the militia launching the largest manhunt Moscow had ever seen, they'd found no trace of Fraera and her gang. Clamorous calls for their capture were answered with failure. The press reported nothing of these events, opting for celebrations of industrial statistics on the days after the most shocking of executions, as if these numbers might dampen the rumours sweeping the streets. Officials were moving their families out of the city. A surge in holiday requests had been submitted. The situation was intolerable. Coveting the glory of being the one who snared Fraera, the mantle of a heroic monster-slayer, Panin saw Lazar as bait. Since they couldn't arrange for Lazar to be released through normal channels, without admitting the State could be held to ransom, the only option was to break him out. Panin had hinted that their project had powerful supporters and was proceeding with the tacit consent of those in charge.

Lazar was a convict in the Kolyma region, Gulag 57. Escape was considered impossible. No one had ever succeeded. Security at many of the Gulags was little more than their location: there was no means of surviving outside the compound. The chances of traversing the vast and unforgiving terrain on foot were negligible. If Lazar went missing he would be declared dead. With Panin's help, it was a simple matter to get into the Gulag, fabricating the necessary paperwork, positioning Leo as a prisoner. Getting out, however, would not be so easy.

Vibrations raced through the hull. The ship's bow veered to the side. Leo sat bolt upright. They'd hit ice.

Genrikh rushed forward, peering over the side. A sunken mass of ice slowly passed by, its pinnacle no larger than a car, the majority of its bulk underwater appearing as a vast dark-blue shadow. The hull appeared intact. There was no shouting from the prisoners down below. No water was leaking in. Feeling sweat under his reindeer fur, he signalled to the captain that the danger had passed.

In the first voyages of the year the bows occasionally knocked against remnants of the ice mass, collisions that made an ominous noise against the ageing hull. In the past these collisions used to terrify Genrikh. The *Stary Bolshevik* was a sickly vessel: no good for trade or commerce, suitable only for convicts – barely able to cut a path through water let alone brush aside ice. Built for a speed of eleven knots, the coal-fired steamer never managed much above eight, puffing like a lame mule. Over the years the smoke coming from the single funnel, located towards the stern, had turned darker and thicker, the vessel moved slower while the creaking had become louder. Yet despite the ship's worsening health Genrikh had gradually lost his fear of the sea. He could sleep through storms and hold down meals even when plates and cutlery clattered from side to side. It wasn't that he'd grown brave. Another more pressing fear had taken its place – a fear of his fellow guards.

On his first voyage he'd made a mistake that he'd never been able to put right, one that his comrades had never forgiven. During Stalin's reign the guards frequently colluded with the *urki* — the career criminals. The guards would organize a transfer of one or two female prisoners into the male hold. Sometimes the women's cooperation was bought with false promises of food. Sometimes they were drugged. Sometimes they were dragged, fighting and screaming and shouting. It depended on the tastes of the *urki*, many of whom enjoyed snuffing out a fight as much as sex. Payment for this transaction was information on the politicals — convicts sentenced for crimes against the State. Reports of things said, conversations overheard, information that the guards could translate into valuable written denunciations when the ship reached land. As a small bonus the guards took final turns with the unconscious women, consummating an allegiance as old as the Gulag system itself. Genrikh had politely declined to join in. He hadn't threatened to report them or shown any disapproval. He'd merely smiled and said:

Not for me.

Words that he'd come to regret more bitterly than anything he'd ever done. From that moment he'd been shunned. He'd thought it would last a week. It had lasted seven years. At times, trapped on board, surrounded by ocean, he'd been mad with loneliness. Not every guard joined in the rapes all of the time but every guard joined in some of the time. However, he was never offered the chance to put good his mistake. The initial insult stood uncorrected since it didn't express a preference such as *I don't feel like it today* but a gut reaction: *This is wrong*. On occasion, pacing the deck at night, longing for someone to talk to, he'd turned to see the other guards gathered away from him. In the darkness all he could make out were their smouldering cigarettes, red fag ends glowering at him like hate-filled eyes.

He'd stopped worrying that the sea might swallow this ship or that ice might rip the hull. His fear had been that one night he'd fall asleep only to wake, his arms and feet held fast by the other guards, dragged, as those women were dragged, fighting, screaming, thrown over the side, falling into the black, freezing ocean where he would splash helplessly for a minute or two, watching the lights of the ship grow smaller and smaller.

For the first time in seven years those fears no longer troubled him. The entire guard contingent of the ship had been replaced. Perhaps their removal had something to do with the reforms sweeping the camps. He didn't know. It didn't matter: they were gone, all of them, except for him. He'd been left behind, excluded from their change in fortune. For once, exclusion suited him just fine. He found himself among a new group of guards, none of whom hated him, none of whom knew anything about him. He was a stranger again. Anonymity felt wonderful, as if he'd been miraculously cured of a terminal sickness. Presented with an opportunity to start afresh, he intended to do everything in his power to make sure he was part of the team.

He turned to see one of the new guards smoking on the other side of the deck, staring at the dusk skyline, no doubt brought outside by the noise of the collision. A tall, broad-shouldered man in his late thirties, he had the poise of a leader. The man — Iakov Messing — had said very little during the journey. He'd volunteered no information about himself and Genrikh still had no idea if Iakov was staying aboard the ship or whether he was merely en route to another camp. Tough with the prisoners, reticent with the other guards, a brilliant card player and physically strong, there was little doubt that if a new group were going to form, as it had done on the last ship, it would form with Iakov at its centre.

Genrikh crossed the deck, greeting Iakov with a nod of his head and gesturing at his pack of cheap cigarettes.

— *May I?*

Iakov offered the pack and a lighter. Nervous, Genrikh took a cigarette, lit it and inhaled deeply. The smoke was coarse on his throat. He smoked infrequently and tried his best to pretend that he was enjoying the experience, sharing a mutual pleasure. It was imperative he made a good impression. However, he had nothing to say. Iakov had almost finished his cigarette. He'd soon be going back inside. The opportunity might not arise again, the two of them alone – this was the time to speak.

— *It's been a quiet voyage.*

Iakov said nothing. Genrikh flicked ash at the sea, continuing:

— *This your first time? On board, I mean? I know it's your first time on board this ship, but I was wondering if, maybe, you've . . . been on other ships. Like this.*

Iakov answered with a question:

— *How long have you been on board?*

Genrikh smiled, relieved to have solicited a response.

— *Seven years. And things have changed. I don't know if they've changed for the better. These voyages used to be something—*

— *How so?*

— *You know . . . all kinds of . . . Good times. You know what I mean?*

Genrikh smiled to underscore the oblique innuendo. Iakov's face was impassive.

— *No. What do you mean?*

Genrikh was forced to explain. He lowered his voice, whispering, trying to coax Iakov into his conspiracy.

— *Normally, around day two or three, the guards—*

— *The guards? You're a guard.*

A careless slip: he'd implied he was outside the group and now he was being asked whether that was the case. He clarified:

— *I mean me, us. We.*

Emphasizing the word — *we* — and then saying it again for good measure.

— *We talk to the* urki, *to see if they're willing to make us an offer, a list of names, a list of the politicals, someone who'd said something stupid. We ask what they'd want in return for this information: alcohol, tobacco . . . women.*

— *Women?*

— *You've heard of "taking the train"?*

— *Remind me.*

— *The line of men who take their turn, with the female convicts. I was always the last carriage, so to speak. You know, of the train of men, who took their turn.*

He laughed.

— *Last was better than nothing, that's what I say.*

He paused, looking out at sea, hands on his hips, longing to scrutinize Iakov's reaction. He repeated, nervously:

— *Better than nothing.*

Squinting in the dim dusk light, Timur Nesterov studied the face of this young man as he boasted about his history of rape. The man wanted to be patted on the back, congratulated and assured that those times were the good times. Timur's cover as a prison guard, as officer Iakov Messing, depended upon remaining invisible. He couldn't stand out. He couldn't kick up a fuss. He was not here to judge this man or to avenge those women. Yet it was difficult not to imagine his wife as a convict aboard this ship. In the past she'd come very close to being arrested. She was beautiful and she would've ended up at the mercy of this young man's desire.

Timur tossed the cigarette into the sea, moving indoors. He was almost at the tower door when the guard called out after him:

— *Thanks for the smoke!*

Timur stopped, wondering at this muddle of manners and flippant savagery. To his eye, Genrikh was more like a child than a man. Just as a child might try to impress an adult, the young officer pointed up to the sky.

— *Going to be a storm.*

Night was closing, and in the distance flashes of lightning silhouetted black clouds — clouds shaped like the knuckles of a giant fist.

Lying on his back in the darkness, Leo listened to the heavy rain pummelling the deck. The ship had begun to roll and pitch, lumbering from side to side. He traced the vessel in his mind, picturing how it might hold in a storm. Stubby, like a gigantic steel thumb, it was wide and slow and stable. The only section — aside from the steam funnel — that rose above deck was the tower where the guards and crew quarters were located. Leo took reassurance from the vessel's age: it must have survived many storms in its lifetime.

His bunk shook as a wave thumped the side, breaking over the deck — a sloshing noise that carried with it a visual imprint — the deck briefly merging with the sea. Leo sat up. The storm was growing. He was forced to grip the sides of the bunk as the ship lurched violently. Prisoners began crying out as they were shaken off their bunks, cries echoing around the darkness. It had become a disadvantage to be so high. The wooden frame was unstable. The structure wasn't secured to the hull. The bunks might fall, tipping their occupants to the floor. Leo was about to climb down when a hand grabbed his face.

With the wind and the waves, the commotion, he hadn't heard anyone approach. The man's breath smelt like decay. His voice was gruff.

— *Who are you?*

Sounding authoritative, he was almost certainly a gang leader. Leo was sure the man wasn't alone: his men must be nearby, on the other bunks, to the sides, underneath. It was impossible to fight: he couldn't see the man he was fighting.

— *My name is—*

The man cut him off.

— *I'm not interested in your name. I want to know who you are. Why are you here, among us? You're not a* vory. *Not a man like me. Maybe you're a political. But then, I see you doing sit-ups, I see you exercising and I know you're not a political. They hide in the corner and cry like babies about never seeing their families again. You're something else. Makes me nervous, not knowing what's in a person's heart. I don't mind if it's murder and stealing, I don't even mind if it's hymns and prayers and goodness, I just like to know. So, I say again, who are you?*

The man seemed entirely indifferent to the fact that the ship was now being tossed like a toy by the storm. The entire bunk was rocking: the only thing keeping it fixed was the weight of the people on it. Prisoners were jumping to the floor, scrambling over each other. Leo tried to reason with the man.

— *How about we talk when this storm's over?*

— *Why? There something you need to do?*

— *I need to get off this bunk.*

— *You feel that?*

The tip of a knife touched Leo's stomach.

Abruptly, the ship lifted up, a movement so sudden and powerful it felt as though the hand of a sea god were underneath them, pushing them out of the ocean and racing them towards the sky. As suddenly the movement stopped, the velocity vaporized, the watery hand turning to spray and the *Stary Bolshevik* fell, plunging straight down.

The bows smacked into the water. With the force of a detonation, the impact cracked through the ship. With a synchronized snap every bunk splintered and collapsed. For a second Leo was suspended in darkness, falling, with no idea what lay beneath him. He rotated so that he'd land face down, pushing his hands out towards the floor. There was a crunch of bones breaking. Unsure whether he was injured, whether his bones had broken, he lay still, breathless and dazed. He didn't feel any pain. Patting the ground underneath him he realized he'd landed on another prisoner, across a man's chest. The noise was the man's ribs fracturing. Leo searched for a pulse only to find a splintered fragment of wood jutting out of the man's neck.

Staggering to his feet, the ship rolled to the side, then back the other way. Someone grabbed his ankles. Worried that it was the nameless, faceless gang leader he kicked them away only to realize that it was more likely someone desperate for help. With no time to put right that wrong, the ship rose up again, at an even sharper angle than before, rocketing towards the sky. The smashed bunks, now free to move, slid towards him, piling up. Sharp, lethal fragments pressed against his arms and legs. Prisoners unable to maintain their grip on the sloping floor tumbled down, knocking into him, an avalanche of wood and dead bodies.

Pushed down by the ragged wall of people and timber, Leo tried blindly, hopelessly, to find something to steady himself, something to grab on to. The ship was at a forty-five-degree angle. Something metallic caught him in the side of the face. Leo fell, tumbling, rolling, until he arrived against the back wall, against the hot planks that separated the convicts from the roaring coal engine. The wall was four deep with prisoners tipped from their beds, waiting for the ship's climb to reverse and slip into the inevitable fall. Groping for anything fixed that they could hold on to, they feared being tossed forward into the unknown. Leo clasped the hull – it was smooth and cold. There was nothing to grip. The ship stopped its upward climb, perched on the crest of a wave.

Leo was about to be thrown forward. He'd be helpless, everyone behind him landing on top of him, crushing him. Unable to see anything, he tried to remember the layout of the hold. The steps up to the deck hatch were his only chance. The ship tipped into a free fall, accelerating down. Leo threw himself in the direction where he guessed the steps were located. He collapsed into something hard – the metal steps – and managed to clasp an arm around them just as the ship's bow thumped into the water.

A second detonation-like impact, the force was tremendous. Leo was convinced the entire ship had split apart, a nutshell smashing under a hammer. Waiting for a wall of water, instead he heard the sound of breaking wood, like tree trunks splitting in half. There were screams. Leo's arm, locked around the step, was yanked so hard, he was sure it had been dislocated. Yet there was no wall of water rushing in. The hull was intact.

Leo looked behind him and saw smoke. He couldn't just smell the smoke, he could see it. Where was the light coming from? The noise of the engine had intensified. The timber partition had broken apart. The engine room was exposed. At its centre was a red, glowering hub surrounded by the smashed debris of bunks and twisted bodies.

Leo squinted, his eyes adjusting from permanent darkness. The hold was no longer secure: the prisoners – the most dangerous men in the penal system – now had access to the crew quarters and the captain's deck, which could be reached from the engine room. The officer in charge of keeping the engine running, covered in coal dust, raised his hands in surrender. A convict leapt at him, flinging him against the red-hot engine. The officer screamed: the stink of burning flesh filled the air. He tried to push himself free from the metal but the convict held him fast, gloating as the man was cooked alive, his eyes rolling, gurgling on spit. The jubilant prisoner called out:

— *Take the ship!*

Leo recognized that voice. It was the man on his bunk, the gang leader with the knife, the man who'd wanted him dead.

Flung from side to side, Timur zigzagged down the *Stary Bolshevik*'s narrow corridors, colliding with walls, scrambling to secure the two access doors that led up from the engine room. He'd been on the bridge when the ship had dropped from the crest of a wave, as though it had sailed off a crumbling cliff of water, the bow falling for thirty metres before smashing into the base of an ocean-trough. Timur had been thrown forward, catapulted over the navigation equipment, tumbling to the floor. The vessel's steel panels reverberated with the impact's energy. Standing up, look-ing out of the window, all he could see was foaming water rushing towards him – churning grey and white and black – convinced that the ship was sinking, plunging straight down to the bottom, only for the bow to be lifted once again, angled towards the sky.

Attempting to ascertain the damage, the captain had rung down to the engine room. There was no response – calls went unanswered. There was still power, the engine was still working, the hull couldn't have been breached. The upward movement of the ship discounted extensive flooding. If the outer hull was intact the only other explanation for the loss of communication was that the timber partition wall must have snapped like a twig. The convicts were no longer secure: they could enter the engine room and climb the stairs, accessing the main tower. If the prisoners reached the upper levels they'd kill everyone and plot a new course for international waters where they'd claim asylum in exchange for anti-Communist propaganda. Five hundred convicts against a crew of thirty of which only twenty were guards.

Control of the lower levels, those below deck, was lost. They couldn't recapture the engine room or save the crew working there. However, it was still possible to seal those compartments, trapping the convicts in the lower levels of the ship. From the engine room there were two separate access points. Timur was heading towards the first. Another group of guards had been dispatched to the second. If either door were open, if either fell into the convicts' hands, the ship would be lost.

Turning right and left, hurtling down the last flight of stairs, he was at the base of the tower. He could see the first access door straight ahead: at the end of the corridor. It was unlocked, swinging backwards and forwards, clanging against the steel walls. The ship veered upwards, tilting sharply, throwing Timur forward to his hands and knees. The heavy steel door swung open revealing a horde of convicts climbing up from the engine room, as many as thirty or forty faces. They saw each other at the same time: the door being the midway point between them, both sides stared at each other across the divide between freedom and captivity.

The convicts exploded forward. Timur countered, launching himself off the floor, running, leaping into the door just as a mass of hands pressed against the other side, pushing in the opposite direction. There was no way he could hold them for long: his feet were sliding back. They were almost through. He reached for his gun.

The storm jerked the ship to the side, tipping the convicts off the door while throwing Timur's weight against it. The door slammed shut. He spun the lock, clamping it tight. Had the storm tilted the ship the other way, he would have been thrown to the floor and the convicts would have spilled out over him like a stampeding herd, overwhelming him. Denied freedom, their fists pounded against the door, banging and cursing. But their voices were faint and their blows hopeless. The thick steel door was secure.

Timur's relief was temporary, interrupted by the sound of machine-gun fire from the other side of the ship. The convicts must have passed through the second door.

Running, staggering, past abandoned crew quarters, Timur turned the corner, seeing two officers crouched, firing. Reaching their position, he drew his gun, aiming in the same direction. There were bodies on the floor between them and the second access door, prisoners shot, some alive, motioning for help. The critical door down to the sub-deck levels – now the only remaining access point for the convicts – had been wedged open by a plank of wood, protruding from the middle. Even if Timur made a run for the door there was no way to shut it. The officers, panicking, were firing aimlessly, bullets sparking off steel, pinging with lethal randomness around the corridor. Timur gestured for the officers to lower their weapons.

Pools of water on the floor mimicked the wild movements of the sea, sweeping from one side to the other. The prisoners weren't pushing forward, remaining safe behind the door. No doubt they were finding it difficult, among their cut-throat team, to conjure up the twenty or so willing to sacrifice their lives by surging forward to seize control of the corridor. At least that many would die before the guards were overpowered.

Timur took possession of one of the machine guns, aiming at the protruding wood stump. He fired, splintering it, walking forward at the same time. The stump was disintegrating under a barrage of steady gunfire. The door could be shut, locked, the final access point closed. Timur sprang forward. Before he could reach the handle, three more stumps were pushed through. There was no way to shut the door. Out of ammunition, Timur pulled back.

Four additional guards had arrived, stationed at the end of the corridor, making seven in total – a pitiful force to hold off five hundred. Since their early losses, the prisoners hadn't attempted a second advance. If a proportion weren't prepared to sacrifice their lives, there was no way to progress. They were almost certainly devising another means of attack. One of the officers whispered:

— *We stick our guns in the gap in the door! They don't have weapons! They'll drop the wood: we'll shut the door.*

Three officers nodded, running forwards.

They hadn't taken more than a couple of steps when the door was flung open. Panicked, the officers opened fire – to no avail. The foremost prisoners were using the injured crew as a human shield: burnt bodies carried like battering rams, skinless, charred faces screaming.

The officer nearest the advance tried to backtrack, his weapon firing uselessly into his colleague. The convict launched the body at him, knocking the officer to the floor. The guards redirected their bullets towards the prisoners' feet. Several fell, but there were too many of them, moving too fast. The column of prisoners continued to advance. In minutes they would control the corridor, from which point they would spread to the rest of the ship. Timur would be lynched. Paralysed, he couldn't even fire his handgun. What use were six shots against five hundred? It was as pointless as shooting at the sea.

Struck by an idea, he turned, hurrying to the outer door, the door that opened onto the deck. He threw it wide open, exposing the wild sea, a dizzy mass of water. Each of the guards wore a safety belt. He clipped his hook to the wire that ran around the tower, a system designed to prevent men from being washed overboard.

Glancing back at the gunfight, there were only two officers remaining. Scores of prisoners were dead but a seemingly inexhaustible number were packed behind them. Timur called out to the sea, challenging it, rallying it:

— *Come on!*

The ship plunged down, pointing Timur into a deep trough. Then, slowly, it rose up. A mountain of water was rolling straight towards him, the crumbing white surf high above, blotting out the sky. It crashed into the side of the ship, flooding the corridor. Timur was swept back, immersed in the sea. Water filled the space entirely. The cold stunned him. He was helpless — unable to move, or think, washed down the corridor.

His safety hook pulled him to a standstill. The wave had broken over the ship. The ship countered the movement, tipping back the other way. The water drained away as quickly as it had swept in. Timur fell to the floor, gasping, surveying the results of the flood. The wall of prisoners had been smashed back, some to the floor, most down the steps. Before they were able to recover, he unclipped himself, ran forward, his clothes soaked and heavy, his boots squelching over the shot-up bodies of guards and prisoners, victims of the skirmish. He slammed the door shut, locking it. The sub-deck levels were secure.

There was no time to waste. The door to the sea was wide open: another mountain of water might flood the interior, toppling the entire ship. Timur moved back towards the outer deck door. A hand grabbed him. One of the prisoners was alive, tripping Timur over. The prisoner clambered on top of him, pointing a machine gun at his head. There was no chance he'd miss. The prisoner pulled the trigger. Out of ammunition, or ruined by the sea, the gun didn't fire.

Granted a reprieve, Timur sparked back into life, smashing the prisoner's nose with a punch, spinning him onto his front and forcing his face into a puddle of water. Once more the ship began to tilt down, this time to Timur's disadvantage, the water draining away, saving the prisoner who could now breathe. Dead bodies slid down the corridor, out onto the deck. Timur and the injured prisoner were slipping in the same direction, wrestling with each other, only metres from tumbling into the sea.

As they passed through the door Timur reached up and grabbed hold of the safety line, kicking the injured prisoner, sending him out onto the deck. A second wave was racing towards them. Timur pulled himself inside, shutting the door. Staring through the small plate-glass window, directly into the eyes of the prisoner, the wave hit. The vibrations rippled through his hands. When the water cleared, the prisoner was gone.

Leo watched from the bottom of the stairs as the newly appointed leader of their uprising tugged the steel door, trying to pull it open. They were trapped, with no way of getting to the bridge. He'd lost many of his very gang in the attempt to break free. Needless to say, he'd commanded from the back, avoiding the bullets. The surge of water had swept him downstairs. Leo glanced at the floor — he was ankle-deep in a mass that was rolling from side to side, destabilizing the vessel. There was no way to pump it out, not in the midst of the current hostilities. There was no chance of cooperation. If any more came in, the ship would capsize. They'd sink, in the darkness, unable to break out, locked in a freezing steel prison. Yet the ship's precarious condition was of little interest to their newly self-appointed leader. A convict revolutionary, he was determined to succeed or die.

The coal engine began to splutter. Leo turned back to assess the damage. The engine had to be kept running. Addressing the remaining prisoners, he called out for help.

— *We have to keep the coal dry and the fire fed*.

The convict leader re-entered the engine room, snarling.

— *If they don't free us we'll smash the engine*.

— *If we lose power the ship can't navigate, it will sink. We need the engine to keep working. Our lives depend upon it*.

163

— *So do theirs. If we cut the power, they've got to talk to us —* *they've got to negotiate.*

— *They will never open those doors. We smash the engine:* *they'll abandon ship. They've got life rafts, enough for them and* *none of us. They'd rather let us drown.*

— *How do you know?*

— *They've done it before! Aboard the* Dzhurma*! Prisoners* *broke into the store, stole food and set fire to the rest, the rice sacks,* *the wooden shelves, expecting the guards to come rushing down. They* *didn't. They let it burn. All the prisoners suffocated.*

Leo picked up a shovel. The convict leader shook his head.

— *Put it down!*

Leo ignored him, shovelling the coal, feeding the engine. Neglected, it was already markedly cooler. None of the other men were helping, waiting to see how the conflict played out. Assessing his opponent, Leo wasn't convinced he could overpower him. It had been a long time since he'd fought anyone. Leo tightened his grip on the shovel, preparing himself. To Leo's surprise, the convict smiled.

— *Go ahead. Shovel the coal like a slave. There's another way* out.

The convict grabbed a second shovel and climbed through the smashed partition wall into the prisoner hold. Leo stood, uncertain whether to continue shovelling or follow the man. Within moments the clamour of steel smashing against steel rang out. Leo rushed through the gap in the partition wall, returning to the gloom of the hold. Squinting he saw that the *vory* was at the top of the stairs, using the shovel to land blows against the hatch. To an ordinary man the task would be futile. But his strength was such that the hatch was beginning to buckle upwards, arching under the pressure. Eventually the steel would tear. Leo called out:

— You break the hatch and water will flood in. There's no way to close it again. If the hold fills the ship will sink!

Standing at the top of the steps, pounding the hatch with colossal force, the convict sang out to his fellow inmates:

— Before I die, I'm going to be free! I'm going to die a free man!

Seemingly tireless, he was denting the hatch, targeting each blow where the previous blow had landed.

There was no way of knowing how much longer until the hatch was broken. Once broken, it couldn't be repaired. Leo had to act now. Fighting him alone would be an impossible task. He needed to enlist the help of the other prisoners. He turned to them, ready to rally them.

— Our lives depend on

His voice failed to rise over the clanging blows and the storm. No one was going to help him.

Compensating for the rocking of the ship, Leo lunged for the bottom step, steadying himself. The convict had twisted his legs around the steel frame of the stairs, fixing himself in position as he continued to thunder blows against the hatch. Seeing Leo climbing towards him he pointed his mangled shovel. Leo's opponent had the higher position. The only chance would be to take out his legs, bringing him down. The prisoner took up a defensive position, angling the shovel back.

Before Leo could reposition himself bullets punched through the hatch into the convict's back. His mouth full of blood, the *vory* looked down at his chest, perplexed. The storm shook him free from the top step, throwing him down. Leo dodged out of the way, letting the man crash into the water. More bullets punctured the hatch, zipping past Leo's face. He jumped, landing in the water, out of the line of fire.

Leo peered across. The *vory* was dead, lying face down. A new

165

danger had been created. The hatch was criss-crossed with bullet holes. Water was pouring in, a dense shower every time a wave broke over the deck. If they couldn't fill those holes, the water level would rise and the ship would capsize. It was essential that Leo climb the steps to plug the holes. The ship continued to be tossed from side to side, water gushing in through the hatch. The water level in the hold was rising, splashing onto the cooling coal engine. Leo couldn't wait any longer. The ship was already struggling to right itself. He had to act now.

Leo stripped the clothes from the dead convict, ripping them into rags. With thick streams of water soaking him from the damaged hatch he tentatively put his foot on the bottom step, ready to climb. His life depended on the intelligence of the unseen guard.

Euphoric, Genrikh clung to the gun turret, waves breaking around him as though he was riding the back of a monstrous whale. Because of his bravery the convicts' attempted escape had failed. He'd saved the ship. From a coward to a hero in one night! Earlier, inside the tower, hearing the battle erupt between the guards and the prisoners, he'd taken refuge in the crew quarters, cowering. He'd seen his friend Iakov run past and he'd done nothing, remaining hidden. Only once he was certain that the convicts had lost, that they'd been beaten back and the ship was secure, did he emerge, belatedly understanding the different kind of danger he was in. The surviving crew would accuse him of being a deserter. They'd hate him as the previous crew had hated him. He'd be condemned to another seven years of isolation. Bleak with despair, redemption had landed in his lap – the clang of steel against steel. He'd been the only crewmember to hear the convicts smashing the hatch. They were trying to seize the ship from the deck. The hatch had not been constructed to withstand sustained attacks. Normally no prisoner would dare touch it for fear of being shot. In the storm, however, the gun turret was unmanned. This was his opportunity to prove himself. Rejuvenated by the prospect, he'd run across the deck from the base of the tower. He'd taken aim and fired. Giddy with excitement he'd cried out, firing a second and third burst through the hatch. He'd stay out here for as long as the storm lasted. Everyone in the tower would witness his extraordinary courage. If any convict tried to break through, if any convict even came near the hatch, he'd kill him.

*

Standing on the bridge, choked with rage at Genrikh's stupidity, Timur couldn't allow him to fire again. The ship was low in the water, the captain barely able to pull up over the waves. If they took on any more water they'd sink. The storm showed no sign of abating. Timur knew, as the others did not, how much water had already flooded the vessel when he'd opened the outer doors. Having saved the ship from the convicts, he now had to save it from a guard.

Running down the flights of stairs, he braced himself before throwing open the door to the deck. Wind and rain whipped around him as if personally insulted by his presence. He closed the door behind him, hooking himself onto the safety wire. The distance between the base of the tower and the gun turret was perhaps fifteen metres, a clear stretch of deck – if he was caught by a wave crossing that space he'd either be slammed into the side of the deck or taken out to sea. His safety cord would count for little, dragging him along in the sea like fish bait until the line snapped. He glanced at the bullet holes in the hatch. Something caught his eye: a rag pushed up – plugging the hole. Genrikh was lining up another shot.

Timur darted across the deck just as a wave began to sweep over the side, rushing towards him. He dived forward, grabbing the side of the turret and pushing the gun into the air. Genrikh fired. The wave hit. For a split second Timur's legs were lifted up.

Had he not been holding on he would've been swept out to sea. The water cleared, his legs fell back down. With a mouth and nose full of salt water, Timur spluttered. Recovering, he grabbed hold of Genrikh by the scruff of the neck, losing control, furious, shaking him like a rag doll. He pushed him back, pulling the ammunition clip out of the gun and tossing it into the sea.

With the gun disarmed Timur staggered back towards the tower, checking the hatch as he passed. More rags were being stuffed into the holes. Almost at the tower, he felt the impact of another wave. Turning around, he saw water rushing at him. Smacked off his feet, he was pounded against the deck. Silence, all he could see was a million bubbles. Then the water drained from the deck, the sounds of the storm returned. He sat up, looking out. The machine-gun turret was gone: ripped out like a rotten tooth. The wreckage had been swept to the bows of the ship. Genrikh was caught up in the twisted steel.

Timur had enough slack in his cord to pull himself along the side and grab hold of the young guard. Pitiful, Genrikh tried to free himself from the metal. He was stuck. If the wreckage went overboard it would take him with it. Timur could save him. Yet Timur hadn't moved. He glanced out at the sea. They were climbing another wave, soon they'd be plunging down, into the trough, and the force that had swept a bolted machine-gun turret off the deck would sweep them out too.

Turning his back on Genrikh, Timur took hold of the cord and pulled himself towards the tower. The ship's angle reversed, plunging down. He reached the door, climbing inside, sealing it shut.

*

Genrikh rose with a wave, splashing to keep afloat. The water was so cold he couldn't feel anything below his waist. Washed overboard, there'd been intense pain when the steel had ripped him. Numb with shock, it was as if the icy waves had bitten him in half. For a second he saw the lights of the ship, and then they were gone.

TEN KILOMETRES
NORTH OF MOSCOW

8 APRIL

Zoya's wrists and ankles were bound with thin steel wire, coiled so tight that when she tried to adjust her position it cut into her skin. She was blindfolded and gagged, lying on her side. There was no blanket underneath her — nothing to cushion the bumps in the road. Judging by the noise of the engine and the amount of space around her, she was in the back of a truck. She could feel the accelerations and vibrations through the steel floor. Each abrupt stop rolled her backwards and then forwards, more like a carcass than a living person. Once she'd recovered from the disorientation she began to visualize her journey. At the outset they'd made frequent turns, negotiating traffic. They'd been in a city — Moscow, although she couldn't be sure of that. Right now they were travelling straight, at a constant speed. They must have left the city. Except for the truck's gruff engine there was no other noise, no traffic. She was being taken somewhere remote. Based on this and the disregard for her safety — stuffing a rag so far down her throat she almost choked — she was certain that she was about to die.

How long had she been a captive? She had no way to know —

the passing of time had become difficult to judge. After being snatched from the apartment, she'd been drugged. Bundled into the car she'd seen Raisa fall. That was the last thing she remembered before waking up, her head thumping, her mouth as dry as dust, sprawled on the floor of a windowless brick chamber. Even though she'd been unconscious when she'd been brought in, she had an acute sense that she was deep underground. The air was always cool and damp: the bricks never grew warm, giving no clue as to the cycles of day and night. The stench strongly suggested a sewer system. She often heard the sound of water. Sometimes the vibrations were so strong it felt as if there were rivers rushing through adjacent tunnels. She was given food and bedding, her captors making no attempt to conceal their identities. They didn't speak to her except for a series of curt commands and questions, showing little interest in her beyond the bare necessities of keeping her alive. Yet from time to time she was vaguely aware of someone watching her, hiding in the gloom of the corridor outside her cell. As soon as she moved closer, trying to catch a glimpse of them, they'd slip away into the darkness.

Over these past couple of weeks she'd thought about death, turning the subject over and over like sucking a boiled sweet. What exactly *was* she living for? She nurtured no dreams of being rescued. The idea of freedom did not bring tears of joy to her eyes. Freedom had been life as an unpopular, unhappy schoolgirl – hated and hateful. She felt no more alone in captivity than she had done in Leo's home. She felt no more like a prisoner now than she had done before. The setting had changed. Her captors had changed. Life was the same. She didn't cry at the memory of her bedroom, or of a hot meal eaten together around the kitchen table. She didn't even cry at the memory of her sister. Maybe Elena would be happier without her – maybe she was holding her little sister back, stopping her from leading a normal life and growing close to Leo and Raisa.

Why can't I cry?

She'd pinch herself. But it was no good. She couldn't cry.

She hoped Raisa had survived the fall. She hoped Elena was safe. Yet even these hopes, sincere though they were, felt detached, as if they were other people's ideas of what she should be feeling rather than deeply held emotions. A crucial cog in her internal machinery was missing, instead of connecting emotions to experiences — wheels spun aimlessly. She should be afraid. But instead she felt as if she were floating in a bath of lukewarm resignation. If they wanted to kill her, they could. If they wanted to free her, they could. Bravado aside, it was honestly all the same to her.

*

The truck turned off the road, rattling over a dirt track. After some time, slowing down, it made several further turns before coming to a stop. Front doors opened and shut. Feet crunched across the ground, approaching the back. Tarpaulin was pulled aside. Like freight, Zoya was lifted up and placed on her feet, barely able to stand, the wire lacerations around her ankles making it difficult to balance. The ground consisted of coarse mud and small stones. Queasy from the journey, she wondered if she was going to be sick. She didn't want her captors thinking she was weak and afraid. Her gag was removed. She breathed deeply. A man began to laugh, condescending laughter, smug and deep and slow, as the steel wire was unwound and the blindfold was removed.

Zoya squinted at the daylight that seemed as bright as if she was only a hand's length away from the surface of the sun. Like a subterranean ghoul caught outside its lair, she turned her back on the sky. Her eyes adjusting, the surroundings slowly came into focus.

She was standing on a dirt track. In front of her, on the verge, were tiny white flowers, spread unevenly like splashes of spilled milk. Looking up, she saw woodland. Deprived of stimuli, her eyes behaved like a desiccated sponge dropped into water, widening, expanding – absorbing every drop of colour before her.

Remembering her captors, she turned around. There were two of them – a squat man with thick arms and a thick neck, an oversized muscular torso. Everything about him was stout and squashed, as though he'd been grown in a box too small. In contrast, standing beside him, was a boy, perhaps thirteen or fourteen years old, her age. He was lean and sinewy. His eyes were sly. He regarded her with open disdain, as if she was beneath him, as if he was an adult and she was nothing but a little girl. She disliked him intensely.

The squat man gestured at the trees.

— *Walk. Stretch your legs. Fraera doesn't want you getting weak.*

She'd heard that name before – *Fraera* – catching fragments of conversations when the *vory* were drunk and boisterous. Fraera was their leader. Zoya had met her only once. She'd swept into her cell. She hadn't introduced herself. She didn't need to. Power hung around her like a robe. While Zoya hadn't been afraid of the other thuggish men, whose strength could be measured by the thickness of their arms, she had been afraid of this woman. Fraera had studied her with cool calculation, a master craftsman examining a second-rate watch. Though it had been an opportunity to ask the question – *What are your plans for me?* – Zoya had been unable to speak, stupefied into silence. Fraera had spent no more than a minute in the cell before leaving, having not said a word.

Free to walk, Zoya stepped off the dirt track, entering the woods, her toes sinking into the damp soil and vegetation. Maybe they'd kill her as she walked towards the trees. Maybe the guns were already raised. She glanced back. The man was smoking. The boy was following her every move. Misunderstanding her glance, he called out:

— *Run and I'll catch you.*

She prickled at his superior attitude. He shouldn't be so sure of himself. If there was one thing she could do, it was run.

Twenty paces into the forest, she stopped, pressing her hand against a tree trunk, eager for sensations different from the monotony of cool, damp bricks. Despite being watched she quickly lost her self-consciousness and crouched down, squeezing a fist full of earth. Trickles of dirty water ran down the sides of her hand. As a child brought up on the *kolkhoz*, she'd worked alongside her parents. From time to time, tending the fields, her father would bend down and take a handful of soil, rubbing it through his fingers, breaking up clods, squeezing the earth as she was squeezing it now. She'd never asked him why. What did it tell him? Or was it just habit? She regretted not finding out. She regretted many things, every wasted second, sulking and playing silly games and not listening when he wanted to talk and misbehaving and causing her parents to lose their temper. Now they were gone and she would never speak to them again.

Zoya unclenched her fist, hastily brushing the soil off. She didn't want to remember any more. If she couldn't see the point of life, she could certainly see the point of death. Death would mean the end of all these sad memories, the end of regrets. Death would feel less empty than life. She was sure of it. She stood up. These woods were too much like the woods in Kimov, near the *kolkhoz*. Better the monotony of cool, damp bricks – they reminded her of nothing. She was ready to go.

Zoya turned back to the truck. She jumped, startled to find the squat muscular man standing directly behind her. She hadn't heard him approach. Looking down at her he grinned, revealing a mostly toothless smile. He'd tossed a cigarette aside and she watched where it landed, smouldering on the damp ground. He'd already taken off his coat. Now he rolled up his shirtsleeves.

— *Fraera's orders were for you to get some exercise. And you haven't had any.*

He reached out, touching the top of her shirt, running his finger over her face as though wiping away a tear. His nails were coarse, bitten down. He lowered his voice.

— *We're not tamed, like you. We're not polite, like you. If we want, we take.*

Zoya struggled to maintain her brave facade, stepping away as he stepped forward.

— *Taking is what we do best. Submission is what young girls do best. You might call it rape. I call it . . . exercise.*

Fear was what this man desired — fear and domination. She would give him nothing.

— *If you touch me, I'll kick you. If you pin me down, I'll scratch your eyes. If you break my fingers, I'll bite your face.*

The man laughed out loud.

— *And how will you do that, little girl, if I knock you unconscious first?*

Every step Zoya took, he matched, his wide body caging her, until she was pressed against a tree, unable to move any further. Out of sight, her hands patted the tree trunk, searching for something she could use to defend herself. Breaking off a small branch, she rubbed her fingertip over the end. It would have to do. She looked to the boy. He was idling near the truck. Following the direction of her glance, the man turned to the boy.

— *She thinks you're going to save her!*

Zoya swung the branch with all her strength, smashing the jagged end into his face. She expected blood. But the branch broke apart, crumbling in her hand. Blinking in surprise, the man stared at her hand, at the remains of the branch and realizing what had happened, he laughed.

Zoya sprang forward. The man lunged. She ducked out of reach. Heading in the direction of the truck, running as fast as she could, she sensed he was close behind. Surely the boy would cut her off but she couldn't see him. Grabbing the door to the driver's cabin, she opened it and threw herself inside. Her pursuer was only metres away, no longer smiling. Taking hold of the handle, she slammed the door shut just as he crashed against it. She pushed down the lock, hoping he didn't have the keys. He didn't — they were in the ignition. Scrambling across to the driver's seat she turned the key. The engine spluttered into life.

With only a vague idea of what to do she took hold of the gear stick, scratching it forward — the sound of metal scraping. Nothing happened. The man had taken off his shirt, wrapping it round his fist: he swung his arm back shattering the side window, showering the cabin with glass. Unable to reach the gas pedal, Zoya slid off the seat, pressing her foot down, revving the engine. The truck rolled forward as the man opened the door, leaning across the passenger seat. She sank down as far as she could. He grabbed her hair, pulling her up. She cried out, scratching his hands.

Inexplicably, he let go.

Zoya fell back to the floor of the cabin, crouching, breathing fast. The engine chugged. The truck was no longer moving. The man was gone. The door was open. She cautiously stood up, glancing over the passenger seat. She could hear the man. He was swearing. Peering further forward, she saw him lying on the ground.

177

Confused, Zoya noticed the boy standing close by. There was a knife in the boy's hand. The blade was smeared with blood. The man was clutching the back of his ankle. It was bleeding heavily: his fingers were red. The boy stared at her, saying nothing. Unable to stand, the man snatched at the boy's legs. The boy sidestepped out of reach. The man tried to stand, quickly falling, rolling onto his back. The tendons in his ankle had been sliced. His left foot hung uselessly. His face scrunched up, he shouted out terrible threats. Yet he was unable to implement any of them, limping along the ground, a peculiar sight – lethal yet pathetic at the same time.

Ignoring the man entirely, the boy turned to Zoya.

— *Get out of the truck.*

Zoya stepped out of the cabin, keeping her distance from the injured man. He was using his shirt to bind his foot, tying it around his ankle. The boy wiped the blade of his knife and the knife disappeared into the folds of his clothes. Keeping one eye on the man, Zoya said:

— *Thank you.*

The boy frowned.

— *Had Fraera ordered me to kill you, I would've.*

She waited before asking:

— *What is your name?*

He hesitated, unsure whether or not to answer. Finally he mumbled:

— *Malysh.*

Zoya repeated the name.

— *Malysh.*

Zoya peered down at the injured man and then at the truck. She'd driven it off the track. The man pounded the ground, crying out:

— *Wait till the others hear what you've done. They'll kill you!*

Zoya looked at the boy, concern passing across her face.

— *Is that true?*

Malysh considered.

— *That's not your problem. We're going to walk back. If you try and run, I'll slit your throat. If you let go of my hand, just to pick your nose . . .*

Pleased that, at last, she knew the identity of her secret admirer, Zoya finished his sentence:

— *You'll slit my throat?*

Malysh cocked his head to the side, regarding her with suspicion — no doubt wondering if she was mocking him. To put him at ease, Zoya reached out and took hold of his hand.

PACIFIC COAST
KOLYMA
THE PORT OF MAGADAN
STARY BOLSHEVIK PRISON SHIP

SAME DAY

The steps and stairways were the only solid structures offering elevation from the floodwater and were consequently crowded with prisoners, squeezed together, perched like crows on a power line. Those less lucky were huddled on the wreckage of collapsed bunks – broken planks piled high to create a makeshift timber island surrounded by lapping, icy water. The bodies of those who'd died had been pushed away and were bobbing on the surface. Leo was one of the privileged few high above the water, on the steel steps that led up to the bullet-ridden and cloth-stuffed hatch.

Once the holes in the hatch had been plugged Leo had been forced to keep the coal engine burning, his chest and face roasted by the fire while his legs, knee deep in water, went numb with cold – his body sliced into opposite sensations. Shaking with exhaustion, barely able to lift the shovel, he'd worked without help. The other convicts had sat in the damp darkness like cave creatures, motionless and dumb. Facing a lifetime of hard labour, why add another day? If the engine died and the ship ceased to move, drifting in the open sea, that was an issue the guards needed to address. They could shovel their own coal. These men weren't about to help in their transportation to prison. Leo didn't have the energy to convince them of the dangers of doing nothing. He knew that if the guards were forced to descend into the hold, after the attempted uprising, they'd shoot indiscriminately.

Alone, he'd continued for as long as he could. Not until he'd dropped an entire load, the shovel slipping from his hands, did another man emerge from the gloom to take his place. Leo had mumbled inaudible thanks, climbing the steps – the prisoners making space for him – and slumping at the very top. If it could be called sleeping, he'd slept, shivering and delirious with thirst and hunger.

*

Leo opened his eyes. There were people on deck. He could hear footsteps overhead. The ship had come to a stop. Trying to move, he found his body was stiff – his limbs calcified into a foetal shape. He stretched his fingers, then his neck: joints cracking in quick succession. The hatch was thrown open. Leo looked up, squinting at the bright light. The sky seemed as dazzling as molten metal. His eyes adjusting slowly, he accepted that it was in fact a dull grey.

Guards appeared around him: machine guns pointing down. One man shouted, addressing the hold:

— *Try anything and we'll scuttle the ship with you all locked in. We'll drown the lot of you.*

The convicts could barely move, let alone mount a serious challenge to their authority. There was no gratitude that they'd kept the engine running, no appreciation that they'd saved the ship, just the muzzle of a machine gun. A different voice called out:

— *On deck! Now!*

Leo recognized the voice. It was Timur. The sound of his friend revived him. Moving slowly, he sat upright. Like a creaky wooden puppet, yanked up by its strings, he climbed from the steps to the deck.

The battered steamer was listing, askew in the water. The gun was gone. All that remained were threads of twisted steel. It was hard to imagine that the sea, now still and smooth and calm, could have been so ferocious. Making only the briefest eye contact with Timur, Leo observed his friend's face, the dark lines under his eyes. The storm had been gruelling for him too. They'd have to compare stories at a later date.

Moving past, Leo made his way to the edge of the deck, pressing his hands against the rail and taking his first look at the port of Magadan, gateway to the most remote of regions, a part of his country that he was both intimately connected with and a stranger to at the same time. He'd never been here before yet he'd sent hundreds of men and women here. He hadn't allocated them to any particular Gulag, that hadn't been his responsibility. But it was inevitable that many had ended up on board this ship, or one like it, shuffling forward in single file, as he was now, ready for processing.

Considering the region's notoriety he'd expected more obvious and sinister drama in the landscape. But the port, developed some twenty years ago, was small and hushed. Wooden shacks mingled with the occasional angular concrete municipal building, the sides decorated with slogans and propaganda, an awkward glimpse of colour in a muted palette. Beyond the port, in the distance, lay a network of Gulags spread among the folds of snow-tipped hills.

The hills, gentle near the coast, grew in size further inland, their vast curved tops merging with the clouds. Tranquil and menacing in equal measure, it was a terrain that made no allowances for frailty, smoothing weakness off its Arctic-blasted slopes.

Leo climbed down to the dock where there were small fishing boats: evidence of life other than the imprisonment system. The Chukchi, the local people who'd lived off this land long before it was colonized by Gulags, carried baskets of walrus tusk and the first cod catches of the year. They spared Leo only a cursory, unsympathetic glance, as if the convicts were to blame for their land's transformation into a prison empire. Guards were stationed on the dock, herding the new arrivals. Dressed in thick furs and felt, layered over their uniforms, they wore a mixture of Chukchi handcrafted clothes and meanly cut, mass-produced, standard-issue uniforms.

Behind the guards, gathered for the delayed voyage home, were prisoners being released. They'd either served their term or had their sentence quashed. They were free men except by the looks of them their bodies didn't know it yet – their shoulders were hunched and their eyes sunken. Leo searched for some sign of triumph, some malicious yet understandable pleasure in seeing others about to set off for the camps that they were leaving behind. Instead, he saw missing fingers, cracked skin, sores and wasted muscles. Freedom might rejuvenate some, restoring them to a semblance of their former selves, but it would not save all of them. This is what had become of the men and women he'd sent away.

*

On deck, Timur watched as the prisoners were marched towards a warehouse. Leo was indistinguishable from the others. Their assumed identities were intact. Despite the storm, they'd arrived unharmed. The journey by sea had been a necessary part of their cover. Although it was possible to fly into Magadan, organizing such a flight would have prevented them from slipping into the system unobserved. No prisoners were ever flown in. Fortunately stealth was unnecessary on the return journey. A cargo plane was standing by at Magadan airstrip. If all went as planned, in two days' time, he and Leo would be returning to Moscow with Lazar. What had just passed on the ship had been the easiest part of their plan.

He felt a hand on his shoulder. Standing behind him was the captain of the *Stary Bolshevik* and a man Timur had never seen before – a high-ranking official, judging from the quality of his attire. Surprisingly for a man of power, he was exceptionally thin, prisoner-thin, an unlikely solidarity with the men he oversaw. Timur's first thought was that he must be sick. The official spoke, the captain nodding obsequiously before the man had even finished his sentence.

— *My name is Abel Prezent, Regional Director. Officer Genrikh . . .*

He turned to the captain.

— *What was his name?*

— *Genrikh Duvakin.*

— *Is dead, I'm told.*

At the mention of that name, the young man he'd left to die on deck, Timur felt a knot tighten inside him.

— *Yes. He was lost at sea.*

— *Genrikh was a permanent post on the ship. The captain now has need of guards for the return voyage. We have a chronic shortage. The captain remarks that you did a fine job on board with the attempted mutiny. He's personally requested that you become Genrikh's replacement.*

The captain smiled, expecting Timur to be warmed by the compliment. Timur flushed with panic.

— *I don't understand.*

— *You're to remain on board the* Stary Bolshevik *for the return journey.*

— *But I've been ordered to Gulag 57. I'm to become the second in charge of the camp. I have new directives from Moscow to implement.*

— *I appreciate that. And you will be stationed at 57 as designated. It will take seven days to Buchta Nakhodka if the weather allows, and then another seven days back here. You'll be at your post in two or three weeks, at the most.*

— *Sir, I must insist that my orders be followed and that you find someone else.*

Prezent became impatient, his veins protruding like a warning sign.

— *Genrikh is dead. The captain has requested you replace him. I will explain to your superiors my decision. The matter is settled. You will remain on the ship.*

MOSCOW

Malysh was standing beside his accuser Likhoi, the *vory* whose tendon he'd cut. His ankle was heavily bandaged and he was pale and feverish with loss of blood. Despite his injuries he'd insisted that the *skhodka*, a trial to mediate between disputing gang members, go ahead.

— *Fraera, what of our code? One* vory *may never harm another? He has shamed you by injuring me. He has shamed all of us.*

Supported by a crutch, Likhoi refused to sit since it would be a sign of weakness. There was froth on the corners of his lips, tiny bubbles of spit that he hadn't bothered to wipe away.

— *I wanted sex. Is that a crime? Not for a criminal!*

The other *vory* smiled. Confident he had their support, he returned his attention to Fraera, dropping his head in respect, lowering his voice.

— *I ask for Malysh's death.*

Fraera turned to Malysh.

— *Your reply?*

Glancing at the hostile faces surrounding him, he answered:

— I was told to keep her safe. They were your orders. I did as I was told.

Not even the prospect of death made him more articulate. Though Malysh was convinced that Fraera did not want to sanction his death, his actions had left her little room to manoeuvre. It was undeniable – he'd breached their code. It was forbidden for a *vory* to harm another *vory* without authorization from Fraera. They were supposed to protect each other as if their lives were interwoven. In clear violation, he'd acted impulsively, siding with the daughter of their enemy.

Malysh watched as Fraera paced within the circle of her followers, judging the mood of her gang. Popular opinion was against him. In moments such as these power became ambiguous. Did she have the authority to overrule the majority? Or did she have to side with the majority to preserve her authority? Malysh's position was weakened by the fact that his accuser was a popular figure. The man's *klikukha* – 'Likhoi' – referred to his vaunted sexual prowess. In contrast 'Malysh' was a lowly *klikukha*, meaning 'young one', referring to his inexperience, both sexual and criminal. His membership to the gang was recent. Whereas the other *vory* had met in the labour camps, Malysh had joined their ranks by chance. From the age of five, he'd worked as a pickpocket at Leningrad's Baltiysky Rail Terminal. A street child, he'd quickly earned a reputation as the most skilful of thieves. One of the people that he'd robbed was Fraera. Unlike many, she'd noticed her loss immediately and given chase. Surprised by her speed and determination he'd needed all his skill and knowledge of the terminal building to escape, scrambling out of a window barely big enough for a cat. Even so, Fraera had still managed to grab hold of one of his shoes. Expecting that to be the end of the matter, Malysh had returned to work the next day, at a different rail station, only to find Fraera waiting for him, holding his shoe. Instead of a confrontation, she'd offered him the opportunity to leave his union of pickpockets and join her. He was the only pickpocket who'd ever managed to give her the slip.

Despite his skills as a thief his appointment to *vory* status had been controversial. The others looked down on his background of petty crime. It didn't seem worthy of entry into their ranks. He'd never murdered, he'd never spent time in a Gulag. Fraera brushed these concerns aside. She'd taken a liking to him even though he was solemn and withdrawn, rarely speaking more than a couple of words. The others accepted, reluctantly, that he was now one of them. He accepted, reluctantly, that he was one of them. In reality, he was hers and everyone knew it. In return for her patronage Malysh loved Fraera in the same way that a fierce, fighting dog would love its owner, circling her feet, snapping at anyone who came too close. All the same, he was not naive. With her authority under scrutiny their history counted for nothing. Fraera was determinedly unsentimental. Malysh had not only drawn the blood of another *vory*, he'd jeopardized her plans. Unable to drive the truck, he and the girl had been forced to walk back into the city, a journey on foot that had taken almost eight hours. They could've been stopped and arrested. He'd explained to the girl that if she screamed for help, or let go of his hand, he'd slit her throat. She'd obeyed. She hadn't complained about being tired, never asking to rest. Even in crowded streets where she could have caused him problems, she'd never let go of his hand.

Fraera spoke.

— *The facts are not in dispute. According to our laws, the punishment for harming another* vory *is death*.

Death wasn't meant in the ordinary sense of the word. He wouldn't be shot or hanged. Death meant exile from the gang. A tattoo would be forced upon him in a visible place, his forehead or the backs of his hands, a tattoo of an open vagina or anus. Such a tattoo was a signal for all *vory*, no matter what allegiance they held, that the bearer of the tattoo was deserving of any kind of physical and sexual torment, which could be delivered without fear of recourse from the other gang. Malysh loved Fraera. But he would not accept this punishment. Moving his leg, his hand slipped into position. There was a knife secreted in the folds of his trousers. He freed it from the fabric, his finger ready on the spring mechanism, as he calculated his escape.

Fraera stepped forward. She'd come to a decision.

*

Fraera studied the faces of her men, expressions of intense concentration fixed upon her, as if this alone would deliver the verdict they desired. She'd spent years earning their loyalty, generously rewarding obedience and ruthlessly striking at dissent. Despite this, so much now hinged on so slight an incident. An uprising needed a unifying cause. Popular, dumb – Likhoi had rallied her men. They saw him as the epitome of a *vory*. They understood his urges as their urges. If he was on trial, so were they. Trivial though the disagreement was, the problems this *skhodka* created were far from simple. To their minds, there was only one acceptable verdict: she would have to authorize Malysh's death.

Listening to them quote *vory* law as though it was sacred, she marvelled at their lack of self-awareness. Her rule was founded upon transgressions of traditional *vory* structures as much as abidance by them. Most obviously, they were men led by a woman, unprecedented in *vory* history. In contrast to other *derzhat mast* – the leader of a community of thieves – Fraera wasn't motivated by a desire to exist apart from the State. She sought revenge upon it and those who served it. She described that revenge to them in terms they could understand, claiming that the State was nothing other than a larger, rival gang, with which she was in the most bitter of blood feuds. Yet at heart she knew *vory* were conservative. They would prefer a male leader. They would prefer to be concerned only with money and sex and drink. Her agenda of revenge was something they tolerated, as indeed was her gender – tolerated only because she was brilliant and they were not. She funded them, protected them and they depended on her. Without her, the centre would fall apart and the gang would break into squabbling, irrelevant factions.

Their unlikely alliance had been formed in Minlag Gulag, a northern camp south-east of Arkhangelsk. Originally a political prisoner convicted under Article 58, at that time Anisya, as she'd been known, had no interest in the *vory*. They existed within separate social spheres, layers like water and oil. The focus of her life had been her newly born son – Aleksy. He'd been something to live for, a child to love and protect. After three months of nursing him, three months of loving him more than she'd ever imagined she was capable of loving, the child had been taken from her. She'd woken in the middle of the night to find that he was gone. At first the nurse had claimed that Aleksy had died in his sleep. Anisya had grabbed her, shaking her, demanding her child back until beaten off by a guard. The nurse had spat at her that no woman convicted under Article 58 deserved to bring up a child:

— *You'll never be a mother.*

The State was Aleksy's parents now.

Anisya had fallen ill, sick with grief. She'd lain in bed, refusing food, delirious with dreams that she was still pregnant. She'd felt it kicking and moving and screaming for her help. The nurses and *feldshers* had impatiently waited for her to die. The world had arranged every possible reason for her to die and given her every opportunity. However, something inside her resisted. She'd examined this resistance forensically, like an archaeologist carefully sweeping away fine dust, wanting to know what lay beneath. She'd unearthed not the face of her son, nor the face of her husband. She'd found Leo, the sound of his voice, the feel of his hand on hers, the deceit and betrayal, and like a magical elixir she drank these memories in one long gulp. Hatred had brought her back from the brink. Hatred had rejuvenated her.

The idea of seeking revenge on an MGB officer, a man hundreds of miles away, would have been laughable had she spoken it aloud. Far from depressing her, her powerlessness was a source of inspiration — she would start from nothing. She would build her revenge from nothing. While other patients slept, doped on doses of codeine, she spat her pills out, collecting them. She'd stayed in the infirmary, feigning sickness while secretly regaining her strength and accumulating dose after dose of medicine, pills that she hid in the lining of her trousers. Once she'd accumulated a significant quantity she'd left the infirmary, much to the nurses' surprise, returning to the camp with nothing except her wits and trousers lined with pills.

Until her arrest Anisya had always been defined in relation to someone else: one man's daughter, another man's wife. On her own, she'd set about redefining herself. Each of her weaknesses she'd appointed to the character of *Anisya*. Each of her strengths were gathered together and knitted into a new identity — the woman she was about to become. Overhearing the *vory*, familiarizing herself with their slang, she'd selected a new name for herself. She would be known as Fraera, the outsider. A *vory* term of contempt, she would take that insult and make it her strength. She'd traded the codeine with the leader of a gang, seeking his favour, asking permission to join them. The *vory* leader had scoffed, agreeing to her suggestion only if she proved herself by executing a known informer. He'd taken all the codeine as a non-refundable down-payment, setting her a challenge he considered beyond her skills. Only three months previously she'd been nursing her baby. Even if she dared to make some attempt on the informer's life, she would be caught and sent to an isolation unit, or executed. The *derzhat mast* had never expected that he would need to honour his promise. Three days later the informer had started to cough during dinner, falling to the floor, his mouth full of blood. His stew of cabbage and potato had been laced with slithers of razor blade. The *derzhat mast* had been unable to go back on his agreement – the *vory* code forbade him. Fraera had become the first female member of his gang.

Fraera had no intention of remaining a subordinate. Her plans required that she be in charge. Using the education they'd given her, she'd sought her independence. They had taught her to see her body as a commodity to be traded like any other, a resource to which they attached no concept of shame. She'd set about seducing the Gulag commander. Since he could order any woman to his office for sexual gratification, Fraera had needed him to fall in love with her. She'd viewed her revulsion as merely another obstacle to overcome. Within five months, at her request, he'd transferred the entire *vory* gang to another camp, leaving Fraera free to start her own.

Since no self-respecting *vory* would accept a woman's patronage, Fraera had turned to the outcasts, the outsiders – the *vory* scavenging on scrap heaps, sucking on fish bones and munching rotten vegetables. They'd been shunned due to a disagreement, or a betrayal, or some act of incompetence. Some had fallen to the level of a *chuskhi*, so disgraced that it was forbidden for another *vory* to even touch them. According to their laws such disgrace was irreversible. Despite this, she'd offered them a second chance when no other *vory* would condescend to utter their name. Some had been terminally weakened, mentally or physically. Some had repaid the debt by attempting to over-throw her as soon as they'd regained their strength. Most had accepted her patronage.

With Stalin's death freedom had come early – women and chil-dren granted an amnesty. The members of her gang were already on shorter sentences since they were not political criminals. Fraera had no intention of hunting Leo down, plunging a knife in his back or putting a bullet in his head. He needed to suffer as she had suffered. Her ambitions required time and resources. Many gangs traded in black-market goods. The opportunities such a market presented were limited since there was already in place a highly developed system. She had no interest in being a small-time trader, cutting a modest profit from imported groceries, not when she had access to a far more precious commodity.

During the persecution of the Church, at the high-watermark of the anti-religious movement, many artefacts had been hidden: icons, books and silverware, all of which would've been burnt or melted down. Most priests had taken action to save the Church's heritage. They'd buried items in fields, stashed silver in chimneys and even wrapped paintings in waterproof leather, hiding them inside the engines of disused, rusting tractors. No maps were drawn. Only a few knew the locations, whispered from one to another, beginning with the words:

— *In case I die . . .*

Most of the guardians of these secrets had been arrested, shot, starved in the Gulags or worked to death. Of those who knew, Fraera had been among the first to be released. She'd unearthed the treasures one by one. Using her *vory*'s knowledge of the black-market infrastructure, the people who needed to be bribed, she'd shipped items out of the country, negotiating sales to Western religious organizations as well as private buyers and foreign museums. Some had baulked at the idea of purchasing another Church's treasures. Yet Fraera's sales technique had been savagely effective: were her prices not met, the safety of the items could no longer be assured. She'd sent her buyers a seventeenth-century icon of St Nikolas of Mozaisk. Once painted in bright colours, the egg tempera had discoloured, and to recapture the brilliance it had been covered in gold and silver sheet. She'd imagined the priests weeping as they'd opened the parcel to find the icon smashed into fragments, the saint's face scratched off except for the eyes. Fraera had not confessed to her role in this vandalism. In the interests of maintaining a functioning business relationship, she'd blamed over-zealous party members. After that, she'd been able to name her price, depicting herself as a saviour, rather than a profiteer.

Paid in gold, she'd brought in the riches that she'd always promised her *vory*, unearthing each treasure one by one in case any should consider her leadership redundant. Cautious, trusting no one, the first thing she'd spent money on was a cyanide tooth which she'd proudly displayed to her men, assuring them if they thought she could be tortured for the locations of the missing artefacts they were wrong. She would die to spite them. Judging from the reactions of the gang, two men had been thinking along those lines. She'd killed them before the week was out.

One final loose end had been the Minlag camp commander, who'd come seeking a life with Fraera, as they'd dreamed, and to collect his share of her profits.

Here's your share.

A knife dragged up through his stomach, it hadn't been fair — she owed him her life. It had taken him a little less than an hour to die, wriggling on the floor, wondering how he'd been so wrong. Up until the moment the blade tip had entered his stomach he'd been sure that she loved him.

*

The room was heavy with anticipation. Fraera raised her hand.

— *We do not follow ordinary* vory *laws. You once had nothing. You could not feed yourselves. I saved you when the law said I should let you die. When you fell sick, I gave you medicine. When you were well, I gave you opium and drink. My only demand has been obedience. That is our only law. In this regard, Likhoi has failed me.*

No one moved. Their eyes flicked from side to side; each man trying to figure out what the next man was thinking. Leaning on his crutch, Likhoi's mouth twisted into a snarl.

— *Let's kill the bitch! Let us be governed by a man! Not some woman who thinks fucking is a crime.*

Fraera stepped closer to him.

— *Who would run this new gang, you, Likhoi? You once licked my boot for a crust of bread. You are governed by impulse and made stupid by it. You would lead a gang to ruin.*

Likhoi turned to the men:

— *Let us make her our whore. Let us live like men!*

Fraera could have stepped forward and slashed Likhoi's throat, ending his challenge. Understanding that she needed to win this argument by consent, she countered with the statement:

— *He has insulted me.*

It was now up to her *vory* to decide.

No one did anything. Then a hand grabbed Likhoi and

another – his crutch was kicked away. Pushed to the ground, his clothes were ripped from him. Naked, he was pinned down: one man crouched on each arm and leg. The remaining men turned to the stove, taking a red-hot coal from the fire. Fraera looked down at Likhoi.

— *You are no longer one of us.*

The coal was pressed against his tattoos, the skin bubbling. His skin would be rendered blank, disfigured so no new tattoos could take their place. According to practice, he should then be let go, exiled. But Fraera – who knew the pull of vengeance too well – would make sure his injuries left him no chance of survival. She glanced at Malysh, communicating her desire. He drew his knife, flicking open the blade. He would cut the tattoos off.

*

In her cell Zoya gripped the bars, listening to the screams as they echoed through the corridor. Her heart beating fast, she concentrated on the sounds. They were the screams of a man, not a young boy. She felt relief.

They were standing side by side, staring at the next man's shoulder, rocking with the motion of the freight truck. Although there was no guard stopping them from sitting down, there were no benches and the floor was so cold that they'd taken a collective decision to stand, shuffling to keep warm, like a captured herd of animals. Leo occupied a space closest to the tarpaulin sheet. It had come loose, rendering the compartment's temperature sub-zero but offering, by way of exchange, a partial view of the landscape as the material flapped open. The convoy was climbing into the mountains following the Kolyma highway – a surface that unrolled meekly across the landscape as though conscious it was trespassing across a wilderness. In the convoy, there were three trucks in total. Not even a car bothered to follow behind to make sure prisoners didn't jump down and try to escape. There was nowhere to escape to.

Abruptly the highway steepened, the rear of the truck tilting down, angled towards the snow-covered valley to such an acute degree that Leo was forced to grip the steel frame, the other prisoners pressing against him as they slid down. Unable to make the climb, the truck remained stationary, teetering and ready to roll back. The handbrake was yanked up. The engine stopped. The guards unlocked the back, spilling the prisoners onto the road.

— *Walk!*

The first two trucks had managed to climb over the crest of the hill, disappearing from view. The remaining truck — without the weight of the prisoners — started its engine and accelerated up the hill. Left behind, the convicts trundled, huffing like old men, the guards at the back, guns ready. Set against the terrain, the guards' swagger seemed slight and absurd — an insect strutting. Observing them through a convict's eyes, Leo marvelled at how different the guards believed themselves to be — men marshalling cattle. He wanted to say, just to see their surprise:

— *I am one of you.*

The idea caught him short. Was he one of them? Smug with power, stupefied by State-allocated importance: he was certain that he had been.

At the crest the highway flattened out. Leo paused, catching his breath, surveying the landscape before him. Blasted by cold air, his eyes watering, he was confronted by the surface of a moon — a sprawling plateau as wide as a city, smoothed with ice and permafrost, pockmarked with craters. The lonely highway sliced an uncertain diagonal, heading towards a mountain larger than any they'd encountered so far: rising out of the plateau like a monstrous camel's hump. Somewhere at the base was Gulag 57.

As the convicts climbed back into the truck, Leo glanced at the other two vehicles. He had to face up to the fact that Timur wasn't in the convoy. There was no chance that his friend would've got into one of those vehicles without making contact, even if it was nothing more than a glance across a crowd. Leo hadn't seen him since yesterday, passing him on the deck of the *Stary Bolshevik*. After that he'd been shepherded into the transit camp at Magadan where he'd been deloused, inspected by a doctor who'd declared him fully fit, assigned to TFT, *tyazoly fezichesky trud*, heavy labour, no limitations placed on work duties. Duly processed, he'd waited in one of the large tents erected for the arrivals, the smell of canvas reminding him of makeshift medical facilities during the Great Patriotic War, hundreds of beds crammed together. They'd agreed to find each other that night. Timur hadn't appeared. Leo had reassured himself with various explanations. there had been some delay and they'd find each other in the morning. It was too risky to ask after him aside from jeopardizing their cover Leo might be mistaken for an informer. Unable to sleep, he'd risen early, expecting to see his friend. When they'd been loaded into the trucks, Leo had held back. Comforting explanations for Timur's absence had become harder to concoct.

Leo was about to meet Lazar for the first time in seven years. Their first encounter, the moment they laid eyes on each other, was perhaps the most dangerous moment in the entire plan. There could be no question of Lazar's hatred being eroded by time. If he didn't try to kill Leo outright, he'd announce that Leo was a Chekist, an interrogator, a man responsible for the incarceration of hundreds of innocent men and women. How long could he survive surrounded by those who had been tortured and interrogated? This was why Timur's presence was essential. They'd predicted a violent reunion. More than that, they'd factored it into their calculations. As a guard Timur could intervene and stop any altercation. Regulations stipulated that Leo and Lazar would be pulled out of the conflict and ordered to the isolator, individual punishment cells. In adjacent cells, Leo would have an opportunity to explain that he was here to free him, that his wife was alive and that there was no chance he'd ever be released by ordinary means. He either accepted Leo's help or died a slave.

Running his icy fingers across his newly shaven head, Leo frantically improvised a solution. There was only one option – he'd have to postpone meeting Lazar until Timur caught up. Hiding wouldn't be easy. Gulag 57 had contracted since Stalin's death, both in prisoner numbers and geographical sprawl. Previously it had been composed of many *lagpunkts* scattered over the mountainside, sub-colonies within a colony, some positioned in such exposed topography and in such poor mining yields that their purpose can only have been death. Gulag 57 had closed all of these smaller barracks, a prison empire whittled back to the main base at the foot of the mountain, the only place where the gold mine had ever produced a viable return. From Leo's assessment of the blueprints even this central complex was rudimentary. The *zona*, the controlled area, was rectangular. Although a curved design would have suited the terrain better, law dictated that the *zona* must be of regular design. There were no rounded edges in a Gulag except for the barbed wire, coiled across poles six metres high, sunk two metres deep, forming an outer perimeter. Inside the perimeter there were several sleeping barracks, a communal eating barracks, closed off from the administration centre by an inner rectangle of barbed-wire fencing, divisions within divisions, zones within zones. Security was provided by six small guard towers and two substantial *vakhta* towers, one either side of the main gate with mounted heavy machine guns and log-panel protective walls. At each corner of the *zona* was a smaller tower where officers surveyed the ground through telescopic sights. If the guards fell asleep, or passed out drunk, freedom depended upon scaling the mountain or crossing kilometres of exposed plateau.

Upon arrival Leo would be herded into the inner prisoner zone. Since there were three barracks he could in theory remain inconspicuous, at least for another twenty-four hours. That might give Timur enough time to catch up.

The truck slowed. Wary of being picked off by a zealous sniper in the *vakhta*, Leo glanced out, his eye drawn to the mountain. The slopes were perilously steep. Against the mountain's colossal bulk the mine, a series of trenches and man-made streams where clods of earth were washed and sifted for gold, appeared insignificant.

There were shadows in the tops of the two *vakhta*: guards watching the new arrivals. The towers were fifteen metres high, accessed by a series of rickety ladders that could be pulled up at any time. In between the towers the gates were opened by hand. Guards pushed the timber frames, scratching them across the snow. The trucks entered the compound. From the back of the truck Leo watched as the gates closed behind him.

Stepping down from the back of the truck, Leo was ushered into a single line by the guards. Side by side, single file, the convicts stood shivering, ready for inspection. With no scarf and an ill-fitting hat, Leo had stuffed rags around his jacket collar. Despite his best efforts he was unable to stop his teeth tapping. His eyes roamed the *zona*. The simple timber barracks were raised off frozen soil, supported on squat stilts. The horizon was barbed wire and white sky. The buildings and structures were so rudimentary it was as if a once-mighty civilization had de-evolved, skyscrapers replaced with huts. This was where they died: the men and women he'd arrested, the men and women whose names he'd forgotten. This was where they'd stood. This was what they saw. Except he did not feel how they'd felt. They would have had no plans to escape. They would have had no plans at all.

Waiting in silence, there was no sign of Gulag 57's commander, Zhores Sinyavksy, a man whose reputation had spread beyond the Gulags, carried out by the survivors and cursed across the country. Fifty-five years old, Sinyavksy was a veteran of the Glavnoe upravlenie lagerei – GULAG for short: his entire adult life had been dedicated to enforcing lethal servitude. He'd overseen con-vict construction projects including the Fergana Canal and the aborted railway at the mouth of the Ob River, a set of tracks that never connected with their intended destination, the Yenisei River, falling many hundreds of kilometres short, rusting in the ground like the remains of a prehistoric steel beast. Yet the failure of that project, costing many thousands of lives and billions of roubles, hadn't damaged his career. While other supervisors gave in to demands that prisoners rest and eat and sleep, he'd always met his targets. He'd forced prisoners to work in the dead of winter and at the height of summer. He hadn't been building a railway. He'd been building his reputation, chiselling his name into other men's bones. It didn't matter if the sleepers hadn't been strengthened, if they cracked in the July sun and buckled in the January ice. It didn't matter if workers collapsed. On paper his quota had been fulfilled. On paper he was a man to trust.

Flicking through his file, it was self-evident that for Sinyavksy this was more than a job. He didn't crave privileges. He wasn't motivated by money. When he'd been offered comfortable administrative posts in temperate climates, overseeing camps not far from cities, he'd refused. He desired to rule over the most hostile terrain ever colonized. He'd volunteered to work in Kolyma. He'd seen the desolation and decided this was the place for him.

Hearing the creak of wood, Leo looked up. At the top of the stairs Sinyavksy stepped out of the command barracks, wrapped in reindeer furs so thick they doubled his size. The coat was as decorative as it was practical, hung across his shoulders with such aplomb the implication was that he'd killed the animals in a heroic battle. The theatricality of his appearance would surely have been ludicrous in any other man and in any other place. Yet here, on him, it seemed appropriate. He was emperor of this place.

Unlike the other prisoners whose survival instincts were more sharply tuned, having spent several months on trains and in transit camps, Leo stared openly at the commander with reckless

fascination. Belatedly remembering that he was not a militia officer any more, he turned away, redirecting his gaze down at the
ground. A convict could be shot for making eye contact with a
guard. Though regulations had changed in theory, there was no
way of knowing if the changes had been implemented.

Sinyavksy called out:

— *You!*

Leo kept his eyes fixed down. He could hear the stairs creaking
as the commander descended from the elevated platform, reaching the ground, footsteps crunching across snow and ice. Two
beautifully tailored felt boots stepped into view. Even now Leo
kept his eyes down like a scolded dog. A hand gripped his chin,
forcing him to look up. The commander's face was lined with
thick dark grooves, skin like cured meat. His eyes were tinged with
an iodine yellow. Leo had made a rudimentary mistake. He'd stood
out. He'd been noticed. A common technique was to make an
example out of a convict upon arrival to show the others what
they could expect.

— *Why do you look away?*

Silence, Leo could feel the other prisoners' relief emanating
from them like heat. He'd been picked, not them. Sinyavksy's
voice was peculiarly soft.

— *Answer.*

Leo replied:

— *I did not wish to insult you.*

Sinyavksy let go of Leo's chin, stepping back and reaching into
his pocket.

Anticipating the barrel of a gun, it took Leo several seconds to
adjust. Sinyavksy's arm was outstretched – yes – but his palm was
turned up to the sky. On the flat of his hand were small purple
flowers, each no bigger than a shirt button. Leo wondered if this

was a moment's insanity as a bullet passed through his brain, a confusion of images, memories smashed together. But time passed, the delicate flowers were fluttering in the wind. This was real.

— *Take one.*

Was it a poison? Was he to writhe in pain in front of the others? Leo didn't move, arms flat by his side.

— *Take one.*

Obedient, powerless, Leo reached out, his thumb and forefinger trembling, stumbling across Sinyavksy's palm as if they were the legs of a drunken man, almost knocking the flowers off. Finally, he took hold of one. It was dried, the petals brittle.

— *Smell it.*

Once again, Leo did nothing, unable to comprehend his instruction. It was repeated.

— *Smell it.*

Leo lifted it to his nose, sniffing the tiny flower, smelling nothing. There was no scent. Sinyavksy smiled.

— *Lovely, yes?*

Leo considered, unsure if this was a peculiar trap.

— *Yes.*

— *You love it?*

— *I love it.*

He patted Leo on the shoulder.

— *You shall be a flower-grower. This landscape looks barren. But it is full of opportunities. There are only twenty weeks in the year when the topsoil thaws. During those weeks I allow all prisoners to cultivate the land. You can grow whatever you like. Most grow vegetables. But the flowers that grow here are quite beautiful, in their modest way. Modest flowers are often the prettiest, don't you agree?*

— *I agree.*

— *Do you think you will grow flowers? I don't want to force it upon you. There are other things you can do.*

— *Flowers . . . are . . . nice.*

— *Yes, they are. They are nice. And modest flowers are the nicest.*

The commander leaned close to Leo, whispering:

— *I shall save you a good patch of soil. Our secret . . .*

He squeezed Leo's arm, affectionately.

Sinyavksy stepped away, addressing the entire line of prisoners, his hand outstretched, displaying the small purple flowers.

— *Take one!*

The prisoners hesitated. He repeated the order:

— *Take! Take! Take!*

Frustrated with their sluggish response he threw the flowers into the air, purple petals fluttering around their shaven heads. Reaching into his pocket, taking another handful he threw them again, over and over, showering them. Some men looked up, tiny purple petals catching in their lashes. A few men were still looking at the ground, no doubt convinced this was a trick of the most devious kind that only they had passed.

Still holding his flower, balanced in the cup of his hand, Leo didn't understand, he couldn't make sense of it – had he read the wrong file? This man with pockets full of flowers couldn't be the same man who had ordered prisoners to work while their comrades' bodies rotted beside them, couldn't be the commander who'd supervised the Fergana Canal and the Ob River railway. His supply of flowers finished, the last petals spinning to the snow, Sinyavksy continued his introduction speech.

— *These flowers grew from the meanest, cruellest soil in the world! Beauty from ugliness: that is our belief here! You are not here to suffer. You are here to work just as I am here to work. We are not so different, you and I. It is true that we will do different kinds of work. Perhaps your work is harder. Yet we will work hard together, for our country. We will improve ourselves. We will become better people, here, in this place where no one expects to find goodness.*

The words seemed heartfelt. They were uttered with genuine emotion. Whether because the commander was racked with guilt, or remorse, or fear at being judged by the new regime, it was quite obvious that he'd gone insane.

Sinyavksy gestured to the guards; one hurried towards the mess-hall barracks, returning moments later with several prisoners, each carrying a bottle and a tray of small tin cups. They poured a thick, dark liquid into the cups, offering one to each convict. Sinyavksy explained.

— *The drink,* khvoya, *is an extract of pine needles combined with rose water. Both are rich in vitamins. They will keep you healthy. When you are healthy you are productive. You will lead a more productive life here than you did outside the camp. My job is to help you become a more productive citizen. In so doing, I become a more productive citizen. Your welfare is my welfare. As you improve, so do I.*

Leo hadn't moved. He hadn't changed position. His hand was still outstretched. A breeze caught the flower and blew it to the ground. He bent down and picked it up. When he stood up, the prisoner with the pine-needle concentrate had arrived. Leo took hold of the small tin cup, his fingers briefly touching the fingers of the prisoner. For a split second they were strangers and then recognition sparked.

Lazar's eyes appeared enormous, black-rock moons with a red sun blazing behind them. He was thin, his body boiled down to a concentrate of its former self – his features starker, more pronounced, skin stretched tight except for the left side of his face where his jaw and cheek had slipped, as though they'd been made from wax and left too close to the fire. Leo reasoned he must have suffered a stroke, before remembering the night of the arrest. His fist clenched involuntarily – the same fist he'd used to punch Lazar again and again until his jaw had turned soft. Surely seven years was long enough to heal, long enough for any injury to heal. But Lazar would have received no medical treatment in the Lubyanka. The interrogators might even have made use of the injury, twisting the broken bone whenever his answers were unsatisfactory. He would've received limited treatment in the camps, no reconstructive surgery – the idea was fanciful. That impulsive, senseless act of violence, a crime Leo had forgotten about as soon as his knuckles ceased being sore, had been immortalized in bone.

Lazar made no discernible reaction to their reunion except to pause from his duties as their eyes cracked against each other. His face was inscrutable, the left side of his mouth dragged into a permanent grimace. Without saying a word, he moved away, down the line of prisoners, pouring small cups of pine-needle extract for the new arrivals, not glancing back, as though nothing was amiss, as though they were strangers again.

Leo clutched his small tin cup, fingers clamped tight around it, remaining in the same position. The gelatinous syrup quivered as his hand trembled. He'd lost the ability to think or strategize. The camp commander called out, in good humour:

— *You there! Friend! Flower-lover! Drink! It will make you strong!*

Leo brought the cup to his lips, tipping the thick black liquid down his neck. Intensely bitter, it lined his throat like tar, making him want to cough it up. He closed his eyes, forcing it down.

Opening his eyes he watched Lazar finish his duties, returning to the barracks, walking at an unhurried pace. Even as he passed by he didn't look back, showing no sign of agitation or excitement. Commander Sinyavksy continued to speak for some time. But Leo had stopped listening. Inside his clammy fist, he'd crushed the dried purple flower to powder. The prisoner standing to his right hissed:

— *Pay attention! We're moving!*

The commander had finished talking. Introductions were over; the convicts were being shepherded from the administration zone into the prisoner zone. Leo was near the back of the line. The sun had set, extinguishing the horizon. Lights flickered in the guard towers. No powerful spotlights searched the ground. Except for the dull glow of the hut windows, the *zona* was completely dark.

They passed through the second wire fence. The guards remained at the border of the two zones, guns ready, ushering them towards the barracks. No officer entered this zone at night. It was too dangerous, too easy for a prisoner to smash their skull and disappear. They were only concerned with maintaining the perimeter, sealing the convicts in and leaving them to their own devices.

Leo was the last to enter the barracks — Lazar's barracks. He would have to face him alone, without Timur. He'd reason with him, talk to him. The man was a priest: he would hear his confession. Leo had much to tell. He had changed. He'd spent three years trying to make amends. Like a man walking to his execution, he climbed the flight of steps with heavy legs. He pushed on the door, breathing deeply, inhaling the stench of an overcrowded barracks and revealing a panorama of hate-filled faces.

SAME DAY

Leo had blacked out. Coming round, he found that he was on the floor, dragged by his ankles, submerged beneath waves of kicking prisoners. His fingers touched his scalp, finding the skin sticky with blood. Unable to focus, unable to fight, helpless at the epicentre of this ferocity, he couldn't survive for long. A glob of spit hit his eye. A boot slammed into the side of his head. His jaw hit the floor, his teeth scratching against each other. Abruptly, the kicking and spitting and shouting abated. In unison the mob pulled away, leaving him spluttering, as though washed up by a storm. From roaring hatred to silence, someone must have intervened.

Leo remained where he was, afraid that these precious seconds of calm would end as soon as he dared to look up. A voice sounded out:

— *Get up.*

Not Lazar's voice, a younger man. Leo unravelled from his foetal position, peering up at the figures looming over him – there were two, Lazar and standing beside him, perhaps thirty years old, a man with red hair and a red beard.

Wiping the phlegm from his face, the blood from his lips and nose, Leo awkwardly rotated himself into a sitting position. Some two hundred or so convicts were watching, perched on

211

the top bunks, standing close by, as though attending a theatrical performance with different grades of seating. The new arrivals were in the corner: relieved that attention wasn't focused on them.

Leo got to his feet, hunched like a cripple. Lazar stepped forward, examining him, circling, before returning to the spot directly in front, eye to eye. His expression flickered with tremendous energy, taut skin trembling. Slowly he opened his mouth, closing his eyes as he did, clearly in terrible pain. The word he uttered was less than a whisper, a tiny exhalation of air, carrying on it the faintest sound.

— *Max . . . im.*

Everything Leo had planned to say, the story of how he'd changed, tales of his enlightenment, the entire edifice of his transformation, disintegrated like snow on hot coal. He'd always comforted himself that he was a better man than most of the agents he'd worked alongside, men who had a set of gold teeth fashioned from the mouths of their interrogated suspects. He had not been the worst: not by far. He was in the middle, perhaps even lower, hiding in the shadows of the monsters that had murdered above him. He had done wrong, a modest kind of wrong – he was at best a mediocre villain. Hearing that name, the alias he'd chosen himself, he began to cry. He tried to stop but to no avail. Lazar reached out and touched one of these tears, collecting it, holding the drop on the end of his finger. Peering at it for some time, he returned it to the exact spot he'd taken it from – pressing his finger hard against Leo's cheek and smearing it down contemptuously, as if to say:

— *Keep your tears. They count for nothing.*

He took hold of Leo's hand – palm scarred from the chase through the sewers – and placed it against the left side of his face.

His cheek felt uneven, like rubble, a mouth full of gravel. He opened his mouth again, wincing, closing his eyes. As though the laws of physics had been reversed, smell travelling faster than light, an odour of decay struck Leo first, teeth rotten and diseased. Many were missing altogether: the gum deformed, black streaks with patchy, bloody stubs. Here was transformation, here was change: a brilliant orator, thirty years of speeches and sermons, turned into a stinking mute.

Lazar closed his mouth, stepping back. The red-haired man offered Lazar the side of his face as though it was a canvas to be painted upon. Lazar leaned so close that his lips were almost touching the man's ear. As he spoke his lips hardly seemed to move, tiny movements. The red-haired man delivered his words.

— *I treated you as a son. I opened my home to you. I trusted you. I loved you.*

The man didn't translate first person into third, speaking as though he was Lazar. Leo replied:

— *Lazar, I have no defence. All the same, I beg you to listen. Your wife is alive. She has sent me here to free you.*

Leo and Timur had speculated as to whether Lazar might have already been sent a coded letter containing Fraera's plans. However, Lazar's surprise was genuine. He knew nothing of his wife. He knew nothing of how she'd changed. With a gesture of irritation he waved at the red-haired man, who sprang forward, kicking Leo to his knees:

— *You're lying!*

Leo addressed Lazar.

— *Your wife is alive. She is the reason I'm here. It's the truth!*

The red-haired man glanced over his shoulder, awaiting instructions. Lazar shook his head. Taking his cue, the red-haired man translated:

— *What do you know of the truth? You're a Chekist! Nothing you say can be trusted!*

— *Anisya was freed from the Gulags three years ago. She's changed, Lazar. She has become a* vory.

Several of the vory watching laughed, ridiculing the notion that the wife of a dissident priest could enter their ranks. Leo pressed on regardless.

— *Not only is she* vory, *she's a leader. She no longer goes by the name Anisya. Her* klikukha *is Fraera.*

The cries of incredulity soared. Men were shouting, pushing forward, insulted at the notion that a woman could rule them. Leo raised his voice.

— *She's in charge of a gang, sworn upon revenge. She is not the woman you remember, Lazar. She has kidnapped my daughter. If I cannot secure your release she'll kill her. There's no chance of you ever being released. You will die here, unless you accept my help. All our lives depend upon your escape.*

Outraged by his story, the crowd fermented into a second fury of abuse, standing up and closing around him, ready to attack again. However, Lazar raised his hands, ushering them back. He evidently had some standing among them for they obeyed without question, returning to their bunks. Lazar ushered the red-haired man to his side, speaking into his ear. The man nodded, approving. Once Lazar had finished the red-haired man spoke with an air of self-importance.

— *You are a desperate man. You would say anything. You are a liar. You always have been. You have fooled me before. You will not fool me again.*

If Timur had arrived he would've offered Fraera's letter as proof that she was alive. She'd written it to answer these exact doubts. Without the letter, Leo was helpless. He said, desperate:

— *Lazar, you have a son.*

The room fell silent. Lazar shook, as if something inside him were trying to break out. He opened his mouth, a twisted motion and despite his outrage, the word he muttered was almost inaudible.

— *No!*

His voice was as deformed as his cheek, a cracked sound. The pain of projecting even that one word had left him weak. A chair was brought and he sat down, wiping the perspiration from his pale face. Unable to speak any more, he gestured at the red-haired man, who, for the first time, spoke as himself.

— *Lazar is our priest. Many of us are his congregation. I am his voice. Here he can speak about God and not fear that he's saying the wrong thing. The State cannot send him to prison if he is already here. In prison, he has found the freedom they would not give him outside. My name is Georgi Vavilov. Lazar is my mentor, as he once tried to be yours. Except that I would rather die than betray him. I despise you.*

— *I can get you out too, Georgi.*

The red-haired man shook his head.

— *You thrive on men's weaknesses. I have no desire to be anywhere but by my master's side. Lazar believes that it is divine justice that you have been sent to him. Judgement shall be passed upon you and by men upon whom you once passed judgement.*

Lazar turned to an elderly man standing at the back of the barracks, so far uninvolved in the proceedings. Lazar indicated that the man should step forward. He did so, slowly, walking crookedly. The elderly man addressed Leo.

— *Three years ago I met the man who'd interrogated me. Like you, he had been sent into the prisons, a place where he'd sent so many. We devised a punishment for him. We composed a list of*

215

every torture we, as a group, had ever suffered. The list detailed over one hundred methods. Every night we inflicted one of those tortures on the interrogator, working our way down the list, torture by torture. If he could survive them all, we would allow him to live. We did not want him to die. We wanted him to experience every method. To this end, we stopped him from hanging himself. We fed him. We kept him strong so that he might suffer more. He reached thirty before he deliberately ran towards the edge of the zona and was shot by the guards. The torture that he inflicted upon me was the first torture on the list. It is the torture you will face tonight.

The elderly convict rolled up his trouser legs, revealing knees that were purple, blackened and deformed.

10 APRIL

The cloud level had sunk a thousand metres, obliterating the view. Silver-gilded droplets hung in the air — a mist part ice, part water, part magic — out of which the drab highway appeared metre by metre, a grey, lumpish carpet unravelling in front of them. The truck was making slow progress. Frustrated with the additional delay, Timur checked his watch, forgetting that it was broken, smashed in the storm. It clung uselessly to his wrist, the glass cracked, the mechanism jammed with salt water. He wondered how badly it had been damaged. His father had claimed it to be a family heirloom. Timur suspected this was a lie and the way in which his father, a proud man, had disguised giving his son a battered second-hand watch for his eighteenth birthday. It was because of the lie, rather than despite it, that the watch had become Timur's most treasured possession. When his eldest son turned eighteen he intended to hand it down to him, although he'd not yet decided whether to explain the sentimental importance of the lie, or merely perpetuate the mythology of its origins.

Despite the delay, Timur took great comfort from the fact that at least he'd avoided being sent back across the Sea of Okhotsk on the return voyage to Buchta Nakhodka. Yesterday evening he'd been on board the *Stary Bolshevik*, the ship ready to depart: repairs had been made to the hold, the water pumped out and the newly released prisoners loaded in, their faces knotted in contemplation of freedom. Unable to see a way out of his predicament Timur had stood on deck, paralysed, watching as the harbour crew unfastened the ropes. In another couple of minutes the ship would've been at sea and he would've had no prospect of reaching Gulag 57 for another month.

In desperation, Timur had walked into the captain's bridge, hoping sheer force of circumstance would compel him to come up with a plausible excuse. As the captain turned to him he blurted out:

— *There is something I have to tell you.*

An inept liar, he'd remembered it was always easier to tell a version of the truth.

— *I'm not actually a guard. I work for the MVD. I've been sent here to review the changes being implemented in the system following Khrushchev's speech. I've seen enough of the way in which this ship is managed.*

At the mere mention of the speech, the captain paled.

— *Have I done wrong?*

— *I'm afraid the contents of my report are secret.*

— *But the journey here, the things that happened, that wasn't my fault. Please, if you file a report describing how I lost control of the ship . . .*

Timur had marvelled at the power of his excuse. The captain had moved closer, his voice imploring:

— *None of us could've foreseen the partition wall would fail. Don't let me lose my job. I can't find another. Who would work with me? Knowing what I'd done for a living? Running a prison ship? I would be hated. This is the only place for me. This is where I belong. Please, I have nowhere else to go.*

The captain's desperation had become embarrassing. Timur had stepped away:

— *The only reason I'm telling you is because I can't make the return voyage. I need to talk to Abel Prezent, Regional Director. You'll have to manage the ship without me. You can offer some excuse to the crew for my absence.*

The captain had smiled obsequiously, bowing his head.

Stepping off the ship onto the harbour, Timur had congratulated himself on chancing across such a potent excuse. Confident, he'd entered the administrative section of the prisoner processing centre, climbing the stairs to the office of Regional Director Abel Prezent, the man who'd assigned him to the *Stary Bolshevik*. Prezent's face had scrunched up with irritation.

— *Is there a problem?*

— *I've seen enough of the ship to write my report.*

Like a cat sensing danger, Prezent's body language changed.

— *What report?*

— *I've been sent by the MVD to collect information about how the reforms are being implemented since Khrushchev's speech. The intention was for me to remain unknown, unidentified, so that I might more accurately judge the way in which the camps are being managed. However, since you reassigned me to the* Stary Bolshevik, *against my orders, it has forced me to come forward. Needless to say I'm not carrying identification. We did not think*

it necessary. We did not anticipate that my duties would be chal-
lenged. However, if you need proof, I know the exact details of your
employment record.

Timur and Leo had carefully studied the files of all the key figures in the region:

— You worked at Karlag, Kazakhstan, for five years, and
before that—

Prezent had interrupted, politely, raising a finger, his voice constricted, as though invisible hands were squeezing his thin, pale
throat:

— Yes, I see.

He stood up, considering, his hands behind his back.

— You are here to write a report?

— That is correct.

— I suspected something like this would happen.

Timur had nodded, pleased with the credibility of his improvised cover story:

— Moscow requires regular evaluations.

— Evaluations . . . that is a lethal word.

Timur had not anticipated this meditative and melancholic
reaction. He tried to soften the implied threat.

— This is fact-gathering and nothing more.

Prezent had replied:

— I work hard for the State. I live where no one else wants to
live. I work with the most dangerous prisoners in the world. I have
done things no one else wanted to do. I was taught how to be a
leader. Then I was told those lessons were wrong. One minute it is
law to do a certain kind of thing. The next minute it is a crime. The
law says I should be strict. The law says I should be lenient.

Timur's lie had been swallowed whole. Mere reference to the
Secret Speech had them cowering. Unlike the captain, Prezent did

not implore, or beg for a favourable report. He'd become nostalgic for a time gone by, a time where his place and purpose had been clear. Timur pressed his advantage.

— *I need immediate transport to Gulag 57.*

Prezent had said:

— *Of course.*

— *I must leave right now.*

— *The journey into the mountains can't be made at night.*

— *Hazardous or not, I would prefer to make it now.*

— *I understand. I've delayed you. And I apologize. But it's simply not possible. The first thing tomorrow, that is the earliest. There is nothing I can do about the darkness.*

*

Timur turned to the driver.

— *How long till we're there?*

— *Two, three hours – the mist is bad, three hours, I say.*

The driver laughed, before adding:

— *I never heard of anyone being in a hurry to get to a Gulag before.*

Timur ignored the joke, channelling his impatient energy into reassessing his plans. Success required several elements to slot into place. Out of their control was Lazar's cooperation. Timur had in his possession a letter written by Fraera, the contents of which had been read and re-read, checking for a warning or some secret instruction. They'd found none. As an additional persuasive measure, unbeknown to Fraera, Leo had insisted they bring a photo of a seven-year-old boy. The child in the photo wasn't Lazar's son but he had no way of knowing that. The apparent sight of him might prove more powerful than the mere idea of him. Should this fail then Timur had in his possession a bottle of chloroform.

The truck slowed to a stop. Up ahead was a timber bridge, simple in design. It spanned a deep fault line, a crack in the landscape. The driver made a snaking movement with his hand.

— *When the mountain snow melts, it flows fast . . .*

Timur strained forward in his seat, peering at the rickety bridge. The far side disappeared into the mist. The driver frowned.

— *That bridge was built by prisoners. You can't trust it!*

There was one other guard travelling with them, who was asleep. Judging from the smell of his clothes, he'd been drunk last night, probably drunk every night of his life. The driver shook him.

— *Wake up! Useless . . . lazy . . . wake up!*

The guard opened his eyes, blinking at the bridge. He wiped his eyes, scrambled out of the cabin, jumped to the ground. He belched loudly and began waving the truck forward. Timur shook his head.

— *Wait.*

He stepped out of the cabin, climbed down and stretched his legs. Shutting the door, he walked to the beginning of the bridge. The driver was right to be concerned: the bridge wasn't much wider than the truck. There were maybe thirty centimetres to spare on either side, nothing to stop the tyres slipping off if the approach wasn't exactly aligned. Glancing down, Timur saw the river some ten metres below. Tongues of smooth, dripping ice jutted out from either side of the bank. They'd begun to melt, rapid drips feeding a narrow undulating flow. In a matter of weeks, when the snows melted, there'd be a torrent.

The truck crept forward. The hungover guard lit a cigarette, content to shirk responsibility. Timur gestured for the driver to align the truck to the right: it was edging off course. He gestured again. Visibility was poor but he could see the driver, the driver must be able to see him. Timur called out:

— To the right!

Even though it hadn't made the necessary adjustments the truck accelerated. At the same time, its headlights flared up, a bright sulphur yellow blinding him. The truck was coming straight towards him.

Timur dived out of the way but too late: the steel bumper smashed into him while he was midair, crushing his body, before spitting him out over the ravine. Briefly suspended in the air, upturned towards the shimmering sky, then falling, his body spinning, twisting towards the river, directly above one of the ice lips. He crashed face down. Bone and ice splintered simultaneously.

Timur lay with his ear flat to the ice, like a safe-cracker. He couldn't move his fingers or his legs. He couldn't move his neck. He felt no pain.

Someone shouted down:

— Traitor! You'd spy on your own kind! We stick together! Us against them!

Timur couldn't turn his neck to look up. But he recognized the voice as the driver's.

— There will be no reports, no blame and no guilt – not in Kolyma, maybe in Moscow, but not here. We did what we had to do! We did what we were told to do! Fuck Khrushchev's speech! Fuck your report! Let's see you write it from down there.

The hungover guard chuckled. The driver addressed him.

— Go down.

— Why?

— Otherwise everyone will see his body.

— Who will? There's no one here.

— I don't know, someone like him, if they send another.

— I don't need to go down there. The ice will melt.

223

— In three weeks it will, who knows who'll drive by in that time. Just go down there and push him in the river. Do this right.

— I can't swim.

— He's on the ice.

— But if the ice breaks?

— You'll get your feet wet. Just get down! No mistakes.

Staring into the river, his breathing ragged and rasping, Timur listened as the reluctant executioner, whining like a lazy teenager, clambered down the steep bank — the clumsy sound of his approaching murderer.

For as long as he could remember his greatest fear had been a member of his family dying in the Gulags. He'd never worried about himself. He'd always been sure he could cope and that somehow, no matter what, he'd find a way home.

These were the last minutes of his life. He thought of his wife. He thought of his sons.

*

Annoyed at being bossed around, his head pounding from a hangover, forced to slip and slide down the ravine wall, risking spraining his ankle, the guard finally reached the riverbank. His heavy boots touched the ice sheet tentatively, testing its strength. In an attempt to distribute his weight evenly, he lowered himself to his hands and knees, crawling to the body of the guy sent from Moscow. He tapped the traitor with the barrel of his gun. He didn't move.

— He's dead!

The driver called out:

— Check his pockets.

He pushed his hand into the pockets, finding a letter, some money and a knife — odds and ends.

— *There's nothing!*

— *What about his watch?*

He unclipped it.

— *It's broken!*

— *Push the body into the water.*

Sitting on the ice, using his boots, he kicked out, pushing the body towards the river. The man was heavy but his body slid across the smooth ice without too much trouble. On the edge of the ice lip, he saw the man's eyes were open. They blinked – the man, the Moscow spy, was still alive.

He's alive!

— *Not for long. Push him in. I'm getting cold.*

He watched the man blink once more before kicking him off the edge of the ice into the river. There was a splash. The body rocked up and down before being taken away, downstream, into a wilderness where no one would ever see him again.

Still sitting on the ice, the guard studied the watch. Cheap and smashed, it was worthless. But something stopped him from tossing it into the water. Cracked glass or not, it seemed a shame to throw it away.

MOSCOW

Elena asked:

— *When is Zoya coming home?*

Raisa replied:

— *Soon.*

— *When I get back from the shops?*

— *No, not that soon.*

— *How soon?*

— *When Leo returns, he'll bring Zoya with him. I can't say when that will be, exactly, but it will be soon.*

— *You promise?*

— *Leo's doing everything he can. We have to be patient for a little longer. Can you do that for me?*

— *If you promise that Zoya's OK.*

It was a promise Raisa had no choice but to make.

— *I promise.*

Elena asked the same questions every day. On each occasion it was as if she'd never asked them before. She wasn't necessarily seeking new information; rather that she was attuned to the tone of the response, listening for minute variations. Any hint of

226

impatience or irritation, any suggestion of doubt, and she'd slip back into the catatonic despondency that had struck her down immediately after Zoya's capture. She'd refused to leave her room, crying until she was unable to cry any more. Leo had refused the doctor's instruction that she be sedated, sitting with her every night, hour after hour. Only when Raisa had returned from hospital did Elena begin to improve. The most dramatic progress had occurred when Leo left Moscow, but not because she wanted him gone: it was the first concrete evidence that action was being taken to bring Zoya back. Her mind easily digested the concept that when Leo returned, Zoya would return with him. Elena didn't need to know where her sister was, or what she was doing, just that she was coming home, and coming home soon.

Leo's parents were waiting by the front door. Still weak from her injuries, Raisa depended upon their help. They'd moved into the gated ministerial complex, cooking and cleaning, creating a sense of domestic normality. Ready to leave, Elena paused.

— *Can't you come with us? We'll walk very slowly.*

Raisa smiled.

— *I'm not feeling strong enough. Give me a day or two, then we'll go out together.*

— *With Zoya? We can go to the zoo. Zoya liked that. She pretended that she didn't but I know she did. It was her secret. I'd like Leo to come too. And Anna, and Stepan.*

— *We'll all go.*

Elena smiled as she shut the door, the first smile that Raisa had seen from her in a long time.

Alone, Raisa lay down on Zoya's bed. She'd moved into the girls' room. Elena would fall asleep only when she was by her side. Security had been increased at the ministerial complex, as it had across the city. Agents, retired and active, were reviewing their living arrangements, putting additional locks on the door, bars on windows. Though the State had tried to stop the release of information there had been too many murders for rumours not to circulate. Everyone who'd ever denounced their friend or colleague took additional precautions. The profiteers of fear were afraid exactly as Fraera had promised.

*

Raisa opened her eyes, unsure how long she'd been asleep. Though she was facing the wall and unable to see behind her, she was certain that there was someone else in the room. Turning onto her back and lifting her head, she saw the outline of an officer in the doorway, an androgynous silhouette. There was a dreamlike quality to the experience. Raisa felt no fear or surprise. This was their first encounter and yet there was a peculiar familiarity between them, an immediate intimacy.

Fraera took off her cap, revealing cropped hair. She stepped into the room, remarking:

— *You can scream. Or we can talk.*

Raisa sat up.

— *I'm not going to scream.*

— *No, I didn't think so.*

Raisa had heard that tone many times: as a man might patronize a woman, peculiar from the lips of another woman only a couple of years her elder. Fraera noticed her irritation.

— *Don't be offended. I had to be sure. It hasn't been easy, getting in to see you. I've tried many times. It would be a shame to cut this visit short.*

Fraera sat on the opposite bed, Elena's bed – her back against the wall, her legs crossed, unbuttoning her uniform jacket. Raisa asked:

— *Is Zoya safe?*

— *She's safe.*

— *Unharmed?*

— *Yes.*

Raisa had no reason to believe her. Yet she did.

Fraera picked up Elena's pillow, squeezing it, in no particular rush.

— *This is a nice room, filled with nice things for two nice girls, given to them by two nice parents. How many nice things does it take to compensate for a murdered mother and father? How soft do the sheets have to be for a child to forgive that crime?*

— *We've never tried to buy their affections.*

— *Hard to believe, looking around.*

Raisa struggled to control her anger.

— *Would we have been more of a family if we'd bought them nothing?*

— *But you're not a family. Sure, if someone didn't know the truth they might mistake you for a family. I wonder if that was what Leo had in mind: the illusion of normality. It wouldn't be real, he'd know that, but he could enjoy it, reflected in other people's eyes. Leo is good at believing in lies. That would make the girls little more than props, dressed up in pretty outfits, so he can play at being a father.*

— *The girls were in an orphanage. We offered them a choice.*

— *A choice between sickness, impoverishment and malnutrition, or living with the man who murdered their parents . . . that's not much of a choice.*

Raisa paused, uncertain, unable to disagree.

— *Neither Leo nor I were ever under the impression that the adoption would be straightforward.*

— *You didn't correct me when I said "the man who murdered*

229

their parents". I expected you to say: Leo didn't shoot them. He tried to save them. He was a good man among bad. But you don't believe that, do you?

— *He was an MGB officer. He's done terrible things.*

— *Yet you love him?*

— *I didn't always.*

— *You love him now?*

— *He has changed.*

Fraera leaned forward.

— *Why can't you answer? Do you love him?*

— *Yes.*

— *I want to hear you say it: I love him.*

— *I love him.*

Fraera sat back, considering. Raisa added by way of explanation:

— *He's not the man who arrested you. He's not the same.*

— *You are right. He is not. There is one crucial difference. In the past he was unloved. Today he is loved. You love him.*

Fraera unbuttoned her shirt, restricted by the collar, revealing the top of the tattoos that unravelled across her body like the symbols of an ancient witchcraft.

— *Raisa, how much do you know about him? How much do you know about his past?*

— *He infiltrated your husband's church. He betrayed you, he betrayed your congregation and he betrayed Lazar.*

— *And for those things alone, he deserves to die. However, did you know that before he revealed his betrayal, he proposed to me? Like a young lover under a full moon?*

Raisa dropped her head and nodded.

— *Yes, he asked you to leave Lazar. At the time I'm sure he believed you would want to become his wife. He was deluded. He has been deluded about many things, love included. Love, particularly.*

Fraera seemed disappointed, wanting to pick open a secret. She continued, her enthusiasm notably diminished.

— *He thought he was trying to save me. In fact, he was trying to save himself. Had I accepted his offer, he would've tricked himself into believing that he was, at heart, a decent man. I would not excuse his crimes so easily. I made him a promise. I swore that he would never be loved. I was sure that I was right because how could such a monster be loved? Who would love him?*

Raisa felt flustered under Fraera's stare.

— *I will not defend the things he did.*

— *But you must. You love him. I've seen the two of you together. I've watched you, spied on you, as Leo once spied on me. You make him happy. What's worse, he makes you happy. Your love for him is everything. That is why I am placing it on trial. That is why I am here. I want to find out how it is possible that you can live with him. Sleep with him. I thought at first you might be stupid: an officer's trophy, beautiful and unquestioning. I thought you didn't care about the crimes Leo has committed.*

Fraera stood up, crossing the divide and sitting on the same bed as Raisa, positioned like two best friends sharing secrets in the middle of the night.

— *Yet you exhibit no mindless loyalty to the State. There were even rumours of you being a dissident. Your love for Leo became an even greater mystery, one that I had to solve at all costs. I was forced to delve into your past. May I share my findings?*

— *You have my daughter. You may do as you please.*

— *Your family was killed during the war. You lived as a refugee.*

Raisa was paralysed as Fraera wielded information like a knife.

— *During those years you were raped.*

Raisa's mouth opened, a fraction, enough to serve as confirmation. She didn't try to deny it, sensing there was more to follow.

— How did you know?

— Because I visited the orphanage where you abandoned your child.

Raisa felt something far more powerful than surprise. The most intimate secrets from her past, events that she'd carefully buried and laid to rest were being dug up and brandished before her. Scrutinizing Raisa's reaction, Fraera took hold of her hand.

— Leo doesn't know?

Raisa held Fraera's hopeful stare, answering:

— He knows.

Once again Fraera looked disappointed.

— I don't believe you.

— It took many years for me to tell him but I did. He knows, Fraera: he knows it all. He knows I can't have children, he knows why, he knows that the only child I will ever give birth to I gave away. He knows my shame. I know his.

Fraera touched Raisa's face.

— That is why you married Leo? You sensed how desperate he was to be loved. He would gladly have accepted the opportunity to be father to your child. You saw him as an opportunity. You would bring your child back from the orphanage.

— No, I knew my child had died before I met Leo. I went to the orphanage as soon as I was strong enough, as soon as I'd found a home, as soon as I was able to be a mother again. They told me that my son had died of typhus.

— So why did you marry Leo? What reason was there for saying yes to him?

— Since I'd already given up my son in order to survive, in comparison it didn't seem too much of a compromise to marry a man I feared rather than loved.

Fraera leaned forward and kissed Raisa. Pulling back, she said:

— I can taste your love for him. And your hatred of me . . .

— You have taken my child.

Fraera stood up, walking to the door, buttoning up her shirt.

— She is not yours. As long as you love Leo you leave me no choice. Your love for him is the reason he can live with himself. He has committed unspeakable crimes and yet, despite this, he is loved. He has murdered and he is loved. And by a woman any man would admire, by a woman I admire. Your love excuses him. It is his redemption.

Fraera fastened her jacket, returning the cap to her head, disappearing into her disguise.

— I spoke to Zoya before I came to see you. I wanted to hear what life was like in this sham of a family. She is intelligent, broken, messed-up. I like her very much. She told me that she made you an offer. Leave Leo and she could be happy.

Raisa was appalled. Zoya was supposed to be a hostage. Yet she was confiding in Fraera, talking about Raisa, equipping their enemy with all the family secrets she needed. Fraera continued:

— I'm surprised you could be so cruel as to dismiss her request with a declaration of love for Leo. This is a girl so disturbed that she takes a knife from your kitchen and stands over Leo while he sleeps, planning to cut his throat.

Raisa's guard fell. She didn't know what Fraera was referring to – what knife? A knife held over Leo? After several attempts Fraera had finally landed upon a weakness – a lie, a secret. She smiled.

— It seems there is something Leo hasn't told you. It's true, Zoya used to stand by his side of the bed, holding a knife. Leo caught her. And he didn't tell you?

In an instant Raisa fitted together the discrepancies. When she'd found Leo sitting at the kitchen table, brooding, he hadn't been concerned about Nikolai, he'd been thinking about Zoya. She'd asked him what was wrong. He'd said nothing. He'd lied to her.

Fraera was now in control.

— *Bearing that incident in mind, think carefully about what I'm about to say. I will repeat Zoya's offer. I will return Zoya to your care, unharmed. In exchange you and the girls must never see Leo again. Love the girls, or love Leo, that has been the reality of your situation for the past three years. And, Raisa, now, you must choose.*

KOLYMA
GULAG 57

SAME DAY

Leo could barely stand, let alone dig. Working in a crude system of trenches three metres below the topsoil, his pickaxe pinged uselessly against the permafrost. There were vast smouldering fires, like the funeral pyres of fallen heroes, slow burning to soften the frozen ground. But Leo was near none of them, deliberately located by the leader of his work brigade in the coldest and most remote corner of the gold mines, in the least developed trench system where, even had he been at full strength, it would've been impossible to fulfil his *norm*, the minimum amount of rock he needed to break to be fed a standardized ration.

Exhausted, his legs quivered, unable to support his weight. Swollen and bubbled, his kneecaps were sunk behind sacs of fluid, swirls of purple and blue. Last night he had been forced onto his knees, his hands tied behind his back, his ankles lifted and bound to his wrists so that his entire body weight was supported on his kneecaps. To keep him from falling over he'd been secured to the steps of a bunk. Hour after hour he'd been unable to relieve the pressure: skin stretched tight, bone grinding against wood, sandpapering his skin. At each shift in position he'd cried out through his gag. They'd slept while he'd remained on his knees, teeth chomping like a mad horse against the filthy rag, which the prisoners had prepared by rubbing it across their weeping boils. While snores had criss-crossed the barracks one man had remained awake – Lazar. He'd watched over Leo the entire night, removing the gag when he'd needed to vomit, retying it after he'd finished, displaying a paternal dedication: a father tending to a sickly son, a son who needed to be taught a lesson.

At dawn Leo had spluttered back into consciousness as ice-cold water had been poured over his head. Untied, his gag removed, he'd slumped, unable to feel his feet, as though his legs had been amputated below the knees. It had taken several excruciating minutes before he'd been able to stretch them and several minutes more before he'd been able to heave himself up – hobbling – aged a hundred years. His fellow prisoners had allowed him to take breakfast, to sit at a table, to eat his ration, his hands shaking. They wanted him to live. They wanted him to suffer. As a man wandering in a desert might dream of an oasis, Leo's mind concentrated on the shimmering image of Timur. Since it was impossible to make the journey from Magadan at night there was only a narrow window, in the early evening, when his friend, his saviour, might arrive.

Arms shaking with fatigue, Leo lifted the pickaxe above his head only for his legs to give way. Falling forward, his puffy knees slammed into the ground. On impact the fluid sacs burst, popping like ripe adolescent spots. He opened his mouth, a silent scream, his eyes streaming as he toppled onto his side, taking the pressure off his knees and lying at the bottom of a trench. Exhaustion smothered any sense of self-preservation. For a brief moment, he would've been content to shut his eyes and go to sleep. In these temperatures he'd never have woken up.

Remembering Zoya, remembering Raisa and Elena, his family, he sat up, placing his hands on the ground, slowly pushing himself up. Struggling to his feet, someone grabbed him, hissing in his ear:

— *No rest, Chekist!*

No rest, no mercy either – that was Lazar's verdict. The sentence was being carried out with vigour. The voice in his ear didn't belong to a guard: it was a fellow prisoner, the leader of his brigade, driven by an intense personal hatred, refusing to allow Leo a single minute when he didn't experience pain or hunger or exhaustion, or all these things together. Leo hadn't arrested this man or his family. He didn't even know the man's name. That didn't matter. He'd become a talisman for every prisoner: an ambassador for injustice. *Chekist* had become his name, his entire identity, and seen in that way, everyone's hatred was personal.

A bell was rung. Tools were downed. Leo had survived his first day at the mine, a modest ordeal compared to the coming night – a second as yet unannounced torture. Dragging his legs up the ramp, limping out of the trench, following the others back, his only source of strength was the prospect of Timur's arrival.

Approaching the camp and the dim daylight, diffuse among the sunken cloud cover, Leo had almost completely disappeared. Emerging out of the darkness, he saw the headlights of a truck on the plateau. Two fists of yellow light, fireflies in the distance. Had it not been for his knees, Leo would have dropped to the ground and wept with relief, prostrate before a merciful deity. Pushed and shoved by the guards who dared curse him only out of earshot of their reformed, enlightened commander, Leo was herded back inside the *zona*, his eyes constantly thrown over his shoulder,

237

watching as the truck grew closer. Failing to keep his emotions under control, his lip trembling, he returned to the barracks. No matter what torture they'd planned, he'd be saved. He stood by the window – eyes and nose pressed up against the glass, like an impoverished child outside a sweet shop. The truck entered the camp. A guard stepped down from the cabin, then the driver. Leo waited, fingernails digging into the window frame. Surely Timur was among their number, perhaps seated in the back. Minutes passed, no one else stepped out. He continued to stare, desperation overwhelming logic, until he finally accepted that no matter how long he watched the truck, there was no one else on board.

Timur hadn't arrived.

Leo couldn't eat, his hunger displaced by disappointment so strong it filled his stomach. In the mess hall he remained at the table long after the other prisoners had left, lingering until the guards angrily ordered him out. Better to be punished by them than by his fellow inmates, better to spend the night in the isolator – the freezing punishment cells – than to go through another torture. After all, weren't these guards operating under the changed commander Sinyavksy? Hadn't he spoken about justice and fairness and opportunity? As the guards pushed him towards the door, in a deliberate act of provocation Leo lashed out, swinging a punch. He was slow and weak: his fist was caught. A rifle butt smashed into his face.

Dragged by his arms, legs trailing in the snow, Leo wasn't taken to the isolator. He was dumped in the barracks – left sprawled in the middle of the room. He heard the guards leave. His eyes focused on the timber beams. His nose and lips were wet with blood. Lazar looked down at him.

Stripped bare, wet towels wrapped tight around Leo's chest, tied behind his back, they rendered him unable to move, arms pinned by his sides. He felt no pain. Although he'd never served as an official interrogator, he had first-hand knowledge of their methods. From time to time he'd been forced to watch. Yet this technique was new to him. He was lifted up and left lying on his back. The prisoners continued with their evening activities. His stomach was cold and wet with the towels. But he was too exhausted to care and seizing the opportunity, he shut his eyes.

He woke, partly due to the sound of prisoners getting into bed, mostly because of the tension around his chest. Slowly he began to understand the torture. As the towels dried they became tighter, constricting incrementally, steadily crushing his ribs together. The subtle dynamic of the punishment was the knowledge that the pain would only get worse. While the other men readied for bed, Lazar took his regular place on a chair beside Leo. The red-haired man, Lazar's voice, approached.

— *Do you need me?*

Lazar shook his head, ushering him to bed. The man glared at Leo like a sulking, jealous lover, before retreating as ordered.

By the time the prisoners were asleep the pain was so intense that had he not been gagged Leo would've cried out for mercy. Watching his face slowly contort, as if screws were being tightened, Lazar knelt beside Leo in a gesture of prayer, lowering his mouth to his ear, his bottom lip touching Leo's lobe as he spoke. His voice was as faint as the shuffle of autumn leaves:

— *It is hard . . . to watch another suffer . . . no matter what they have done . . . It changes you . . . no matter how right you are . . . to desire revenge . . .*

Lazar paused, recovering from the exertion of these words. His pain had never stopped, living with it as a companion, knowing that it would never get better and that he would never know another moment without it.

— I have asked the others . . . Was there one Chekist *who helped you? Was there one good man . . . ? Everyone . . . said . . . no.*

He paused again, wiping the sweat from his brow, before returning his lips to Leo's ear.

— The State chose you . . . to betray me . . . Because you have a heart . . . I would've spotted a man without one . . . That is your tragedy . . . Maxim, I cannot spare you . . . There is so little justice . . . We must take what we can get . . .

Pain became delirium: so intense it took on euphoric properties. Leo was no longer aware of the barracks: the timber walls were dissolving, leaving him alone in the middle of an icy white plateau – a different plateau, whiter and softer and brighter and not at all awful or cold. Water fell from the sky, freezing rain, directly above him. He blinked, shaking his head. He was in the barracks, on the floor. Water had been poured over him. The gag had been removed. The towels were untied. Even so, he could inhale only the tiniest gulps of air: his lungs had grown accustomed to their constriction. He sat up, making slow, shallow gasps. It was morning. He'd survived another night.

Prisoners trudged past him, snorting disdain, on their way to breakfast. Leo's gasps began to slow, his breathing returning to normal. He was alone in the barracks and he wondered if he had ever felt this alone in his life. He stood up, needing to lean against the bed frame to support his weight. A guard called out to him, furious at his lingering behind. He dropped his head, shunting forward, unable to lift his feet, sliding them along the smooth wood like an infirm ice-skater.

Entering the administration zone, Leo stopped. He couldn't endure a second day of work. He couldn't endure a third night. His imagination crackled with the memory of the various tortures he'd witnessed. What would come next? The mirage of Timur was too faint to sustain him. Their plans had gone wrong. Nearby a guard called out:

— *Keep moving!*

Leo had to improvise. He was on his own. Facing in the direction of the camp commander's office, he called out:

— *Commander!*

At the violation in etiquette, guards ran towards him. From the dining barracks, Lazar watched. Leo needed to catch the commander's attention quickly.

— *Commander! I know about Khrushchev's speech!*

The guards arrived by his side. Before he could say any more Leo was struck across his back. A second blow struck him in the stomach. He crouched, huddling, as more blows landed.

— *Stop!*

The guards froze. Unravelling himself, Leo glanced up at the administration barracks. Commander Sinyavsky was standing at the top of the steps.

— *Bring him to me.*

Guards hustled Leo up the stairs and into the office. The commander had retreated to the corner beside a squat, fat-bellied stove. The log-lined room was decorated with maps of the region, framed photos of the commander with prisoners at work — Sinyavksy smiling, as if in the company of friends, the prisoners' faces impassive. There were shadows around the frames indicating that other photos, of different shapes and sizes, had recently been taken down and these ones put up in their place.

Dressed in tattered clothes, his body beaten, Leo stood hunched, trembling like a *bezprizornik*, a ragged street child. Sinyavksy ushered the guards away.

— *I wish to speak to the prisoner alone.*

The guards glanced at each other. One uttered:

— *This man attacked us last night. We should stay with you.*

Sinyavksy shook his head.

— *Nonsense.*

— *You are not safe with him.*

Considering their rank, their tone was inappropriately threatening. Evidently the commander's power was being questioned. Addressing Leo:

— *You will not attack me, will you?*

— *No, sir.*

242

— *No, sir! He's even being polite. Now, all of you: leave, I insist.*

The guards retreated, reluctantly, making no attempt to conceal their contempt for this softness.

Once they were gone, Sinyavksy moved to the door, checking that they weren't standing outside. He listened to the creak of the guards' footsteps as they descended the stairs. Certain of privacy, he bolted the door and turned to Leo.

— *Please, sit.*

Leo sat in the chair positioned in front of the desk. The air was warm and smelt of wood chips. Leo wanted to sleep. The commander smiled:

— *You must be cold.*

Without waiting for an answer, Sinyavksy walked to the stove. He picked up a pan on the top and poured amber liquid into a small tin cup, the same sort of cup that had been used for the pine-needle extract. Holding it by the rim, he offered it to Leo.

— *Careful.*

Leo glanced down at the steaming surface. He raised it to his lips. The smell was sweet. The liquid tasted like melted honey and wildflowers. None of it made it to the back of his throat: like the first rains falling on a desiccated, cracked-mud riverbed, the warm sugars and alcohol were absorbed instantly. Blood rushed to his head. His cheeks flushed red. The room began to swirl. The feeling subsided into a gentle, intoxicated mellowness, a lullaby sensation, as if Leo had swallowed happiness in nectar form.

Sinyavksy sat down opposite, unlocking a drawer, taking out a cardboard box. He placed it on the desk in front of them. The top was stamped:

NOT FOR PRESS

The commander tapped it.

— *You know what's inside?*

Leo nodded.

— *You're a spy, aren't you?*

Leo shouldn't have taken that drink. Starved suspects were routinely rendered drunk, their tongues loosened. He needed his wits. It was a mistake of the most obvious kind to trust in this man's benevolence. Entering the room, he'd intended to reveal his true identity, detailing his intimate knowledge of the commander's career, supported with the names of his superiors. This allegation, coming from nowhere, caught him flat-footed. The commander cut across his silence.

— *Don't try to think of a lie. I know the truth. You're here to report back on the progress of our reforms. Like your friend.*

Leo's heart rose in his chest.

— *My friend?*

— *While I am committed to change, many in this region are not.*

— *You know about my friend?*

— *They are looking for you, the two officers who arrived last night. They are convinced more than one man has come to spy on them.*

— *What has happened to him?*

— *Your friend? They executed him.*

Leo's grip loosened around the rim of the tin cup but he did not let it fall to the floor. The strength seeped out of his back: his spine turned soft. He leaned forward, his head dropped, staring down at the floor. The commander continued:

— *I fear they will kill us too. Your outburst about the Secret Speech has revealed your identity. They will not allow you to leave. As you saw, it was difficult even getting a moment alone with you.*

Leo shook his head. He and Timur had survived impossible situations. He couldn't be dead. There was some mistake. Leo sat up.

— *He's not dead.*

—*The man I'm referring to arrived on board the* Stary Bolshevik. *He was due to come here as my second in command. That was a cover story. He was sent here to write a report. He admitted as much. He claimed he was here to assess us. So they killed him. They will not be judged. They will never allow it.*

Timur must have invented that story to reach the camp and save him. He should never have asked for Timur's help. He had been so preoccupied with rescuing Zoya he'd only briefly considered the risks to Timur. He'd seen them as small, so convinced was he of his plans and their abilities. He'd broken a loving family in the attempt to piece back together an unhappy one, ruining something wonderful in the pursuit of Zoya's affections. He began to cry as the realization sank in that Timur, his friend, his only friend — a man adored by his wife and sons, decent and loyal, a man whom Leo loved very much — was dead.

When Leo eventually looked up, he saw that Zhores Sinyavksy was crying too. Leo stared in disbelief at the old man's red eyes and tear-glistening, leathery cheeks and wondered how a man who'd built an incomplete railway out of innocent lives could cry at the death of a man he didn't even know, a man whose death he wasn't responsible for. Perhaps he was crying for every death he'd never cried for, every victim who'd passed away in the snow, or the sun, or the mud, while he smoked a cigarette, satisfied that his quota had been achieved. Leo wiped his eyes, remembering Lazar's contempt for them. He was right. Tears were worthless. Leo owed Timur more. If Leo didn't survive, Timur's wife and sons would not even know how he'd died. And Leo would never have the chance to say sorry.

The guards were intent that he should never make it back to Moscow. They were protecting their fiefdom. Leo was a spy, hated by both sides – prisoners and guards alike, alone except for the commander, a man whose mind seemed warped by guilt. He was, at best, an unpredictable ally and no longer in control of the camp. Like wolves, the guards were circling the administration barracks, waiting for him to emerge.

Looking around the room, his mind spinning through ideas, Leo saw the tannoy on the desk. It was connected to speakers set up around the *zona*.

— *You can address the entire camp?*

— *Yes.*

Leo stood up, taking the tin cup and filling it to the brim with the warm amber alcohol. He handed it to the commander:

— *Drink with me.*

— *But—*

— *Drink to the memory of my friend.*

The commander swallowed it in one gulp. Leo filled the cup again.

— *Drink to the memory of all who have died here.*

The commander nodded, finishing the cup. Leo filled it again.

— *And all those innocent deaths across our country.*

The commander tossed back the last of the spirit, wiping his lips. Leo pointed to the speaker.

— *Turn it on.*

In the mess hall, Lazar contemplated Leo's decision to throw himself at the commander's mercy. A recent convert to compassion, Zhores Sinyavksy might protect him. The other prisoners were furious at the prospect of justice being snatched from them. They'd already planned the third torture, the fourth, fifth – each man eagerly anticipating the night on which Leo would suffer as they'd suffered, when they would see in his face the pain they'd experienced and he'd cry out for mercy and they'd have the long-dreamed-of chance to say:

— *No*.

As for Leo's story about his wife – Anisya – it nagged at him. But the *vory* in the barracks had assured him it was impossible that a woman who once sang hymns and cleaned and cooked could rise to lead her own gang. Leo was a liar. This time Lazar would not be fooled.

Hissing static emitted from the tannoy speakers outside. Although it was nothing more than a background noise, their daily routine was so rigid and unchanging that Lazar flinched at this occurrence. Standing up, moving around the crowd of prisoners eating breakfast, he opened the door.

The speakers were set up on tall timber poles, one overhanging each of the prisoner barracks and one in the administration zone, positioned outside the kitchen and the mess hall. They were rarely used. A handful of curious prisoners gathered behind him, including Georgi, his voice, who never left his side. Their eyes fixed on the nearest loudspeaker, battered by the winds, hanging crooked. A wire snaked around the pole reaching the icy ground where it ran to the commander's office. Static hissed again, modulating into the tinny voice of their commander. He sounded uncertain.

— *Special report . . .*

He paused, then began again, louder this time:

— *Special report to the 20th Congress of the Communist Party of the Soviet Union. Closed session. 25th February 1956. By Nikita Sergeyevich Khrushchev, First Secretary, Communist Party of the Soviet Union.*

Lazar descended the steps, walking towards the speaker. The guards had stopped what they were doing. After a moment's confusion they whispered among themselves, evidently uninformed of the commander's intention. A small group broke off, pacing to the administration barracks. Meanwhile the commander continued to read aloud. The more he read, the more agitated the guards became.

— *What took place during the life of Stalin, who practised brutal violence, not only towards everything which opposed him, but also towards that which seemed, to his capricious and despotic character, contrary to his concepts . . .*

Hurrying, the guards climbed the stairs, banging against the door, urgently calling out to the commander, trying to ascertain if he was acting under duress. One shouted out, with simpleminded earnestness:

— *Are you a hostage?*

The door remained shut. It didn't sound to Lazar as if the

commander was reading under duress. His voice was growing into the role.

— *Stalin created the concept Enemy of the People. The term made possible the use of the cruellest repression, violating all norms of Revolutionary legality, against anyone who disagreed with Stalin . . .*

Lazar's head angled upwards towards the speaker, his mouth open in awe, as if a celestial miracle were being performed in the sky.

The entire prison population abandoned their breakfast or carried their bowls with them, gathering around the single speaker, a vast human knot, staring up, hypnotized by the crackling words. These were criticisms of the State. These were criticisms of Stalin. Lazar had never heard anything like them before, not in this form, words that weren't muttered between two lovers, or by two prisoners across bunks. These words were from their leader, words that had been spoken aloud in Congress, transcribed and printed and bound, distributed into the furthest reaches of their country.

— *How is it that a person confesses to crimes that he has not committed? Only in one way: the application of torture, bringing him to a state of unconsciousness, deprivation of his judgement, taking away his human dignity . . .*

The man beside Lazar put an arm around him. The prisoner beside him did the same and soon every prisoner was linked together, arm across shoulder.

Lazar tried not to pay the guards any attention, concentrating on the speech, but he was distracted by their dilemma – they were grappling with the decision of whether to stop the commander from reading, or to stop the prisoners from listening. Deciding it was easier to deal with one man than one thousand, they banged their fists against the door, ordering their commander to cease immediately. Intended to protect against Arctic conditions, the door was made of thick logs. The small windows were fitted with shutters. There was no easy way in. Desperate, one guard fired his machine gun, bullets splintering uselessly up and down the wood. It didn't open the door but it achieved the desired result. The reading stopped.

Lazar felt the silence like a loss. He was not alone. Angry at having the speech cut short, prisoners to the left and right began to stamp their feet, quickly joined by others, by everyone, two thousand legs up and down, beating against the frozen ground:

— *More! More! More!*

The energy was irresistible. Before long his foot was also pounding the ground.

*

Leo and the commander listened to the commotion outside. Unable to risk opening the shutters, for fear of the guards shooting them, they couldn't see what was going on. The vibrations from the stamping travelled through the floorboards. The sound of the chanting travelled through the thick walls.

— *More! More! More!*

Sinyavksy smiled, placing a hand to his chest, seeming to interpret their response as an affirmation of his reformed character.

The mood in the camp was volatile, exactly as Leo desired. He gestured at the pages of the speech that he'd been hastily editing, condensing the document, compressing it to a series of shocking admissions. He handed the commander the next page. Sinyavksy shook his head.

— *No.*

Leo was taken aback.

— *Why stop now?*

— I want to give my own speech. I've been . . . inspired.

— What are you going to say?

Sinyavksy raised the microphone to his mouth, addressing Gulag 57.

— My name is Zhores Sinyavksy. You know me as the commander of this Gulag, where I have worked for many years. Those who arrived recently will think me a good man, fair and just and generous.

Leo doubted that. However, he tried to appear convinced by these declarations. The commander was treating his speech with absolute seriousness.

— Those who have been here longer will not think upon me so kindly. You have just listened to Khrushchev admitting mistakes made by the State, admitting Stalin's acts of cruelty. I wish to follow the example of our leader. I wish to admit my own mistakes.

Hearing the word – *follow* – Leo wondered if the commander was driven by guilt or by a life of unquestioning obedience. Was this redemption or imitation? If the State reverted to terror, could Sinyavksy return to brutality with the same suddenness that he'd embraced leniency?

— I have done things of which I am not proud. It is time I asked for your forgiveness.

Leo realized that the potency of his confession might be even greater than the admissions made by Khrushchev. The prisoners knew this man. They knew the prisoners that he'd killed. The chanting and stamping stopped. They were waiting for his confession.

*

Lazar noticed that even the guards were no longer trying to break down the door, waiting for the commander's next words. After a pause, the tinny voice of Sinyavksy sounded out across the camp:

— Arkhangelsk, my first posting: I was tasked with supervising prisoners working in the forest. They would cut down trees, readying the timber for transportation. I was new to the job. I was nervous. My orders were to collect a fixed amount of timber each month. Nothing else mattered. I had norms just like all of you. After the first week I discovered a prisoner had been cheating in order to fulfil his norm. Had I not caught him, my count would have been short and I would've been accused of sabotage. So you see . . . it was about survival, nothing else. I had no choice. I made an example of him. He was stripped naked, tied to a tree. It was the summer. At sunset his body was black with mosquitoes. By the morning he was unconscious. By the third day he was dead. I ordered his body to remain in the forest as a warning. For twenty years, I didn't think about that man. Recently, I think about him every day. I do not remember his name. I don't know if I ever knew his name. I remember that he was the same age as me at the time. I was twenty-one years old.

Lazar noted how the commander moderated honesty with qualifications.

I had no choice.

With those words thousands died, not with bullets but with perverse logic and careful reasoning. When Lazar returned his attention to the speech, the commander was no longer talking about his career in the forests of Arkhangelsk. He was discussing his promotion to the salt mines of Solikamsk.

— In the salt mines, as an efficiency measure, I ordered men to sleep underground. By not moving the men up and down at the end of each shift, I saved thousands of precious work hours, benefiting our State.

The prisoners shook their heads, imagining the conditions of that underground hell.

— My purpose was to discover new ways of bringing benefit to our State! What could I say? Had I not thought of this, my junior officer might have proposed it and I would've been punished. Did these men need daylight more than the State needed salt? Who had the authority to make that argument? Who dared to speak up for them?

One of the guards, a man Lazar had never seen before, strode towards them, brandishing a knife. They were going to cut the wire and kill the speech. The guard was smiling, pleased with his solution.

— Out of my way.

The foremost prisoner stepped forward, standing on the wire, blocking the guard. A second prisoner joined him, and a third, a fourth, keeping the wire out of reach. Smiling threateningly, as if to say he would remember this for later, the guard moved to another exposed stretch of wire. Responding, the prisoners quickly pushed forward, filling the space, protecting the wire. The knot of prisoners reshaped until there was a dense line of prisoners standing side by side stretching from the timber pole supporting the speaker to the base of the administration barracks. The only way the guard could get to the wire was by crawling under the barracks, something his pride stopped him from doing.

— Get out of my way.

The prisoners didn't move. The guard turned to face the two *vakhta*, the fortified towers overlooking the camp. He waved at the gunners, pointing towards the prisoners before hurrying away.

There was a burst of gunfire. In unison the prisoners dropped to their knees. Lazar look around, expecting to see dead and injured. No one seemed to be hurt. The volley must have been targeted over their heads, hitting the side of the barracks, a warning shot. Slowly everyone stood up. Voices from the back cried out:

— *We need help!*

— *Bring the* feldsher*!*

Out of sight, Lazar couldn't see what was going on. The calls for medical assistance continued. But no one came. The guards did nothing. Soon the cries stopped – there were no more calls for help. Explanations rippled through the crowd. A prisoner had died.

Sensing the mood darken, the guard put away his knife and drew his gun. He fired at the speaker, missing several times, until finally it sparked and crackled, falling silent. The other four speakers in the prisoner zone were still working but they were some distance away: the commander's voice was reduced to an inaudible background sound. Keeping his gun drawn, the guard announced:

— *Back to the barracks! And no one else will die!*

The threat was misjudged.

Picking up the wire from the ground, a prisoner darted forward, wrapping it around the guard's neck, throttling him. The prisoners surrounded the fight. Other guards ran to intervene. A prisoner grabbed the officer's gun, firing at the approaching guards. One man fell, wounded. The others drew their weapons, firing at will.

The prisoners scattered. An understanding flashed through them instantaneously. If the guards regained control, the reprisals would be savage, no matter what speeches were being given in Moscow. At this point, both towers opened fire.

*

The commander was still talking, recounting bloody confession after bloody confession, seemingly oblivious of the gunfire. His mind had snapped: under Stalin his character had been pulled with such extreme force in one direction. Now he was being pulled in the opposite direction. He had no resistance, no idea who he really was, neither a good man nor a bad man but a weak one.

Allowing the commander to carry on, Leo opened the shutter, cautiously looking out. Rioting prisoners were running in every direction. There were bodies on the snow. Calculating the forces on both sides, Leo guessed a ratio of one guard for every forty inmates, a high ratio, in part explaining why the camps were so expensive to run — the forced labour failing to earn back the cost of keeping the convicts fed, housed, transported and enslaved. A central expense was the guards, paid a premium for working in such remote conditions. This was the reason they were killing to cling on to authority. They had no lives to go back to, no families or neighbourhoods that wanted them. No factory-floor community would accept them. Their prosperity depended upon the prisoners. The fight would be equally desperate on both sides.

There was a flash of gunfire from the towers — the window shattered. Leo dropped, glass falling around him, bullets hitting the floorboards. Safe behind the thick log walls, Leo slowly reached up, trying to close the shutters. The wood broke apart in a shower of splinters. The room was exposed. On the desk the tannoy equipment, kicked around by the bullets, was lifted up, spinning in the air before clattering to the floor. Sinyavksy fell back, curling into a ball. Over the noise Leo cried out:

— *Do you have a gun?*

Sinyavksy's eyes flicked to the side. Leo followed them to a wooden crate tucked in the corner, padlocked. He stood up, running towards it only to find the commander running to block him, putting his hands up.

— *No!*

Leo knocked the commander aside, bringing the heavy base of the steel desk lamp crashing down against the lock. With a second blow the lock smashed off and he pulled it free. The commander once again leapt forward, throwing himself over the crate.

— *I beg you . . .*

Leo pulled him off, opening the lid.

Inside there was nothing more than a collection of odds and ends. There were framed photos. They showed the commander standing proudly beside a canal: emaciated prisoners toiled in the background. Leo guessed they were the photos that had originally hung on the office wall. He tossed them aside, rooting through files, certificates, awards and letters congratulating Sinyavksy on meeting a quota – the detritus of his great career. There was a hunting rifle at the bottom. On the handle were notches, twenty-three kills. Certain that these notches didn't refer to wolves or bears, Leo loaded the rifle with the fat, finger-length bullets, moving back to the window.

The two primary towers, the *vakhta*, were strategically crucial, constructed on high wooden stilts. The guards had already pulled up the ladders, making it impossible to scale their positions. Protected behind thick log walls, the top of each tower housed podium-mounted machine guns capable of firing hundreds of rounds a minute, a collective firepower far greater than anything on the ground. Leo had to draw their fire away from the prisoners. He took aim at the guard tower directly ahead. There was little chance his shot would be accurate enough to penetrate the gap in the log walls. He fired twice, shuddering under the massive recoil of the rifle. They stopped firing at the prisoners, redirecting their volley of bullets at him.

Ducking down, crouched against the floor, Leo glanced at Sinyavksy. He was in the corner, reading the remaining pages of the Secret Speech, calmly, as if nothing was amiss while his office was torn apart by gunfire. He looked up at Leo, reading:

— *Let my cry of horror reach your ears: do not remain deaf, take me under your protection; please, help remove the nightmare of interrogations and show that this is all a mistake!*

Sinyavksy stood up.

— *This is all a terrible mistake! This should never have happened!*

Leo shouted at him:

— *Get down!*

A bullet hit the commander in the shoulder. Unable to watch him die, Leo jumped up, knocking the commander flat. Landing on his injured knees, he almost passed out with the pain. Sinyavksy whispered:

— *That speech has saved my life.*

Leo smelt smoke. He rolled onto his back, taking the pressure off his knees. He stood up awkwardly, moving to the window. There was no more heavy gunfire. Through the smashed window he cautiously surveyed the *zona* and saw the source of the smoke. Directly underneath the base of the cabin was a fire, flames climbing the structure. Barrels of fuel had been rolled underneath and set alight, the cabin roasted like meat on a skewer. For the men inside there was no escape. Unable to climb down the ladder, the guards tried to squeeze out through the gap in the log walls. The gap was too narrow: one man was stuck, wedged in, unable to go forwards or back as the fire took hold. He began to scream.

The second tower was trying to protect itself from a similar fate: shooting at the prisoners carrying materials to build a fire. But there were too many convicts, coming from too many sides. Once underneath, there was nothing the guards in the tower could do except wait. A new fire was started. Both towers had been defeated. The balance of power had shifted. The prisoners now had control of the camp.

An axe cracked into the commander's door, a second blow, a third, the steel end jutting through the timber. Before they had a chance to break through, Leo put the rifle down and unlocked the door, stepping back, arms up, indicating surrender. A small force of prisoners stormed the room, brandishing knives and guns and steel bars. The man in charge regarded his captives.

— *Bring them outside.*

The prisoners grabbed Leo by his arms, hurrying him down the steps, herding him together with the guards that had been captured — their roles reversed. Battered and bloody, they sat on the snow watching the *vakhta* burn. Columns of smoke rose up, blocking out a wide streak of sky, announcing their revolution to the entire region.

Scrunching his face in concentration, Malysh studied the handwritten list. He'd been told it was composed of the names of the men and women Fraera planned to murder. Since he was unable to read, the list appeared to his eye as nothing more than a collection of unintelligible symbols. Until recently it had never troubled him that he couldn't read or write, able only to recognize the letters of his *klikukha*. For this reason, during his initiation he'd been savvy enough to insist that none of his tattoos contain words for fear that his fellow *vory* might exploit his ignorance and print something insulting. Though it was forbidden under penalty of death to create a false tattoo, an outright lie, that rule might not prevent them making a joke at his expense, calling him Little Prick, instead of Little One.

He was smart and he didn't need a certificate or a diploma to prove it. He didn't need to read or write. What good were those skills to him? He didn't expect a teacher to pick a lock or throw a knife. Why should anyone expect a thief to read? While that reasoning still made sense to him, something had changed. Embarrassment was inside him and it had begun to grow since the moment Zoya had taken hold of his hand.

She couldn't know that he was illiterate. Maybe she presumed the worst, seeing him as little more than a *chiffr*-addicted thug. He didn't care. She should be more worried about whether he was going to slit her throat than passing judgement on him. He was winding himself up. Breathing deeply, he returned his attention to the names in front of him – the retired Chekists. He knew from listening to Fraera that the list contained names, addresses and a description of each individual's crimes – whether they were an investigator, interrogator or an informer. Running a dirty thumbnail over each line he could identify which column contained their names: that was the column with the fewest words. The column with numbers in it: that was their address. And by deduction the final column, which contained the most words, must be the description of their crimes. Who was he trying to fool? This wasn't reading. This wasn't even close. He threw the list down, pacing the sewer tunnel. It was her fault – that girl, she was the reason that he felt like this. He wished he'd never seen her.

Unsure what he was going to do, he ran along the tunnel, entering their stinking lair. Fraera claimed they were living in the remains of an ancient library, the lost library of Ivan the Terrible which once held a priceless collection of Byzantine and Hebrew scrolls. Illiterate and hiding in a library – the irony had never occurred to him before, not until Zoya arrived. Ancient library or not, he considered their base little more than a network of ugly, damp stone chambers. Avoiding the others, who were drinking as always, he made his way silently towards Zoya's cell.

He retrieved the footstool and stood on it, looking through the bars. Zoya was asleep in the corner, curled up on her mattress. There was a lantern hanging from the ceiling – out of reach, always lit so that she was under constant scrutiny. Immediately Malysh's anger changed. His eyes drifted over her body, watching her sleep, the slow rhythm of her chest rising and falling. Though he was a *vory* he was also a virgin. He'd murdered but he'd never had sex, a source of great amusement to the others. They teased him, saying if he didn't use his prick soon it would get infected and fall off and he'd be nothing more than a girl. After his initiation they'd taken him to a prostitute, pushing him into the room and closing the door, ordering him to *grow up*. The woman had been sitting on the bed, bored, naked, goosebumps on her arms and legs. She'd been smoking a cigarette – a long stub of ash arching off the end – and all Malysh could think about was whether the hot ash was going to fall on her breasts. She'd tapped it onto the floor and asked what he was waiting for, nodding at his crotch. He'd fumbled at his belt, taking it off and then putting it back on again, telling her he didn't want to have sex, she could keep the money just so long as she said nothing to the others. She'd shrugged, told him to sit down, they'd wait five minutes and then he could go, no one would believe he could last longer than that anyway. They'd waited five minutes. He'd sat on the bed and then he'd left. As he'd walked down the corridor, preparing his lie, she'd called out to the others that they'd been right. He'd chickened out. The *vory* had cackled like witches. Even Fraera had seemed disappointed in him.

Hearing someone behind him, Malysh spun round, drawing his knife. His hand was caught, fingers gripped, the knife taken from him. Closing the blade and handing him the knife back, Fraera leaned over his shoulder, looking into the cell.

— *Beautiful, isn't she?*

Malysh didn't reply. Fraera looked down at him.

— *It's rare that anyone is able to sneak up on you, Malysh.*

— *I was checking on the prisoner.*

— *Checking?*

He blushed. Fraera put her arm around Malysh, adding:

— *I want her to accompany you on your next job.*

Malysh looked up at Fraera.

— *The prisoner?*

— *Use her name.*

— *Zoya.*

— *She has more reason than most to hate* Chekists. *They murdered her parents.*

— *She can't fight. She'd be useless. She's just a girl.*

— *I was just a girl, once.*

— *You're different.*

— *So is she.*

— *She might try to run away. She'd shout for help.*

— *Why don't you ask her? She's listening.*

There was a silence. Fraera called into the cell:

— *I know you're awake.*

Zoya sat up, turning to face them. She spoke out:

— *I didn't claim that I wasn't.*

— *You are brave. I have a proposition for a brave young girl. Do you want to accompany Malysh on his next assignment?*

Zoya stared at him.

— *To do what?*

Fraera answered:

— *To murder a Chekist.*

SAME DAY

The two *vakhta* had collapsed into smouldering heaps, the bulk of
the timber burnt through, reduced to red embers and occasional
flickering flames. Wisps of smoke trailed the night sky, carrying up
the ashes of at least eight guards: their final act on earth to block
out a streak of stars before being scattered across the plateau.
Fallen Gulag guards, those killed outside the firetrap of the *vakhta*,
lay where they'd died, dotted across the camp. One body hung out
of a window. The ferocity with which he'd been killed suggested
that he'd been particularly vicious in his duties – chased by angry
prisoners, eventually caught, beaten and stabbed as he'd desperately tried to clamber out. His body had been left draped over the
windowsill, the flag of their newly formed empire.

The surviving guards and Gulag personnel, some fifty in total,
had been gathered in the centre of the administration zone. Most
were injured. Without blankets or medical care, huddled on the
snow, their discomfort was met with indifference, a lesson well
learnt by the prisoners. In evaluation of Leo's ambiguous status
he'd been classified as a guard rather than a prisoner, forced to sit,

shaking with cold, observing the old power structures collapse and new ones form.

As far as he could ascertain there were three unelected leaders, men whose authority had been established within the microcosm of their barracks. Each man had his own band of followers, distinctly defined. Lazar was one leader. Those who followed him were older prisoners, the arrested intellectuals, craftsmen — the chess players. The second leader was a younger man: athletic, handsome, perhaps a former factory worker — the perfect Soviet, and yet imprisoned all the same. His followers were younger, men of action. The third leader was a *vory*. He was perhaps forty, with thin eyes and jagged teeth, a shark's smile. He'd taken possession of the commander's coat. Too long for him, it dragged across the snow. His followers were the other *vory*: thieves and murderers. Three groups, each represented by their leader, each with competing points of view. The clashes of opinion were immediate. Lazar, voiced by red-haired Georgi, counselled caution and order.

— *We must establish lookouts. We must take up arms along the perimeter.*

After many years of practice Georgi was able to speak at the same time as listening to Lazar.

— *Furthermore, we must protect and ration our food supplies. We cannot run amuck.*

The square-jawed worker, clipped from a reel of a propaganda movie, disagreed.

— *We are entitled to as much food as we can get our hands on and any drink we can find as compensation for lost wages, as a reward for winning our freedom!*

The reindeer-coat *vory* made only one demand:

— *After a lifetime of rules, disobedience must be tolerated.*

There was a fourth group of prisoners, or rather a non-group, individuals who followed no leader, intoxicated on liberty, some running like wild horses, bolting from barrack to barrack, exploring, whooping at unidentifiable pleasures, either turned mad by the violence, or mad all along and able to express it at last. Some were asleep in the guards' comfortable beds: freedom being the ability to close their eyes when they were tired. Others were doped up on morphine, or drunk on their former captors' vodka. Laughing, these men cut strips out of the wire fences, turning the hated barbed wire into ornamental trinkets with which they decorated the guards who once commanded them, pressing barbed-wire crowns onto their heads, mockingly referring to them as the sons of God and calling out:

— *Crucify the fuckers!*

Witnessing the anarchy orbiting them, Lazar pressed his argument, whispering to Georgi, who repeated:

— *We must protect supplies as a matter of urgency. A starving man will eat himself to death. We must stop cutting the wire. It is protection from the forces that will inevitably arrive. We cannot counsel absolute freedom. We will not survive.*

Judging from the reindeer-coat *vory*'s muted reaction, much of the looting had already been done. The most precious resources were already in his group's hands.

The square-jawed worker, whose name Leo didn't know, agreed to take some of the steps proposed, practical measures, as long as they dealt with the pressing matter of punishments for the captured guards.

— *My men must have justice! They have waited years! They have suffered! They cannot wait a moment longer!*

He spoke in slogans, every sentence ending in an exclamation mark. Though Lazar was reluctant to postpone the practical measures, he compromised in order to win support. The guards were to be placed on trial. Leo was to be placed on trial.

*

One of Lazar's followers had once been a lawyer, in his former life, as he referred to it, and took a prominent role in setting up the tribunal by which Leo and the others were to be judged. He devised his system with relish. After years of submissive grovelling, the lawyer delighted in returning to a tone of authority and expertise, a tone that he considered naturally his.

— *We agree that only the guards will be tried. The medical staff and the former prisoners who now work for the Gulag administration are exempt.*

This proposal was agreed. The lawyer continued:

— *The steps to the commander's office will serve as the court's stage. The guard will be led to the bottom step. We, the free men, will call out examples of their brutality. If an incident is considered valid the guard will take a step up. If the guard reaches the top he will be executed. If he does not reach the top, even if he reaches the penultimate step and no more crimes can be found against him, the guard will be allowed to descend the stairs and sit down.*

Leo counted the steps. There were thirteen in total. Since they started on the bottom step that meant twelve crimes to reach the top: twelve to die, eleven or less to live.

Dropping his voice, striking a note of deliberate gravitas, the lawyer called out:

— *Commander Zhores Sinyavksy.*

Lead to the first step, Sinyavksy faced his court. His shoulder had been crudely bandaged, the bleeding stopped in order to keep him alive long enough to face justice. His arm hung uselessly.

Despite this, he was smiling like a child in a school play, searching for a friendly face among the gathered prisoners. There was no single representative for the defence or the prosecution: both sides were to be debated by the assembled prisoners. Judgement was collective.

Almost immediately a chorus of voices called out. There were insults, examples of his crimes, overlapping, unintelligible. The lawyer raised his arms, calling for silence:

— *One at a time! You raise your hand, I will point and then you will speak. Everyone will have a say.*

He pointed at a prisoner, an older man. The prisoner's hand remained raised. The lawyer remarked:

— *You can lower your hand. You're free to speak.*

— *My hand is the proof of his crime.*

Two fingers were cut off at the knuckle, blackened stumps.

— *Frostbite. No gloves. Minus fifty degrees: so cold that when you spit it turns to ice before it hits the ground. He still sent us out, in conditions not suitable for spit! He sent us out! Day after day after day! Two fingers, two steps!*

Everyone cheered in agreement. The lawyer straightened his grey prison-issue cotton coat as if it were a formal gown.

— *It is not about the number of fingers you lost. You cite inhumane work conditions. The crime has been agreed. But that is one example and therefore one step.*

A voice from the crowd:

— *I lost a toe! Why doesn't my toe count for a step?*

There were more than enough deformed and blackened fingers and toes to force the commander to the top. The lawyer was losing control, unable to scramble enough rules into place to sedate the animated crowd.

Cutting across the debate, the commander called out:

— *You are right! Your injury is a crime. Each of the injuries you have suffered is a crime.*

The commander took another step up. The interjections faded, the arguments silenced as they listened.

— *The truth is that I have committed more crimes than there are steps. Were there steps up to the mountaintop, I would have to climb them all.*

Aggrieved that his system had been bypassed by this confession, the lawyer responded:

— *You accept that you deserve to die?*

The commander answered indirectly.

— *If you can take a step up, can you not also take a step down? If you can do wrong can you not also do good? Can I not try to put right the wrongs that I have done?*

He pointed at the prisoner who'd lost his toe.

— *You lost your toe to frostbite and for that I have taken a step up. But last year you wanted to send your wages to your family. When I told you that because our system has not been fair you hadn't earned as much as they needed, didn't I take from my own salary to make up the difference? Didn't I personally ensure your wife received the money in time?*

The prisoner glanced around, saying nothing. The lawyer asked:

— *Is it true?*

The prisoner nodded reluctantly.

— *It is true.*

The commander took a step down.

— *For that act, can I not take a step down? I accept that I have not yet done enough good to offset my wrongs. So why not allow me to live? Allow me to spend the rest of my life trying to make amends? Is that not better than dying?*

— *What about the people you killed?*

— *What about the people I saved? Since Stalin's death, the mortality rate in this camp is the lowest in Kolyma. That is the result of my changes. I increased food rations. I have given you longer rest periods and shorter working days. I have improved medical care. The sick no longer die! The sick recover. You know this to be true! The reason you were able to overpower the guards is because you are better fed, better rested and stronger than you have ever been before! I am the reason this uprising is even possible!*

The lawyer stepped up to the commander, flustered that his system was in disarray.

— *We said nothing about being able to take a step down.*

The lawyer turned to the triptych of convict leaders.

— *Do we wish to change the system?*

The square-jawed leader turned to his comrades.

— *The commander asks for a second chance. Do we grant it?*

It began as a murmur, the answer growing louder and louder as more joined in.

— *No second chance! No second chance! No second chance!*

The commander's face dropped. He genuinely believed he'd done enough to be spared. The lawyer turned to the condemned man. Clearly they hadn't thought the process through. No one had been designated the role as executioner. The commander took from his pocket one of the small dried purple flowers, clutching it in his fist. He climbed to the top of the stairs, staring up at the night sky. The lawyer spoke, his voice quivering under the pressure.

— *We offer a collective judgement. We must perform a collective punishment.*

Guns were drawn. The lawyer stepped clear. The commander cried out:

— One last thing . . .

Handguns, rifles and bursts from a machine gun – the commander fell back, as if flicked over by a giant finger. Villainous in life, in the face of death he had achieved a kind of dignity. The prisoners resented him for it. They would allow him no more words.

The mood in the makeshift court turned from excitement to solemnity. Clearing his throat, the lawyer asked:

— What shall we do with the body?

Someone said:

— Leave it there, for the next one to see.

It was agreed. The body would be left.

— Who is next?

Leo tensed. Georgi declared:

— Leo Stepanovich Demidov.

The lawyer peered out over the guards.

— Who is this? Who is Leo?

Leo didn't move. The lawyer called out:

— Stand up or you will forfeit your trial and we will execute you immediately!

Slowly, not entirely sure that his legs wouldn't give way, Leo stood up. The lawyer ushered him to the bottom step, where he turned to face his court. The lawyer asked:

— Are you a guard?

— No.

— What are you?

— I am a member of the Moscow militia. I was sent here undercover.

Georgi called out:

— He's a Chekist!

The crowd, his jury and judge, burst into a flurry of anger. Leo glanced at his accuser. Georgi was acting independently. Lazar was reading a sheet of paper, a list of Leo's crimes, perhaps. The lawyer asked:

— *Is this true? Are you a Chekist?*

— *In the past, I was a member of the MGB.*

The lawyer called out:

— *Examples of his crimes!*

Georgi replied:

— *He denounced Lazar!*

The prisoners jeered. Leo took a step up. Georgi continued:

— *He beat Lazar! Smashed his jaw!*

Leo was guided up the next step.

— *He arrested Lazar's wife!*

Leo was now standing on the fourth step.

— *He arrested members of Lazar's congregation!*

Standing on the fifth step, Georgi had run out of things to say. No one else in the compound knew Leo. No one else could name his crimes. The lawyer declared:

— *We need more examples! Seven more!*

Frustrated, Georgi called out:

— *He's a Chekist!*

The lawyer shook his head.

— *That is not an example.*

According to the rules of their system, no one knew him well enough to convict him, no one that is, except Leo himself. The prisoners were dissatisfied. They were rightly certain that, as a Chekist, there must be many more examples unknown to them. Leo sensed that the system would not protect him. Had he not witnessed the commander's execution, he might have climbed to the top and admitted his wrongdoings. But he had no speech more eloquent than the commander's. His life depended upon the rules of their system. They would need seven more examples. They did not have them.

Georgi, refusing to give up, cried out:

— *How many years were you a Chekist?*

After serving in the army, Leo had been recruited into the secret police. He had been a Chekist for five years.

— *Five years.*

Addressing the assembled convicts, Georgi asked:

— *Is it not easy to believe that he wronged at least two people each year? Is that so hard to believe of a Chekist?*

The crowd agreed: two steps for each year. Leo turned to the lawyer, hoping he would overrule this amendment. The lawyer shrugged, the suggestion became law. He gestured Leo to the top. He had been sentenced to death.

Unable to comprehend that this was the end, Leo didn't move. A voice cried out:

— *To the top or we'll shoot you where you stand!*

Light-headed, Leo climbed to the top, standing over the commander's bullet-ridden body, an array of guns pointed at him.

A voice, the man who hated him, Georgi, cried out:

— *Wait!*

Leo watched as Lazar spoke into Georgi's ear. Unusually, Georgi wasn't translating simultaneously. When Lazar had finished Georgi looked at him, questioning. Lazar indicated that he repeat his words. Georgi turned to Leo, asking:

— *My wife is alive?*

Georgi took the paper from Lazar's hand, carrying it to Leo and offering it to him. Leo crouched down, recognizing the letter written by Fraera, proof that she was alive and containing information only she could've known. Timur had been carrying it. Before he'd been killed, the guards must have stripped him of all his belongings.

— *It was found in the pocket of a guard. You were not lying.*

— *No.*

— *She is alive?*

— *Yes.*

Lazar indicated that Georgi return, whispering into his ear. With reluctant obedience Georgi announced:

— *I request that he be spared.*

MOSCOW

Like two mongrel cats, Zoya and Malysh sat side by side on the roof of Apartment Block 424. Zoya remained close to Malysh, keen to reassure him that she didn't want to escape. After the exertion of travelling several kilometres through sewer systems, climbing ladders, sidestepping slime-thick walls, both of them were damp with sweat and it was pleasant on the rooftop, fanned by a cool night breeze. Zoya felt invigorated. Partly that was due to the exercise after many sedentary days and nights. Mostly it was because she was with him. This felt like the childhood stolen from her – mischievous adventure with a kindred spirit.

Zoya glanced at the photo pinched between Malysh's fingers.

— *What is her name?*

— *Marina Niurina.*

Zoya took the photo from him. Niurina was a woman in her thirties, stern and prim. She was wearing a uniform. Zoya returned the photo.

— *You're going to kill her?*

Malysh gave a small nod, as if someone had asked him if they could have a cigarette. Zoya wasn't sure whether she believed him or not. She'd seen him attack the *vory* who'd tried to rape her. He was skilled with a knife. Reticent and moody, he didn't seem like someone who made idle brags.

— *Why?*

— *She's a Chekist.*

— *What did she do?*

Malysh looked at her quizzically, not understanding. Zoya expanded the question.

— *Did she arrest people? Did she interrogate them?*

— *I don't know.*

— *You're going to kill her but you don't know what she did?*

— *I told you. She's a Chekist.*

Zoya wondered how much he knew about the secret police. She remarked, cautiously:

— *You don't know much about them. Do you, the secret police? Not really, I mean?*

— *I know what they did.*

Malysh thought about this for a while before adding:

— *They arrested people.*

— *Don't you need to know a little more about a person before you kill them?*

— *Fraera has given me orders. I don't need any other reason.*

— *That's what they would say, the Chekists, about the things they did: that they were just following orders.*

Malysh became irritated.

— *Fraera has said you can help. So you can help. She didn't say anything about asking a lot of stupid questions. I can take you back to your cell if that's what you want.*

— *Don't get angry. I would've asked why, that's all. Why are we killing this woman?*

Malysh folded the photo in half and put it back in his pocket.

Zoya had pushed him too far. She'd been excited and she'd stepped over the line, her brashness getting the better of her. She remained silent, hoping she hadn't ruined everything. Expecting peevish irritation, she was surprised when Malysh spoke in an almost apologetic tone.

— *Her crimes were written down in a list. I didn't want to ask anyone to read it aloud.*

— *You can't read?*

Scrutinizing her reaction, he shook his head. She was careful to keep her face blank, alert to his insecurity.

— *Didn't you go to school?*

— *No.*

— *What happened to your parents?*

— *They died. I grew up in train terminals, mostly, until Fraera came along.*

Malysh asked:

— *You think it's bad that I can't read?*

— *You've never had the opportunity to learn.*

— *I'm not proud of it.*

— *I know.*

— *I'd like to read, and write too. I'm going to learn, someday.*

— *You'll learn quickly, I'm sure.*

They sat in silence for the next hour or so, watching as the lights in the surrounding buildings went dark, one by one, the occupants turning in for bed. Malysh stood up, stretching, a nocturnal creature that only stirred when everyone else slept. Out of the pockets of his baggy trousers he took a reel of stiff wire, unwinding it. At the end of the wire he fastened a shard of mirror, wrapping the wire round and round until it was secure. He carefully tilted the mirror so that it was at a forty-five-degree angle. Walking to the edge of the building, he lay on his stomach and lowered the wire until the mirror was in line with the bedroom window. Zoya joined him, lying by his side and glancing down. The curtain was closed but there was a small gap. In the dark room he could make out a figure in bed. Malysh pulled the wire up, taking the mirror off the end, winding the wire up and putting the items back in his pocket.

— *We enter the other side.*

Zoya nodded. He paused, muttering:

— *You can stay here.*

— *On my own?*

— *I trust you not to run away.*

— *Malysh, I hate Chekists as much as Fraera. I'm with you.*

Taking off their shoes, leaving them neatly side by side on the roof, they scaled down the brickwork, holding on to the drainpipe for support. It was a short descent: a metre or so. Malysh reached the windowsill as easily as if there'd been a ladder. Zoya followed tentatively, trying not to look down. They were on the sixth floor and a fall would be fatal. Flicking out his knife, Malysh lifted the catch, opened the window and entered the apartment. Wary of Zoya making a noise, he turned around, offering his hand. She waved it aside, gingerly lowering herself to the floorboards.

They'd broken into the living room, a large room. Zoya whispered in Malysh's ear:

— *Does she live alone?*

He nodded, curtly, not appreciating the question – any question. He wanted silence. The size of the apartment was remarkable. By adding up the square metres of empty floor space, Zoya could guess the scale of this woman's crimes.

Up ahead the bedroom door was closed. Malysh reached out, taking hold of the handle. Before he opened the door, he indicated that Zoya stay behind, out of sight, in the living room. Although she wanted to follow, he wasn't going to allow her any further. Zoya nodded, pulling back, waiting while Malysh opened the door.

*

Malysh stepped into the dark room. Marina Niurina was in bed, lying on her side. Readying his knife, stepping up to her, he paused, as though balancing on the brink of a cliff. The woman in bed was much older than the woman in the photograph – she had grey hair, a wrinkled face, she was at least sixty years old. He hesitated, wondering if he had the wrong address. No, the address was correct. Perhaps the photo had been taken many years ago. He leaned closer, taking out the folded photo to compare. The old lady's face was in shadow. He just couldn't be sure. Sleep made everyone seem innocent.

Suddenly Niurina opened her eyes and lifted her arm from under the covers. She was holding a gun, levelling it between Malysh's eyes. Her legs swung out of bed, revealing a floral nightgown.

— *Step back.*

Malysh obeyed, arms raised, knife in one hand, photo in the other, calculating whether he was fast enough to disarm her. She guessed his thoughts, cocking the gun and firing at the knife in his hand, taking off the tip of his finger. He cried out, clutching the injury as the knife clattered across the floor. Niurina said:

— *That shot will bring up the guards. I'm not going to kill you. I'm going to let them torture you. I might even join in myself. I'm going to find out where your companions are. Then we're going to kill them too. Did you really think we were going to roll over and let you and your mob kill us one by one?*

Malysh pulled back. She stood up, off the bed.

— *If you suppose that by running away you'll have an easy death, a bullet in the back, think again. I'll shoot your foot off. In fact, better to shoot your foot off now, just to be sure.*

*

Her heart thumping, barely able to breathe, Zoya had to act quickly, not stand in the middle of the room, dumbstruck like a stupid child. The old woman couldn't possibly have seen her. Looking around, there was nowhere to hide except under the writing desk. Wounded, Malysh was retreating from the bedroom towards her, his hand dripping blood. He was careful not to look at her, not to give her away. She was his only chance. The woman was almost at the door. Zoya darted under the desk.

From her hiding place Zoya caught sight of the woman for the first time. She was much older than the photograph but it was the same woman. She was smiling, or sneering, enjoying the power of her gun, following Malysh closely. If Zoya did nothing, if she remained under the desk, the guards would come, Malysh would be arrested — she would be saved, reunited with Elena and Raisa, reunited with Leo. If she did nothing, her life would return to normal.

Zoya leapt up, crying out, charging for the gun. Taken by surprise, Marina Niurina turned the gun in her direction. Zoya grabbed the woman's wrist, sinking her teeth as far in as they would go. A shot was fired, deafeningly loud beside her ear, the bullet smashing into the wall — Zoya felt the vibrations of the recoil through her teeth. Using her free hand, the woman struck Zoya and struck her again, knocking her to the floor.

Helpless, Zoya looked up as the woman aimed the gun at her. Before she could fire, Malysh scampered up her back, sinking his fingers into her eyes. She screamed, dropping the gun, scratching

279

at his hands only causing him to press harder. Malysh looked down at Zoya:

— *The door!*

With the woman screaming, spinning round and round, Zoya ran to the front door, locking it at the same time as the guards thumped up the stairs. When Zoya turned, Niurina dropped to her hands and knees, Malysh still riding her back. He pulled his fingers free, leaving a bloody mess where her eyes had been. Malysh picked up the gun, gesturing for Zoya to follow him: running to the window.

Behind them the guards kicked at the door. Malysh fired through the wood, halting their progress. With the chamber empty, he dropped the gun, following Zoya out onto the window ledge. Using a spread of machine-gun fire, the guards replied in kind, bullets hitting all sides of the living room. Malysh and Zoya began climbing the outside wall. Zoya reached the roof first, pulling herself up. She heard the door to the living room being smashed down, the guards exclaiming at the bloody scene before them.

Zoya leaned down, helping Malysh up. With both of them on top of the roof, she grabbed her shoes, about to run off. Malysh caught hold of her wrist.

— *Wait!*

Hearing the guards at the window below, Malysh picked a slate from the roof, readying himself. A guard's hand grabbed the ledge. As the guard lifted himself up, Malysh smashed the slate into his face. The guard let go, falling to the street. Malysh cried out:

— *Run!*

They ran across the roof, jumping the gap to the adjacent building. Looking down, they saw swarms of officers in the street. Malysh remarked:

— It was a trap. They were watching the apartment.

They'd expected Niurina to be a target.

With their original escape route blocked, they were forced to enter the new apartment block, climbing into a bedroom. Malysh called out:

— Fire!

In the overcrowded buildings, ancient timber structures, with faulty electrics, fire was a constant fear. Grabbing Zoya's hand he ran out into the corridor, both of them now shouting:

— Fire!

Even without smoke, the corridor was crowded within seconds. Panic quickly spread through the building, feeding off itself. On the stairs Zoya and Malysh dropped to their hands and knees, crawling between people's legs.

Outside, on the street, inhabitants surged out of the building, merging with the KGB and the militia. Zoya grabbed hold of a man's arm, pretending to be distraught. Malysh did the same and the man, sympathetic, guided the two of them past the officials who presumed them to be a family. As soon as they were free they let go of the man's arm, slipping off.

Reaching the nearest manhole, they pulled back the steel cover, climbing down into the sewers. At the bottom of the ladder Zoya ripped off a portion of her shirt, wrapping it around Malysh's bleeding finger, round and round, until it became as thick as sausage. Catching their breath, both of them began to laugh.

KOLYMA
GULAG 57

The morning light was as clear and sharp as Leo had ever seen — a perfect blue sky and white plateau. Standing on the roof of the administration barracks, he raised the burnt, twisted remains of the binoculars to his eyes. Salvaged from the fire, only one cracked lens was usable. Searching the horizon like a pirate in the bows of his ship, Leo saw movement at the far end of the plateau. There were trucks, tanks and tents — a temporary military encampment. Alerted by yesterday's flaming towers, beacons of dissent, overnight the regional administration had established a rival base for its counter-operations. There were at least five hundred soldiers. Though the prisoners were not outnumbered they were vastly out-gunned, having only collected together two or three heavy machine guns, several clips of ammunition and an assortment of rifles and handguns. Against long-range weaponry, Gulag 57 was hopelessly exposed while the wire fence would offer no protection against advancing armour. Completing his bleak assessment, Leo lowered the binoculars, handing them back to Lazar.

A cluster of prisoners had gathered on the roof. Since the destruction of the towers, it had become one of the highest vantage points in the camp. Aside from Lazar and Georgi there were the two other leaders and their closest supporters: ten men in all. The *very* leader asked Leo:

— *You're one of them. What will they do? Will they negotiate?*

— *Yes, but you can trust nothing they say.*

The younger convict leader stepped forward.

— *What about the speech? We are not under Stalin's rule any more. Our country has changed. We can make our case. We were being treated unfairly. Many of our convictions should be reviewed. We should be released!*

— *The speech might force them to negotiate in earnest. However, we are a long way from Moscow. The Kolyma administration may have decided to deal with this insurrection in secret, to prevent moderate Moscow influences becoming involved.*

— *They want to kill us?*

— *This uprising is a threat to their way of life.*

On the ground, a prisoner shouted:

— *They're calling!*

The prisoners hurried to the ladder, bottle-necking in their haste to clamber down. Leo was last to descend, unable to hurry since bending his legs caused a sharp pain in both knees, the damaged skin stretching. By the time he reached the bottom of the ladder, he was sweating, short of breath. The others were already by the radio.

A radio transceiver was the sole means of communication between the various camps and the administrative headquarters in Magadan. One of the prisoners with some rudimentary knowledge of the equipment had taken charge. He was wearing earphones and repeated the words he could hear:

— Regional Director Abel Prezent . . . He wants to speak to whoever is in charge.

Without discussion the young leader took the microphone, launching into a rhetorical outburst.

— Gulag 57 is in the hands of the prisoners! We have risen up against the guards! They beat us and killed at their whim! No more . . .

Leo said:

— Mention that the guards are alive.

The man waved Leo aside, swollen by his own importance.

— We embrace our leader Khrushchev's speech. In his name, we want every prisoner's sentence reviewed. We want those who should be free, granted freedom. We want those who have done wrong, treated humanely. We demand this in the name of our Revolutionary forefathers. That glorious cause has been corrupted by your crimes. We are the true heirs of the Revolution! We demand you apologize! And send us food, good food, not convict gruel!

Unable to conceal his disbelief, Leo shook his head.

— If you want to get everyone killed, ask for caviar and prostitutes. If you want to live, tell them the guards are alive.

The man added, peevishly:

— I should tell you that the guards are alive. We are holding them in humane conditions, treating them far better than they treated us. They will remain alive as long as you do not attack us. If you attack, we have taken precautions to ensure every last guard will die!

The voice on the radio crackled in reply, words that the man repeated:

— He requests proof of life. Once that is given he will listen to our demands.

Leo moved close to Lazar, petitioning him as the voice of reason.

— *The injured guards should be sent over. Without medical attention they will die.*

The *vory* leader, annoyed at being sidelined, interjected:

— *We shouldn't give them anything. It is a sign of weakness.*

Leo countered:

— *When those guards die of their injuries they will be worthless to you. This way you gain some value from them.*

The *vory* sneered:

— *And no doubt you want to be included in the truck that carries them out?*

He'd guessed Leo's intention exactly. Leo nodded.

Lazar whispered in Georgi's ear, words that he announced with his own note of surprise:

— *And I want to go with him.*

Everyone turned to Lazar. He continued, whispering to Georgi:

— *Before I die I would like to see my wife and son. Leo took them from me. He is the only person who can reunite us.*

*

The freight truck was loaded with the most severely injured guards, six in total, none of whom would survive another twenty-four hours without medical attention. Lifted on planks, improvised stretchers, Leo assisted the transfer of the final guard from the barracks. Laying him down in the back of the truck, they were ready to go.

About to leave, Leo caught a glimpse of the guard's watch. It was cheap, gold plated, unremarkable except for the fact that it was Timur's. There was no doubt: he'd seen that watch countless times. He'd listened to Timur's story of how his father had passed it off as a family heirloom despite it being worthless. Crouching down, Leo ran his fingertip across the cracked glass. He looked at the injured guard. The man's eyes were nervous. He understood its significance. Leo asked:

— *You took this from my friend?*

The guard said nothing.

— *This belonged to my friend.*

Leo felt anger rising through his body.

— *This was his watch.*

The guard began to shake. Leo tapped the watch, commenting:

— *I'm going to have to take it back.*

Leo tried to unclip the worthless watch. As he did, he lifted his leg, pressing his knee against the man's injured, bloody chest, pushing down hard:

— *You see . . . this is a family heirloom . . . it now belongs to Timur's wife . . . and his sons . . . his two sons . . . two wonderful sons . . . two wonderful boys . . . It belongs to them because you murdered their father . . . you murdered my friend . . .*

The guard began to bleed from his mouth and nose, his arms feebly patting Leo's leg, trying to push it away. Leo kept his knee steady, maintaining pressure on the injured torso. The pain from his bruised knee caused his eyes to water. They weren't tears for Timur. This was hatred, revenge, the force of which made him push down harder and harder. Leo's trousers were soaked with the guard's blood.

The watchstrap unclipped, coming free from the guard's limp wrist. Leo put it in his pocket. The remaining five men in the back of the truck were looking at him, terrified. He walked past them, calling out to the prisoners on the ground:

— *One of these guards is dead. We have space for another.*

While they offloaded the body, an event which none of the prisoners questioned, Leo examined the watch. As the rage began to seep away, he felt weak, not out of regret or shame, but tiredness as the most powerful of stimulants – revenge – flushed out of his system. That depth of anger must be how Fraera felt about him.

Leo peered at the injured guard walking to the truck, the replacement for the one he'd just killed. His arm was wrapped in bloody bandages. Something was wrong. The man was nervous. Perhaps he'd also been involved in Timur's murder. Leo reached out, stopping him, taking hold of the bandages and pulling them back, revealing a long, superficial cut stretching from his elbow to his hand, self-inflicted. The same was true for the injuries to his head. The man whispered:

— *Please . . .*

If caught he'd be shot. If the prisoners thought the guards were exploiting their kindness, a kindness they'd never been shown, the entire operation would be at risk. After the execution of the other guard, Leo hesitated only briefly before allowing him into the back of the truck.

Lazar, speaking through Georgi, was addressing the other prisoners, explaining to his followers the reasons for wanting to leave:

— *I do not expect to live much longer. I am too weak to fight. I thank you for letting me go home.*

The young leader responded:

— *Lazar, you have helped many men. You have helped me. You have earned this request.*

The other prisoners chimed in agreement.

Leo approached Lazar, assessing his appearance.

— *We need to dress as guards.*

Leo, Lazar and Georgi stripped three dead guards of their uniforms. They hastily got changed, hurrying, fearful the prisoners would change their minds. Dressed in ill-fitting uniforms, Leo took the wheel, Georgi in the middle, Lazar on the other side. Prisoners opened the gates.

Suddenly the young leader banged his hand on the truck door. Leo was ready to accelerate off, should he need to. But the man said:

— *They've agreed to accept the wounded as a sign of good faith. Good luck, Lazar, I hope you find your wife and son.*

He stepped away from the truck. Leo put the vehicle into gear, driving past the remains of the two guard towers, through the perimeter gates and onto the highway, heading directly to the military encampment on the other side of the plateau.

*

Running as fast as he could, the radio operator arrived at the outer gates. The prisoners were watching as the truck set off along the highway. Out of breath, the operator exclaimed:

— *They're leaving already? But we haven't told the regional commander. We haven't told him we're sending the sick and injured. Should I run back and tell him?*

The young leader grabbed the man's arm, stopping him.

— *We're not going to tell him. We cannot fight a revolution with men who want to run away. We must make a lesson out of Lazar. The others must learn that there is no option but to fight. If the soldiers open fire on their own injured guards, so be it.*

SAME DAY

Leo drove slowly, edging along the highway towards the temporary encampment. With only two kilometres remaining, midway between rival camps, his eye was caught by a single puff of smoke on the horizon.

The view disappeared, engulfed in a cloud of dust. An explosion dug up the highway, only metres in front of the truck. Dirt and ice and shrapnel cracked against the windscreen. Leo swerved, avoiding the crater. The right tyre slipped off the tarmac. The truck almost rolled over, shaking as it passed through the smoke, lopsided. Heaving the steering wheel, he pulled the truck level, skidding back into the middle of the highway. Leo checked his rear-view mirror, staring at the scooped-out portion of tarmac.

Another puff of smoke appeared on the horizon, then a second and a third, mortar rounds fired one after the other. Leo slammed his foot on the gas pedal. The truck surged forward, trying to accelerate under their trajectory, exploiting the fractional lag between firing and impact. The engine growled, its speed slowly building. Only now did Lazar and Georgi turn to Leo for an explanation. Before they could speak, the first shell landed directly behind – so close the rear of the truck lifted up. For a fraction of a second only the front tyres were touching the highway and Leo could no longer see anything except the road, the cabin facing directly down, angled towards the tarmac. Convinced the truck was going to spin over and land upside down, he felt more surprised than relieved when the rear sat back with a jolt, knocking them out of their seats. Leo struggled with the wheel, trying to regain control. The second shell landed wide, missing the highway, showering the truck with ragged chunks from the plateau, shattering the side window.

Leo swerved, abandoning the highway just as the third shell landed – a perfect shot, detonating exactly where the truck had been. The tarmac was ripped up, the remains thrown into the air.

Crashing across the uneven icy tundra, bumping up and down, Georgi cried out:

— *Why are they firing?*

— *Your comrades lied! They haven't called in!*

In the side mirrors Leo saw the injured guards, confused and panicked and bloody, peering around the canvas, trying to work out why they were under fire. Using his elbow, Leo knocked out the cracked side window, sticking his head through and shouting at the guards:

— *Your uniforms! Wave them!*

Two of the guards stripped off their jackets, waving them like flags.

Four puffs of smoke appeared on the horizon.

Unable to accelerate across the tundra, Leo had no other option except to hold the truck steady and hope. He imagined the shells arcing in the air, rushing up, then whistling down towards them. Time seemed to stretch – a second becoming a minute – and then the explosions sounded out.

The truck was still bumping along. Glancing in the mirror, Leo saw four columns of dust rising behind the truck. He smiled.

— *We're beyond their range!*

He hammered the steering wheel in relief.

— *We're too close!*

The relief melted away. Up ahead, at the edge of the temporary encampment, two tanks rotated their turrets towards them.

The nearest tank fired, an orange burst. Leo's body involuntarily tensed, the air sucked out of his lungs. But there was no explosion — in the wing mirror he saw the shell had ripped through the truck's tarpaulin and exited the other side. The gunner would not make the same mistake twice, directing the next shell at the steel cabin where it was sure to detonate. Leo punched the brakes. The truck stopped. He threw open the door, climbing onto the roof of the cabin, taking off his jacket, waving, shouting:

— *I'm one of you!*

Simultaneously both tanks lurched forward, their caterpillar tracks splintering across the tundra. Leo remained on the top of the cabin, waving his uniform from side to side. Less than a hundred metres away one tank came to a halt. The hatch opened. The tank operator peered out, mounted machine gun at the ready. He called out:

— *Who are you?*

— *I'm a guard. I've got wounded officers in the back.*

— *Why didn't you radio?*

— *The prisoners told us they had. They told us they'd spoken to you. They tricked us! They tricked you! They wanted you to kill your own men.*

The second tank circled the rear of the truck, its turret aimed squarely at the occupants. The wounded guards pointed to their uniforms. The hatch to the second tank opened, the operator calling out:

— *All clear!*

*

At the perimeter of the temporary military encampment Leo stopped the truck. The injured were unloaded, carried to a medical tent. Once the last man was helped off, Leo would start the engine and drive down the highway, back towards the port of Magadan. The back of the truck was empty. They were ready to go. Georgi tapped his arm. A soldier was approaching.

— *Are you the ranking officer?*

— *Yes.*

— *The director wants to speak with you. Come with me.*

Leo indicated that Lazar and Georgi remain in the truck.

The command centre was under a snow-camouflage canopy. Senior officers surveyed the plateau with binoculars. Detailed maps of the region were spread out, blueprints of the camp. A gaunt, sick-looking man greeted Leo.

— *You were driving the truck?*

— *Yes, sir.*

— *I'm Abel Prezent. Have we met?*

Leo couldn't be sure that every officer didn't meet Prezent at one stage or another but he was unlikely to remember every guard.

— *Briefly, sir.*

They shook hands.

— *I apologize for firing on you. But with no communication, we were forced to consider you a threat.*

Leo didn't need to fake his indignation.

— *The prisoners lied. They claimed to have spoken to you.*

— *They'll soon get their comeuppance.*

— *If it's of any use, I can detail the prisoners' defences. I can mark their positions . . .*

The prisoners hadn't made any defences but Leo thought it prudent to seem helpful. However, the Regional Director shook his head.

— That won't be necessary.

He checked his watch.

— Come with me.

Unable to get away, Leo had no choice but to follow.

Leaving the cover of the canopy, Abel Prezent looked up to the sky. Leo copied the direction of his gaze. The sky was empty. After a moment Leo heard a distant humming noise. Prezent explained:

— There was never any question of negotiating. We risk anarchy if their demands are met. Every camp would start a revolution of its own. No matter what they say in Moscow, we must not allow ourselves to become soft.

The humming grew louder and louder until a plane roared over the plateau, flying low, the numbers on its steel belly visible as it passed directly overhead, levelling out on a course towards Gulag 57. It was a Tupolev TU-4, an ageing bomber reverse-designed from the American Fortress planes – four propeller engines, a forty-metre wingspan and a fat silver cylindrical frame. On a direct approach, the underside hatch opened. They were going to bomb the base.

Before Leo had a chance to question the decision a large, rectangular object fell from the hatch, a parachute opening immediately. The TU-4 veered up, climbing sharply to clear the mountain while the bomb swung through the sky, rocking on its parachute, perfectly positioned, guided into the centre of the camp. It drifted out of sight, landing, the parachute spreading across the roof of a barracks. There was no explosion, no firestorm: something had gone wrong. The bomb hadn't detonated. Relieved, Leo checked on the Regional Director, expecting him to be furious. Instead he seemed smug.

— They requested food. We have given them a crate containing the kind of food they haven't seen in years, tinned fruit, meats,

sweets. They will eat like pigs. Except we have added a little some-thing . . .

— The food is poisoned? They'll make the guards eat it first.

— The food is laced with a toxin. In six hours they'll fall uncon-scious. In ten hours they'll be dead. It doesn't matter if they test it on the guards. There are no immediate symptoms. In eight hours we'll storm the camp, injecting our fellow guards with the antidote and leaving the rioters to die. Even if every prisoner doesn't try the food, most will and the number of prisoners will be heavily depleted. We must resolve this revolution before Moscow and her spies start to interfere.

There was no doubt in Leo's mind: this was the man who had ordered Timur's death. Barely containing his anger, Leo remarked:

— An excellent plan, sir.

Prezent nodded, smirking at his murderous ingenuity. He thought so too.

Dismissed, Leo returned through the command headquarters to the truck. He reached the cabin, climbing in, feeling the same rage he'd experienced upon seeing Timur's watch. He looked out of the smashed window in the direction of Abel Prezent. They had to leave now. This was their only chance. Everyone was preoccu-pied with the plane. Yet he couldn't – he wouldn't allow Prezent to get away with it. He opened the cabin door. Georgi grabbed his arm.

— Where are you going?

— There's something I have to take care of.

Georgi shook his head.

— We need to go now, while they're distracted.

— This won't take long.

— What do you have to do?

— That's my concern.

— *It is ours too.*

— *That man murdered my friend.*

Leo pulled free. But Lazar leaned across, taking Leo's arm, indicating that he wanted to speak. Leo lowered his ear, Lazar whispered:

— *People don't always get . . . what they deserve . . .*

With those faint words, Leo's indignation was extinguished. He dropped his head, accepting this truth. He hadn't come here for revenge. He'd come here for Zoya. Timur had died for Zoya. They had to leave now. Abel Prezent would get away with murder.

SAME DAY

The shadow cast by the mountain enveloped Gulag 57, stretching across the plateau, reaching out towards the temporary military encampment. Abel Prezent checked his watch: the toxin would be taking effect very soon; prisoners would be falling unconscious. They'd timed it carefully. At night, no one in the camp would think it odd that prisoners were tired. Before their suspicions were aroused, the ground troops would advance, unseen, cutting through the fence and regaining control. The prisoners would be killed, except for a token number necessary to fend off accusations of a massacre. News of the success would spread through the region. Every other camp would receive the clear message that the riot had failed and that the Gulags were here to stay, that they were not the past – that they were part of the future, that they would always be part of their future.

— *Excuse me, sir?*

A bedraggled guard stood before him.

— *I was on the truck, from Gulag 57. I'm one of the injured officers they released.*

The man's arm was bandaged. Abel smiled, condescendingly:

— *Why aren't you in the medical tent?*

— *I faked my injuries to get on board the truck. I'm not seriously hurt. The doctor says I'm fit to report for duty.*

— You needn't worry about your comrades. We'll be launching our rescue soon.

Abel was about to move away. The man persisted:

— Sir, it wasn't about them. It was about the three men driving the truck.

Driving along the highway at night, guided by dim headlights, Leo strained forward, clutching the steering wheel, peering into the darkness. Nothing more than adrenaline was holding back exhaustion. The journey towards Magadan had been made possible by the monotonous simplicity of the descent with only the narrow timber bridge proving difficult. Now, for the first time, the lights of Magadan could be seen at the foot of the hills on the edge of the sea — a vast black expanse. The airstrip was close, just north of the port.

There was a whistling noise. Ahead of their position an orange flare hung in the night sky fizzing phosphorous light. Launched from the edge of the town, a second flare was fired, then a third, a fourth — orange stars along the highway. Leo slammed on the brakes.

— *They're searching for us.*

He killed the headlights. Leaning out of the smashed window, he looked behind them. In the distance were numerous sets of headlights, snaking down the mountain.

— *They're coming from both directions. I'm going to have drive off-road.*

Georgi shook his head.

— *If we stay on the highway they'll find us in minutes.*

— *Off-road, how long then? You need more time.*

Georgi turned to Lazar.

— I've accepted that I will never leave Kolyma. I accepted that fact a long time ago.

Lazar shook his head. But Georgi, the man who'd served as his voice, was adamant.

— For once, Lazar, listen to me. I was never going with you to Moscow. Let me do this.

Lazar whispered to Georgi, words that for once he didn't have to voice out loud, words that were for him alone.

A second wave of flares was launched, sweeping light up the highway, moving ever closer. Leo got out of the truck, Lazar followed. Georgi took the steering wheel. He paused, glancing through the smashed window at Lazar, before uncertainly driving off, towards Magadan. Lazar had lost a part of himself — he'd lost his voice.

On foot, Leo and Lazar stumbled in the dark over uneven icy terrain towards the flickering lights of the airstrip. Georgi had been right. The ground was so uneven the truck would've become stuck within a matter of minutes. Spasms of pain shot through Leo's legs, causing him to fall. Lazar helped him up, supporting him. Arms wrapped around each other's shoulders, they were an unlikely team.

Another barrage of flares was launched into the sky, their orange Cyclops' eyes concentrated on the highway. There was gunfire. Leo and Lazar paused, turning around. The truck had been found. It accelerated towards a roadblock. Under heavy fire, the truck seemed to veer left and right, out of control, continuing briefly along the highway before skidding off and rolling onto its side. The authorities would find only one body. They would quickly widen the search. Leo observed:

— We don't have long.

Approaching the perimeter of the airstrip, Leo paused, studying its primitive layout. There were three parked planes. The only one that could make the journey across the Soviet Union was the twin-engined Ilyushin Il-12.

— *We walk to the Ilyushin, the largest plane – we walk slowly, like nothing's wrong, like we're supposed to be here.*

They stepped out into the open. There was a handful of ground crew and soldiers. There were no patrols, no sense of urgency. Leo knocked on the plane's door. He'd been promised they would be ready to fly at a moment's notice. Since there'd always been a chance that the escape might be delayed, Panin had assured Leo that there would always be someone on board no matter what time they arrived.

Leo knocked again, a frantic impatience building as each second passed. The door opened. A young man, not much more than twenty years old, peered out. He'd evidently been dozing. A faint smell of alcohol leaked from the cabin. Leo said:

— *You're here under Frol Panin's orders?*

The young man rubbed his eyes.

— *That's right.*

— *We need to fly back to Moscow.*

— *There are supposed to be three of you.*

— *Things have changed. We need to go now.*

Without waiting for an answer, Leo climbed up into the plane, helping Lazar in, shutting the door. The young man was puzzled.

— *We can't fly.*

— *Why not?*

— *The pilot and co-pilot aren't here.*

— *Where are they?*

— *Having dinner, in town. It will only take thirty minutes to bring them back.*

Leo estimated they had about five minutes at the most. He concentrated on the young man.

— *What is your name?*

— *Konstantin.*

— *Is the plane ready to fly?*

— *If we had a pilot.*

— *How many times have you flown?*

— *This plane? Never.*

— *But you're a pilot?*

— *I'm training. I've flown smaller planes.*

— *But not this plane?*

— *I've watched them pilot it.*

That would have to do.

— *Konstantin, listen to me very carefully. They're going to kill us, you as well, unless we take off right now. We can either die here or we can try to fly this plane. I'm not threatening you. These are our options.*

The young man stared at the cabin. Leo took hold of him

— *I believe in you. You can do this. Ready the plane.*

Leo took the co-pilot's seat, an incomprehensible panel of gauges and buttons before him. His knowledge of planes was rudimentary. Konstantin's hands were shaking.

— *I'm starting the engine.*

The propellers shuddered and began to spin. Leo glanced out of the window. They'd attracted the soldiers' attention. Officers were moving towards them.

— *We need to hurry.*

The plane taxied onto the airstrip. The radio crackled into life but before the control hut could address them Leo turned it off. He didn't need the young pilot hearing their threats. Lazar, seated behind, tapped Leo on the shoulder, pointing out of the window. The soldiers were running for the plane. Their guns were drawn.

— *Konstantin, we have to take off.*

The plane began to build up speed.

The soldiers were sprinting, running parallel with the cabin. As the plane accelerated, leaving them behind, they began to fire, bullets ricocheting off the engine. Ready for take off, they were going to get away and Leo looked up. The Tupolev TU-4 bomber was descending directly towards them.

The young pilot shook his head, slowing down. Leo said:

— *Don't slow down. This is our only chance!*

— *What chance!*

— *We have to take off!*

— *We'll crash! We can't get over the bomber!*

— *Fly at the Tupolev. They'll pull up. Do it!*

They were coming towards the end of the runway.

The Ilyushin took off, on course for a mid-air collision with the bomber. Either the Tupolev abandoned its descent or the two planes would crash. Konstantin called out:

— *They're not moving! We've got to land!*

Leo gripped Konstantin's hand, holding their course steady: if they crash-landed they'd be caught and shot. They had nothing to lose. The bomber crew did.

The Tupolev veered upwards, a steep climb, just as the Ilyushin flew underneath, the tail fin skimming the bomber's underbelly as the two planes passed each other. Ahead of them for the first time was clear sky. Konstantin smiled, the confounded smile of a man who couldn't believe that he was alive.

Leo climbed out of his seat, joining Lazar in the back. Magadan was nothing more than a collection of lights in a vast darkness. This was the world that Leo had banished Lazar to — a wilderness that had been his home for the past seven years.

MOSCOW

SAME DAY

Raisa sat on Elena's bed, watching her sleep. Since Fraera's visit, Elena's questioning had become more assertive, as if she sensed the situation had changed. Promises that Zoya's return was imminent were no longer enough. She'd become immune to assurances, content for an hour or so before the effect faded and a deep unease returned.

The phone rang. Raisa hurried out, rushing to the receiver.

— *Hello?*

— *Raisa, it's Frol Panin. We've made radio contact with Leo. The plane is on its way. He'll be in the city in less than five hours. Lazar is with him.*

— *You've contacted Fraera?*

— *Yes, we're waiting to receive instructions for the exchange. You'll want to meet Leo at the airport?*

— *Of course.*

— *I'll have a car sent over when his plane is nearing. We're almost there, Raisa. We almost have her.*

Raisa hung up the receiver. She remained by the phone, pondering those words.

We almost have her.

Panin was talking about catching Fraera: he had little interest in her daughter. Despite Panin's considerable charms, Raisa agreed with Leo's assessment of his character: there was something cold about him.

Elena was standing in the hallway. Raisa stretched out her hand. Elena stepped forward. Guiding her into the kitchen, Raisa sat her down at the table. She warmed milk at the stove, tipping it into a mug. She put the mug down in front of her.

— *Is Zoya coming home tonight?*

— *Yes.*

Elena picked up the mug and took a satisfied sip.

There was no more time to consider Fraera's offer. Raisa no longer believed in Leo's plan. Having met Fraera for herself, having listened to her anger, it didn't make sense to hand Zoya over to Leo and make him a hero. He would achieve in that prisoner exchange everything Fraera was determined he should never have — a daughter, happiness, a family reunited. The premise was wrong. Leo's belief in it was naive. Zoya was in danger. Leo was not the one to save her.

Raisa opened a drawer, taking out a tall red candle. Placing it on the windowsill, in clear view of the street below, she struck a match and lit the wick. Elena asked:

— *What are you doing?*

— *Lighting a candle so that Zoya can find her way home.*

Raisa glanced out into the street. The candle was lit. The signal was given. She would accept Fraera's offer. She would leave Leo.

Malysh sat on a ledge, listening to the racing sewer water. Two months ago the world had made sense. Now he was confused. Someone liked him, not because he could handle a knife, not because he was useful, someone liked him because . . . he couldn't exactly say. Why did Zoya like him? He'd never been liked before. There was no logic to it. She'd saved his life for no reason. Presented with an opportunity to escape, she'd not only turned it down, she'd risked her life for him.

Fraera approached, sitting beside him, their legs dangling side by side like friends on a riverbank, except instead of fish and fallen leaves passing them by, the city's waste flowed beneath their feet. Fraera asked:

— *Why are you hiding here?*

Malysh wanted to remain silent, petulant, but it was an unforgivable insult to not reply, so he muttered:

— *I don't feel well.*

To his surprise Fraera laughed.

— *Two months ago you would've killed that girl and not thought anything of it.*

She rested a hand on his shoulder.

— *I need to know if you will do anything I order, without question.*

— *I have never disobeyed you.*

— *You have never disagreed with anything I've ordered you to do.*

Malysh couldn't counter – it was true, he'd never had a contrary opinion, until now. She'd pushed him together with Zoya in order to test him. She'd manufactured his relationship with Zoya to measure it against her relationship with him.

— *Malysh, when I was imprisoned, I heard a story, told by a Chechen convict. It comes from a Nartian epic, about a hero called Soslan. It is the custom of Narts to avenge not only wrongs committed against them but any committed against their family or ancestors, no matter how ancient the crime. Quarrels last for hundreds of years. Soslan spent his entire life in pursuit of revenge. When you come of age, Malysh, you will need a new name. I had hoped it would be Soslan.*

Though her voice hadn't changed, Malysh sensed danger. Fraera stood up.

— *Follow me.*

Malysh followed her through the tunnels and chambers to Zoya's cell. She unlocked the door. Zoya was standing in the corner, having heard them approach. She sought confirmation in Malysh's eyes that something was wrong. Fraera took hold of Zoya's wrist, pulling her towards the door. Confused, Malysh didn't know whether to obey or protest. Before he could make up his mind, Fraera slammed the door, locking him in.

Having flown the width of the Soviet Union from the Pacific coast to the capital, the Ilyushin's fuel gauge was tapping empty. They had one chance to put down. A storm had closed over them, the plane burrowing through furious black clouds. Lazar was in the back, chewing biscuits with the good side of his mouth. Leo was strapped into the co-pilot's chair, trying to keep Konstantin's confidence from crumbling. Flying towards Stupino military airstrip on the outskirts of Moscow, the plane made its final descent. Panic in his voice, Konstantin declared:

— *I should be able to see the lights by now!*

Passing through the cloud's base, instead of lights being stretched out in the distance they were coming up directly underneath. The plane was too high. Panicking, Konstantin lurched into a steeper drop: a catastrophic gradient. Frantically adjusting, he levelled out, belly-flopping the plane onto the runway. The wheels smashed down, spinning briefly before snapping off, the steel stubs scratching along the tarmac, ripping the plane open as if it were being unzipped. The wing tip hit the ground, swinging the disembowelled plane on its torn stomach one hundred and eighty degrees, slingshotting it off the edge of the runway, propellers digging up mud.

Dazed, his forehead bleeding, Leo unbuckled himself, standing up, pushing open the cockpit door and revealing a cabin torn in half. Lazar had survived, positioned on the opposite side to the damage, a halo of the plane's shell intact around him. Still in his seat, the young pilot started to laugh, hysterical whoops of delight – turned quite mad – rain streaming onto his face through the cracked window.

Leo doubted the plane would catch on fire: there was no fuel and the rain was intense, dousing the smoking engines. With it being safe to leave the pilot behind, he helped Lazar out of the torn midriff, clambering through the wreckage, using the detritus of the wing to step down into the mud. Emergency vehicles raced towards them, medics approached. Leo waved them aside.

— *We're OK.*

He was Lazar's voice now. Frol Panin stepped out of his executive ZiL limousine, a guard moving in perfect synchronization, opening an umbrella above him. He offered his hand to Lazar.

— *My name is Frol Panin. I'm sorry I couldn't arrange your freedom more conveniently. Your wife's actions made any official release impossible. Come, we must hurry. We can speak in the car.*

In the back of the limousine Lazar studied the soft leather upholstery and walnut panels with an infant-like fascination. There were ice cubes in a small silver jug, a bowl of fresh fruit. Lazar picked up an orange, cupping it in his hands, squeezing it. Panin politely ignored the behaviour: the bewilderment of a convict surrounded by luxury. He handed Leo a map of Moscow.

— *That's all we received from Fraera.*

Leo examined the map. A central location was marked with an ink crucifix:

— *What's there?*

— *We couldn't find anything.*

The car began to move.

— *Where is Raisa?*

— *I spoke to her earlier. She was going to wait for the car. When the car arrived, they found your parents looking after Elena. Raisa had gone out.*

Alarmed, Leo sat forward.

— *She's supposed to be under protective custody.*

— *We can't protect someone who doesn't want to be protected.*

— *You don't know where she is?*

— *I'm sorry, Leo.*

Leo sat back. There was no doubt in his mind that Fraera was involved in Raisa's disappearance.

*

It was two in the morning by the time they arrived in the city centre. The contrast to the wilderness of Kolyma was so pronounced that Leo felt sick with disorientation, a sensation exacerbated by sleep deprivation and drumming anxiety. They stopped in the middle of Moskvoretskaya Naberezhnaya, the main road that followed the Moskva, at the point marked on the map. The driver got out. Panin's bodyguard joined him. The two officers checked the area, returning to the car.

— *There's nothing here!*

Leo stepped out. The rain was heavy: he was soaked through in a matter of seconds. The street was empty. He could hear the rain running down the drain. He crouched down. The manhole cover was under the car.

— *Drive forward!*

The limousine moved forward, exposing the cover. Leo wrenched it open, pushing it aside. The guards were either side of him, guns ready. The drop was deep. There was no one on the ladder.

309

Leo returned to the car.

— *Do you have flashlights?*

— *In the trunk.*

Leo opened the trunk, checking the flashlights, handing one to Lazar.

Leo took the lead, climbing down first, gripping the ladder, the shudder-inducing memory of torn skin combining with the real-time pain he felt in his knees. Sheets of rain spilled over the edge, splashing his hands, his neck and face. Lazar followed. Panin called down:

— *Good luck.*

As soon as they were both below street level the manhole was closed, the steel lid clattering shut, cutting off the streams of rainwater and the street light. In the pitch-black darkness they paused, turning on their flashlights, before continuing down.

Reaching the bottom of the ladder Leo surveyed the main tunnel. It was filled with a torrent of white, swirling water. The heavy rain had caused an overflow. Instead of modest, filthy streams, cascades of crashing water were channelling across the city. Unsure whether it was possible to proceed, Leo was forced to suppose the existence of some kind of ledge. Testing his theory he hung down, tentatively exploring with his boot. The narrow ledge was submerged under water.

Leo shouted to Lazar, projecting his voice above the noise:

— *Say close to the wall!*

Lazar climbed down, Leo guiding him. Pressed flat against the wall, the two of them criss-crossed their lights in every direction searching for some instruction. In the distance, a hundred or so metres down the tunnel, there was a light.

As they set off towards the light, along the narrow ledge, the water level in the tunnel was rising, splashing around their knees.

Each step required ferocious concentration. Only metres away, Leo saw a lantern fixed to the wall above the outline of a door. Scraping at the thick slime that covered the walls, he pushed the door open. Water poured in, down a flight of concrete stairs descending further underground. They hurried, closing the door behind them, cutting off the water — relieved to be clear of the perilous ledge.

Inside the narrow spiral staircase the air was dank and hot. They descended in silence, their breathing echoing around the closed chamber. After fifty or so steps they came across another door. Leo pushed hard on the steel frame, the hinges creaking. There was no stench of sewage, no flowing water, just silence. Leo turned to Lazar:

— *Stay here.*

Leo entered the new tunnel, exploring it with his flashlight. The walls were dry. His foot kicked a steel track — they were in a metro tunnel.

Like an underground sunrise a soft yellow light appeared, emanating from an old-fashioned mining lantern, a flickering gas flame held by a man. He was alone, his proportions grotesquely muscular, tattoos stretched across his hands and neck.

— *Don't move.*

The *vory* searched Leo and Lazar. Finished, he shut the steel door that led up to the sewers, locking it. He swung around, indicating the direction they were going to walk. They set off, Leo in front, Lazar just behind, the *vory* at the back, commenting as they went:

— *This metro line isn't on any map. After it was completed the workers were executed so that its existence would remain a secret. It's called the* spetztunnel *and it runs from the Kremlin to Ramenkoye, an underground town fifty kilometres away. If the West attacks, our leaders will descend, sitting on silk cushions, while Moscow burns.*

After some distance the *vory* stopped walking.

— *Here.*

There was a steel door in the wall. Leo opened it, shining his torch up at the concrete stairway, thankful that it climbed upwards. The *vory* closed the door on them. Seconds later there was a hissing sound: the lock was rendered useless with acid. No one could follow them.

Damp with sweat, they reached the top of the steps, finding the door unlocked, and exited into Taganskaya metro station. Leo walked out of the station into the middle of Taganskaya Square, exasperated, searching for what to do next. Lazar raised his arm, pointing in the direction of the river some two hundred metres away. There was a woman standing in the middle of Bolshoy Krasnokholmskiy Bridge.

Leo hurried, Lazar by his side. Reaching the riverbank, without the protection of the buildings, the wind doubled in strength. The bridge was a stark concrete arch, and swirling below, the Moskva was tumultuous with the night's downpour. The woman remained in the middle of the bridge, waiting for them, rain sloshing off her jacket. Drawing close, Leo recognized that jacket. It belonged to him.

Raisa lowered her hood.

Running forward, reaching her side, taking her hands, he was befuddled with emotions — concern and relief. Raisa shook her hands free of his grip.

— *Why didn't you tell me about Zoya? She held a knife over you. You told me nothing was wrong. You lied to me, about something like that? What did we promise? No more lies! No more secrets! We promised, Leo!*

— *Raisa, I panicked. I wanted a chance to put things right before telling you. After you came out of hospital, I was preparing to go to Kolyma. You were still weak.*

— *Leo, I wasn't weak. You were! This isn't about being a hero. It's about what's best for Zoya and Elena. I met Fraera. She came to me. There's no way she's going to hand Zoya over to you. It's never going to happen.*

On the south side of the bridge car headlights appeared, beams of light blurred by the downpour. The car accelerated towards them, causing Leo to raise his hand, shielding his eyes from the lights. The car braked. Doors opened. The driver was a *vory*. Fraera stepped out of the passenger side, indifferent to the rain. She glanced at Leo, then at Raisa, before concentrating her attention on Lazar, her husband.

Lazar walked towards her, uncertain, evidently shocked, despite Leo's warnings, at her transformation. They stood opposite each other. Exploring his appearance, she touched the side of his face, feeling the shape of his injured jaw. He winced at her touch but didn't pull away. She said:

— *You have suffered.*

Leo watched as Lazar mouthed the words:

— *We have . . . a son?*

— *Our son is dead. Your wife is dead.*

A gunshot, a flash of light – Lazar fell to his knees, clutching his stomach.

Leo ran forward, catching Lazar as he fell. His teeth were red with blood. Stunned by the senseless execution, Leo turned to Fraera.

— *Why?*

She didn't reply, looming over him, offering no explanation. He looked down at Lazar's body, cradled in his arms. The man he'd betrayed, and rescued, the man who'd saved his life, was dead. Leo lowered his body, laying him down on the road.

Fraera grabbed Leo by the shirt.

— *Get in the front of the car.*

She waved her gun at Raisa.

— *You too!*

Leo stood up, climbing into the driver's seat. Raisa was in the passenger seat. Zoya was in the back, her wrists and ankles bound. Her mouth was gagged – her eyes were terrified. The car had been modified. There was a grate between them. Raisa and Leo simultaneously pressed their hands up against the wire.

— *Zoya!*

Zoya pressed her face against the other side, pleading through the gag for help. Their fingers touched. Leo shook the grate but it held fast.

The back door was opened: Fraera leaned in, grabbing Zoya, pulling her, lifting her out. Leo spun around, trying to open the door. It was locked. Raisa tried her door, to no avail. Fraera and the *vory* carried Zoya to the trunk. The *vory* picked up a grain sack, opening it while Fraera lowered Zoya in.

Leo swivelled round, aiming his boots squarely at the side window. Like a mule, he kicked out again and again, his soles bouncing off, the glass remaining intact. Raisa cried out:

— *Leo!*

Leo scrambled across to Raisa's side of the car, the side nearest to the river. The *vory* and Fraera were carrying the sack, Zoya was struggling to break out, thrashing and twisting, fighting for her life. The *vory* slapped her across the face, knocking the resistance out of her for long enough to push her down and secure the sack. The pair of them together lifted the sack. It was weighted. The unconscious Zoya was heaved up onto the ledge. Leo's face was flat against the glass as he watched the sack pushed off the bridge. He caught a glimpse of it plummeting towards the river.

Fraera perched on the bonnet of the car, squatting, her face close to the windscreen, eyes on fire, lapping up their pain like a cat licking cream. Exploding with rage, Leo pummelled the windscreen, uselessly banging his fists, trapped behind reinforced glass. Fraera watched, delighting in his helplessness, before jumping down and mounting the back of a bike. Leo hadn't even noticed that two motorbikes had pulled up alongside them.

Trapped in the car, Leo kicked the ignition, exposing the wiring. Sparking the connections, he put his foot down on the accelerator, revving the engine, driving as if in pursuit of Fraera. Raisa called out:

— *Leo! Zoya!*

Leo wasn't chasing Fraera. Picking up enough speed, he swung the car violently left, towards the barricade. The car smashed against the edge of the bridge, ripping the side off, tearing it open. With the engine smoking, the wheels spinning on the kerb, Leo turned to his wife. Raisa had cut her head, but she was already out of her seat, climbing out of the smashed side. He staggered after her, reaching the point where Zoya had been dropped.

Raisa jumped first, Leo after her. Falling, he saw Raisa enter the water, shortly before his legs crashed through the surface. Underwater, the current pulled down. Sucked deeper, he resisted his impulse to return to the surface and kicked down with the force of the current, directing himself to the bottom where Zoya would've come to a rest. He didn't know how deep the river was, he kicked harder and harder — his lungs burning, fighting his way down. His hands touched the thick silt at the bottom. He looked around, unable to see anything. The water was black. Pulled upwards, he tried to search, spinning round, but it was no good —

he couldn't see anything. Desperate for air, forced back to the surface, he gasped. Glancing around, the bridge was already in the distance behind him.

Leo breathed deeply, preparing to dive again. He heard Raisa cry out:

— *Zoya!*

It was a hopeless cry.

SIX
MONTHS
LATER

MOSCOW

Filipp broke the bread, studying the way the still-warm dough pulled apart, stretching briefly before tearing into ragged strips. He dug out a chunk and placed it on his tongue, chewing slowly. The loaf was perfect, which meant the batch was perfect. He wanted to gorge himself, spreading a thick layer of butter that would soften and melt. Yet he was unable to swallow even this modest mouthful. Standing over the bin he spat out the sticky ball of dough. The waste of food appalled him but he had no choice. Despite being a baker, one of the best in the city, forty-seven-year-old Filipp could only consume liquids. Persistent and untreatable stomach ulcers had plagued him for the past ten years. His gut was pockmarked with acid-filled craters – the hidden scars of Stalin's rule, testimony to nights lying awake worrying about whether he'd been too stern with the men and women working under him. He was a perfectionist. When mistakes were made he lost his temper. Disgruntled workers might have written a report naming him and citing bourgeois, elitist tendencies. Even today, the memory caused his gut to burn. He hurried to his table, mixing a chalk solution and gulping down the foul-tasting white water, reminding himself that these worries belonged in the past. There were no more midnight arrests. His family was safe and he had denounced no one. His conscience was clear. The price had been the lining of his stomach. All things considered, even for a baker and a lover of food, that price was not so high.

The chalk water soothed his gut and he berated himself for dwelling on the past. The future was bright. The State was recognizing his talents. The bakery was expanding, taking over the entire building. Previously he'd been limited to two floors with the top floor designated as a button factory, a cover for a secret government ministry. Locating it above a bakery had never made sense to him: the rooms were filled with flour dust and roasted by the heat from the ovens. In truth, he wanted them gone not because he needed the space but because he'd never liked the look of the people who'd worked there. Their uniforms and cagey demeanour aggravated his stomach.

Making his way to the communal stairway, he peered up at the top floor. The previous occupants had spent the past two days clearing out filing cabinets and office furniture. Reaching the landing, he paused by the door, noting the series of heavy locks. He tried the handle. It clicked open. Pushing on the door, he studied the gloomy space. The rooms were empty. Emboldened, he entered his new premises. Fumbling for the light switch he saw a man slumped against the far wall.

Leo sat up, blinking at the bulb overhead. The baker came into focus, a man as thin as wire. Leo's throat was dry. He coughed, getting to his feet, brushing himself down and surveying the gutted offices of the Homicide Department. The classified case files, evidence of the crimes he and Timur had solved, had been removed. They were being incinerated, every trace of the work he'd done these past three years destroyed. The baker, whose name he didn't know, stood awkwardly – the embarrassment of a compassionate man witnessing the misfortune of a fellow citizen. Leo said:

— *Three years of passing each other on the stairs and I never asked your name. I didn't want to . . .*

— *Worry me?*

— *Would it have?*

— *Honestly, yes.*

— *My name is Leo.*

The baker offered his hand. Leo shook it.

— *My name is Filipp. Three years, and I never offered you a loaf of bread.*

Leaving the Homicide office for the last time, Leo glanced back before shutting the door. Feeling an awful kind of light-headedness, he followed Filipp downstairs where he was handed a round loaf – still warm, the crust golden. He broke the bread, biting into it. Filipp studied his reaction carefully. Realizing his opinion was being sought, Leo finished the mouthful and said:

— *This is the best bread I've ever eaten.*

And it was true. Filipp smiled. He asked:

— *What did you do up there? Why all the secrecy?*

Before Leo had a chance to reply, the question was retracted.

— *Ignore me. I should mind my own business.*

Still eating, Leo ignored the retraction.

— *I was in charge of a specialist division of the militia, a homicide department.*

Filipp was silent. He didn't understand. Leo added:

— *We investigated murders.*

— *Was there much work?*

Leo gave a small nod.

— *More than you might think.*

Accepting another loaf to take home, as well as the remains of the one he'd started, Leo turned to leave. Filipp called out, trying to end on a positive note:

— *It gets hot here in the summer. You must be pleased to be moving to another location?*

Leo looked down, studying the pattern of flour footprints.

— *The department isn't moving. It's closing down.*

— *What about you?*

Leo looked up.

— *I'm to join the KGB.*

The Serbsky Institute was a modest-sized building with curved steel balconies around the top-floor windows, more like a block of attractive apartments than a hospital. Raisa paused, as she always did at this point, fifty metres away, asking herself if she was doing the right thing. She glanced down at Elena, standing by her side, holding her hand. Her skin was supernaturally pale, as though her body was fading. She'd lost weight and was unwell with such regularity that sickness had become her usual state. Noticing Elena's scarf had come loose, Raisa crouched down, fussing over her.

— *We can go home. We can go home at any time.*

Elena remained silent, her face blank, as if no longer a real girl but a replica created with tissue-paper skin and green pebble eyes, emitting no energy of her own. Or was it the other way round? Was Raisa the replica, fussing and caring in an imitation of the things a real mother would do?

Raisa kissed Elena on the cheek, and garnering no response, felt her stomach knot. She had no resilience to this indifference, indifference that had begun when she'd knelt down, her eyes filled with tears, and whispered into Elena's ear, expecting an outburst of grief.

Zoya is dead.

323

Elena hadn't reacted. Six months later, she still hadn't reacted, not in any ordinary, outward sense.

Raisa stood up, checking on the traffic, crossing the road and approaching the main entrance. The Serbsky Institute was a desperate measure but she was desperate. Love wasn't going to save them. Love simply wasn't enough.

Inside – stone floors, bare walls – nurses in crisp uniforms pushed steel trolleys equipped with leather restraints. Doors were bolted. Windows were barred. There could be no doubt that the institute's reputation as the city's foremost psychiatric centre was a point of notoriety rather than acclaim. A treatment centre for dissidents, political opponents were admitted for insulin-induced comas and the latest in pyrogenic and shock therapy. It was an improbable place to seek assistance for a seven-year-old girl.

In their discussions Leo had repeatedly stated his opposition to psychiatric help. Many of those he'd arrested for political crimes had been sent into a *psikhushka*, a hospital such as this. While Leo agreed, as indeed he had to, that there might be good doctors working within a brutal system, he didn't believe the risk in searching for those men and women warranted the potential gain from their expertise. Declaring yourself unwell was tantamount to positioning yourself on the fringes of society, not a place any parent, or guardian, would want for their child. Yet his stance seemed less like caution and more like mulish stubbornness – a blind determination to be the one that fixed his family even as it crumbled in his hands. Raisa was no doctor, but she understood that Elena's sickness was as threatening as a physical ailment. She was dying. It was primitive to hope the problem would merely pass.

The woman behind the front desk glanced up, recognizing them from previous visits.

— I'm here to see Dr Stavsky.

Working behind Leo's back, talking to friends, colleagues, she'd secured an introduction to Stavsky. Despite a career in treating dissidents, with all that entailed, Stavsky believed in the value of psychiatry beyond the political sphere and disapproved of the excesses of punitive treatments. He was motivated by a desire to heal and he'd agreed to examine Elena without making any official record. Raisa trusted him as much as a person lost at sea would put their faith in a drifting plank. She had little choice.

Upstairs, summoned in, Dr Stavsky crouched down in front of Elena.

— Elena? How are you?

Elena didn't reply.

— Do you remember my name?

Elena didn't reply. Stavsky stood up, addressing Raisa in a whisper.

— This week?

— No change, not a word.

Stavsky directed Elena to the scales.

— Please take off your shoes.

Elena didn't respond. Raisa knelt down, taking Elena's shoes off, guiding her onto the scales. Stavsky peered at the display, noting her weight. He tapped his pen against his pad, running his eyes across the numbers accumulated these past weeks. He stepped back, perching on his desk. Raisa moved forward to help Elena off the scales but Stavsky stopped her. They waited. Elena remained on the scales, facing the wall, doing nothing. Two minutes became five minutes became ten minutes and Elena still hadn't moved. Finally, Stavsky indicated that Raisa should help Elena off the scales.

Fighting back tears, Raisa finished tying Elena's laces and stood up, about to ask a question, only to see Stavsky on the telephone. He hung up, placing his pad on the desk. She didn't know how or why but she knew she'd been betrayed. Before she could react, he said:

— *You came to me for help. It is my view that Elena needs professional, full-time supervision.*

Two male orderlies entered the room, closing the door behind them like a trap slamming shut. Raisa wrapped her arms around Elena. Stavsky slowly approached.

— *I have arranged for her to be admitted to a hospital in Kazan. I know the staff well.*

Raisa shook her head, in disbelief as much as to rebut his proposal:

— *This is no longer up to you, Raisa. The decision has been made in the interest of this young girl. You are not her mother. The State has appointed you her guardian. The State is taking back guardianship.*

— *Doctor . . .*

She spat the word out with contempt.

— *You are not taking her.*

Stavsky moved closer, whispering:

— *I will tell Elena she is going with these nurses to Kazan. I will tell her that she will not see you again. I am quite certain that she will not react. She will walk out of this room, with those two strangers, and she won't even look back. If she does that, will you believe you cannot help her?*

— *I refuse to accept that test.*

Ignoring Raisa, Stavsky crouched down and spoke slowly and clearly.

— *Elena, you are going to be taken to a special hospital. They will try to make you better. It is possible that you will never see*

Raisa again. However, I will make sure you are well looked after.
These men will help you. If you do not wish to go, if you wish to
stay, if you wish to remain here with Raisa, all you have to do is
say so. All you have to do is say no. Elena? Do you hear me? All
you have to say is no.

Elena did not reply.

Inessa, Timur's widow, opened the door. Leo entered the apartment. For several months after returning from Kolyma he'd expected that Timur would appear from the kitchen, explaining that he hadn't been killed, he'd survived and found a way home. It was simply impossible to imagine this home without him. He'd been his happiest here, surrounded by his family. However, the designation of accommodation was without compassion. According to the system, Timur's death meant the family needed less space. Furthermore, their modern apartment was a perk of his job. Inessa worked in a textiles factory and the men and women she worked alongside made do with far more modest living arrangements. Using his *blat*, his influence, Leo had fought to keep the family where they were, requesting that Frol Panin intervene. Perhaps feeling a sense of responsibility for Timur's death, Panin had agreed. Yet to Leo's surprise Inessa had been tempted by the prospect of moving out. Every room was seeped in memories of her husband. They left her breathless, so sad she could barely function. Only when Leo had shown her the apartment blocks where she would be relocated, a single room, shared facilities, thin walls, did she relent and only then because of her two sons. Had she been alone, she would've moved out that day.

Leo gave Inessa a hug. Separating, she accepted the loaf of bread.

— *Where did this come from?*

— *The bakery underneath our offices.*

— *Timur never brought home bread.*

— *The people who worked there were too scared to talk to us.*

— *But not now?*

— *No.*

Like the movement of a shadow, sadness passed across Inessa's face. The Homicide Department had been Timur's too. It was gone.

Her two sons, Efim, ten years old, and Vadim, eight, hurried out of their bedroom to greet Leo. Though Timur had died working for Leo, his sons bore him no ill will. On the contrary, they were pleased by his visits. They understood that he had loved Timur and that their father had loved Leo. All the same, for Leo, their affection was a fragile pleasure, certain one day to break. They did not yet know the details of what had happened. They did not yet know their father had died trying to put right the wrongs of Leo's past.

Inessa ran her hand through Efim's hair as he spoke excitedly about his schoolwork, the sports teams he was playing for. As the elder son, Timur's watch would be given to him when he turned eighteen. Leo had replaced the cracked glass and the interior mechanism, which he'd kept for himself, unable to throw it away, occasionally taking it out and resting it on the palm of his hand. Inessa had not yet decided what story she would tell Efim about the watch's origins, whether to lie about it being a treasured family heirloom. That decision was for another day. Addressing Leo, she said:

— *Will you eat with us?*

Leo was comfortable here. He shook his head.

— *I have to go home.*

*

Back at his apartment, he discovered that Raisa and Elena weren't home. The security officers on duty said that the pair had left for school in the morning, they'd seen nothing out of the ordinary. Unaware of any plans, he couldn't imagine what Raisa was doing out at this time of night with Elena. No clothes had been packed: no bags had been taken. He phoned his parents; they didn't have any answers. His fear wasn't that Fraera was involved. Zoya's murder had been her last act of revenge against State Security personnel. After a six-month absence he doubted Fraera would return. There was no need. Leo had been hurt exactly as she desired.

Hearing the noise of someone approach he rushed to the hall-way, throwing open the door. Raisa staggered forward, catching the doorframe as if drunk. Leo supported her, taking her weight. He checked the corridor. It was empty.

— *Where's Elena?*

— *She's . . . gone.*

Her eyes rolled, her head slumped. Leo carried her into the bathroom, placing her under the shower, running it cold.

— *Why are you drunk?*

Raisa gasped, shaken awake by the shock of the water.

— *Not drunk . . . drugged.*

Leo turned the shower off, wiping Raisa's hair out of her eyes, sitting her on the side of the bath. Her bloodshot eyes were no longer rolling shut. She stared at the puddles forming around her shoes, her speech no longer slurred.

— *I knew you'd disagree.*

— *You took her to see a doctor?*

— *Leo, when someone you love is sick, you seek help. He said it would be unofficial, no paperwork.*

— *Where?*

— *Serbsky.*

At the sound of the name Leo went numb. Many of the men and women he'd arrested had been sent there for treatment. Raisa began to cry.

— *Leo, he sent her away.*

Dumb incomprehension, then rage.

— *What is the doctor's name?*

— *You can't save her, Leo.*

— *What is his name!*

— *You can't save her!*

Leo raised his hand, arching it back, ready to strike her across the face. In a flash, diverting his anger, he grabbed the mirror from the wall and smashed it in the sink. The shards cut his skin, drawing blood, red lines rolling around his wrists, down his arms. He dropped to the floor, bloody fragments scattered around him.

Taking a towel, Raisa sat beside him, pressing it against his injured hand.

— *You think I didn't fight? You think I didn't try to stop them? They sedated me. When I woke up, Elena was gone.*

Leo turned the defeat over in his mind. It was complete. His hopes of a family had been destroyed. He'd failed to save Zoya's life and failed to persuade Elena that life was worth living. Three years of honesty and trust between himself and Raisa had been wiped out. He'd lied to her, a lie forever preserved by the calamities that had followed from it. He didn't feel any anger at Raisa for accepting Fraera's offer, for agreeing to leave him. Raisa claimed it was tactical and nothing more, a desperate bid to save Zoya. She'd taken their family's well-being into her own hands. The only mistake she'd made was waiting too long.

The three-year pretence had come to an end. He was no father, no husband and certainly no hero. He would join the KGB. Raisa would leave him. How could she not? There would be nothing between them except a sense of loss. Each day he'd know that Fraera had been right about him: he was a man of the State. He had changed, but far more importantly he'd changed back. He remarked:

— *There was a moment when I thought we had a chance.*

Raisa nodded.

— *I thought so too.*

Leo wasn't sure how much time had passed. They hadn't moved – Raisa by his side on the floor, leaning against the bathtub, the tap dripping behind them. He heard the front door open yet still he couldn't stand up. Stepan and Anna appeared at the bathroom doorway. No doubt concerned by Leo's earlier phone call, his parents had travelled over. They took in the room, seeing the blood, the smashed mirror:

— *What happened?*

Raisa squeeze his hand. He answered:

— *They took Elena.*

Neither Stepan nor Anna said a word. Stepan helped Raisa to her feet, wrapping a towel around her, guiding her to the kitchen. Anna took Leo into the bedroom, examining the cut. She dressed the wound, behaving as she had done when he'd been a boy and had hurt himself. Finished, she sat beside Leo. He kissed her on the cheek, stood up, walked into the kitchen, stretching out his hand to Raisa.

— *I need your help.*

*

Frol Panin was Leo's most influential ally but he was unavailable, out of the city. Although they weren't friends, three years ago

Major Grachev had supported Leo's proposal to create an autonomous homicide department. Leo had reported to him directly for the first two years until Grachev had stepped aside, making way for Panin. Since then Leo had seen the major infrequently. However, a proponent of change, Grachev believed that the only way to govern was by making amends, seeking to admit and redress, in moderation, the wrongs perpetrated by the State.

With Raisa by his side, Leo knocked on Grachev's apartment door, instinctively checking the length of the communal corridor. It was late but they couldn't wait until morning, fearful that if their efforts lost momentum a sense of crushing despondency would return. The door opened. Accustomed to the major in pristine uniform, it was a shock to see him scruffily dressed, his glasses smudged with fingerprints, his hair wild. Normally formal and restrained, he embraced Leo affectionately, as though reunited with a lost brother. He bowed affectionately before Raisa.

— *Come in!*

Inside there were boxes on the floor, items being packed. Leo asked:

— *You're moving?*

— *No. I'm being moved. Out of the city, far away, I couldn't even tell you where, really I couldn't. They did tell me. But I'd never heard of the place. Somewhere north, I think, north and cold and dark, just to make the point even clearer.*

His sentences were tumbling out one after the other. Leo tried to focus him:

— *What point is that?*

— *That I am no longer a man in favour, no longer the man for the job, any job it seems, other than running a small office in a small town. You remember this punishment, Leo? Raisa? Exile. You both suffered it yourself.*

Raisa asked:

— *Where is your wife?*

— *She left me.*

Pre-empting their condolences, Grachev added:

— *By mutual agreement. We have a son. He has ambitions. My relocation would ruin his chances. We have to be practical.*

Grachev stuffed his hands into his pockets.

— *If you came for my help, I am afraid my situation has deteriorated.*

Raisa glanced at Leo, her eyes asking whether it was worth explaining their predicament. Grachev spotted her reaction.

— *Talk to me, if not because I can help, then as conversation between like-minded friends.*

Embarrassed, Raisa blushed.

— *I am sorry.*

— *Think nothing of it.*

She quickly explained:

— *Elena, our adopted daughter, has been taken from us and admitted to a psychiatric hospital in Kazan. She never recovered from the murder of her sister. I had arranged for her to see a doctor on an unofficial basis.*

Grachev shook his head, interjecting:

— *Nothing is unofficial.*

Raisa tensed.

— *The doctor promised not to make any records of her treatment. I believed him. When she didn't respond to his treatment . . .*

— *He committed her in order to protect himself?*

Raisa nodded. Grachev considered, before adding, as an afterthought:

— I fear none of us will recover from Zoya's murder.

Surprised by this comment, Leo sought an explanation:

— None of us? I don't understand.

— Forgive me. It is unfair to compare the wider consequences to the grief you must feel.

— What wider consequences?

— We needn't go into that now. You're here to help Elena . . .

Leo interrupted:

— No, tell me, what wider consequences?

The major perched atop a box. He looked at Raisa, then Leo.

— Zoya's death changed everything.

Leo stared at him blankly. Grachev continued:

— The murder of a young girl to punish a former State Security officer, along with some fifteen or more retired officers hunted down and executed, several tortured. These events shook the authorities. They'd released this very woman from the Gulags. What was her name?

Leo and Raisa replied at the same time:

— Fraera.

— Who else might they have released? Many hundreds of thousands of prisoners are coming home; how will we govern if even a fraction of their number behave like her? Will her revenge start a chain reaction culminating in the collapse of rule and order? There will be civil war once more. Our country will be ripped down the middle. This is the new fear. Steps have been taken to prevent this.

— What steps?

— An air of permissiveness has crept into our society. Did you know there are authors writing satirical prose? Dudintsev has written a novel – Not By Bread Alone. *The State and officials are openly mocked, in print. What follows next? We allow people to criticize. We allow people to oppose our rule. We allow people to*

*take revenge. Authority that once was strong suddenly seems
fragile.*

— *Have there been similar reprisals across the country?*

— *When I spoke about wider consequences I wasn't merely referring to incidents within our country. There are reprisals across all
the territories under our rule. Look at what happened in Poland.
Riots were precipitated by Khrushchev's speech. Anti-Soviet sentiment is stirring throughout Eastern Europe, Hungary,
Czechoslovakia, Yugoslavia . . .*

Leo was shocked.

— *The speech has travelled?*

— *The Americans have it. They have printed it in their news-
papers. It has become a weapon against us. It is perceived that we
have dealt ourselves a terrible blow. How are we to continue the
global revolution when we confess to such murderous acts against
our own people? Who would want to join our cause? Who would
want to become our comrades?*

The major paused, wiping sweat from his brow. Leo and Raisa
were now crouching before him, like children captivated by a
story. He continued:

— *After Zoya's murder everyone who argued for reform, including me, was silenced. Even Khrushchev was forced to retract many
of the criticisms he made in his speech.*

— *I didn't know that.*

— *You were grieving, Leo. You buried your daughter. You
buried your friend. You were not paying attention to the world
around you. While you mourned, a revised speech was written.*

— *Revised how?*

— *The admissions of summary executions and torture were cut.
This document was published one month after Zoya's murder. I'm
not claiming Fraera's revenge was the only contributing factor. But*

those murders were important. They made a graphic case for the traditionalists. Khrushchev had no choice: a Central Committee resolution rewrote his speech. Stalin was no longer a murderer: he merely made errors. The system wasn't at fault. Any minor mistakes were Stalin's alone. It was the Secret Speech, without the secrets.

Turning these facts over, Leo remarked:

— *My department's failure to stop these murders was the reason they closed us down.*

— *No. That's an excuse. They never approved of the Homicide Department. They never liked me for helping to create it. Your department was part of the creeping culture of permissiveness. Leo, we moved too quickly. Freedoms are won slowly, bit by bit — they have to be fought for. The forces that desire change, me included, marched too far and too fast. We were arrogant. We overreached ourselves. We underestimated those who want to protect and preserve power as it was.*

— *They've ordered me to rejoin the KGB.*

— *That would be a potent symbol. The reformed MGB agent folded back into the traditional power structures. They're using you. You must allow yourself to be used. If I were you, Leo, I would be very careful. Do not believe that they will behave any more kindly than Stalin. His spirit lives on, not in one person, but diffused, in many people. It's harder to see but make no mistake: it is there.*

*

Outside the apartment Leo took hold of Raisa's hands.

— *I've been blind.*

BLIZHNYA DACHA
KUNTSEVO
TWENTY KILOMETRES WEST
OF MOSCOW

21 OCTOBER

This was Frol Panin's second visit to Blizhnya Dacha, one of Stalin's former residences, now open to families of the ruling elite as a retreat. The decision had been taken that the residence was not to be closed down or turned into a museum. The dacha was to remain filled with children playing, staff cooking and the ruling elite slouching on creaking leather chairs, ice cubes clinking as they sipped their drinks. Upon Stalin's death it had been discovered that the drinks cabinet contained bottles filled with imitation alcohol, weak tea instead of Scotch, water for vodka, so that Stalin might remain sober while his ministers lost control of their tongues. No longer needed, the imitation alcohol had been poured away. Times had changed.

Having eaten sparingly from a five-course meal, picking at three types of bloody meat, ignoring three wines, Frol's social duties were finished for the night. He climbed the stairs, listening to the heavy rain. Loosening his shirt, he entered his suite. His young

sons were in the room next door, put to bed by a maid. His wife
was getting undressed, having excused herself from the end of the
meal, as was expected of the wives, enabling husbands to talk of
weighty matters, an excruciating routine since most were drunk
with nothing to say. Entering the living room and shutting the
door he felt relief. The evening was over. He hated coming here,
particularly with his children. To his mind the dacha was a place
where people lost their lives. No matter how many children now
played in the grounds, no matter how loudly they laughed —
those ghosts remained.

Frol turned off the living-room lights, heading towards the bedroom and calling out to his wife.

Nina was on the edge of the bed. Seated beside her was Leo.
Soaked by rain, his trousers were mud-stained, his hand was bandaged and the bandages were soaked too. Dirty water seeping from
his clothes had formed a circular stain on the sheets. In Leo's face
Frol observed stillness belying an enormous kinetic force inside,
tremendous anger bubbling under a thin sheet of glass.

Frol calculated quickly:

— *Why don't I sit beside you Leo, instead of my wife?*

Without waiting for a reply, Frol gestured for Nina to approach.
She tentatively stood up, moving slowly. Leo didn't stop her. She
whispered to Frol.

— *What is going on?*

Frol replied, making sure Leo could also hear.

— *You have to understand that Leo has experienced a terrible
shock. He's grief-stricken and not thinking straight. To break into
a dacha could result in his execution. I'm going to work very hard
to see that doesn't happen.*

He paused, then addressed Leo directly:

— *May my wife check on my children?*

Leo's eyes sparked.

— *Your children are safe. You have some nerve asking me that.*

— *You're right, Leo, I apologize.*

— *Your wife stays here.*

— *Very well.*

Nina sat on a chair in the corner. Frol continued:

— *This is concerning Elena, I take it? You could have come to my office, made an appointment, I would've arranged for her release. I had nothing to do with her admission to hospital. I was appalled to hear about it. Completely unnecessary, the doctor was acting on his own authority. He believed he was doing the right thing.*

Frol paused

— *Why don't we call for some drinks?*

Leo emptied his pockets.

— *I pose no threat to you. I haven't brought a gun. If you called for your guards, they'd arrest me.*

Nina stood up, about to shout for help. Frol indicated that she remain silent. He asked:

— *Tell me then, Leo, what do you want?*

— *Was Fraera working for you?*

— *No.*

Frol sat down beside him.

— *We were working together.*

*

Leo had expected Frol Panin to deny it. But there was no reason for him to lie. Powerless, Leo could do as little with the truth as he could do with a denial. Panin stood up, taking off his jacket, undoing some of his shirt buttons.

— *Fraera came to me. I didn't know who she was. I didn't have any knowledge of* vory *in Moscow. They'd always been an irrelevance. She broke into my apartment and was waiting for me. She knew everything about you. Not only that, she knew about the struggle between the traditionalists in the party and the reformists. She proposed that we work together and claimed that our aims overlapped. She would be granted the freedom needed to take revenge on those involved in her arrest. In exchange, we could exploit that series of murders, using it for our own purposes, creating a sense of fear.*

— *She never cared about Lazar?*

Panin shook his head.

— *She saw Lazar as someone from her former life, nothing more. He was a pretext. She wanted you to go to the Gulag as a punishment, to force you to see the world you sent so many people to. From our point of view, we needed you out of the way. The Homicide Department was the only independent investigative force. Fraera required a free hand. Once you and Timur were gone, she could kill as she pleased.*

— *The KGB never looked for her?*

— *We made sure they never got close.*

— *The officers you appointed to run the Homicide Department in my absence?*

— *Were our men, they did as they were told. Leo, you almost managed to stop the murder of the Patriarch. That murder was a vital part of our plan. His death shocked the entire regime. Had you remained in the city, Fraera would have been forced to kill you. For her own reasons, she didn't want to. She preferred to send you away, to stretch out your punishment into something altogether more awful.*

— *And you agreed?*

Panin seemed puzzled by that statement of the obvious.

— *Yes. I agreed. I removed Major Grachev and positioned*

myself as your closest adviser in order to help you make the right decisions, the decisions we wanted you to make. I arranged the paperwork that enabled you to break into Gulag 57.

— You and Fraera planned this?

— We were waiting for the right moment. When I heard Khrushchev's speech, I knew it was time. We had to act. The changes were going too far.

Leo stood up, walking towards Nina. Concerned, Panin also stood up, tense. Leo put his hand on her shoulder.

— Isn't this how we used to interrogate our suspects? A loved one present, the implications clear, if the suspect failed to give the correct answer, the loved one would be punished?

— I'm answering your questions, Leo.

— You authorized the murder of men and women who served the State?

— Many of them were murderers themselves. In my position, they would have done the same thing.

— What position is that?

— Leo, these hasty reforms – more than Stalin's crimes, more even than the West – pose the greatest threat to our nation. Fraera's murders were an illustration of the future. The millions we, as a ruling party, have wronged would revolt, just as the prisoners on board the Stary Bolshevik *rose up, just as they did in that Gulag. Those scenes would be repeated in every city in every province. You haven't noticed, Leo, but we are engaged in a silent battle for our nation's survival. It has nothing to do with whether or not Stalin went too far. He did. Of course he did. But we cannot change the past. And our authority is based on the past. We must behave as we have always behaved: with an iron rule. We cannot admit mistakes and hope our citizens will love us all the same. It is unlikely we will ever be loved, so we must be feared.*

Leo removed his hand from Nina's shoulder.

— *You have what you wanted. The Secret Speech has been retracted. You don't need Fraera any more. Let me have her. Give me my revenge as you gave it to her. You should have no compunction about betraying her. You've betrayed everyone else.*

— *Leo, I understand that you have no reason to trust me. But my advice is this: forget Fraera. Forget that she exists. Let me arrange for Elena to be released from hospital. You and Raisa can move out of the city, away from all these memories. I'll find you another job. Whatever you want.*

Leo turned to face Panin.

— *She's still working for you?*

— *Yes, she is.*

— *On what?*

— *That speech weakened us domestically and internationally. In response, we need a clear show of our strength. For this reason we're working to manufacture an uprising abroad, in parts of the Soviet Bloc, small, symbolic uprisings that we will crush mercilessly. The KGB has established a series of foreign cells attempting to stimulate disorder, scattered across Eastern Europe. Fraera is in charge of one of those cells.*

— *Where?*

— *Take my advice, Leo, this is not a fight you can win.*

— *Where is she?*

— *You cannot beat her.*

— *How could she hurt me more?*

— *Because, Leo, your daughter, Zoya, is alive.*

SOVIET CONTROLLED
EASTERN EUROPE
HUNGARY
BUDAPEST

22 OCTOBER

Zoya walked as fast as she could on her way to the Operehaz, the drop point for her illicit cargo. Her pockets were brimming with bullets, one hundred rounds in total, each tip etched with a cross to ensure it quartered upon entering the body. Though it was a cold night she felt hot and flustered. Wearing a knee-length coat tied at the waist, a black beret slanted across her forehead, she looked older than fourteen, more like a Hungarian student than a Russian orphan. Nervous, clammy with perspiration, she snatched the beret off her head, pressing it into her pocket, atop the bullets, muffling their telltale jingle.

Reaching the main boulevard, Sztalin ut, not far from the Operehaz, Zoya paused, checking that no one was following. Taking her by surprise, someone grabbed her shoulders. She turned around, finding herself surrounded by a group of men, convinced that they were the Hungarian secret police. One man kissed her cheek, pressing a sheet of paper into her hand. It was a poster of some kind. The men were talking in rapid bursts. Although she'd been in the city for five months she'd picked up only a handful of Hungarian phrases. Judging by their attire, the men were students or artisans, not officers, and she relaxed. Even so, she had to be careful: if they realized she was Russian there was no knowing how they'd behave. She smiled, meekly, hoping they'd consider her shy and let her go. They were hardly interested in her anyway, unravelling another poster and plastering it to the front of a shop window. Zoya pulled away, hurrying to her destination.

Arriving at the Operehaz, climbing the stone stairs, she hid behind the pillars, out of view from the street. She checked her watch, a gift from Fraera. She was early and she pulled back into the shadows, nervously waiting for her contact to show up. This was the first task she'd handled alone. Normally she worked with Malysh. They were a team – a partnership forged in Moscow five months ago.

Taken from her cell that night, Zoya had been certain Fraera was going to execute her in order to punish Leo. Facing death, as she had done only days earlier, Zoya had discovered that she was no longer indifferent to the prospect. She'd cried out:

— *Malysh!*

Fraera had set her down on the ground.

— *Why did you call his name?*

— *Because I . . . like him.*

Fraera had smiled, a smile turning into a laugh, slowly at first, then getting louder, her *vory* laughing beside her, a chorus of scorn. Zoya had blushed, her face burning with shame. Humiliated, she'd run at Fraera, arms raised, fists clenched. Before she'd landed a blow Fraera had caught hold of her hand.

— *I will give you a chance, one chance. If you fail, I will kill*

you. If you succeed, you will become one of us. You and Malysh
can remain together.

Driven to the middle of Bolshoy Krasnokholmskiy Bridge, that
night had unfolded as Fraera predicted. Leo and Raisa had been
waiting. Soaked by the rain, they had climbed into the front of the
car. Separated by a steel grate, Zoya had witnessed Raisa's face
crumple with distress. In that moment Zoya had experienced
doubts. But it was too late to change her mind. Pressing her hands
against the grate she'd bidden farewell to her unhappy life: a decision that necessitated leaving her little sister behind. She'd feigned
resistance as she'd been dragged out of the car. Out of sight, she'd
voluntarily climbed into the sack. Already inside, Malysh had been
waiting for her.

The sack had been carried to the edge of the bridge while Zoya
continued to make a show of struggling until the *vory* had struck
her, entirely unexpectedly. She'd collapsed. The sack had been
zipped shut. In the darkness Malysh had wrapped his arms around
her, supporting her as they'd been dropped. Briefly midair, in each
other's arms, in the darkness — then they'd crashed into the water.

Steel weights had carried the sack straight down. The waterproof waxed canvas had shrouded them in a minute's worth of air.
The steel had thudded against the riverbed toppling Malysh and
Zoya to the side. Working blind, Malysh had flicked open his knife
and cut through the material. Freezing water had rushed in, filling the sack in an instant. Malysh had helped Zoya out. Holding
hands, they'd kicked their way back up to the surface. Swimming
to the riverbank, they'd watched the final moments on the bridge
as Leo and Raisa had jumped, mistakenly believing they were
going to save her.

Struggling upstream against the torrent, Zoya and Malysh had
pulled themselves along the high stone sides of the riverbank.

Reaching the timber jetty they'd been reunited with Fraera as she'd listened to Raisa and Leo's distant, desperate cries, savouring their grief for a child they thought was lost.

*

There was a man lingering at the bottom of the steps to the Operehaz. Zoya emerged from her hiding place. The man checked up and down Sztalin ut before moving towards her. Zoya emptied her pockets, filling his satchel with the customized bullets. He pulled out a handgun, loading the chamber. The bullet was a match. He filled the other chambers while Zoya continued to transfer the bullets from her pockets to his bag. Finished, the man hid his gun, dropping his head in thanks before hurrying down the steps. Zoya counted to twenty before setting off again, making her way back home.

It was odd to think of this city as home. Six months ago Zoya had known nothing of Hungary except that it was a loyal ally of the Soviet Union, part of a brotherhood of nations, a front-line state in the global Revolution. Fraera had corrected this classroom propaganda, explaining that Hungary had never been given any choice. Liberated from Fascist forces, it had been occupied and placed under Soviet rule. Hungary was a sovereign nation with no sovereignty. The leader for many years, Matyas Rakosi, had been appointed by Stalin and had imitated his master exactly, torturing and executing citizens. He'd created the AVH – the Hungarian secret police – modelled on the Soviet secret police. The language and location were different but the terror had been the same. With Stalin's death, the struggle had begun for reform, electrified by dreams of independence. Zoya was a foreigner here, an outsider, yet not since her parents had died had she felt more at home here in a country that, like her, had been adopted against its will.

Relieved that the night was almost over and that she was no longer carrying bullets, Zoya swung down Nagymezo ut. Directly ahead, a small crowd had gathered. At its centre were the men she'd bumped into previously, sitting on each other's shoulders to transform the entire height of a street light into a totem pole of postered text. A woman in the crowd saw Zoya approach. In her thirties, stout and stocky, the woman was drunk – her cheeks were red. Wrapped around her, like an enormous shawl, was the Hungarian flag. Zoya glanced at the street light and pulled the same crumpled poster from her pocket as if to say – *I know, I know!* Not content with this gesture, the woman pulled her into the throng, talking good-naturedly, but nothing Zoya could understand. The woman began to dance and sing. The others joined in, all of them knowing the words, except for Zoya. She could only laugh and smile in the hope that they would eventually let her go. Keen to leave before they noticed she wasn't speaking, she attempted to extricate herself from the stranger's affections. But the woman was no longer flushed with happiness. A van had swung off the main boulevard and was accelerating towards them. It skidded to a halt. Two AVH officers jumped out.

The crowd closed ranks around the street light as though it was territory to be defended. One of the officers grabbed the flag, which was wrapped around Zoya, pulling it free, holding it up contemptuously. It was only now that Zoya noticed the Communist hammer and sickle in the centre had been cut out, leaving a gaping hole in the middle of the material. Unable to understand a word he was saying, the AVH officer sounded like a barking dog. He searched Zoya's pockets, infuriated by her silence. Finding nothing apart from the beret he threw it back at her. A single bullet trapped inside the material fell to the street.

The officer picked up the bullet, staring directly at Zoya.

Before he could speak the drunk woman reached out and scooped up the beret from the street, placing it proudly on her head. It looked ridiculous, too small for her. The officer turned to the woman and Zoya didn't need to speak Hungarian to understand that he was asking if the beret belonged to her. The officer raised the bullet to the woman's face. Did this also belong to her, he must have asked. In reply, she spat in his face. While the officer wiped the glob of phlegm from his cheek, the woman flicked Zoya a glance: *Run!*

Cutting a diagonal across the street, Zoya ran. Mid-sprint, she turned around, peering over her shoulder. She saw the AVH officer swing a punch, connecting with the side of the woman's face. As if the punch had connected with her own face, Zoya's legs crumbled and she collapsed — her hands scraping across the ground. Rolling onto her back, looking over the tips of her shoes, she saw the woman fall. A man jumped forward, grabbing the officer. A second man joined the fray. Scrambling to her feet, Zoya lurched into another run, this time reaching the side street. Out of sight, she didn't stop. She had to get help. Fraera would know what to do.

Fraera and her *vory* occupied several apartments within a small courtyard set back from Rakoczi ut. Accessed by a narrow passageway, the apartments couldn't be seen or spied upon from the street. Reaching them, Zoya stopped running. No one was following her. In the unlit passageway, relieved to be off the street, she felt a hand on her shoulder. It was Malysh. They hugged. He said:

— *Are you OK?*

She shook her head.

They entered the courtyard. There were six floors of apartments. Those Fraera occupied spread across various floors, each put to different use. There was a small printing press, producing leaflets and posters. In another apartment there were stocks of guns and ammunition. A third served as a meeting place, to eat and sleep and discuss. Entering the communal apartment, Zoya was surprised by the number of people – far more than usual. On one side were Hungarian men and women, most aged in their twenties, arguing passionately. On the other side were the *vory*. Most had not made the journey from Moscow to Budapest, remaining behind, preferring the certainty of the criminal underworld. They didn't understand the deal Fracra had made with Panin. They couldn't conceive of a life outside Russia. Only a small number of her most ardent supporters had followed her, partly out of loyalty, mostly because they knew no other *vory* gang in Moscow would want them. From fifteen, only four remained.

Fraera was in the middle, in between the two groups, listening even when Hungarian was being spoken, sensitive to body language and gestures. She saw Zoya immediately, spotting her distress.

— *What happened?*

Zoya explained. Fraera's eyes came alive, she turned around, addressing her translator, a Hungarian student named Zsolt Polgar.

— *Find as many Hungarian flags as you can. Cut the sickle and hammer out of them, so there's a hole in the middle. This is the symbol we've been waiting for!*

Fraera had no interest in the woman who'd risked her life to save Zoya. Upset, Zoya left the apartment. She leaned against the balcony rail. Malysh joined her. He lit a cigarette, a habit he'd copied from the other *vory*. She took the cigarette from his lips, stubbing it out under her foot.

— It makes you smell.

She regretted her words. The smoke did make him smell: it made him smell like all the other *vory*. But she hadn't meant to embarrass him. Hurt, he slid off the rail, skulking back inside the apartment. She needed to remember that he was not her little sister to boss around.

At the memory of Elena, guilt clutched her throat like a hand. She'd contemplated her decision countless times — had she not joined Fraera, she would've been killed. Yet the truth was that she had wanted to leave, to run away, and had there been a free choice, had Fraera offered her a chance to go home or come with her — she would've left her little sister behind.

— You're angry?

Startled, she faced Fraera. Although they'd lived together for six months, Fraera remained intimidating and inaccessible, more like a source of energy than a person. Zoya composed herself.

— The woman with the flag saved me. There's a chance she'll die for it.

— Zoya, you should prepare yourself . . . many innocent people are about to lose their lives.

Descending the stairway and leaving the courtyard, Fraera checked that no one had seen her. It was late at night. The streets were empty. There was no sign of the AVH officers that Zoya had described. She set off, frequently stopping with calculated abruptness, turning around and making sure she wasn't being followed. She trusted no one, including her supporters. The workers, students and representatives of various underground anti-Soviet resistance movements were indulgent and impractical, preoccupied with irrelevant theoretical debates. It would be easy for the AVH to infiltrate their ranks. They'd be too self-absorbed to notice the signals, putting all of them in danger. Despite Fracra being here under Frol Panin's instructions, the AVH knew nothing of her operations. If she was caught she would be shot. No one outside of the conspirators in Moscow had been trusted with information regarding the plans to trigger an uprising. If her dissident supporters found out that she was simultaneously working with Soviet ministers, they'd kill her.

Bending down, Fraera scooped up a leaflet fluttering in the gutter – a copy of the revised sixteen points, sixteen demands for change. The points had been formulated yesterday afternoon in a crowded meeting at the Technological University. Unable to pass for a student, Fraera had loitered outside. When she'd heard that the intention of the meeting was to debate whether the students should leave DISZ, the campus Communist Party organization, as a protest against their Soviet rulers, she'd decried their lack of ambition, encouraging her student acquaintances to divert the discussion on to bolder issues. Fraera had been working in this fashion for the past four months, applying pressure, offering material support and stoking resentment against the occupation as best she could. While the anger was real and deep, she'd struggled to convert sentiment into direct action. There was only so much she could do herself. Her role was to professionalize amateur dissidents. Yesterday, finally, there'd been success. With a determination and clarity that surprised her, the students had distilled their debate into sixteen points.

> *We demand the immediate withdrawal of all*
> *Soviet troops, in accordance with the*
> *declaration of the peace treaty.*

On the scruffy handwritten notes carried out from the hall, that demand had been ranked fourth. Fraera had hurried back to her apartment, transcribing the notes and making one amendment: placing the demand for troop withdrawal at the top. Within hours her *vory* were handing out revised copies, at every street corner, interlaced with the most provocative extracts from the Secret Speech.

Outside of the few *vory*, the remnants of her gang, Fraera's closest associate was Zsolt Polgar, her translator, an engineering student she'd met in a revolutionary underground bar, located in a factory basement. With low ceilings that were never visible because of the thick haze of cigarette smoke, Fraera had found the venue's population rich in ambition. Zsolt – the son of a wealthy

Hungarian diplomat, destined for power and money were he only to conform to the Soviet occupation and find his place within it – spoke fluent Russian and Hungarian and had quickly become Fraera's most valued intermediary. She humoured him, slept with him, beguiling him with stories of her ruthlessness. Appreciating his skills, she flattered him as a libertarian and revolutionary. In reality, she saw him as little more than a rebellious young man, kicking out against his father whom he despised as a sycophantic Soviet appeaser. Regardless of his motivation, he was brave and idealistic, easy to manipulate. He had suggested a demonstration in support of the sixteen points – an inspired notion. As it happened, the idea had been duplicated around the city and Fraera wondered if that might be the work of one of Panin's other cells. Either way, the result was that tomorrow two marches would set out at the same time, one from either side of the city, joining at Palffy Square. There had been previous shows of disquiet in the capital, none of which had amounted to anything. Fraera was certain that only when people were standing side by side, feeding off each other, was there any chance that the anger would transform, like a pupa to a butterfly, from bitter obedience into glorious violence.

Reaching the Astoria Hotel, several blocks from her apartment, Fraera took a moment to observe the crossroads before glancing up at the hotel's top floor. In the last window along, on the corner, a red candle was burning, the quaint signal that she'd devised. In this context it meant she was to come upstairs. Moving round to the back of the hotel, entering through the deserted kitchens, she climbed to the top floor, walking to the room at the far end of the corridor. She knocked. A guard opened the door, gun drawn. There was a second guard behind him. She stepped into the suite and was frisked before being ushered next door.

Seated at a table, glancing out of the window like a contemplative poet, was Frol Panin.

An alliance with Panin, or any man like him, had never been part of Fraera's plans. Arriving in Moscow, she'd accepted that unless she was content with merely plunging a knife in Leo's back she needed assistance. Similarly, Budapest had never been part of her plans. It was another improvisation. With the illusion of Zoya's death, her original ambition – to bring ruin down on Leo's hopes of happiness – had been achieved. Leo was tortured as she'd been tortured: the loss of a son paid for with the loss of a daughter. He was broken, forced to live with grief and not even allowed the fire of righteous indignation that had sustained her through those same emotions. Her revenge complete, she'd been faced with what to do next. It had become apparent that she couldn't untangle herself from Panin and melt away. If she stopped being useful to him he would order her death. If she escaped it would be a life of wealth and growing old, a life she had no interest in. Hearing of his international operations, his attempts to agitate disturbances within the Soviet Bloc, she'd volunteered herself and her men. Panin had been sceptical but Fraera had pointed out that she was likely to make a far more convincing agitator against Soviet Russia than the loyal KGB agents he was using.

Panin offered his hand – a polite, formal gesture that she found absurd. Nevertheless she shook it. He smiled.

— *I've flown over to monitor progress. Our troops are in position on the border. They have been for some time. Yet there is nothing for them to do.*

— *You'll get your uprising.*

— *It needs to happen now. It is of no use to me a year from now.*

— *We're on the brink.*

— *My other cells have had considerably more success than you. Poland, for example . . .*

— *The riots you instigated in Poznan were crushed with no serious loss of face for Khrushchev. They did not have the impact you required otherwise you wouldn't be bothering with Budapest.*

Panin nodded, admiring Fraera's gift for weighing up situations exactly. She was right. Khrushchev's plans to scale back the conventional military had not been derailed. They were a central platform of his reforms. Khrushchev had argued that the Soviet Union no longer needed so many tanks and troops. Instead, it had a nuclear deterrent and was building an experimental missile-delivery system that required no more than a handful of engineers and scientists, not millions of soldiers.

Panin considered the policy foolhardiness of the most dangerous kind. Aside from the inadequacies of the missiles, Khrushchev had fundamentally misunderstood the importance of the military, just as he'd misunderstood the impact of his Secret Speech. The military existed not solely to protect against external aggressors; its real purpose was to hold the Soviet Union together. The glue between the nations of the Soviet Bloc wasn't ideology but tanks and troops and planes. His proposed cuts, combined with the reckless sabotage inflicted by his speech, were putting their nation in peril. Panin and his allies were arguing that not only must they maintain the size of the conventional army but they must also extend and re-arm it. They must increase spending, not decrease it. A disturbance in Budapest, or indeed in any other Eastern European city, would prove that the entire fabric of the Revolution depended upon its conventional military might, not merely its nuclear arsenal. Several million men with rifles were useful in reminding the population, at home and abroad, who was in control.

Panin said:

— *What news do you have for me?*

Fraera handed him the leaflet printed with the sixteen points.

— *There's going to be a demonstration tomorrow.*

Panin glanced at the sheet of paper.

— *What does it say?*

— *The first demand is for Soviet troops to leave the country. It is a call for freedom.*

— *And we can trace the inspiration back to the speech?*

— *Certainly. But the demonstration won't be enough.*

— *What else do you need?*

— *A guarantee that you will fire on the crowd.*

Panin placed the leaflet on the desk.

— *I'll see what I can do.*

— *You must succeed. Despite everything these people have been through, the arrests, the executions, they will not become violent unless provoked. They are not like . . .*

— *Us?*

Ready to leave, Fraera hesitated by the door, turning back to face Panin.

— *Was there anything else?*

Panin shook his head.

— *No. Nothing else.*

SOVIET UNION–
HUNGARIAN BORDER
THE TOWN OF
BEREHOWE

23 OCTOBER

The train was crowded with Soviet soldiers, raucous conversations criss-crossing the carriage. They were being mobilized in preparation for the planned uprising, of which they knew nothing. There was no sense of anxiety or trepidation, their jovial mood contrasting starkly with Leo and Raisa, the only civilians on board.

When Leo had heard the news — *Zoya is alive* — relief had been muddled with pain. In disbelief he'd listened to Panin's explanation: the re-telling of events on the bridge, including Zoya's calculated pretence and her willing collaboration with a woman who wanted nothing other than to make Leo suffer. Zoya was alive. It was a miracle, but a cruel one, perhaps the cruellest good news Leo had ever experienced.

In explaining events to Raisa, he'd witnessed the same shift from relief to anguish. He'd knelt before her, apologizing repeatedly. He'd brought this upon them. She was being punished because she loved him. Raisa had controlled her response, concentrating on the details of what had happened and what it revealed about Zoya's state of mind. For her there was only one question: how they were going to bring their daughter home?

Raisa had no difficulty in accepting that Panin had betrayed them. She understood the logic of Fraera's cooperation with him in order to enact her revenge in Moscow. However, Panin's attempts to initiate uprisings within the Soviet Bloc was political manoeuvring of the most cynical kind, condemning thousands to death in order to consolidate the position of Kremlin hard-liners. Raisa couldn't understand what part of this appealed to Fraera. She was siding with the Stalinists, men and women who thought nothing of her imprisonment or the loss of her child, or indeed the loss of any child. As for Zoya's defection, if that was the right way of looking at it, from one dysfunctional family to another, Raisa was less puzzled. It was easy to imagine Fraera's intoxicating appeal to an unhappy teenager.

Leo had made no attempt to talk Raisa out of accompanying him to Budapest. The opposite was true: he needed her. Raisa stood a much better chance of getting through to Zoya. Raisa had asked Leo whether they were prepared to use force if Zoya refused to come, confronting Leo with the grim prospect of kidnapping his daughter. He nodded.

Since neither Leo nor Raisa spoke Hungarian, Frol Panin had arranged for them to be accompanied by forty-five-year-old Karoly Teglas. Karoly had worked as an undercover operative in Budapest. Hungarian by birth, he'd been recruited by the KGB after the war, serving under the hated leader Rakosi. He had recently been in Moscow on a temporary basis, advising them on the potential crisis in Hungary. He'd agreed to act as a guide and translator, accompanying Leo and Raisa.

Returning from the toilet, Karoly wiped his hands on his trousers, taking his seat opposite Leo and Raisa. With a portly stomach, plump cheeks and round glasses, there was hardly a straight line anywhere in his appearance. A collection of curves, he appeared, at a glance, an unlikely operative, definitively non-lethal.

The train slowed, nearing the town of Berehowe on the Soviet side of the heavily fortified border. Raisa leaned forward, addressing Karoly directly.

— *Why has Panin allowed us to go to Budapest when Fraera is working for him?*

Karoly shrugged.

— *You would have to ask Panin himself. It is not for me to say. If you want to turn back, that is up to you. I have no power over your movements.*

Karoly looked out of the window, remarking:

— *The troops are not crossing the border. From here on, we behave like civilians. Where we are going, Russians are not loved.*

He turned to Raisa.

— *They won't make any distinction between you and your husband. It doesn't matter that you're a teacher and he's an officer. You'll be hated just the same.*

Raisa prickled at being spoken down to.

— *I understand hatred.*

*

At the border, Karoly handed over the papers. He glanced back, watching Leo and Raisa, in conversation, seated in the back of the car – paying careful attention not to glance at him, a giveaway that they were debating how far they could trust him. They would be wise not to trust him in any way. His orders were simple. He was to delay bringing Leo and Raisa into the city until an uprising had begun. Once Fraera had served her purpose, Leo, a man reported to be of great tenacity and zeal, a trained killer, could be allowed his revenge.

SOVIET-CONTROLLED
EASTERN EUROPE
HUNGARY
BUDAPEST

SAME DAY

Exhilarated, Zoya clutched Malysh's hand, not wanting to lose him among the thousands of people pooling into Parliament Square from every street and junction. Having spent so many years romanticizing death, certain it was the only answer to her loneliness, she now felt like jumping up and down, as if she owed the world an apology, shouting out — *I am alive!*

The march had far exceeded expectations. No longer merely made up of students and dissidents, the whole city seemed to be gathering in the square, drawn out of their apartments, offices, factories, unable to resist the demonstration's gravitational pull, which grew stronger with each new person joining. Zoya understood the significance of their location. A parliament should be the centre of power, the place where a nation's destiny was decided. In reality, the building was irrelevant, an ornate, majestic front for Soviet authority. Its beauty somehow made the insult worse.

The sun had set. Yet the night didn't diminish the excitement.

More and more people were arriving, disregarding habits of prudence and caution, the influx continuing even though the square was already full, the new arrivals forcing the crowd closer together. Far from claustrophobic, the atmosphere was affectionate. Strangers talked and laughed and hugged each other. Zoya had never been caught up in a public assembly like this before. She'd been compelled to attend May Day celebrations in Moscow but this was different. It wasn't the scale. It was the disorder, the absence of authority. No officers stood in the corner. No formations of tanks rolled by. No troops goose-stepped as they passed rows of hand-picked children waving flags. A fearless protest, an act of defiance: everyone was free to do as they pleased, to sing and clap and chant:

— *Russkik haza! Russkik haza! Russkik haza!*

Hundreds of feet stamped the three-beat rhythm and Zoya joined in, fists clenched, punching the air, overcome with an indignation that was, considering her nationality, absurd.

Russians go home!

She didn't care if she was Russian. Home was here, among people who had suffered as she'd suffered and who understood oppression as she understood it.

Shorter than the men and women around her, Zoya strained on tiptoe. Suddenly she felt two hands clasp her waist as Fraera lifted her up, placing her on her shoulders, giving her a view of the entire square. The crowd was larger than she'd supposed, stretching up to the Parliament building and the river behind it. There were people across roads and lawns and tram tracks, clambering onto pillars and statues.

Without warning the Parliament lights shut off, plunging the square into darkness. There was confusion among the crowd. There was power in the side streets. It must be a deliberate act against them, an attempt to drive them away, to break their resolve with darkness as a weapon. A cheer sounded out. Zoya saw a single burning torch, a newspaper rolled up. Quickly, more spots of fire appeared, improvised torches. They would make their own light! Fraera handed Zoya a rolled-up copy of the daily journal *A Free People*. A *vory* lit the end, turning it slowly, until the flame spread. Zoya held it above her head, the flames tinted blue-green by the ink. She waved it from side to side and a thousand burning torches waved back.

As Fraera lowered her to the ground, flushed with emotion, Zoya strained forward and kissed her on the cheek. Fraera froze. Even though Zoya's feet were on the ground, Fraera's hands remained tight around her waist, not letting go. Zoya waited, holding her breath, fearful that she'd made a terrible mistake. In the darkness she was unable to see Fraera's reaction until a nearby man lit a newspaper. The flickering red light revealed Fraera's expression, shaken as if by the sight of a ghost.

*

Fraera felt the kiss lingering on her cheek, burning hot. She pushed Zoya aside, touching the place where she'd been kissed. It had been a mistake to place Zoya on her shoulders. Unwittingly she'd allowed Anisya to return, her former self, mother and wife. Tenderness, affection, characteristics that she'd exorcized, had crept back. Drawing her knife, she raised the blade to the side of her face and pulled down, scraping the skin, shaving off the remains of the kiss. Feeling relieved, she wiped the edge of the blade and put the knife away.

Having regained her composure, she stared at the rooftops of the surrounding buildings, furious with Panin for failing to post snipers. Zsolt Polgar followed her glance, asking:

— *What are you looking for?*

— *Where are the AVH?*

— *You're worried about our safety?*

Fraera hid her scorn at his naivety, replying:

— *There's no one to fight against.*

— *At the radio station students are trying to broadcast the six-teen points. Rumour has it that the station management is refusing. The AVH is protecting the building to make sure it remains under Soviet control.*

Fraera took hold of his shoulders.

— *That's it! That's where we will make our fight!*

Elbowing through crowds, Fraera worked her way free from the peaceful assembly, suffocated by their passivity. Further away from Parliament Square the mood changed. Along Muzeum korut, towards Nemzeti muzeum, people were running in a chaos of directions, some scared, others angry, carrying slabs of rock, ripped-up paving stones. The focus of their activity was the radio station, situated along Brody Sandor ut, a narrow street that ran beside the museum. Whatever peaceful protest might have begun here had evolved into a violent mob – the radio-station windows were smashed, glass shards on the street crunching underfoot like frozen puddles. A van lay overturned in the middle of the road, wheels spinning, the front crumpled. The radio-station doors were shut and secured.

Zsolt questioned the nearby men and women and returned to Fraera, switching from Hungarian to Russian, speaking in hushed tones.

— *The students demanded to read the sixteen points. The woman running the station—*

— *Who is she?*

— *Her name is Benke, a loyal Communist, but not too smart it*

*seems. She proposed a compromise. They couldn't have access to the
station but she'd give them a mobile broadcasting van. The van
arrived. The students read the points.*

Fraera was already ahead of him.

— *It was a trick?*

— *The van wasn't transmitting. Instead, the station continued to
broadcast orders for everyone to go home, condemning the disruption. The students flipped the van over and rammed it against the
doors. Now they want the station, nothing less; they say it's the
national station and it belongs to them, not the Soviets.*

Fraera glanced around, assessing the mob's strength.

— *Where are the AVH?*

— *Inside.*

Fraera glanced up. Figures appeared at the top-floor windows —
officers. There was a hissing noise, plumes of smoke unravelled
within the confines of the street. Tear gas was twisting out of steel
canisters like vengeful genies released from bottles, swelling, rising
up. Fraera pulled her men back, checking on Zoya and Malysh,
retreating, clambering over the rails, towards the museum as the
gas chased them. Reaching the top of the museum steps, they
turned. White wisps swirled around their ankles but posed no
danger. The bulk of the tear gas had been funnelled down the
street, spewing onto the main road. Out of the chemical fog
emerged men and women, dropping to their knees, retching.

As the gas began to thin, Fraera moved closer, surveying the
empty street. A gloomy stillness prevailed. The mob was broken.
The fight had been extinguished. Fraera shook her head. If tonight
passed without serious incident the authorities would regain
initiative, control would be reasserted. Fraera strode towards the
station.

— *Follow me.*

The gas hadn't cleared. Fraera wasn't going to wait, climbing over the rails, walking into the middle of the street, plumes of gas hugging her. She covered her mouth and nose with her hand. Almost immediately she began to cough but she continued, staggering towards the radio-station entrance, her eyes streaming.

Zoya grabbed Malysh's arm.

— *We have to follow her!*

Malysh ripped his shirt, fashioning a mask each for himself and Zoya. Climbing over the rails, they entered the street, the two of them standing beside her. The gas was lifting, circulating into the broken windows of the radio station, making it easier to breathe on the street and forcing the figures back from the windows. Slowly the mob reassembled around the nucleus of Zoya, Malysh and Fraera. The *vory* returned with steel bars. They took to the doors, trying to splinter them open.

Zoya looked up. AVH officers were at the windows, this time armed with rifles. She grabbed Malysh, rushing forward. They pressed themselves flat against the wall just as a volley of shots rang out. Everyone in the street ducked, stooping, checking to see who'd been hit. No one had been hurt. The shots had been fired above their heads into the walls of the building opposite. The volley had been intended to cower them, timed exactly as the front doors to the station opened.

Puffed up with resolve, AVH officers stepped out, rifles ready, a Greek phalanx protecting the radio station. The officers divided into two lines, back to back — one line moving up the street, the other moving down, cutting the mob in half. With bayonets fixed, they advanced. Malysh and Zoya were being pushed down, towards the museum. Zoya looked at the young girl next to her, perhaps eighteen years old. Far from being scared, she grinned triumphantly at Zoya, locking arms with her. They'd stand together.

She called out at the officers, cursing them. Inspired by the girl's defiance, Zoya bent down, scooping up a rock no larger than her palm and throwing it, striking an officer on the cheek. Elated, she was still smiling when he swung his rifle in her direction.

There was a flash. Zoya's legs buckled, she fell. Breathless, unsure whether she was hit, she rolled onto her side, staring into the eyes of the girl who'd linked arms with her. The bullet had struck the girl in the neck.

The officers continued advancing. Zoya couldn't move. She had to get up. The officers would trample her underfoot. They would kill her. Yet she couldn't leave this girl. Suddenly Fraera crouched down, scooping up the dead girl in her arms. Malysh helped Zoya up – the two of them ran. Behind them, the officers stopped their advance, holding their position.

Fraera laid the girl down, crying out in raw anger, as if she were her mother, as if she loved this girl. Zoya stood back, watching as men and women knelt beside the young victim, drawn in by the sound of Fraera's cries. Was this grief a performance? Before Zoya could think about it further, Fraera stood up, drawing a gun and firing at the line of officers. It was the cue her *vory* had been waiting for. From both sides of the street, they drew their guns, opening fire. The formation of officers began to break up, retreating to the station, no longer certain that they could maintain control. The officers had presumed, like men fighting beasts, that they were the only ones armed with guns. Under attack, they hastened back to the safety of the radio station.

Zoya remained by the dead girl's body, staring at her lifeless eyes. Fraera pulled her aside, offering her a gun.

— *Now we fight*.

Zoya replied:

— *I killed her*.

369

Fraera slapped her across the face.

— *No guilt. Just anger. They shot her. What are you going to do about it? Cry like a child? You've been crying all your life! It's time to act!*

Zoya grabbed the gun and charged towards the radio station, aiming at the figures in the windows, pulling the trigger and firing all six shots.

Dawn, and Zoya hadn't slept. Far from being dulled by fatigue, her senses seemed heightened, her eyes picking up every detail of her surroundings. To her side, broken coffee cups were inexplicably heaped in the gutter, hundreds piled knee-high as if marking a burial spot. In front, the remains of a fire composed entirely of charred books, copies of Marx and Lenin, looted from bookstores. Fragile flakes of grey ash rose up towards the sky in reverse of snowfall. Cobblestones were missing, wrenched out of the ground to serve as missiles, gaps in the street's teeth. It was as if the city itself had been in a fight and Zoya had fought on its side. Her clothes smelt of smoke; her fingertips were black, her tongue tasted metallic. Her ears were ringing. Underneath her shirt, pressed against her stomach, was her gun.

The radio station had fallen shortly before sunrise: smoke bellowing from the windows. The timber doors had finally been broken open. The resistance inside had weakened while the attack outside had consolidated with a supply of weapons, rifles from the military academy, fired by the cadets. Fraera had found Zoya and Malysh and ordered them not to take part in storming the building. She didn't want them caught in a pitched battle, fighting in smoke-filled corridors where desperate AVH officers lurked behind doors. She'd given them a different objective:

Find Stalin.

*

Arriving at the end of Gorkii fasor, a street that led out onto the city's main park, the Varosliget, Malysh and Zoya were shocked by the absence of its landmark. At the centre of Heroes Square the vast statue of Stalin – a bronze colossus as tall as four men with a moustache as wide as an arm – was gone. There was the stone plinth but no statue on top of it. Malysh and Zoya approached the mutilated monument. Two steel boots remained: the Generalissimo had been cut off near the ankles, a twisted steel support jutting out of his right boot. His body and head were missing. His statue had been murdered and the corpse stolen. Two men were busy on the plinth trying to affix a modified Hungarian flag to the boot.

Zoya began to laugh. She pointed at the space where Stalin had once been:

— *He's dead! He's dead! The bastard's dead!*

Malysh pounced, slamming his hand over her mouth. She'd shouted out in Russian. The two men on the plinth stopped and turned. Malysh raised his arm, punching the air:

— *Russkik Haza!*

The men nodded half-heartedly, distracted as their flag fell over.

Malysh lead Zoya away, whispering:

— *Remember who we are.*

In reply Zoya kissed him on the lips – a quick, impulsive kiss. She pulled back and before he could react she pretended that nothing had happened, pointing at the deep scratches in the street.

— *That's the direction they dragged the body!*

She set off, heart pounding, following the marks where the bronze had rubbed against the cobblestones.

— *They must have dragged it with a van or a truck.*

Malysh didn't reply and unable to play it cool any longer Zoya stopped.

— *Are you annoyed?*

He slowly shook his head. Her cheeks began to burn. Changing the subject, she gestured at the scratches.

— *I'll race you. First to Stalin's body! On the count of three . . .*

Before a single number had been uttered, they both broke into a run, cheating in perfect synchronization.

Malysh tore ahead but stopped as he lost track of the scratches in the street, forced to run back, searching for clues. Like hounds hunting, they paused at the first junction, heads down, circling the possible turning points. Zoya found the trail, setting off, Malysh now behind. They were heading south and turned down towards Blaha Lujza Square, a large crossroads, a junction lined with shops.

Up ahead they saw the bronze body, flat on its belly, as wide and as long as a tramcar. They accelerated, running flat out. But Zoya had more in reserve, having paced herself, exploiting Malysh's earlier miscalculation about how far they'd have to run. She was ahead of him but only barely. She strained forward, stretching — her fingertips touching Stalin's bronze calf. Panting, smiling, she glanced at Malysh and saw that he was genuinely annoyed. He hated to lose and was trying to think of some reason to annul the race.

To seal her victory Zoya climbed the statue, her flat-soled shoes slipping over Stalin's smooth bronze thighs until she wedged her toes into the folds of his coat and pushed herself up. Standing on top she saw that Stalin's head was missing, severed at the neck, a crude decapitation. She walked the line of his back, one foot carefully in front of the other – a trapeze artist pacing a tightrope. Malysh remained on the street, hands in pockets. She smiled at him, expecting him to blush. Instead, he returned her smile. A burst of pleasure exploded inside her chest, and in her mind she performed celebratory cartwheels along Stalin's spine.

Reaching the bronze neck, she ran her fingers over the rough edge where the head appeared to have been chipped and smashed and blowtorched off. Standing up, hands on hips, conqueror, giant-slayer, she surveyed the square. There was a small crowd on the opposite side near Jozsef korut. As they moved she caught a glimpse of Stalin's head. Supported on the remains of his zigzag neck, he seemed to be staring at her, stupefied at his humiliation. A hole had been smashed in his forehead, buckling his hairline, out of which protruded a street sign: 15KM. The truck that had dragged the statue into the district had also dragged the head from the body. There were chains still attached. Zoya lowered herself to the street, peeking into the Stalin's dark stomach – hollow and black and cold, just as she suspected – before hurrying to the assembled crowd.

Malysh caught up with her, grabbing her hand.

— *Let's go back*.

— *Not yet*.

Zoya pulled free, passing through the crowd, walking straight up to Stalin's face and spitting at his huge, smooth eye. After having run so fast Zoya's mouth was dry and very little spit came out. It didn't matter. There was laughter. Pleased, she was ready to leave. But before she could retreat Zoya was lifted up and placed on top of Stalin's head, mounted on his bronze fringe. A discussion broke out in the crowd. They addressed her directly. Without any idea what they were saying she nodded. Two men hurried to the truck, talking to the driver, while another man handed her the newly modified Hungarian flag. The truck started its engine, slowly driving forward. The slack chains running from the back of the truck to Stalin's head rose up from the street. As soon as the chains were taut the head shifted position, rotating, as though it were coming to life. Zoya grabbed the protruding 15KM sign, steadying herself. Everyone was talking at once: she understood they were asking if she was OK. She nodded. They signalled to the driver. He accelerated. Stalin's head lurched forward, bumping over the tramlines.

Trying to figure out how to stop the giant head from bucking her off, she positioned her feet wide, riding the crest of Stalin's hair, hands clasped around the protruding street sign. Zoya gained confidence, standing up straight. Spotting Malysh's concerned face she smiled to reassure him, ushering him forward, wanting him to join her but he refused, crossing his arms, staying back, annoyed at her recklessness. Ignoring his grumpiness, she played to the crowd, pointing forward like an empress atop her chariot. The truck was moving at a steady pace: Stalin's head dragged at walking speed, the Hungarian flag lank behind her, trailing along the ground. She gestured to the driver – faster.

The truck accelerated. Sparks crackled from the bottom of Stalin's jaw. Zoya's hair was flapping. Picking up enough speed, the flag began to flap as well, spreading out behind her. In that second, she became an emblem of their defiance, Stalin's head under her feet, the modified Hungarian flag sweeping out. She looked around hoping to see admiration in the crowd's eyes, hoping a camera might capture this moment.

Her audience had disappeared.

At the end of Jozsef korut there was a tank, turret pointed directly at them, tracks grinding over the street, advancing at speed. The truck braked. The chains fell slack. Stalin's head stopped so suddenly it flipped forward, nose hitting the street, throwing Zoya off. Dazed, winded, she lay sprawled in the middle of the square.

Malysh grabbed her. She sat up, bruised, seeing the tank rolling straight towards them, only a couple of hundred metres away. Leaning on Malysh she stood up, staggering away. Trying to find cover, they hurried towards the nearest shop. She looked back. The tank fired: a burst of yellow, a whistling noise. The shell hit the street behind them – a cloud of smoke, fragments of stone, streaks of fire. Zoya and Malysh were smashed down.

Out of the cloud, Stalin's giant head appeared, blasted off the ground and swinging like a ball at the end of a chain, arcing towards them, as if taking revenge for its desecration. Zoya pushed Malysh flat just as it passed over, Stalin's jagged neck only centimetres above them, before crashing through the shop window, showering them with glass. Where the head travelled, the truck followed, dragged by the chains, flipped over onto its back, rotating round, crunching into the street, the driver hanging upside down.

Before they could get up, the tank appeared out of the smoke, a metallic monster. They crawled backwards, reaching the devastated pharmacy window. There was nowhere to go, no way to escape. But the tank didn't fire. The hatch was opened. A soldier appeared, taking control of the mounted machine gun. Paralysed by fear, they remained stationary. As the soldier spun the machine gun towards them a bullet struck his jaw. More bullets struck the tank, fired from every side of the square. Under bombardment the dead soldier was pulled down. Before he could close the hatch two men ran at the tank, arms raised high, holding bottles, a rag burning in each. They tossed them inside, filling the tank with fire.

Malysh grabbed Zoya.

— *We have to go*.

For once, Zoya didn't disagree.

SOVIET-CONTROLLED
EASTERN EUROPE
HUNGARY
BUDAPEST
BUDA HILL

27 OCTOBER

Leo had become frustrated at their guide's apparent lack of urgency. They had been making slow progress. It had taken two days to travel a thousand kilometres to the Hungarian border and yet three days to travel the remaining three hundred kilometres to Budapest. Not until Karoly had heard radio broadcasts announcing that disturbances were breaking out in Budapest had he picked up the pace. Quizzed, he could offer no more than a translation of the radio reports – *minor civil unrest perpetrated by bands of Fascists*. From those words it was impossible to judge the scale of the unrest. The radio broadcasts were censored and almost certainly underplaying the disruption. The request for the trouble-makers to go home suggested the authorities were no longer in control. With insufficient information, Karoly decided it was too dangerous to enter the city directly; he was driving in a circular route, avoiding several Soviet army blockades. They'd looped around to the residential Buda district, bypassing the centre, the civic buildings and Communist headquarters – flashpoints for an insurgency.

It was sunrise by the time Karoly parked the car on the vantage point of the Buda Hill, several hundred metres above the city. The adjacent streets were deserted. At the bottom of the hill the Danube divided the city into two – Buda and Pest. While the Buda half remained largely quiet, on the other side of the river there was the crackle of gunfire. Thin wisps of smoke rose from several buildings. Leo asked:

— *Have Soviet troops stormed the city yet? Is the insurgency beaten?*

Karoly shrugged

— *I know as much as you.*

Raisa turned to him.

— *This is your home. These are your people. Panin is using both to settle a political dispute. How can you work for him?*

Karoly became annoyed.

— *My people would be wise to put aside dreams of freedom. They will only get us killed. If this flushes out those troublemakers, so much the better for the rest of us . . . Whatever you may think of me, I wish only to live in peace.*

Abandoning the car, Karoly set off down the hill.

— *First, we go to my apartment.*

It was nearby, just below the castle on the slopes overlooking the Danube. Climbing the stairs to the top floor, Leo asked:

— *Do you live alone?*

— *I live with my son.*

Karoly had made no previous mention of his family and offered nothing more, entering the apartment, pacing from room to room. Finally, he called out:

379

— *Victor?*

Raisa asked:

— *How old is your son?*

— *He's twenty-three.*

— *I'm sure there's a simple explanation for where he is.*

Leo added:

— *What does he do?*

Karoly hesitated before replying:

— *He recently joined the AVH.*

Leo and Raisa remained silent, belatedly understanding their guide's apprehension. Karoly stared out of the window, speaking more to himself than Leo or Raisa:

— *There's nothing to worry about. The AVH would have called all officers into their headquarters at the onset of the uprising. He is there, for sure.*

The apartment was stocked with food, paraffin, candles and a selection of weapons. Karoly had been carrying a gun since they'd crossed the border. He suggested that Leo and Raisa follow his example since being unarmed offered no guarantee that they'd be treated as non-combatants. Leo selected the TT-33, a slim, robust Soviet-made pistol. Raisa reluctantly held it in her hands. Concentrating on the danger poised by Fraera, she forced herself to become familiar with it.

They left the apartment, heading downhill, intending to cross the Danube and enter the other side of town where it was likely that Zoya would be working alongside Fraera, at the centre of the uprising. Passing through Szena ter, they picked their way through the square's improvised fortifications. Young men sat, smoking in doorways, ready-made petrol bombs stockpiled. Tramcars had been toppled, creating a perimeter, blocking access to the streets. From the rooftops, snipers followed their movements. Trying not to arouse suspicions, the three moved slowly, edging towards the river.

Karoly led them across Margit-hid, a wide bridge that connected to a small island in the Danube before reaching Pest. Nearing the middle, Karoly gestured for them to stop. He crouched, pointing at the opposite bridge. There were tanks stationed on it. Heavy armour could be glimpsed around Parliament Square. Soviet troops were evidently engaged, but not in control, judging from the insurgency fortifications. Exposed on all sides, Karoly hunched low, hurrying. Leo and Raisa followed, blasted by the cold winds, greatly relieved when they finally reached the other side.

The city was in a schizophrenic state, neither a war zone nor anything like normality, but both at the same time, switching between the two over small distances. Zoya could be anywhere. Leo had brought two photographs, one of Zoya, a portrait they'd had taken recently as a family. She looked wretched and miserable, pale with hate. The other was Fraera's arrest photograph. She'd changed almost to the point where the photograph was useless. Karoly offered them to passers-by, all of whom wanted to help. There were, no doubt, many families doing exactly the same, searching for missing relatives. The photos were returned with an apologetic shake of the head.

Pressing onwards, they entered a narrow street entirely untouched by fighting. It was midmorning and there was a small café open for business. Customers were sipping coffee as though nothing was out of the ordinary. The only sign that something was amiss was the mass-produced leaflets piled in the gutter. Leo bent down, taking a clutch of the thin papers, cleaning off the dirt. On the top there was a stamp, an emblem — an Orthodox crucifix. Underneath, the text was Hungarian, but he recognized the name: *Nikita Sergeyevich Khrushchev*. This was Fraera's work. Excited at the confirmation of her presence in the city, he took the leaflet to Karoly.

Karoly was standing, transfixed upon a distant point. Leo's eyes followed his gaze to the end of the street. It opened out into a small square. In it there was a single leafless tree. Sunlight filled the space, contrasting with the shadows where they were standing. As his eyes adjusted, Leo focused on the trunk of the tree. It appeared to be swaying.

Karoly broke into a run. Leo and Raisa caught up with him, hurrying past the café, attracting the attention of those at the window. Reaching the end of the street on the brink of sunlight, they stopped. From the thickest branch of the tree, the body of a man hung upside down. His feet were lashed with rope. His arms swayed back and forth like a ghoulish wind charm. A fire had been lit under his body. His head was burnt clean of hair: his skin, flesh, features unrecognizable. He'd been stripped naked but only to his waist, his trousers left in an act of modesty incongruous with the savagery of his murder. The fire had burnt his shoulders, blackening his torso. The untouched skin revealed his youth. His uniform, jacket, shirt and cap were in the ashes below. He'd been burnt to death with his own uniform. As if she were whispering in his ear, Leo could hear Fraera's voice.

This is what they'll do to you.

The man had been a member of the AVH.

Leo turned to see Karoly clawing at his scalp, as though his hair were infested with lice, muttering:

— *I don't . . .*

Karoly edged closer, stretching his hand out to touch the charred face before pulling back, circling the body.

— *I don't know . . .*

He turned to Leo.

— *How can I know if this is my son?*

He dropped to his knees, falling into the cold fire, a puff of ash rising. A crowd gathered, watching the scene. Leo turned to see their expressions — hostility, anger at this display of grief being shown to the enemy, anger at their justice being rebuked. Leo sank down beside Karoly, putting an arm around him.

— *We have to go.*

— *I'm his father. I should know.*

— *It's not your son. Your son is alive. We'll find him. We have to go.*

— *Yes, he's alive. Isn't he?*

Leo helped Karoly up. But the crowd wouldn't allow them to pass.

Leo saw Raisa's hand move closer to her gun, concealed in the top of her trousers. She was right. They were in danger. Several of the crowd began talking — one man had a belt of finger-thick bullets wrapped around his neck. They were accusatory. With tears still in his eyes, Karoly pulled out the photos of Zoya and Fraera. Upon seeing the photos the man with the bullets relaxed, putting a hand on Karoly's shoulder. They spoke for some time. The crowd began to part. Once everyone was gone, Karoly whispered to Leo and Raisa:

— *Your daughter just saved our lives.*

— *That man had seen her?*

— *Fighting near the Corvin cinema.*

— *What else did he say?*

Karoly paused.

— *That you should be proud. She's killed many Russians.*

The approaching Soviet armoured personnel carrier caused panic among the crowd as surely as an explosion detonating in their midst. Every citizen was propelled in a different direction, desperate to get off the street. Raisa ran as fast as she could, men and women and children beside her, their positions interchanging. An elderly man fell. A woman tried to help him, tugging his coat, straining to get him clear of the road. The carrier either didn't see the man or didn't care: prepared to ride over the couple as though they were rubble. Raisa hurried back, heaving the man out of the way as it crunched past – the tracks so close Raisa felt a rush of metallic air.

Raisa checked the street. There was no sight of Leo or Karoly but they were close. Exploiting the confusion created by the carrier, she turned down a side street – any street – running until, exhausted, she stopped. She waited, catching her breath. She'd separated from Leo. She was now free to search for Zoya by herself.

The idea had occurred to her in Moscow more or less as soon as she'd heard that Zoya was alive. Zoya could imagine a life with her. She'd said so. She could not imagine one with Leo. Over these six months Raisa was unable to see how that point of view would've changed. If anything Zoya's position was likely to have become more entrenched. On the train into Hungary her resolve had strengthened as she'd watched Karoly interact with Leo – two former agents, suspicious of each other, yet connected like members of a secret society. Zoya would ask: *Two KGB agents sent to rescue me?* She'd spit at the idea. How little they understood her, the exact sentiment Fraera had no doubt exploited, claiming to empathize with Zoya's sense of isolation.

Raisa doubted that Leo would accept that her disappearance was deliberate. Karoly might guess her true intention. Leo would deny it. That delay gave her a slim advantage. Karoly had provided them with a map of the city, marking his apartment in case they should get separated. She estimated her position to be somewhere near Stahly ut. She needed to travel directly south, keeping off the most obvious routes, to the Corvin cinema, where Zoya had been sighted.

Making slow progress, forced to keep her map hidden, she reached Ulloi ut. The district had seen intense fighting: there were spent tank shells scattered on the broken cobblestones. Despite the street's size Raisa could see very few people, figures darting between doorways and then nothing – eerie stillness for such a key thoroughfare. Remaining close to the edge of the buildings, tentatively advancing, she scooped up a broken brick, ready to duck into a doorway or smash a window and climb through should she need to take cover. As her fingers handled the brick she noticed the underneath was wet. Perplexed, looking down, she saw the street was coated in slime.

Material had been carpeted across the width of the street. It was silk, rolls and rolls of precious silk. Yet it was soaked in a soapy lather. Bemused, Raisa tentatively stepped forward, her smooth-soled shoes slipping so that progress was only possible by keeping one hand on the wall. As though she'd set off an alarm, shouting bellowed out from the windows above. There were men and women on both sides, in the windows, on the roof, heavily armed. Hearing a rumbling, feeling the vibrations, Raisa turned. A tank pulled onto the street, circled, surveying both directions before spinning towards her, pivoting on its tracks and accelerating. Everyone in the windows and on the roof disappeared, pulling back, out of sight. This was a trap. She was in the middle of it.

Raisa hurried across the wet silk, falling over, scrambling up and reaching the nearest shop. The door was locked. The tank was close behind. She swung the brick, smashed the window – large shards falling around her. She clambered inside just as the tank reached the beginning of the frothy silk. Raisa looked back, convinced the tank would ride across this unsophisticated obstacle with ease. But it immediately lurched to the side, no longer gripping, chomping up the slippery silk. There was no traction, no control. Looking up at the rooftop, Raisa saw the waiting forces amassing – a volley of petrol bombs crashed down around the tank, streaking it with fire. The tank angled its turret towards the top of the building, firing a shell. Unable to control its position the shell missed, racing into the sky.

Raisa hurried further into the shop. The walls began to shake. She turned around. Through the smashed window she saw the tank veering towards her. She dived to the floor as the tank crashed into the shop front, the turret spiking through the ceiling above her, walls crumbling. The tank was wedged to a standstill.

In the smoke and dust, Raisa picked herself up, stumbling towards the back of the ruined shop, reaching the stairs only to hear the insurgents coming down from their rooftop positions. Caught between the tank and the descending force, she retreated behind the shop counter, drawing her own gun. With her eye level just above the counter, she saw a Soviet soldier open the tank's hatch.

The insurgents arrived. Raisa caught sight of a machine gun carried by a young woman wearing a beret. The woman cocked her gun, raising it towards the Russian soldier, ready to fire. The young woman was Zoya.

Raisa stood up. Reacting to the movement, Zoya swung around, aiming the gun at her. Face to face after six months, surrounded by swirling brick dust and smoke, the machine gun sagged in Zoya's hands as though it was impossibly heavy. She stood dumb, mouth open. In the background the grimy-faced Russian soldier, perhaps no more than twenty years old, exploited the opportunity. He pointed his gun at Zoya. Reacting instinctively, Raisa aimed her TT-33, pulled the trigger, firing several shots, one hit to the young man's head, flicking it back.

In disbelief at what she'd done, Raisa stared at the soldier's body, her gun still pointing. Pulling herself together, aware that there was very little time, she looked back at Zoya. Stepping forward, she took hold of her daughter's hands.

— *Zoya, we have to go. Please, you trusted me before, trust me again.*

There was conflict in Zoya's expression. Raisa was pleased — there was something to work with. About to make her case, Raisa paused. Fraera had appeared at the bottom of the stairs.

Raisa pulled Zoya aside, taking aim. Caught unawares, Fraera didn't defend herself. Raisa had a clear shot. She hesitated. In that moment she felt the barrel of a gun pressed against her back. Zoya was pointing the gun directly at her heart.

Having spent several hours looking for Raisa, fearing that she might be hurt, Leo finally understood that she must have left him to find Zoya. She didn't believe Zoya would come home with him. Running in an attempt to catch up with her, he arrived at the Corvin cinema, where Zoya had been sighted. It was a defensible oval building set back from the street, connected by a pedestrian walkway that had been blocked off and fortified. A fighter approached. Karoly had been left far behind, unable to keep up. Without his translator, Leo was saved from questioning by the arrival of a Soviet T-34 tank, now in the insurgents' hands, a Hungarian flag hanging from the turret. The fighters surrounded it, cheering. Pushing through the crowd, Leo raised the photograph of Zoya. After examining the photograph one man pointed down the boulevard.

Leo set off, running again. The boulevard was empty. He stopped, bending down – the entire street was covered in ripped silk. Patches of the silk were burnt through, smouldering, while patches were soaking wet. He saw where the captured tank had veered off the street and smashed into a shop front. The corpses of four Soviet soldiers were heaped on the ground. None of them was much older than twenty.

There was no one else around.

Raisa closed her eyes, concentrating on the noises in the surrounding rooms – people running, shouting, items being
dragged, orders being barked in Russian and Hungarian. Injured
men and women cried out in pain. One room was being used to
carry out crude treatments for injuries sustained in the fighting;
another served as a mess hall for Fraera's band of insurgents – the
smell of antiseptic mingling with the smells of cooking, fried meat
and animal fat.

Escorted from the tank at gunpoint, Raisa had barely paid
attention to where she was being led, focused entirely on Zoya as
she'd marched ahead, striding like a soldier, gun over her shoulder – the gun that she'd just pointed at Raisa's heart. Arriving at
an apartment block set back from the street and accessed through
a passageway, Raisa had been taken to the top floor, hustled into
a small room that had been hastily stripped bare and improvised
as a cell.

The walls began to shake. Heavy armour was passing close
by. Raisa peered through the small window. There were skir-
mishes in the street below. Directly above her head there was the
sound of feet on tiles, snipers moving into position. Raisa
crouched by the wall furthest from the window, exhausted,
hands over her ears. She thought about Zoya. She thought

about the young Soviet soldier she'd killed. Finally, she allowed herself to cry.

*

Hearing footsteps outside the room and a key in the lock, Raisa stood up. Fraera entered. Whereas before, in Moscow, she'd been unruffled and in control, she now appeared tired, strained by the pressures of her operation.

— *So, you found me . . .*

Raisa's words trembled with anger:

— *I'm here for Zoya.*

— *Where's Leo?*

— *I'm alone.*

— *You're lying. But we'll find him soon enough. This is not a large city.*

— *Let Zoya go.*

— *You speak as though I stole her. The truth is I rescued her from you.*

— *Whatever problems we had as a family, we love her. You don't.*

Fraera hardly seemed to register the observation.

— *Zoya wanted to join me, so I allowed her to. She is free to do whatever she likes. If she wants to go home with you, she can. I won't stop her.*

— *It's easy to win a child's favour by allowing them to do whatever they want and telling them whatever they want to hear. Give her a machine gun; tell her she's a revolutionary. It's a seductive lie. I don't believe she loves you for it.*

— *I don't ask her to. You and Leo, on the other hand, you demand love. You're both obsessed with it. And the truth is that she was miserable living with you, whereas she's happy with me.*

Over Fraera's shoulder, at the end of the corridor, Raisa could see an injured man spread on the kitchen table. There were no doctors, little equipment to speak of, bloody rags and pots of boiling water.

— *If you stay here, you are going to die. Zoya is going to die with you.*

Fraera shook her head.

— *Concern for her well-being is no proof that you're a parent. The fact is, you're no more her mother than I am.*

*

Raisa awoke. The room was dark and cold and she shivered, pulling the thin bedding around her. It was night. The city was quiet. She hadn't expected to sleep but as soon as she'd lain down her eyes had closed. There was a plate of meat and potatoes on the floor, deposited while she'd been asleep. She reached out, pulling the plate closer. Only now did she notice the door was open.

Standing up, walking forward, she glanced into the hallway. The corridors were empty. To escape would be a matter of leaving the apartment, descending the stairway then exiting to the street. Was it possible that Zoya had opened the door and broken the lock, wanting to help while at the same time concealing her involvement? The enterprise demonstrated stealth and skill yet it was based upon a false assumption. Raisa wasn't here to escape: she was here to bring Zoya home. Zoya would understand that. The method was inconsistent with her character, circumspect while she was bold and brash.

Uneasy, Raisa stepped away. At the same time a shadowy outline appeared in the door. It was the figure of young boy. He spoke in a whisper.

— *Why don't you escape?*

— *Not without Zoya.*

He sprang forward, wrapping a leg around hers, uprooting it and forcing her to the floor, her cry stifled by his hand. She was on her back, pinned down. Raisa felt a knife against her throat. He whispered:

— *You should've run.*

She repeated, speaking through his fingers:

— *Not without Zoya.*

At the mention of Zoya's name she felt his body tense, the blade press against her neck. Raisa asked:

— *You . . . like her?*

There was a shift in his position. His grip around her mouth loosened. She was right. This was about Zoya: the boy was worried about losing her. Raisa said:

— *Listen to me. She's in danger. You are too. Come with us.*

— *She's not yours!*

—*You're right. She's not mine. But I care about her a great deal. And if you do too, you'll find a way to get her out of here. You hear the difference between my voice and Fraera's voice, don't you? You hear that I care? You know that she doesn't.*

The boy removed the knife from her neck. He seemed uncertain. Raisa guessed his thoughts.

— *Come back with us. You're the reason she's happy, not Fraera.*

The boy got to his feet, hurrying out, shutting the door and then opening it again. Remembering the lock was broken, he whispered:

— *Pretend you were trying to break out. If you don't they'll kill me.*

The boy disappeared. Raisa called out:

— *Wait!*

The boy reappeared.

— *What's your name?*

He hesitated.

— *Malysh.*

Leo counted at least thirty tanks, a column advancing along the main boulevard into the city. A deployment of this size, mobilizing at six in the morning, meant a full-scale Soviet invasion was imminent. The insurgency was about to be wiped out.

Leo hastened down the hill, running back to Karoly's apartment. Climbing the stairs, two at a time, he reached the top landing, pushing open the door. Karoly was seated at the table, reading a leaflet. Leo explained:

— *The Soviets have mobilized over thirty tanks. They're entering the city. We have to find Zoya and Raisa immediately.*

Karoly handed him the leaflet. Impatient, Leo glanced at it. At the top there was a photograph. It was of Leo. Karoly translated the text:

— *This man is a Soviet spy. He is disguised as one of us. Report his whereabouts to the nearest revolutionary stronghold.*

Leo put down the leaflet.

— *If Fraera's looking for me, it's proof that Raisa has been captured.*

Karoly remarked:

— *Leo, it's no longer safe for you to go outside.*

Leo opened the door, ready to go.

— *No one is going to care about one Russian spy when there are Russian tanks on every street corner.*

The door to the apartment opposite was ajar. A slice of the neighbour's face was visible. They held eye contact. Then the neighbour shut the door.

Two *vory* entered Raisa's room, grabbed her by the arms, led her into the hallway, out of the front door and onto the balcony. The courtyard below was crowded. Fraera stood at the centre. Seeing Raisa arrive she waved her men aside. They parted, revealing Leo and Karoly on their knees, their arms bound in front of them like slaves ready for sale. Zoya was in among the crowd of onlookers.

Leo stood up. Guns were directed at him. Fraera gestured for them to be put away.

— *Let him speak.*

— *Fraera, we don't have much time. There are over thirty T-34s in the city right now. The Soviets are going to crush this resistance. They're going to kill every man, woman and child holding a gun. There is no chance of victory.*

— *I disagree.*

— *Frol Panin is laughing at you. This uprising is a sham. This isn't about the future of Hungary. You're being exploited.*

— *Maxim, you see everything upside down. I am not being exploited: I am exploiting Panin. I could never have done this on my own. My revenge would have finished in Moscow. Instead of merely being able to take revenge on the men and women involved in my arrest, as I originally planned, he has presented me with an opportunity to take revenge upon the very State that destroyed my life. Here, I am hurting Russia.*

— *No, you're not. The Soviet forces can lose a hundred tanks and a thousand soldiers and it won't matter. They won't care.*

— *Panin has underestimated the depth of hatred here.*

— *Hatred isn't enough.*

Fraera turned her attention to Karoly.

— *You're his translator? An appointment arranged by Frol Panin?*

— *Yes.*

— *You have instructions to kill me?*

Karoly considered, then replied:

— *Either Leo or I was supposed to kill you. Once the uprising began.*

Leo was shocked. Fraera shook her head dismissively.

Did you not realise your true purpose, Leo? You are an unwitting assassin. You are working for Panin, not me.

— *I didn't know.*

— *That is your answer to everything . . . you didn't know. Let me explain. I didn't start this uprising. All I did was to encourage it. You could kill me. It wouldn't make any difference.*

Leo turned to Zoya. She had a gun over her shoulder, grenades on her belt. Her clothes were torn; her hands were scratched. She held his glance, an expression rigid with hatred as if fearful any other emotion might creep through. The boy who'd murdered the Patriarch was beside her. He was holding her hand.

— *If you fight, you will die.*

Fraera addressed Zoya.

— *Zoya? What do you say? Leo is speaking to you.*

Zoya punched the air with her gun.

— *We fight!*

Though Raisa wanted to talk, Leo's body language was set against it. He'd not spoken since being manhandled into the cell. On the other side of the room, Karoly lay sprawled on the bedding, his eyes closed. His leg had been injured during his capture. Breaking the silence, Raisa said:

— *Leo, I'm sorry.*

Leo looked up at her.

— *I made one mistake, Raisa. I should've told you about Zoya. I should've told you about her holding the knife over me.*

Still lying down, his eyes closed, Karoly interjected:

— *The daughter we're trying to rescue, she stands over you with a knife?*

Karoly opened an eye, looking at Raisa, then at Leo.

Leo lowered his voice, trying to cut Karoly out of the conversation.

— *The only way we're going to escape is if we trust each other.*

Raisa nodded.

— *Trust is not going to break us out of this room.*

Leo asked:

— *Do you have any idea how we're going to get Zoya out of here?*

— *She's in love.*

Leo pulled back in surprise.

— *In love with who?*

— *A* vory, *he's young – the same age as her, his name is Malysh.*

— *That boy is a murderer. I watched him kill the Patriarch. He decapitated a seventy-five-year-old man with a length of wire.*

Karoly sat up.

— *They sound like a good match.*

Raisa took hold of Leo's hands.

— *Malysh might be our only hope.*

Zoya lay at the crumbling edge of the house. Damaged by shell-fire, its front had collapsed. Flat on her stomach, with the rifle stretched out before her, Zoya's eye was pressed up against the scope. There were two tanks at the mouth of the Kossuth hid, the bridge near Parliament, no doubt waiting for orders to advance into the city as Leo had predicted.

She'd never expected to see Leo again. She couldn't concentrate, seeing his face. Restless, she needed to pee. Checking on the tanks, seeing no movement, she left her rifle and examined the remains of the bedroom. Since the entire front of the house had fallen down, the room was exposed. The wardrobe offered the only privacy without going too far from her post. She slipped inside and shut the doors, squatting. She felt guilty about dabbing dry with the sleeve of a coat, an odd kind of guilt considering she was about to shoot a man. She'd fired her gun on numerous occasions and it was possible she'd already killed although she hadn't seen anyone die or fall down. Without warning, grabbing a nearby shoe, she threw up, filling it to the toe.

Unsteady, she stepped out of the wardrobe, shutting the doors. The rifle was as she'd left it, lying across the bricks. Shaking, she slowly returned to her position. A Soviet soldier was staggering towards the two tanks. Zoya lined up the injured officer in her crosshairs. She couldn't see his face, only his back — his brown hair. The other officers might come to his aid. Fraera had taught her that these were the officers to shoot, the real prize, before finishing off the injured man.

The wounded soldier fell ten paces from the tank, unable to walk any further. Zoya moved the crosshairs towards the hatch, waiting to see if they'd take the bait. The tank came to life, edging forward, moving as close to the wounded man as possible. They were going to save him. The hatch opened. A soldier cautiously lifted the steel lid, peering out, waiting to see if he'd be shot, ready to duck back down. After a pause, he climbed out, hurrying to the aid of his injured comrade. Zoya had the man in her sights. If she didn't pull the trigger he would help his comrade back into the tank, then they would advance into the city and kill more innocent families and what good would her guilt be then? She was here to fight. They were the enemy. They'd killed children and mothers and fathers.

About to pull the trigger, a hand pushed the gun down. It was Malysh. He lay beside her, their faces close together. She was trembling. He took hold of her rifle, checking on the tanks. She peered over the rubble. The tanks were moving again. But they weren't advancing into the city: they were heading in the opposite direction, back across the bridge. Zoya asked:

— *Where are they going?*
— *I don't know.*

Leo examined the room, searching for a way out. Engrossed in his study of the door, the window, the floorboards, he noticed the relative quiet. The sound of explosions and gunfire had stopped. There were footsteps outside the cell. The door opened. Fraera strode in.

— *Listen!*

A radio in the adjacent room was turned up to full volume. The presenter was speaking Hungarian. Leo turned to Karoly. He listened for several seconds. Impatient, Fraera called out:

— *Translate!*

Karoly glanced up at Leo.

— *A ceasefire has been declared. Soviet forces are pulling out of the city.*

Sensing scepticism, Fraera insisted on a victory tour. They set out, Leo, Raisa and Karoly, surrounded by insurgents and the remains of her gang. Leo counted only four *vory*, excluding Fraera and Malysh, far fewer than in Moscow. Some might have been killed. Others must have abandoned her cause: the life of a revolutionary was not the life of a professional criminal. Fraera didn't seem to care, leading them down the central thoroughfare of Sztalin ut as proudly as if she was marching on Stalin's tomb. Raisa was beside Leo, Karoly just behind, dragging his injured leg. Through the ring of armed men, Leo caught glimpses of Zoya orbiting the group. She walked beside Malysh. Though Zoya ignored Leo completely, from time to time Malysh would flick a hostile glance in his direction. Raisa was correct. They were, unquestionably, in love.

Leo didn't see how a Hungarian triumph was even a theoretical possibility. He'd observed the insurgents armed with bricks and petrol-filled bottles. They fought fearlessly, fighting for their homes, the ground on which they stood. But as a former soldier he saw no strategy. Their campaign was haphazard and improvised. In contrast, the Red Army was the most powerful military force in the world, numerically and technologically. Panin and his co-conspirators intended to keep it that way. The loss of Hungary would never be tolerated, no matter how bloody the conflict became. Yet pacing the streets Leo was forced to accept that there was no longer any Soviet presence in the city. There were no tanks or troops. Many of the Hungarian fighters had abandoned their positions.

Fraera stopped walking. They'd arrived at an office, a medium-sized, unremarkable building. There was a commotion at the front doors, a great number of people entering and exiting. Karoly dragged himself forward, catching up with Leo.

— *This is the headquarters of the AVH.*

Leo replied:

— *Your son?*

— *This is where he works. The officers must have fled as soon as the uprising began.*

Fraera noticed their exchange. She moved through the line of her men, asking:

— *You're familiar with this building? It is the home of the Hungarian secret police. They've abandoned it and are now hiding somewhere. But we will find them.*

Karoly managed to conceal his concerns. Fraera continued:

— *Now that the city is free, the building is open to the public. The secrets held here are secrets no longer.*

Most of the insurgents remained outside. The building was too busy to accommodate the entire gang. Fraera led a smaller group through the doors, entering an internal courtyard. Sheets of paper, typed and stamped, the bureaucracy of terror, fluttered down from the balconies. It was dusk. Electricity was spotty. To compensate, candles were lit, spread across the balconies and floors. The offices were filled with citizens searching through files. Reading by candlelight, men and women thumbed through the information stored about them. Watching many of them cry, Leo didn't need the documents translated. The files contained the names of family and friends who'd denounced them, the words spoken against them. Like a hundred mirrors dropped on the floor, all around he saw faith in mankind shattering. Fraera whispered:

— *Downstairs.*

Whereas the offices had been crowded, the stairs leading to the basement were empty. Taking a candle each they descended. The air was damp and cold. Just as Leo knew the words in those files, he knew what they'd find downstairs — the cells where suspects had been questioned and tortured.

Water dripped onto cracked concrete floors. All the cell doors had been opened. In the first, there was a table and two chairs. In the second, there was a drain in the centre of the room and nothing more. Leo watched Zoya's face, desperate to pick her up and carry her out of this place. She took hold of Malysh's hand. Leo scrunched his fingers into a tight fist, wondering how long Fraera would make them stay down here. To his surprise, Fraera, apparently fearless, seemed shaken by this place. He thought upon the tortures she must have gone through after her arrest. She sighed:

— *Let's drink to the end of all this.*

And briefly, in the darkness, she was human again.

*

In the courtyard of her apartment complex Fraera intended to host the first victory celebration. Open to all, she provided crates of alcohol, spirits, liqueurs and champagne — the preserve of the elite, drinks many had never tasted before, secreted away for exactly this moment. Leo noted these preparations: proof that she always believed victory was possible. To offset the cold, a fire was built in the centre of the courtyard with timber stacked as tall as a man, flames reaching high into the night sky. Crude effigies of

Stalin and his Hungarian equivalent, Rakosi, were dressed in uniforms stripped from the corpses of Soviet soldiers. Leo noted that Fraera photographed the flaming figures, standing on the top-floor balcony, taking care over the shots before putting her camera away.

As the burning uniforms turned to ash, a *cygany* band arrived clutching hand-painted instruments. After a timid start, as if worried that their violins would draw a barrage of Soviet shells, they gradually forgot their anxieties. The music became louder and faster and the fighters began to dance.

Leo and Raisa were sat back from the party, under armed guard, spectators as Zoya became drunk, sipping champagne, her cheeks turning red. Fraera drank from a bottle, which she did not share, always in control. Catching Leo's eye, she joined them.

— *You can dance if you want.*

Leo asked:

— *What are you going to do with us now?*

— *The truth is, I haven't decided.*

Zoya was trying to persuade Malysh to dance. Unsuccessful, she grabbed his hand, pulling him into the ring of people circling the fire. Though she'd seen him clamber up drainpipes, nimble as a cat, he was awkward. Zoya whispered:

— *Pretend it's just you and me.*

Under the pretence that they were alone, they spun around the fire, the world becoming a blur, the fire hot on their faces, dancing faster and faster until the music stopped and everyone clapped. But, for them, the world continued to spin and they had only each other to hold on to.

The fire had burnt down to a mound of red embers and charred stubs. The *cygany* band was no longer playing. The revellers had returned home, those who hadn't passed out. Malysh and Zoya were curled up under a blanket, close to the remains of the fire. Karoly was humming an indistinguishable tune, drunk after having pleaded for alcohol to numb the pain of his leg. As energetic as if she'd rested the entire night, Fraera declared:

— *Why sleep in cramped apartments?*

Forced to take part in Fraera's expedition, they left the courtyard, crossing the Danube, treading wearily towards their destination – the ministerial villas on the lush Buda slopes. Malysh and Zoya accompanied them, along with the *vory* and Fraera's Hungarian interpreter. From the top of Rose Hill, they watched dawn rise on the city. Fraera observed:

— *For the first time in over ten years, the city will wake up to freedom.*

Arriving at a gated villa with high walls, there were, remarkably, guards stationed at the perimeter. Fraera turned to her interpreter.

— *Tell them to go home. Tell them this is now the property of the people.*

The translator approached the gate, repeating her words in

Hungarian. Perhaps having watched the fighting the guards had already come to a similar decision. They were protecting the privileges of a fallen regime. They lifted up the gate, took their things and left. The interpreter returned, excited.

— *The guards say this villa belonged to Rakosi.*

Slurring his words, Karoly remarked to Leo:

— *The play-place of my former boss, the once glorious leader of my country. This is where we used to phone him and ask: do you want us to piss in the suspect's mouth, sir? Do you want to listen while we do it? Yes, he would say, I want to hear it all.*

They entered the immaculately landscaped grounds.

Fraera was smoking a hand-rolled cigarette. From the smell Leo guessed it contained stimulants. Amphetamines would explain how she maintained her ferocious energy levels. Her eyes appeared completely black, pupils like puddles of oil. Leo had used her drug during the all-night arrests and interrogations he'd performed as an officer of the MGB. It would exacerbate aggression. It would make reasoning impossible, skewing her mind towards violence while sealing every decision in unshakeable confidence.

With the keys from the security guard's hut, Fraera ran up the stairs, unlocked the doors and threw them wide open. She bowed to Malysh and Zoya.

— *A new couple should have a new home!*

Malysh blushed. Zoya smiled as she entered the house, her exclamation of amazement echoing around the grand reception hall.

— *There's a pool!*

The swimming pool was covered in a protective plastic sheet, spotted with dead leaves. Zoya dipped her fingers in the water.

— *It's cold.*

The heaters had stopped working. The teak chairs had been

stacked in the corner. A deflated, brightly coloured beach ball was nudged this way and that by the wind.

Inside the house, luxury had decayed. The kitchen was covered with dust, unused since Rakosi was forced to leave Hungary, exiled to the Soviet Union after the Secret Speech. Built to the highest specification, the appliances were foreign. Crystal and fine porcelain filled the cupboards. Bottles of French wine were unopened. Fascinated by the contents of the fridge, trying to identify items turned patchy with mould, Leo and Zoya chanced across each other. Side by side, it was the closest they'd been since his capture.

— *Zoya . . .*

Before he could finish, Fraera called out:

— *Zoya!*

Zoya ran off, obeying the call of her new master.

Following behind, entering the living room, Leo came face to face with Stalin. A vast oil portrait hung from the wall, staring down, a god keeping watch over his subjects. Fraera drew a knife, offering it to Zoya:

— *There's no one to denounce you now.*

Knife in hand, Zoya stepped up onto a chair, her eyes coming level with Stalin's neck. In the perfect position to mutilate his face she did nothing. Fraera called out:

— *Gouge out his eyes! Blind him! Shave off his moustache!*

Zoya stepped down, offering the knife to Fraera.

— *I don't . . . feel like it.*

Fraera's mood switched from elation to irritation.

— *You don't feel like it? Anger doesn't come and go. Anger isn't fickle. Anger isn't like love. It isn't something you feel one minute but not the next. Anger stays with you for ever. He murdered your parents.*

Zoya raised her voice in reply.

— I don't want to think about that all the time!

Fraera slapped Zoya. Leo stepped forward. Fraera drew her gun, pointing it at Leo's chest but continuing to speak to Zoya.

— You forget your parents? Is it that easy? What has changed? Malysh has kissed you? Is that it?

Fraera walked towards him, grabbing Malysh and kissing him. He struggled but she held him fast. Finished, she pulled back.

— Nice, but I'm still angry.

She fired a shot between Stalin's eyes and then another and another, emptying her gun into the portrait, the canvas shaking with each bullet. No bullets left, the trigger clicked against the chamber. Fraera threw gun at his face, the weapon bouncing off, clattering to the ground. She wiped her brow before laughing:

— Bedtime . . .

Loaded with innuendo, she pushed Zoya and Malysh together.

*

Startled, Leo woke, shaken by one of the *vory*.

— We're leaving.

Without any explanation, Leo, Raisa and Karoly were rushed to their feet. They'd been locked in the marble bathroom, using towels to make a bed. They couldn't have snatched more than a couple of hours' sleep. Fraera was outside by the gate. Malysh and Zoya were beside her, everyone exhausted, except for Fraera, jittery with chemical energy. She pointed downhill, towards the centre of town.

— Word is that they've found the missing AVH officers. They've been hiding in the Communist Party headquarters all along.

Karoly's expression changed. His exhaustion disappeared.

It took an hour to descend the hills and return across the river, approaching Republic Square where the party headquarters were located. There was gunfire and smoke. The headquarters was under siege. Tanks under insurgent control shelled the outer walls. Two trucks were on fire. Windows were smashed; chunks of concrete and brick were falling to the ground.

Fraera advanced into the square, taking cover behind a statue as bullets whistled overhead, fired from the rooftops. Held back by the crossfire, they waited. Abruptly the gunfire stopped. A man with a handmade white flag stepped out from the headquarters, petitioning for his life. He was shot. As he collapsed, the foremost insurgents rushed forward, storming the premises.

In the safety of the lull, Fraera led them from behind the statue across the square. A crowd of fighters gathered at the entrance beside the smouldering trucks. Fraera joined them, Leo and the others around her. Under the trucks were the blackened bodies of soldiers. The crowd waited for the captured AVH officers to be fed out to them. Leo observed that not all of the crowd were fighters: there were photographers and members of the international press, cameras hanging around their necks. Leo turned to see Karoly. His earlier expression of hope that he might find his son had transformed into dread, longing for his son to be anywhere but here.

The first of the AVH officers was pulled out, a young man. As he raised his hands he was shot. A second man was pulled out. Leo didn't understand what he was saying but it was obvious the man was pleading for his life. Mid-plea, he was shot. A third officer ran out and seeing his dead friends on the ground tried to run back into the building. Leo saw Karoly step forward. This young man was his son.

Infuriated at his attempt to run from justice, the fighters grabbed the officer, beating him as he clung to the doors. Karoly pushed forward, shrugging Leo off, breaking through the fighters and wrapping his arms around his son. Startled by the reunion, his son was crying, hoping somehow that his father could protect him. Karoly was shouting at the mob. They were together, father and son, for less than a couple of seconds before Karoly was pulled away, pinned down, forced to watch as his son's uniform was ripped off, buttons popping, the shirt shredded. The boy was turned upside down, rope lashed around his ankles, carried towards the trees in the square.

Leo turned to Fraera, to petition for the boy's life, only to see Zoya had already grabbed hold of her arms, saying:

— *Stop them. Please.*

Fraera crouched down, as a parent might when explaining the world to a child.

— *This is anger.*

With that, Fraera took out a camera of her own.

Karoly broke free, staggering lamely after his son, weeping as he saw him strung up, hanging upside down from the tree, still alive — his face bright red, veins bulging. Karoly grabbed his son's shoulders, supporting his weight only for a rifle butt to be smashed in his face. He fell backwards. Petrol was poured over his son.

Moving quickly Leo strode up to one of the *vory*, a man distracted by the execution. He punched him in the throat, winding him, taking his rifle. Dropping to one knee, Leo lined up a shot through the crowd. He'd get one chance, one shot. The petrol was lit. The son was on fire, shaking, screaming. Leo closed an eye, waiting for the crowd to part. He fired. The bullet struck the young man in the head. Still burning, his body hung still. The fighters turned, regarding Leo. Fraera already had a gun pointed at him.

— *Put it down.*

Leo dropped the rifle.

Karoly got up, clutching his son's body, trying to smother the flames, as if he could still be saved. He was now burning too, the skin of his hands bubbling red. He didn't care, holding on to his son even as his own clothes caught alight. The fighters watched the man grieve and burn, no longer boisterous in their hate. Leo wanted to call out for someone to help, to do something. Finally a middle-aged man raised his gun and shot Karoly in the back of the head. His body fell on top of the fire, underneath his son. As they burnt together, many in the crowd were already hastening away.

Back in the apartment, among the hungover *vory* and joyous Hungarian students, Malysh tried to find some space, retreating to the kitchen, making a bed under the table. He took hold of Zoya's hands. As if rescued from a freezing sea she couldn't stop shaking. When Fraera entered the room he could feel Zoya's body tense, as if a predator was nearby. Fraera had a gun in one hand and a bottle of champagne in the other. She crouched down, her eyes blood-shot, her lips cracked.

— *There's a party in one of the squares tonight, thousands of people will be there. Farmers from the country are bringing in food. Pigs will be roasted whole.*

Malysh replied:

— *Zoya isn't feeling well.*

Fraera reached out, touching Zoya's forehead.

— *There will be no police, no State, just the citizens of a free nation, and all of us without fear. We must be there, all of us.*

As soon as she left the room Zoya began to shake again, having contained her emotions during their conversation. The soldiers who lay on the streets, bodies coated in lime, were uniforms more than they were men, symbols of an invading force. The dead Hungarians, flowers thrown over their graves, were symbols of a noble resistance. Everyone, dead or alive, was a symbol of something. Yet Karoly had been first and foremost a father and the officer strung up had been his son.

Malysh whispered to Zoya:

— *We're going to run away, tonight. I don't know where we'll go. But we'll survive. I'm good at surviving: it's the only thing I am good at, except maybe killing.*

Zoya considered for a moment, asking:

— *Fraera?*

— *We can't tell her. We wait until everyone is at the party and then we go. What do you say? Will you come with me?*

*

Zoya drifted in and out of sleep. In her dreams she imagined the place where they'd live, somewhere far away, a remote farm, in a free country, hidden by forests. They didn't have much land: just enough to feed themselves. There was a river, not too wide or fast or deep, where they swam and fished. She opened her eyes. The apartment was dark. Unsure how long she'd been asleep, she looked at Malysh. He raised a finger to his lips. She noticed the bundle he'd prepared and guessed that it contained clothes, food and money. He must have readied it while she was sleeping. Leaving the kitchen, they saw no one in the main room. Everyone was at the party. They hurried out, down the stairs, into the courtyard. Zoya lingered, remembering Leo and Raisa, locked in the top-floor apartment.

A voice called out from the dark passageway:

— *They'll be touched when I tell them how you hesitated, sparing them a thought, before running away.*

Fraera stepped out from the shadows. Quick-witted, Zoya lied:

— *We're coming to the party.*

— *So what's in the bundle?*

415

Fraera shook her head. Malysh stepped forward:

— *You don't need us any more.*

Zoya added:

— *You talk about freedom. Allow us to go.*

Fraera nodded.

— *Freedoms are fought for. I will give you that chance. Draw blood and I'll let you both go – a single graze, a cut, a nick, nothing more. Spill a drop of blood.*

Malysh hesitated, unsure. Fraera began walking towards them.

— *You can't cut me without a knife.*

Malysh drew his knife, ushering Zoya back. Unarmed, Fraera continued walking towards them. Malysh crouched low, ready to strike.

— *Malysh, I thought you understood. Relationships are a weakness. Look at how nervous you are. Why? Because there's too much at stake, her life and your life – your dream of being together, it makes you fearful. It makes you vulnerable.*

Malysh attacked. Fraera sidestepped his blade, grabbing his wrist and punching him in the face. He fell to the ground, the knife now in her hand. She stood over him:

— *You're such a disappointment to me.*

*

Leo turned to the door. Malysh entered first, Zoya followed, a knife pressed against her neck. Fraera lowered the blade, pushing Zoya inside.

— *I wouldn't get too excited. I caught them trying to run off together, happy to leave you behind without so much as a goodbye.*

Raisa stepped forward.

— *Nothing you say makes any difference to the way we feel about Zoya.*

Fraera retorted with mock sincerity:

— *That does seem to be true. No matter what Zoya does, whether she holds a knife over your bed, whether she runs away, pretends to be dead, you still believe there's a chance she'll love you. It's a kind of sentimental fanaticism. You're right: there's nothing I can say. However, there might be something I can say that will change the way you feel about Malysh.*

She paused.

— *Raisa, he is your son.*

Leo waited for Raisa to dismiss the notion. During the Great Patriotic War she'd given birth to a son but he had died. When Raisa finally spoke, her voice was subdued.

— *My son is dead.*

Fraera turned to Leo, smug with secrets, gesturing with her knife.

— *Raisa gave birth to a son. Conceived during the war, the result of soldiers rewarded for risking their lives and being allowed to take whomever they pleased. They took her, over and over, producing a bastard child of the Red Army.*

Raisa's words were washed out, drained, but they were steady and calm.

— *I didn't care who the father was. The child was mine, not his. I swore I would love him even though he'd been conceived in the most hateful circumstances.*

— *Except that you abandoned the boy in an orphanage.*

— *I was sick and homeless. I had nothing. I couldn't feed myself.*

Raisa had not yet made eye contact with Malysh. Fraera shook her head in disgust.

— *I would never have given up my child, no matter how dire my circumstances. They had to take my son from me while I was sleeping.*

418

Raisa seemed exhausted, unable to defend herself.

— *I vowed to go back. Once I was well, once the war was over, once I had a home.*

— *When you returned to the orphanage they told you that your son had died. And like a fool, you believed them. Typhus, they told you?*

— *Yes.*

— *Having had some experience of the lies told by orphanages, I double-checked their story. A typhus epidemic killed a large number of children. However, many survived by running away. Those escapees had been covered up as fatalities. Children who run away from orphanages often become pickpockets in train stations.*

His past rewritten with every word, Malysh reacted for the first time.

— *When I stole money from you, in the station that time?*

Fraera nodded

— *I'd been looking for you. I wanted you to believe our meeting was accidental. I had planned to use you in my revenge, against the woman who'd fallen in love with the man I hated. However, I grew fond of you. I quickly came to see you as a son. I adapted my plans. I would keep you as my own. In the same way, I grew fond of Zoya and decided to keep her by my side. Today both of you threw that love away. With only the thinnest of provocations, you drew a knife on me. The truth is that had you refused to draw that knife, I would've allowed both of you to go free.*

Fraera moved to the door, pausing, turning back to face Leo.

— *You always wanted a family, Leo. Now you have one. You're welcome to it. They are a crueller revenge than anything I could have imagined.*

Raisa turned and faced the room. Malysh was standing before her, his chest and arms covered in tattoos. His expression was cautious, defensive, guarded against denial or disinterest. Zoya spoke first.

— *It doesn't matter if he's your son. Because he's not, not really, not any more, you gave him up, which means you're not his mother. And I'm not your daughter. There's nothing to talk about. We're not a family.*

Malysh touched her arm. Zoya understood it as a reproach.

— *But she's not your mother.*

Zoya was close to tears.

— *We can still escape.*

Malysh nodded.

— *Nothing has changed.*

— *You promise?*

— *I promise.*

Malysh stepped towards Raisa, keeping his eyes on the ground.

— *I don't care either way. I just want to know.*

His question was off-hand, childlike in its attempt to conceal his vulnerability. He didn't wait for Raisa to answer, adding:

— *At the orphanage I was called Feliks. But the orphanage gave me that name. They renamed everyone, names they could remember. I don't know my real name.*

Malysh counted on his fingers.

— *I'm fourteen years old. Or I might be thirteen. I don't know when I was born. So, am I your son, or not?*

Raisa asked:

— *What do you remember of your orphanage?*

— *There was a tree in the courtyard. We used to play in it. The orphanage was near Leningrad, not in the town, in the country. Was that the place, with the tree in the courtyard? Was that where you took your son?*

Raisa replied:

— *Yes.*

She stepped closer to Malysh.

— *What did the orphanage tell you about your parents?*

— *That they were dead. You've always been dead to me.*

Zoya added by way of conclusion:

— *There's nothing more to talk about.*

Zoya guided Malysh into the far corner, sitting him down. Raisa and Leo remained standing near the window. Leo didn't press for information, allowing Raisa to take her time. Finally, she whispered, turning her face away from Malysh's view:

— *Leo, I gave up my child. It is the greatest shame in my life. I never told you, I never told anyone. I never wanted to speak about it again, although I think about it almost every day.*

Leo paused.

— *Is Malysh . . . ?*

Raisa lowered her voice even further.

— *Fraera was right. There was a typhus epidemic. Many children had died. But when I went back my son was still there. He was dying. He didn't recognize me. He didn't know who I was. But I stayed with him until he died. Everything I told you is true. I buried him. Leo, Malysh is not my son.*

Raisa crossed her arms, lost in her thoughts. Working through the events, she speculated:

— *Fraera must have gone back, looking for my son in 1953 or 1954, after she was released. The records would have been shambolic. There was no way she could have found the truth about my son. She wouldn't have known I was there when he died. She found someone close in age to him: maybe she planned to use him against me. Maybe she didn't because she did love Malysh. Maybe she didn't because she couldn't be sure I'd believe her lie.*

— *It might be nothing more than a desperate attempt to hurt us?*

— *And him.*

Leo considered.

— *Why not tell Malysh the truth? Fraera is playing with him too.*

— *What will the truth sound like? He might not take it as a matter of fact. He might feel that I'm rejecting him, devising reasons why he couldn't be my son. Leo, if he wants me to love him, if he's looking for a mother . . .*

*

With her characteristic knack for manipulation, Fraera brought a single, oversized plate of hot stew. There was no option but to sit around, cross-legged, eating together. Zoya refused, at first, to join in, remaining apart. However, the food was turning cold and heat being its sole redeeming quality, reluctantly she joined in, eating with them side by side, metal forks clattering as they spiked chunks of vegetable and meat. Malysh asked:

— *Zoya told me that you're a teacher.*

Raisa nodded.

— *I can't read or write. I'd like to, though.*

— *I'll help you learn, if you want.*

Zoya shook her head, ignoring Raisa and addressing Malysh:

— *I can teach you. You don't need her.*

The plate of food was nearly finished. Soon they'd split off and return to their separate corners of the room. Exploiting the moment, Leo said to Zoya:

— *Elena wants you to come home.*

Zoya stopped eating. She said nothing. Leo continued:

— *I don't want to upset you. Elena loves you. She wants you to come home.*

Leo added no more details, softening the truth.

Zoya stood up, dropping her fork, walking away. She remained standing, facing the wall, before lying down on the bedding, in the corner, her back to the room. Malysh followed, sitting beside her, resting his arm on her back.

*

Leo awoke, shivering. It was early in the morning. He and Raisa were huddled on one side of the room, Malysh and Zoya on the other side. Yesterday Fraera had been absent: food had been brought by a Hungarian freedom-fighter. Leo had noticed a change. A solemnity had fallen across the apartment. There were no more drunken cheers and no more celebrations.

Standing up, he approached the small window, rubbed condensation from the glass. Outside, snow was falling. What should have sealed the impression of a city at peace, clean, white and tranquil, only compounded Leo's sense of unease. He could see no children playing, no snowball fights. The year's first snowfall, in a liberated city, but there was no excitement and no delight. There was no one on the streets at all.

Somewhere in the sky above the apartment a faint whining noise climaxed in a high-pitched boom. A jet plane had flown overhead. Leo sat bolt upright. The room was dark. Raisa woke immediately, asking:

— *What is it?*

Before Leo could answer, explosions sounded out across the city, several in rapid sequence, in many locations. In an instant Leo, Raisa, Malysh and Zoya were up, peering out of the window. Addressing them, Leo said:

— *They're back.*

There was panic in the adjacent rooms, footsteps on the roof, insurgents caught off guard, scrambling into position. Leo could see a tank on the street. Its turret pointed this way and that, before aiming directly at the rooftop snipers.

— *Move away!*

Shooing the others to the far side of the room, there was a split second of stillness, then an explosion. Knocked off their feet, the roof collapsed and the back wall fell away, beams tumbling down. Only a small portion of the room remained, closed by the sloping wreckage. Leo covered his face with the bottom of his shirt, struggling to breathe, checking on the others.

Raisa grabbed the remains of a smashed beam, battering

at the door. Leo joined her, trying to break out. Malysh called
out:

— *This way!*

There was a gap ripped through the base of the wall into the
adjoining room. Flat on their stomachs, with the danger of the
roof collapsing completely, they crawled through, tunnelling out
of the debris, reaching the corridor. There were no guards, no *vory*.
The apartment was empty. Opening the door to the courtyard
balcony they saw occupants fleeing their homes, many huddled,
unable to decide whether to brave the streets or whether they
were safer staying where they were.

Malysh bolted back inside. Leo shouted:

— *Malysh!*

He returned, holding a belt of ammunition, grenades and a
gun. Raisa tried to disarm him, shaking her head.

— *They'll kill you.*

— *They'll kill us anyway.*

— *I don't want you to take them.*

— *If we're going to get out of the city, we need them.*

Raisa looked to Leo. He said:

— *Give me the gun.*

Malysh reluctantly handed it to him. A nearby explosion ended
the debate:

— *We don't have much time.*

Leo looked up at the dark sky. Hearing the drone of jet engines,
he hurried them towards the stairs. There was no sign of any *vory*:
he reasoned they must be fighting or they'd fled. Reaching the
bottom of the stairs, they moved through the terrified crowd,
towards the passageway.

— *Maxim!*

Leo turned, looking up. Fraera was standing on the roof,

machine gun in her arms. Trapped in the middle of the courtyard, they had no chance of reaching the passageway before she gunned them down. He called out:

— *It's over, Fraera! This was never a fight you could win!*

— *Maxim, I've already won!*

— *Look around you!*

— *I didn't win it with a gun. I won it with this.*

Around her neck was a camera.

— *Panin was always going to use the full force of his army. I wanted him to. I want him to smash this city to rubble and fill it with dead citizens! I want the world to see the true nature of our country. No more secrets! No one is ever going to believe in the benevolence of our motherland again! That's my revenge.*

— *Let us go.*

— *Maxim, you still don't understand. I could've killed you a hundred times. Your life is more of a punishment than death. Go back to Moscow, the four of you, with a son wanted for murder, in love with a hate-filled daughter. Just try to be a family.*

Leo separated from the group.

— *Fraera, I am sorry for what I did to you.*

— *The truth is, Maxim . . . I was nothing until I hated you.*

Leo turned around, facing the passageway, expecting a bullet in the back. No bullets were fired. At the exit onto the street he paused, looking back. Fraera was gone.

Inside the remains of an abandoned café with tablecloths wrapped around his hands to protect himself from the glass, Leo lay flat, waiting for the tanks to pass. He lifted his head, peering out of the broken window. There were three tanks, their turrets swivelling from side to side, examining the buildings — searching out targets. The Red Army was no longer deploying isolated units of clumsy, vulnerable T-34s. These were the larger, heavily armoured T-54s. From what Leo had seen so far, the Soviet strategy had changed. Deployed in columns, they responded with disproportionate force — a single bullet would be answered with the destruction of the entire building. The tanks moved on only after the devastation was complete.

It had taken two hours to travel less than one kilometre, forced to seek refuge at almost every junction. Now dawn, they were no longer sheltered by darkness and their progress had slowed yet further, trapped in a city that was being systematically destroyed. Staying indoors was no longer any guarantee of safety. The tanks were equipped with armour-piercing shells that travelled three rooms deep before detonating in the very centre of the house, causing it to collapse.

Witnessing the display of military might, Leo could only speculate as to whether the initial failure to regain control had been deliberate. Not only did it undercut the moderate position of restraint, it illustrated the ineffectiveness of the older armour, defeated by a mere mob. Now the latest hardware strutted on the streets of Budapest like a military propaganda reel. A Moscow audience could draw only one conclusion: plans to scale back the conventional army were flawed. More money was needed, not less, more weapons development – the strength of the Union depended upon it.

Out of the corner of his eye Leo saw a flicker of bright orange, startling among the grey stone rubble and grey morning light. Three young men across the street were readying Molotov cocktails. Leo tried to get their attention, waving at them. Petrol bombs wouldn't work, since the cooling units on the T-54s didn't suffer from the same weakness as the T-34s. They were fighting an entirely different generation of weapons. Their crude devices were useless. One of the men saw him and misunderstanding his wave, made a defiant fist.

The three men stood up, running at the rear tank – they threw the bombs, perfect shots, all three hitting their target, covering the rear of the T-54 with burning fuel. Flames soared. They fled, glancing over their shoulders, expecting an explosion that would never come. The fire roaring on the tank's armour was irrelevant. The men increased their pace, running to shelter. Leo ducked. The tank turned and fired. The cafe shook, the remaining glass shards in the window fell to the ground, smashing all around. Dust and smoke rolled in through the window. Shielded by the cloud, Leo pulled back, coughing, crawling through the smashed crockery to the kitchen where Raisa, Zoya and Malysh were crouched behind the steel units.

— *The streets are impassable.*

Malysh asked:

— *What about the roofs? We can crawl across them*.

— *If they see us, or hear us, they will still fire. Up there it will be much harder to escape. We'd be trapped*.

Raisa said:

— *We're trapped down here*.

On the top-floor landing there were two windows, one onto the main boulevard, the other onto a narrow backstreet, not large enough for a T-54. Leo opened the back window, studying the climb. There was no drainpipe, no foothold, no easy way of reaching the roof. Malysh tapped his leg.

— *Let me look*.

Leo allowed Malysh onto the ledge. Briefly assessing the gap he jumped up, his legs dangling as he hung from the edge. Leo moved to support him, but he said:

— *I'm OK*.

He pulled himself up, swinging a foot onto the edge, then the other foot. He said:

— *Zoya next*.

Raisa glanced down at the drop, some fifteen metres.

— *Wait*.

She picked up the tablecloths that Leo had tied around his hands, knotting them together. She wrapped them round Zoya's waist. Zoya was annoyed.

— *I've survived for months without you*.

Raisa kissed her on the cheek.

— *Which is why it would be particularly embarrassing if you died now*.

Zoya suppressed a smile, squashing it into a frown.

Standing on the window ledge, Leo lifted her up. She took hold of the roof.

— *You have to let go so I can swing my legs!*

Reluctantly Leo let go, watching as she swung her leg. Malysh caught her, pulling her up. The tablecloth safety cord was at full stretch.

— *I'm up.*

Raisa released the cloths, allowing Zoya to pull up her improvised safety line. Raisa was next. Leo was the last to make the climb.

The roof rose to a narrow band. Malysh and Zoya were straddled on the ridge. Raisa was behind, forming a single file. Clambering up, Leo's feet slipped on the tiles, dislodging one – it rattled down the roof before falling off. There was a pause before it could be heard smashing on the street. The four of them froze against the roof. If a tile fell on the other side, onto the boulevard, their position would be given away to the patrolling tanks.

Leo took in the view. Across the city, smoke rose in thick lines. Rooftops were smashed. There were gaps where buildings had once stood. Fighter jets – MiGs – cut low over the city, dropping into attack position, strafing targets. Even on the roof they were exposed. Leo commented:

— *We need to hurry.*

Crawling on all fours, bypassing the dangers below, they were, at last, able to make progress.

Up ahead the houses came to an end: they'd reached the end of the block. Malysh said:

— *We have to climb down, cross the street, and then climb back up on the other side.*

The tiles began to rattle. Leo moved to the edge of the roof, peering down at the main boulevard. Four tanks were passing directly underneath. One by one they turned off the boulevard. To Leo's dismay the fourth tank stopped. It seemed to be guarding the crossroads. They were going to have to sneak around it.

About to return with the bad news, Leo caught sight of movement in the apartment window directly below him. He craned his neck over the edge, watching as two women hung the modified Hungarian flag, the flag with hammer and sickle cut out, from the top-floor window. The tank had seen the protesters. Leo bolted up the roof, gesturing to the others:

Move! Now!

They scrambled as far from the boulevard as they could.

The section of roof behind them mushroomed into the air, debris showering down. The shockwave caused all the tiles to slide. Malysh, closest to the edge, lost his foothold, slipping down, everything giving way beneath him. Zoya threw him the end of the tablecloths. He caught it just as the matrix of tiles avalanched off the roof, taking him with them.

As Malysh fell Zoya was pulled down. She tried to grab onto something and found nothing. Leo reached out, missing her hand but snatching the trail of tablecloths. He managed to steady them – Zoya was on the edge, Malysh was hanging off. If the tank saw him it would fire, killing them all. Leo heaved the sheets up. Raisa reached down.

— *Give me your hand!*

Grabbing Malysh's hand, she pulled him up, the two of them lying side by side. Leo rolled over to the edge, glancing down at the tank. The turret was swinging towards them.

— *Get up!*

On their feet, they ran back across the roof, towards the collapsed apartment on the other side. The shell impacted behind them, at the spot where Malysh had slipped – the corner of the building. All four of them were thrown up and forward, landing on their hands and knees. Ears ringing, coughing in the dust, they studied the devastation in front and now behind them: two gaping holes as if a monster had taken two bites out of the building.

Leo surveyed the shelled-out apartment in front of them. The first shell had hit high, causing the roof to crumble and fall, compressing the top floor with the floor below. They could climb down through the splintered beams. He took the lead, hoping the tank would presume them dead. Reaching the layer of ceiling that had crashed down, he saw the dust-covered hand of the woman who'd hung the flag. No time to linger, he searched for a way out. The stairway was at the back. He pulled at the remains of a door, trying to get access, but it was filled with rubble.

At the front of the damaged apartment, looking out at the boulevard, Raisa said:

— *They're coming around!*

The tank was returning. Trapped, they had nowhere to hide, nowhere to run.

Leo doubled his efforts, trying to clear the stairs, the only way out. Zoya and Raisa joined him. Malysh was gone. He'd fled, saved himself – a *vory* to the end. Leo looked over his shoulder. The tank was taking up position directly outside, lining up a third shot. It would fire again and again, until both houses were rubble. Boxed into the shelled-out apartment, brick walls either side, the stairway blocked, the only chance of escape was to jump down to the street below.

Leo grabbed Zoya and Raisa, running straight towards the tank. At the edge he stopped. Malysh had already scampered down the broken building onto the street. He was making a line for the tank. There was a grenade in his hand.

Malysh pulled the pin, nimbly scaling the front of the tank, clambering up. The tank lifted the gun towards the sky in an attempt to stop him from reaching the opening. But Malysh was too quick, too skilled, wrapping his legs around the barrel, pushing his way up. The hatch opened, an officer was going to shoot Malysh before he could drop the grenade.

Leo drew his gun, firing at the emerging officer, bullets pinging off the armour. The officer was forced to retreat, closing the hatch. Malysh reached the end of the turret, dropping the grenade down. He let go, falling to the street.

The grenade exploded; a fraction later, the shell inside the turret exploded, a much larger blast – the force ripping through the tank. Malysh was picked off his feet and slammed down onto the street. Smoke rose from the tank. No one emerged.

Zoya had already climbed down the building, rushing forward, helping Malysh up. She smiled. Also climbing down and catching up with Zoya, Leo said:

— *We need to get off the street . . .*

Malysh's shirt turned dark red, a stain forming in the centre. Leo dropped to his knees, ripping open the shirt. There was a cut as long as his thumb, a slash across his stomach, a black line – two bloody lips. Checking the boy's back, Leo could find no exit wound.

With Malysh in his arms, Leo rushed into the Second Medical Clinic, Zoya and Raisa by his side. They'd reached the hospital, hurrying along the streets, risking the patrolling tanks. Several turrets had tracked them but none had opened fire. The hospital entrance was filled with injured people, some leaning on friends and family, others lying on the floor. There was blood on the walls, blood on the floor. Searching for a doctor or nurse, Leo saw a flutter of a white coat. He pushed forward. The doctor was surrounded by patients, unable to give each more than a couple of seconds of his time, examining the wounds, sending only the most needy into the hospital. The rest remained in the corridor.

Leo waited in the circle for the doctor's judgement. Finally arriving at Malysh, the doctor touched his face, feeling his brow. The boy's breathing had become faint. His skin was pale. Leo had used Malysh's shirt to press against the wound, the material now soaked with blood. Removing the shirt, the doctor leaned close. His fingers touched the lips of the gash, opening it – blood seeping out. He checked the boy's back, finding no exit wound. For the first time the doctor glanced at Leo. He said nothing, giving an almost imperceptible shake of the head. With that, he moved on.

Zoya grabbed Leo's arm.

— *Why aren't they helping him?*

Leo had been a soldier, had seen injuries like this before. The blood was black: shrapnel had penetrated Malysh's liver. On the battlefield there was no hope of survival. Conditions in this hospital were little better than that. There was nothing they could do.

— *Why aren't they treating him?*

There was nothing Leo could say.

Zoya barged through the crowd, grabbing the doctor's arm, attempting to pull him back towards Malysh. The other people scolded her. But she wouldn't let go until eventually she was pushed back and shouted at. Zoya tumbled to the floor, lost in among their legs. Raisa lifted Zoya up.

— *Why aren't they helping him?*

Zoya began to cry, putting her hands on Malysh's face. She stared up at Leo, her eyes red, imploring:

Please, Leo, please, I'll do anything you want, I'll be your daughter, I'll be happy. Don't let him die.

Malysh's lips moved. Leo lowered his head, listening:

— *Not . . . in . . . here.*

Leo carried Malysh to the entrance, through the blood-soaked arrivals, out of the main doors, away from the reception, finding a place where they could be alone. In the flowerbeds, where the plants had died back and the earth was frozen, Leo sat down, propping Malysh against his legs. Zoya sat beside him. She took hold of Malysh's hand. Raisa remained standing, restless, pacing:

— *Maybe I can find something for the pain?*

Leo looked up, shaking his head. Twelve days into the conflict — there'd be nothing left in the clinic.

Malysh was calm, sleepy, his eyes shutting and opening. He regarded Raisa.

— *I know that . . .*

TOM ROB SMITH

His voice was faint. Unable to hear, Raisa sat beside him. Malysh continued:

— *Fraera lied . . . I know . . . you're not . . . my mother.*

— *I would've wanted nothing more than to be your mother.*

— *I would have liked to . . . have been your son.*

Malysh shut his eyes, turning his head, resting it against Zoya. She lay beside him, her head close to his, as if they were both about to go to sleep. She wrapped her arm around him, whispering:

— *Did I tell you about the farm where we're going to live?*

Malysh didn't reply. He didn't open his eyes.

— *It's near a forest, it's full of berries and mushrooms. There's a river and in the summer, we'll swim . . . We're going to be very happy together.*

Standing on the remains of the roof, Fraera was no longer holding a gun but a camera, photographing the destruction: images that would soon be printed around the world. If this, her last reel of film, didn't survive, it didn't matter. She'd already accumulated many hundreds of photographs, smuggling them out of the city, using the families of the dissidents and insurgents as well as the international press. Her images of dead citizens and buildings destroyed would be published for years to come under the title: *source anonymous*.

Perhaps for the first time since her son had been taken from her nearly seven years ago she was alone, no Malysh by her side, no men ready when she called. The gang that she'd spent years putting together had broken apart. The few remaining *vory* had fled. The band of insurgents had been broken. In the first wave of attacks this morning many had died. She'd photographed their bodies. Zsolt Polgar, her translator, had remained by her side. She'd been wrong about him. He'd died for his cause. As he lay dying, she'd photographed him with particular care.

She had only three photographs left. In the distance a fighter jet circled, coming towards her. She raised the camera, bringing the jet into focus. The MiG dropped into an attack position. Tiles around her began to shatter. She waited until the jet was almost directly overhead. As the roof exploded, fragments of slate burning into her arms and face, she had no doubt her last photograph would be her greatest of all.

TWO
WEEKS
LATER

SOVIET UNION
MOSCOW

His first day at work: Leo's hands were covered in flour and his face was hot from the ovens. Taking out a batch of newly baked loaves, he heard Filipp call out:

— *Leo, you have a visitor.*

An immaculate Frol Panin entered the bakery. He surveyed the premises with condescending good humour. Leo observed:

— *No request we can't accommodate: rye with coriander seeds, or sweetened with honey rather than sugar. Kosher, or oil-free . . .*

He took one of the still-warm loaves, breaking it, offering it to Panin. He accepted, taking a bite. The man who'd betrayed him and who'd collaborated with his enemies, showed no embarrassment, no guilt or shame, chewing contentedly.

— *It's very good.*

Panin put the bread down, dusting the flour off his fingers and checking that Filipp was out of earshot.

— *Leo, no one is going back to Stalinism. There will be no more mass arrests. The camps are closing. Interrogation cells are being ripped out. These changes are in progress. They will continue. But*

they must continue in secret, without any admission of wrongdoing.
We shall go forward . . . without looking back.

Despite everything, Leo couldn't help but admire Panin. He could have arranged for Leo never to have made it out of Budapest. Yet Panin weighed up every decision on a purely practical basis. He did nothing out of malice or spite. With the uprising defeated and Fraera dead, Leo was an irrelevancy and so he'd been allowed to live.

— *Frol Panin, what do you want from me? You won.*

— *I would argue that we all won.*

— *No, I lost a long time ago. I'm just trying not to lose any more.*

— *Leo, whatever you may think of me, my decisions were always for . . .*

— *The greater good?*

Panin nodded, adding:

— *I want you to work for me. We need men like you.*

— *Men like me.*

Leo let the phrase hang before asking:

— *You're going to re-open the Homicide Department?*

— *No, we're not ready for that yet.*

— *When you are, I'll be here.*

— *Baking rye with coriander seeds?*

Panin smiled.

— *Very well, I hope, one day, I can be of some help to you.*

It was an apology, of sorts: a secret apology. Leo accepted the gesture.

— *There is one thing you could do for me.*

SAME DAY

At the reception to the Moscow Conservatory, Leo asked for Piotr Orlov, one of the country's most promising young violinists. He was directed to a rehearsal room. Orlov, in his late twenties, opened the double soundproofed doors, remarking brusquely:

— *Yes?*

— *My name is Leo Demidov. Frol Panin said you could help.*

Hearing Panin's name, the composer became more amiable.

The rehearsal room was small. There was a music stand, an upright piano. Orlov was holding his violin by the neck. His bow was on the stand, along with a stub of resin.

— *What can I do for you?*

Leo opened his folder, taking out a single sheet of paper, a hole burnt through the middle. The hole had been burnt seven years ago using a candle in Lazar's church. As the paper had turned black, Leo had impulsively changed his mind. He'd placed it on the stone floor, stamping out the flames. The charred music – all that remained of the arrested composer's work – had been stored in Lazar's file, evidence of his counter-revolutionary associations.

Orlov stepped up to the stand, examining the few surviving notes. Leo commented:

— *I can't read music so I don't know whether there's even*

enough to get a sense of the whole piece. I wanted to hear it played aloud, as much as is possible.

Orlov raised his violin to his chin, picked up his bow and began to play. Leo was not in the least bit musically minded. He'd expected it to be slow and sad. But it was fast and fun and he liked it very much.

It took him a moment to realize that there was no way Orlov could play for so long with the few notes he'd been given. Confused, he politely waited for Orlov to stop. Eventually, he did.

— *This is very popular, one of the most successful recent compositions.*

— *You must be mistaken. The music was thought to be lost. The composer died before it was ever performed.*

Orlov was puzzled.

— *It was performed last week. The composer is alive.*

*

In the hallway of an exclusive apartment block, Leo knocked on the door. There was a long delay before a middle-aged man opened the door, a servant, dressed in a neat black uniform.

— *Can I help you?*

— *I'm here to see Robert Meshik.*

— *Do you have an appointment?*

— *No.*

— *He won't see anyone without an appointment.*

Leo handed over the burnt sheet of music.

— *He'll see me.*

Reluctantly, the man obeyed.

— *Wait here.*

Some minutes later the man returned, without the music.

— *Please follow me.*

Leo followed him through the expensively furnished apartment to a studio at the back. The composer Robert Meshik was standing by the window, holding the single burnt sheet of music. Addressing his servant, he said:

— *You may leave us.*

The man left. Leo remarked:

— *You have done well for yourself.*

Meshik sighed.

— *In some ways I am relieved. I have been waiting for this moment for many years, for someone to appear, with the evidence, and announce me a fraud.*

— *You knew the real composer?*

— *Kirill, yes, we were friends. We were best friends. We practised together. I was jealous of him. He was a genius. I am not.*

— *You denounced him?*

— *No, never; I loved him. That is the truth. You have no reason to believe me. When he was arrested, of course, I did nothing. I said nothing. He and his music tutor were sent to a labour camp. After Stalin died I tried to find them. I was told that they had not survived. I grieved. I had the idea to copy one of Kirill's pieces, as a memorial to him. They'd been lost but that didn't matter, I'd heard him play them many times. They were in my blood. I made some minor changes. The composition was a success.*

— *But you didn't declare its origins?*

— *I was seduced by the praise. Since then I have copied every piece I could remember, making minor variations, taking all the credit for them, enjoying all the perks. You see, Kirill had no family. He had no one. No one believed in him. No one knew his music except his teacher. And me.*

— *There was one other person.*

— *Who?*

445

— *The wife of a priest.*

— *She is how you found me?*

— *In a way, yes.*

After a silence, the composer asked:

— *Are you going to arrest me?*

Leo shook his head.

— *I don't have the authority to arrest you.*

Meshik seemed not to understand.

— *Then tomorrow, first thing, I will tell the world the truth.*

Leo walked across the room, staring out of the window at the snow that had begun to fall. There were children playing.

— *What will you say? That the State murdered a genius and you stole his music? Who will love you for that confession? Who wants to hear it?*

— *What would you have me do?*

The snow was beginning to settle.

— *Play on.*

Perched on the rooftop of Leo and Raisa's apartment block, Zoya shivered as the snow fell around her. Every day since her return she had climbed up there, scrambling up, staring out over the city. No rooftops were collapsing, no gunfire sounded out and the tiles didn't shake as tanks passed by. She felt as if she was neither in Moscow, nor anywhere else, but in limbo. The sense of belonging she'd experienced in Budapest had nothing to do with that particular city, or the revolution, and everything to do with Malysh. She missed him, or was it that part of her was now missing? He'd taken the weight of loneliness off her shoulders, now that weight felt heavier than ever.

They'd buried Malysh outside Budapest. She hadn't wanted his body left in the hospital, lost among the dead, one of many, with no family or friends to grieve over him. Leo had carried him through the Russian encirclement. Digging in the frozen soil, they'd buried him by a tree, back from the road, tanks and trucks passing by. She used his knife to carve his name into the trunk. Remembering that he couldn't read, she scratched a heart around the letters.

At first, when Zoya had climbed onto the roof, Raisa had hurried after her — no doubt fearful she was going to jump off. Understanding that it was nothing more than a place to sit, Raisa no longer interfered, nor did Leo, allowing Zoya hours there

447

without interruption. She scooped up a clump of snow and watched it melt in her hands.

*

Tidying up after dinner, Raisa turned. Zoya was standing in the doorway, shivering, snow in her hair. Raisa took hold of Zoya's hands.

— *You're cold. Do you want to eat? I put some aside for you.*

— *Is Elena in bed?*

— *Yes.*

— *Leo?*

— *He's not back yet.*

Elena had returned from the hospital, rejuvenated by the miracle of Zoya being alive. Zoya had wept with guilt at the sight of her sister. Elena was dangerously thin. Even without being told, Zoya understood that her little sister would not have survived much longer. Elena hadn't questioned events, overwhelmed with happiness, indifferent to the details of what had happened or why. Her family was alive.

Raisa knelt down before Zoya.

— *Talk to me.*

There was the sound of a key in the front door. Leo entered, red-faced and rushed.

— *I'm sorry . . .*

Raisa replied:

— *You're in time to read to the girls.*

Zoya shook her head.

— *Can I talk to you first? To both of you?*

— *Of course.*

Leo entered the kitchen, pulling up two chairs, sitting beside Zoya.

— *What's wrong?*

— *I've always told Elena everything. Since I got back she's been so happy, I don't want to spoil that. I don't want to tell her what happened. I don't want to tell her the truth. I don't want to tell her that I left her alone.*

Zoya began to cry.

— *If I tell her the truth, will she forgive me?*

Though he wanted to, Leo did not yet feel he could put an arm around her. He said:

— *She loves you very much.*

Zoya looked up at Leo, then at Raisa.

— *But will she forgive me?*

The three of them turned to the doorway. Elena was standing in her nightgown. She'd only been home for a week and already she'd transformed, gaining weight, the colour returning to her skin.

— *What's going on?*

Zoya moved towards her.

— *Elena, I have something to tell you.*

Leo stood up.

— *Before you do, why don't I tell you a bedtime story?*

Elena smiled.

— *One that you made up?*

Leo nodded.

— *One that I made up.*

Zoya wiped away her tears and took hold of Leo's hand.

FURTHER READING

The books I mentioned at the end of *Child 44* were also crucial to the writing of this book and formed the bedrock of the research for this novel. In addition, William Taubman's biography on Khrushchev: *Khrushchev: The Man and His Era* (Simon & Schuster, 2003) was indispensable.

I've already mentioned Michael Korda's book on his experiences in the Hungarian Revolution. Equally inspirational, and important, were Victor Sebestyen's *Twelve Days: Revolution 1956: How the Hungarians Tried to Topple Their Soviet Masters* (Weidenfeld & Nicolson, 2006) and *The Hungarian Revolution of 1956: Reform, Revolt and Repression 1953–1963*, edited by Gyorgy Litvan, English version edited and translated by Janos M. Bak and Lyman H. Legters (Longman, 1966)

I'd like to make special note of one autobiography, *Shallow Graves in Siberia* by Michael Krupa (Minerva Press, 1997). It is an extraordinary story, deeply moving and it reminded me that no matter how oppressive the adversary, someone always manages to find a way above it.

I owe these authors a huge debt. I should note that any inaccuracies are entirely my own.

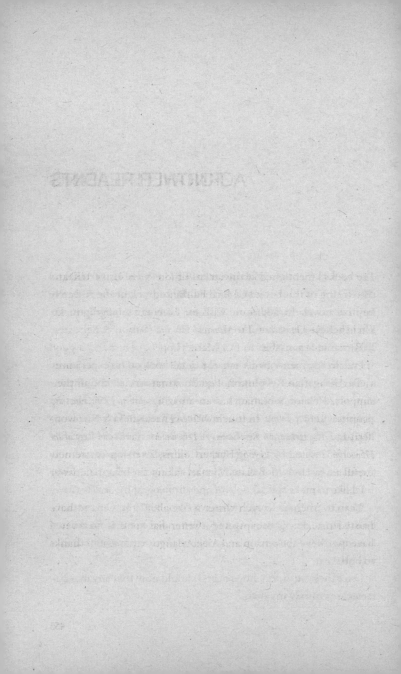

ACKNOWLEDGMENTS

My editors, Suzanne Baboneau at Simon & Schuster UK and Mitch Hoffman at Grand Central Publishing, are quite simply the best editors any writer could wish for. I feel exceptionally lucky. And I am hugely grateful to them.

Particular thanks go to Eva-Marie Hippel at Dumont, a good friend with a meticulous eye for detail. Also thanks to Jonny Geller at Curtis Brown and Robert Bookman at CAA for all their support. Robert Bookman has an amazing gift for connecting people, and he put me in touch with Michael Korda whose wonderful book *Journey to a Revolution: A Personal Memoir and History of the Hungarian Revolution of 1956* (HarperCollins, 2006) was extremely useful research. I appreciate Michael taking the time to answer my questions.

I can't remember which writer spoke about the need to have trusted readers – perhaps every writer has spoken about it. I have two, Ben Stephenson and Alex Arlango, my love and thanks to both.

In the following pages you will find a gripping extract from the beginning of Tom Rob Smith's, as yet untitled, third novel, coming soon from Simon & Schuster. The extract is in its first draft and may be subject to change.

USSR

MOSCOW
THE LUBYANKA
LUBYANKA SQUARE
HEADQUARTERS OF THE SECRET POLICE
21 JANUARY 1950

The safest way to keep a diary was to imagine Comrade Stalin reading every word. Even exercising this degree of caution there was the risk of a slipped phrase, accidental ambiguity – a misunderstood sentence. Praise might be mistaken for mockery, sincere adulation taken as parody. Since even the most vigilant author couldn't guard against every possible interpretation, an alternative was to hide the diary altogether, a method favoured in this instance by the suspect, a young artist called Polina Peshkova. Her notebook had been discovered inside a fireplace, wrapped in waxed cloth and squeezed between two loose bricks. To retrieve the diary the author was forced to wait until the fire died down before inserting a hand into the chimney and feeling for the book. Ironically the elaborate nature of this hiding place had been Peshkova's undoing. A single sooty fingerprint on her writing desk had alerted the investigating agent's suspicions and redirected the focus of his search, an exemplary piece of detective work.

From the perspective of the secret police, the act of concealing a diary was a crime regardless of its content since it was an attempt to separate a citizen's public and private life. In reality no such gap existed. There was no thought or experience that fell outside the Party's authority. For this reason a concealed diary was often the most incriminating evidence an agent could hope for. Since the words weren't intended for any reader, the author tended to lower their guard, resulting in nothing less than an unsolicited confession. From-the-heart honesty made the document suitable for judging not only the author but also their friends and family. A diary could yield as many as fifteen additional suspects, fifteen new leads, often more than the most intense interrogation.

Agent Leo Demidov was in charge of this investigation. In his brief career as a secret-police officer, he'd overseen the examination of many hundreds of journals, pored over thousands of entries in the pursuit of those accused of anti-Soviet agitation. Like a first love, he remembered the very first journal he'd ever examined. Given to him by his mentor, Nikolai Borisov, it had been a difficult case. Leo had found nothing incriminating among the pages. His mentor had then read the same journal, highlighting the apparently innocent observation:

6 December 1936. Last night Stalin's new Constitution was adopted. I feel the same way as the rest of the country, i.e., absolute, infinite delight.

Borisov had been unsatisfied that the sentence conveyed any credible sense of delight. The author was more interested in aligning his feelings with the rest of the country. It was strategic and cynical, an empty sentence intended to hide the author's own doubts. Does a person expressing genuine delight use an abbreviation – i.e. – before describing their emotions? That exact question was put to the suspect in his subsequent interrogation.

INTERROGATOR BORISOV: How do you feel right now?
SUSPECT: I have done nothing wrong.
INTERROGATOR BORISOV: I understand. But my question was: how do you feel.
SUSPECT: I feel apprehensive.
INTERROGATOR BORISOV: Of course you do. That is perfectly natural. But note that you did not say: 'I feel the same as anyone would in my circumstances, i.e., apprehensive.'

The man had no reply. He received fifteen years.

Drawing from the many lessons he'd learned over the years, Leo flicked through Polina Peshkova's diary, observing that for an artist the suspect had inelegant handwriting. Throughout she'd pressed hard with a blunt pencil, never once sharpening the tip. Leo ran his finger over the back of each page, across sentences indented like Braille. He lifted the diary to his nose. It smelt of soot. Against the run of his thumb, the pages made a crackling noise, like autumn leaves. As if he were an animal, he sniffed and peered and weighed the book in his hands — examining it in every way except actually reading it. He turned to the trainee assigned to him. As part of a recent promotion he'd been tasked with supervising new agents, no longer a pupil but a mentor. They would accompany him on his working day and during his night-time arrests, gaining experience, learning from him until they were ready to run their own cases.

Grigori Semichastny was twenty-three years old and the fifth agent Leo had taught. He was perhaps the most intelligent and the least promising. He asked too many questions, queried too many answers. He smiled when he found something amusing and frowned when something annoyed him. To know what he was thinking merely required a glance at his face. Leo was unable to understand why he'd chosen a profession that he was unsuited for. So mismatched was Grigori for the job that Leo had even contemplated advising him to seek another career. Yet such an abrupt departure would place him under scrutiny and would, in all likelihood, condemn him in the eyes of the State. Leo had never heard of anyone successfully changing career. Grigori's only viable option was to stumble along his ill-chosen path and Leo felt it his duty to try to help him as best he could.

Grigori leafed through the pages intently, turning them backwards and forwards as if searching for something in particular. Finally, he looked up and declared:

— *The diary says nothing of any importance.*

Despite remembering his own experience as a novice, Leo was surprised by the answer. He replied:

— *Nothing?*

Grigori nodded.

The notion was improbable. Even if it lacked direct examples of provocation, the things unmentioned in a diary were just as important as the things written down. Why was there no reference to a particular parade? Why in the writing of all these words had there not been the time to declare love for Socialism and hatred for Capitalism? Deciding to offer these wisdoms to his trainee, Leo stood up.

— *Let me tell you a story. A young man once remarked in his diary that on this day he felt inexplicably sad. The entry was dated 23 August. The year was 1949. What would you make of that?*

Grigori shrugged.

— *Not much.*

Leo smiled.

— *What was the date of the Non-Aggression Pact between Nazi Germany and Soviet Russia?*

— *August 1939.*

— *The twenty-third of August 1939. Which means this man was feeling inexplicable sadness on the tenth anniversary of that treaty. Taken together with an absence of any praise for the soldiers who defeated Fascism, for Stalin's military prowess, this man's sadness was interpreted as an inappropriate critique of our foreign policy. Why dwell on mistakes and not express feelings of pride? Do you understand?*

— *Maybe it had nothing to do the treaty. Maybe he was just having a bad day. Maybe it meant nothing more than that.*

Leo became annoyed and his reply was heavy with sarcasm.

— *Maybe there are no enemies? Maybe everyone loves the State? Maybe there are no people who wish to undermine our work? Our job is to reveal guilt, not hope it doesn't exist.*

Grigori stuck by his conclusion.

— *In Polina's diary there are mundane observations and nothing more. This is no case against her.*

*

The artist, whom Leo noted Grigori was informally referring to by her first name, had been commissioned to design and paint a series of public murals. Since there was a risk that she, or indeed any artist, might produce something subtly subversive, a piece of art with a hidden meaning, the MGB were running a routine check. The logic was simple. If her diary contained no secret subversive meaning, it was unlikely that her art would. The task was a minor one and suitable for a novice. The first day had gone well. Grigori had found the diary while Peshkova was at work in her studio. Completing his search, he'd returned the evidence to the hiding place in the chimney in order not to alert Peshkova that she was under investigation. He'd reported back and briefly Leo had wondered if there was hope for the young man: the use of the sooty fingerprint as a clue had been exemplary. During the next four days Grigori maintained a high level of surveillance, putting in many more hours than necessary. Despite the extra work he had made no more reports and offered no observations of any kind. Now he was claiming the diary was worthless.

Leo took the book from him, sensing Grigori's reluctance to let the pages out of his hands. For the first time, he began to read and he agreed that it was hardly the provocative content he had been expecting for a diary so elaborately hidden near a fire. He skipped to the end, reading the most recent entries, written during the past five days of Grigori's surveillance. The suspect described meeting a neighbour for the first time, a man who lived in an apartment block on the opposite side of the road. She'd never seen him before but he'd approached her and they'd spoken in the street. She remarked that the man was funny and she hoped to see him again sometime, coyly adding that he was handsome.

Did he tell me his name? I don't remember. He must have done. How can I be so forgetful? I was distracted. I wish I could remember his name. Now he'll be insulted when we meet again. If we meet again, which I hope we will.

Leo turned the page. The next day she got her wish, bumping into the man again. She apologized for being forgetful and asked him to remind her of his name. He told her it was Isaac and they walked together, talking freely as if they'd been friends for many years. By happy coincidence Isaac was heading in the same direction as her. Arriving at her studio she'd been sad to see him go.

According to her entry, as soon as he was out of sight she began longing for their next encounter.

Is this love? No, of course not. But perhaps this is how love begins?

How love begins – it was sentimental, consistent with the fanciful temperament of someone who writes an inoffensive diary but hides it as carefully as if it contained treachery and intrigue. Leo didn't need a physical description of this friendly young man to know his identity. He looked up at his protégé and said:

— *Isaac?*

Grigori hesitated. Deciding against a lie, he admitted:

— *I thought a conversation might be useful in evaluating her character.*

— *Your job was to search her apartment and observe her activities. No direct contact. She might have guessed you were MGB. She'd then alter her behaviour in order to fool you.*

Grigori shook his head.

— *She didn't suspect me.*

Leo was frustrated by these elementary mistakes.

— *You know that only because of what she wrote in the diary. Yet she could have destroyed the original diary, replacing it with this bland set of observations, aware that she was under surveillance.*

Grigori scoffed, displaying remarkable insolence.

— *The entire diary fabricated to fool us? She doesn't think like that. She doesn't think like us. It's impossible.*

Leo was annoyed at being contradicted by an agent so clearly deficient in his duties. He was a patient man, far more tolerant than other officers, but Grigori was testing him. He snapped back:

— The people who seem innocent are often those we should watch the most carefully.

Grigori looked at Leo with something like pity. However, for once, his expression did not match his reply.

— You're right: I shouldn't have spoken to her. But she is a good person. Of that I am certain. I found nothing in her apartment, nothing in her day-to-day activities that suggests she is anything other than a loyal citizen. The diary is inoffensive. Polina Peshkova does not need to be brought in for questioning. She should be allowed to continue her work as an artist, in which she excels. I can still return the diary before she finishes work. She need know nothing of this investigation.

Leo glanced at her photo, clipped to the front of the file. She was beautiful. Grigori was smitten with her. She was smitten with him. Leo had no choice but to read the diary line by line. He could no longer trust the word of his protégé.

*

Polina Peshkova wrote about her work and life. Her character came through strongly: a whimsical style, punctuated by diversions, sudden thoughts and exclamations. The entries flitted from subject to subject, often abandoning one strand and leaving it unfinished. Having read the entire diary, Leo couldn't deny that there was something appealing about the woman. She frequently laughed at her mistakes, documented with perceptive honesty. Her candour might explain why she hid the diary so carefully. With this thought in mind, Leo gestured for Grigori to sit down. He had remained standing, as if on guard duty, for the entire time Leo had been reading. He was nervous, too nervous to remain seated. Grigori perched on the edge of the chair, looking at Leo with imploring eyes.

— Tell me, if she's innocent, why did she hide the diary?

Seeming to sense that Leo's attitude towards her was thawing,

Grigori became excited. He spoke quickly, rushing through a possible explanation.

— *She lives with her mother and two younger brothers. She doesn't want them snooping through it. Perhaps they'd make fun of her. I don't know. It's nothing more than that. We must be able to distinguish when something is not important.*

Leo's thoughts wandered. He could imagine Grigori approaching the young woman. He struggled to imagine her responding fondly to a stranger's question. Why didn't she tell him to leave her alone? It seemed wildly imprudent of her to be so open. He leaned forward, lowering his voice, not because he feared being overheard but to signal that he was no longer talking to him formally, as a secret police officer.

— *What happened between the two of you? You walked up to her and just started talking? And that . . . that . . .*

Leo hesitated. He didn't know how to finish the sentence. Embarrassed, he asked:

— *And that worked?*

Grigori seemed unsure whether the question was put to him by a friend or by a superior officer. When he understood that Leo was genuinely curious, he answered:

— *More or less, how else do you meet someone except to introduce yourself? I spoke about her art. I told her that I'd seen some of her work — which is true. The conversation continued from there. She was easy to talk to, very friendly.*

Leo found this extraordinary.

— *She wasn't suspicious?*

— *No.*

— *She should have been.*

Briefly they'd been speaking as friends, about matters of the heart; now they were agents again. Grigori sank his head.

— Yes, you're right, she should have been.

He wasn't angry with Leo. He was angry with himself. His connection with the artist had been built on a lie.

Surprising himself, Leo offered the diary to Grigori.

— Take it.

Grigori didn't move, didn't take the diary — looking at Leo, trying to figure out what was happening. Leo smiled.

— Take it. She is free to continue her work as an artist. There's no need to press the case further.

For a moment Grigori seemed not to react, trying to gauge if Leo was serious.

— You're sure?

— Yes. I'm sure. I too found nothing in the diary.

Understanding that she was safe, Grigori smiled. He reached out, taking the diary from Leo's hands. As the pages slipped out of his grip, Leo felt an outline pressed into the paper — it wasn't a letter or a word but some kind of shape, something he hadn't seen.

— Wait.

Taking the diary back, Leo opened the page, examining the top right-hand corner. The space was blank. Yet when he touched the other side he could feel the indented lines. Something had been rubbed out.

He took a pencil, brushing the side of the lead against the paper, revealing the ghost of a small doodle, a sketch not much larger than his thumb. It was a woman standing on a plinth holding a torch, a statue. Leo stared blankly until realizing what it was. It was an American monument. It was the Statue of Liberty.

Leo studied Grigori's face. He turned red and stumbled over his words.

— She's an artist. She sketches all the time.

— Why has it been rubbed out?

He had no answer.

— You tampered with evidence?

There was panic in Grigori's reply.

— When I first joined the MGB, on my first day, I was told a story about Lenin's secretary, Fotieva. She claimed that Lenin asked his chief of security, Felix Dzierzynski, how many counter-revolutionaries he had under arrest. Dzierzynski passed him a slip of paper with the number 1,500 written on it. Lenin returned the paper, marking it with a cross. According to his secretary a cross was used by Lenin to show he had read a document. Dzierzynski misunderstood and executed all of them. That is why I had to rub it out. This sketch could have been misunderstood.

Leo knew the story. It was a wildly inappropriate reference. He'd heard enough.

— Dzierzynski was the father of this agency. To compare your predicament with his is ludicrous. We are not permitted the luxury of interpretation. We are not judges. We don't decide what evidence to present and destroy. If she is innocent, as you claim, that will be found out during questioning. In your misguided attempt to protect her, you've incriminated yourself.

— Leo, she's a good person.

— You're infatuated with her. Your judgement is compromised.

Leo softened his tone.

— Since the evidence is intact, I see no reason to draw attention to your mistake, a mistake that would certainly end your career. Write up your report, mark the sketch as evidence and let those more experienced than us decide.

Leo added, his voice almost a whisper:

— Grigori, I cannot protect you again.

Leo exhaled on the window, causing it steam up. Childlike, he pressed his finger against the condensation and dragged it across. Without thinking, he'd drawn the outline of the Statue of Liberty – a crude version of the sketch he'd seen today. Embarrassed at his idiocy, he hastily rubbed it away with the coarse cuff of his jacket and glanced around. He had no reason to be alarmed. The sketch would have been unrecognizable to anyone except himself. There was only one other passenger: a man seated at the front, wrapped up against the cold in so many layers that the smallest patch of his face was visible.

Except for early in the morning and late at night, the tramcars were crowded. Painted a dirty yellow with a thick brown stripe, they rattled around the city like giant boiled sweets. Often Leo had no choice except to force his way on. With seating for fifty, there was typically twice that number, well over a hundred passengers, the aisles filled with standing commuters jostling for position. Tonight Leo would've preferred the discomfort of a busy carriage, elbows jutting into his side and people pushing past. Instead, he had the luxury of an empty seat, heading home to the privilege of an empty apartment – accommodation he was not obliged to share, another perk of his profession. The measure of a man's status had become defined by how much empty space surrounded him. Soon he'd be designated his own car, a larger home, perhaps even a *dacha*, a country house. More and more space, less and less contact with the people he was charged with keeping watch over.

The words dropped into Leo's head, like pebbles tossed into a pond:

How Love Begins

He'd never been in love, not in the way described in the diary — excitement at the prospect of seeing someone again and sadness as soon as they went away. Grigori had risked his life for a woman he barely knew. Surely that was an act of love? Love did seem to be defined by foolhardiness. Leo had risked his life for his country many times. He'd shown bravery and dedication. If love was sacrifice then his only true love had been for the State.

He slid his hands under his legs, mining the space for any trace of warmth. Finding none, he shivered. The soles of his boots splashed in the shallow puddles of melted snow on the steel carriage floor. There was heaviness in his chest as if he were suffering from the flu with no symptoms except fatigue and dullness of thought. He wanted to lean against the window, close his eyes and sleep. The glass was too cold. He wiped a fresh patch of condensation clear and peered out. The streets were heaped with snow. More was falling, large flakes against the window.

The tramcar slowed to a stop. The front and back doors clattered opened, snow swept in. The driver turned to the open door, calling out into the night:

— *Hurry up! What are you waiting for?*

A voice replied:

— *I'm kicking the snow off my boots!*

— You're letting more snow in than you're kicking off. Get in now or I'll shut the doors!

The passenger boarded, a woman carrying a heavy bag, her boots clad in clumps of snow. As the doors shut behind her she remarked to the driver:

— It's not that warm in here anyway.

The driver gestured outside.

— You prefer to walk?

She smiled, instantly and magically defusing the tension. Caught by her spell, the gruff driver smiled too.

The woman turned, surveying the carriage and catching Leo's eye. He recognized her. They lived near each other. Her name was Lena. A week ago he'd chanced across her on the metro. They'd been so close together that it had felt rude not to say hello. He'd been so nervous, it had taken him several minutes to pluck up the courage to talk to her, delaying for so long that he missed his chance. She'd got off the carriage and Leo, frustrated that he'd squandered the opportunity, followed her even though it wasn't his stop. As she walked towards the exit he'd reached out and touched her on the shoulder. She'd spun around, eyes alert, ready for danger. He'd asked her name. She'd glanced around at the passengers passing them by, before telling him it was Lena and making an excuse about being in a rush. With that, she was gone. There was not the slightest trace of encouragement. Leo hadn't dared to ask anything else. He'd backtracked to the platform, waiting for the next train. It had been an expensive endeavour. He'd turned up to work late that morning, something he'd never done before.

*

Today was the first time he'd seen her since that awkward introduction. Rocking with the motion of the tramcar she passed him by without a word. Leo glanced back. She took a seat near the rear of the carriage. Her bag was on her lap, her eyes fixed on the snow-fall outside. He was hurt at the distance she'd placed between them; each metre was a measure of her dislike for him. If she'd wanted to talk, she would've sat closer. On consideration, that would have been too assertive. It was up to him to go to her. He knew her name. They were acquaintances. There was nothing improper with striking up a second conversation. The longer he waited the more difficult it would become. If the conversation fell flat, all Leo would lose was a little pride.

He stood up, striding towards Lena with a false air of confidence. He took the seat in front of her.

— *My name's Leo. We met the other day.*

She took so long to respond that Leo wondered if she was going to ignore him completely. Finally she said:

— *Yes. I remember.*

Only now did he realize that he had nothing to talk about. Embarrassed, hastily improvising, he remarked:

— *I heard you say just now that it's as cold on this tram as off it. I was thinking the same thing. It is very cold.*

He was speaking nonsense and he blushed at the silliness of his comments, bitterly regretting not having thought this conversation through. Looking at Leo's coat, she commented:

— *Cold? Even though you have such a nice coat?*

Leo's status as an agent provided him access to a range of fine jackets, handcrafted boots, thick fur hats. The coat was tanta-mount to a declaration of his status. Not wishing to admit he worked for the secret police, he decided on a lie.

— *It was a gift from my father. I don't know where he bought it.*

He changed the topic of conversation.

— *I see you around a lot. I wonder if we live nearby.*

— That seems likely.

Leo puzzled over the response. Evidently Lena was reluctant to tell him where she lived. Such caution was not uncommon. He shouldn't take it personally. In fact, he understood it better than anyone. His eyes came to rest on her bag, filled with books, notebooks – school exercise books. Trying to strike a pose of easy familiarity, he reached out, taking one of the books.

— You're a teacher?

Leo glanced at the information written on the front. Lena seemed to straighten slightly.

— That's right.

— What do you teach?

Lena's voice had become fragile.

— I teach . . .

She lost her train of thought, touching her forehead.

— I teach politics. Sorry, I'm very tired.

Leo returned the book.

— I apologize. I'm disturbing you.

Leo stood up, feeling unsteady, and walked back to his seat. Humiliation had replaced the blood in his veins, the sensation pumped around his body – every part of his skin burning. After several minutes of being seated, jaw locked, staring out the window, he noticed that his hands were clenched tight.

MOSCOW
THE LUBYANKA
LUBYANKA SQUARE
HEADQUARTERS OF THE SECRET POLICE

22 JANUARY 1950

Sick with tiredness, the steps and stairways were the only solid Leo felt. He hadn't slept the night before. He'd lain in bed, staring at the ceiling, waiting and waiting for the stinging humiliation to fade. After several hours he'd got up and paced his empty apartment, moving from room to room like a caged animal bumping up against its boundaries, full of hate for the space appointed to him — space he had no one else to share with.

He entered his office, sat at his desk. He was early. There was no one else in, at least not on his floor. There were always people downstairs in the interrogation rooms — those sessions could run for days without interruption. He checked his watch. In an hour or so other staff would start to arrive. Leo began to work, hoping it would push the incident with Lena from his mind. Yet he was wrong, unable to focus on the documents in front of him. With a sudden swipe of his arm, he knocked the papers to the floor. It was intolerable — how could a stranger have such an effect upon him? She didn't matter. He stood up, pacing the office as he'd paced his apartment. He opened the door, walking down the deserted corridor, finding himself in a nearby office where the reports on suspects were held. He checked that Grigori had filed his report, expecting his trainee to have forgotten or to have neglected the duty for sentimental reasons. The file had been submitted, languishing near the bottom of a low-priority stack of case files, many of which would not be read for weeks. This pile dealt with the most trivial of incidents. Leo lifted Peshkova's file, feeling the weight of the diary inside. In a snap decision, he moved it to the highest-priority pile, placing it at the very top – the most serious suspects, ensuring the case would be reviewed today, as soon as the staff arrived.

Back at his desk, Leo's eyes began to close as if having completed that piece of bureaucracy he was finally able to sleep, a load lifting from his mind. His thoughts drifted. Briefly, he was dreaming.

Leo opened his eyes. Grigori was nudging him awake. Leo stood up, embarrassed at being caught asleep at his desk, wondering what time it was.

— *Are you OK?*

Leo considered the question. Pulling his thoughts together, he remembered – the file.

Leo hastened out of the office. The corridors were busy: everyone was arriving for work. He quickened his pace, pushing past his colleagues, reaching the room where active cases were held for review. Ignoring the woman asking if he needed any help, he searched through the stack of files, looking for the documents on the artist Polina Peshkova. The file had been on the top. He'd put it there only sixty minutes ago. Once again the secretary asked if he needed any help.

— *There was a file here.*

— *They've been taken.*

Peshkova's case was already being processed.

INTERVIEW WITH
TOM ROB SMITH

How do you write? For example, do you have a favourite time of day to write? Or a favourite place?

I start early. I'm a morning person, I like those early hours. Midday is the worst time for me writing wise – I go for a walk, take a long lunch and then start again around two. I rarely work later than seven in the evening. It adds up to a lot of hours but it never feels particularly tough as a regime. At the moment I work in a study but I'm not sentimental about it, which is fortunate since it's a rented flat. In fact, I'm about to move, so I'll be working somewhere new in a month or two.

Which book(s) inspired you to become an author?

I don't know if there was any one book. I'm pretty sure it was every book I ever loved. And not just books but also television, film, theatre – I've always liked stories, it's nice to be able to make it my living.

Which other writers do you most admire and why?

The list is long, I wouldn't know where to start – and I'd get nightmares that I'd forgotten someone. Plus, I don't know how meaningful a list it would be anyway: you love different authors for different reasons at different times of the day. Coming up with a list would be like scratching names in fresh cement, I'd be fine with it today, embarrassed by it tomorrow.

What influenced the creation of your first novel, CHILD 44?

The television series *24* was an influence. I wanted to write a book that was as exciting as *24*, a page-turner in the way that the show is compulsive. I buy the DVD box sets. I've watched three or four episodes back to back. I've never watched one episode by itself. I have to force myself to stop and put them aside for at least another day just to make it last. Of course, there are plenty of books like that, books you finish in a day, but I remember very distinctly watching series three of *24* at the beginning of sitting down to write *CHILD 44*.

Without wishing to seem oblique, another big influence was public transport. I used to live in South London and commute to East London: it took an hour with no delays and often it was an hour and a half. There was no way to do that journey without a book, and a certain type of book, a book you could get wrapped up in, a book you could read standing up, a book you'd miss your tube stop for. That was the kind of book I wanted to write. I owe a debt of gratitude to the District line.

And, what influenced the creation of your second novel THE SECRET SPEECH?

THE SECRET SPEECH takes place in a world where the police are the criminals and the criminals are the innocent. A society turned upside down. It struck me that this was an interesting place to set a crime novel, a novel where the detective was, in fact, guilty of far more terrible crimes than the ones he was investigating.

The novel is named after the speech Khrushchev delivered to the 20th Congress of the Communist Party of the Soviet Union. In that speech Khruschchev dealt a devastating blow to the system by admitting to some of the paranoid excesses of his predecessor Stalin's regime. In my book the speech triggers a wave of vicious reprisals against secret policemen who were responsible for brutal acts of repression during Stalin's reign of terror.

Among those in danger is Leo Demidov, the reformed security officer who tracked down a serial killer in *CHILD 44*. When the danger expands to include the family Leo has been trying desperately to hold together, he must confront the terrible mistakes of his past and ask the question: can a person ever truly be redeemed?

What first attracted you to a narrative set in Stalinist Russia?

The story attracted me — the idea of a criminal investigation being hampered by a social theory, the theory that this crime simply could not exist. The story and setting, in that regard, are inextricable. But I didn't suddenly think Stalinist Russia would be a great place to set a novel and go fishing for a story. Having said that, the more research I did, the more I realised what an amazing stretch of history it was and that definitely powered me forward.

Out of all the research, what was the most illuminating or unforgettable piece of information you discovered?

Some facts do stick in your mind, not always because they're the most shocking or the most extreme. I remember reading that Stalin ordered a census of his population, I think in 1937. When the results of the census came back, stating that the population was much lower than Stalin desired it to be (because he'd murdered so many people) he had the census takers shot. It was jaw dropping: executing people because he was annoyed the population wasn't higher, which was his fault anyway. Stalin then released his own inflated figures, figures he could've just made up in the first place.

What works similar to your own would you recommend to the reader who wanted to find out more?

There's a selected bibliography at the back of the novel. I haven't come across a bad book on the period, the histories, the memoirs, diaries – they're all incredible.

What was your favourite childhood book?

I loved Roald Dahl – I must have read everything he wrote. And then there was Tolkein, any adventure stories really, other worlds. I also remember being addicted to a kind of fantasy fiction where you'd read a page and then be forced to make a choice: do you want to go down this tunnel, or climb the ladder? You'd be given different page numbers to turn to and different adventures would unfold depending on the choices you made. I had about forty of those books. You were supposed to follow rules: using a dice to determine if you defeated a monster or not. I'd ignore those rules and cheat my way through. I could never imagine killing myself halfway through a book and starting again. I'd be interested to know if anyone ever did. Anyway, those books must seem quaint now – usurped by computer games where you make those kinds of interactive decisions every single second.

What question would you like here to finish? You pick!

My favourite question I've ever been asked was – 'If you were a kitchen appliance, what appliance would you be?' I've now learned that some questions are best left unanswered. I didn't realize that at the time so I answered this question by claiming I'd be a tap, since it was used a lot. I don't even know what my answer means, it's totally ridiculous. However, you can check out more odd questions I've been asked on my website www.tomrobsmith.com where you can also get in touch, or find out more about the charities that buying copies of my book supports.